HURRICANE BRIDE

Zak Bailey

Contents

CHAPTER 1

SHIN

It had been a month, I felt as if I had been chewed up like a piece of gum. Tasted to test for its flavour then spitted out when they found me inconvenient. There was no instant reasoning why there hasn't been a response to the acceptance of the proposal on our part. So was I devastated? Thoroughly yes. I would lie if I hadn't been looking forward to meeting him. It has been my to do list. Maybe don't marry me. Can't he just go on a simple date with me so I can finally have an experience at it?

Being homeschooled comes with its pros and cons since I was able to avoid social gatherings that kept triggering my social anxiety- I must've celebrated my freedom so early in childhood as I at present struggled with general interactions consequently. I am an adult with zero experience of functioning like a grown-up in society. I at times bless a waitress for serving me. A thank you that transforms to bless you? Sucks to be me. Lucky them, they get my blessing.

Fast forward, year's later I sprouted into a woman with a tolerant mind. Hiding my weakness behind my strong gaze helped me stay tall in any situation. After a decade of worrying about what will happen and if it happens- I gathered that the key to live life is to not give a dime about the future. Live in today rather than lose yourself to tomorrow.

So when I left Seoul last week to attend an international writers conference held in Manila Philippines. I wasn't anticipating the number of writers and beginners pouring in for the lectures. Aren't we readers stereotyped to be the laziest species that roamed the grounds of the earth?

I eat dry cereals if I am out of milk. Going out is- terrifying. To dress, to smile at the cashier, to hold the groceries and to-

I just don't have a life. I do want to go out in the evenings. And weekends. But there is no one I could trap. I am a coward for that. I don't believe in love, but I do believe in having fun and making friends who like you without expectations. They are there to buy you milk for fruit loops, prepare kimchi fried rice to go with it, have long drives at night to an unsafe route, or watch the paintings in the gallery and agree with me that the person is uselessly naked and can't understand what his reasons are.

But no- I get rejected even before a person meets me. Splendid.

My stomach rumbles with hunger, adding to my misery was the man beside me who kept trying to have a conversation with me. He was from United states with German heritage, not more than thirty-five years of age, curly hair, thick brows, and slightly pouch but flat stomach with healthy hairline- he wanted to know my view on freelancing.

"I am up for it. I like to test my abilities to their core. Scoring various skills you see"

He said, his thick German accent in tune with my fake Korean one. I had Australian tutor- so my accent falls somewhere in between, self acquired one.

"That's admirable" I smiled my pearly teeth on display for him by force.

"What do you do? Apart from delivering mind blowing scripts." he whispers, not to disturb the people around us. The room was dark, only the stage with presenter lit with slides who spoke on the topic of Roman philosophy. Everyone was deep into it- exclude me, I was here miles away from home to answer mister Fischer if I would like to work with a target time project "Do you want to try something else?"

There he goes. Grilling me to consider his offer of joining the A list movie director he assists as a screen writer. If he brings this up one more time I would be compelled to speculate that he was only here to convince me to sell my books rights for movie adaptation.

"What do you say?"

There it is.

He is here for it. There is no common manner a man can approach with such big offer out of his pocket. He was sent here.

So I do my part.

"No. I like to leech off my parent's fortune sir"

I politely offer my desire. He looks at me, his prematurely aging eyes squints under the dim fluorescent. Then he cracks out laughing, so hard that it paused the activity in the room for a second. My complex anxiety kicks in when every single eyes in the room diverts at us, swallowing I wipe the greasy sweat off my hot neck with the paw sleeve of the sweater I wore.

I know I must've gone rigid, like a drugged chicken. Blank yet wonderous. Mister Fischer bubbles an apology as I watch him do it effortlessly. When everything falls to its naturalness- he looks at me worried.

"Are you fine miss Han? You went white for a moment there"

Biting my lips I nod, waiting for my heart to relax as I looked ahead.

"You know what? I am freelancing my whole life" then I grab a bottle of water, angrily unscrewing the cap I chug the hydrant down. Crossing my legs and sinking plush on the seat I sigh "I probably also will die a single woman"

The morning I woke up, that's it. I opened my eyes and remained sprawled in bed. Swinging my legs once in a while for movement. Spanning my arms as if to make a snow angel I let out a tired yawn, the white comforter wrinkles at my feline behavior. I practice my jaw exercise so that I can maintain a jawline. I still had some residue of baby fat left behind, people usually mistake me for a teenager because of it. It isn't that pleasant to watch me stretch my mouth, open and close my mouth like a chimp globbing up their meal.

Then I exist and think-

What possibly can I do for today?

Roam around lonely in the streets. Eat alone in a fancy restaurant and also drive with both my hands on wheels with no one to hold one. At twenty-two I was a pathetic excuse- how can they all flirt so easily. As if it's something that comes inherently to them.

That's it.

I Sat up with the cluster of hair falling over my face, rubbing my nose roughly I stared out of the glass wall window from where sunlight streams through. I cringed at the bill I might receive for staying at such a hotel over the week. Mister Fischer was the closest acquaintance I made so far- maybe I can ask him if he wants to go buy matching friendship pajamas with me?

Or I could look into the contract for him.

I've received such offers in the past, but none came from a person so persistent as Mr. Fischer.

Shaking the tempting thoughts off- I groan. It's not possible, this was too big a deal. I need time for this and I know I'll deny it later. I can't have Hollywood ruining a masterpiece because their budget lacks.

I lay their in a fetus position, scrolling through Instagram for an hour. The rule states that you waste your spirit in social media until it's time you realize-

What am I doing?

Then finally you go back to scrolling a minute more- then I got off the bed, my blue silk pants and shirt making it easier for me to slip to the ground as I rolled. We all have different kinds of fears- but mine was mine to me. So I got washed, dressed up, and walked out. I jumped startled when a service boy wished me good morning, I managed one too. It wasn't good riddance I told- a perfect chirpy good morning. Nothing could go wrong in that- he can't judge me for what was to be expected. Then I tapped on the contact of Mister Fischer- he gave me his number, told me I could call him anytime I felt like I needed help. He was a learned scholar and I wrote sappy romance for quick cash.

No offense to Dan Brown. But my books can make one speech-less, it's just so full of spineless characters- that one simply cannot understands what kind of audience it targets. Even though I don't know what prompted it to become a bestseller- so when I step out there was a line of three, two girls, and a boy in the lobby seated with a hardcopy of my previous release. I smile, hugged them, narrated some heartfelt thing about their country and signed their copy.

The boy blushed, he probably was some good year's younger than me, lanky, nerdy, and nervous. I pat his cheeks adoringly. In an alternate dimension, I was passing out because of the attention. My rings click against the metallic pen as I scribbled a note for him,

Thanks for spending your savings on buying a hard copy.

No one ever should be my fan!

As I left I exercised breathing, took a cab met Fischer at a local flower shop. He was there with his beautiful wife and two young daughters. They gawked at my clothing, I had a shirt with skull imprint on, black leather pants wrapped my legs, metallic chains fastened like a chocker across my neck and the dark lipstick I wore did the job of frightening the girls.

I wore every little thing that I wasn't able to wear when my family was around. An emo phase as they call it.

"What a gorgeous little doll" exclaimed Fischer's wife Martha.

Wait- so I don't get judged here?

"You are breathtaking" I breathed, suddenly waved of happiness at her appreciation towards me. She indeed was stunning. Tall, tanned, and typical upper state housewife- someone who belongs in a book where she kills her husband on their fifth anniversary to inherit his thirty-million dollar estate.

I don't tell her that.

But she will be an inspiration for such a book in the market one day.

"My husband here told me everything about you" she hugged me, her green drape dress flows with her shifts. I just crinkle with every step. "Such a bright young mind. I googled you last night"

What did she found?

I just realize my details were a mere click away.

"she has been so restless ever since" he adds

"I can see that" I smile.

"My girls wanted to meet you too" she ushered the children towards me while mister Fischer grinned, he was attractive for a man who has lived almost half of his life. Fit and happy- so when I smiled at the girls Mrs. Fischer began in a sickly sweet voice.

"Go girls, tell the lady how much your father loves their family and doesn't want a stranger to ruin our vacation but he is just too nice to decline any addition made"

Many smiles drop, except hers. Even the plumpy cashier who had been watching the scene with warm motions shook her head in disappointment.

"Darling, you can't " Mr. Fischer said horrified. He must have felt the loss he might endure because of this.

"Yes, I can Aldo. I am not risking you to an innocent-looking young Asian girl who has nothing better to do than tag along with some strangers family"

I did not even know he had a family. But okay.

"I know her" he fought back. She moved to scowl, I looked at the girls sadly. They must be terrified. This does seem like an everyday occurrence. She will be the killer bitch in a book soon. Mark my words.

"He knows you from yesterday, now since you see you are not favored here you may leave" she huffed flinging her satchel.

Committing to her demands I bowed my head lowly, overwhelming emotions clouded me- but before it could pour like a storm I had one last thing to do as I accepted defeat.

"Okay boomer"

Turning around on my heels I leave the shop, sniffing whenever my eyes stung with the hurt I withstood. I walked, left then right then left again on street.

Damn you nice man for being nice when you don't have a nice wife.

So when I bump my shoulder by an iron post I hold onto it tightly. Compression causing my knuckles to flush white as I gritted my teeth. Half a minutes goes by such-

I felt a hand on my shoulder, I flinched at the pain. It was a recent victim of pole attack- so when I looked up and saw Mister Fischer, I groaned. Slapping my hands on my knees in dismay.

"Wasn't the show enough?" I murmured, shoving my hair behind my face snappily.

His stature remained passive. But with his guilty gaze, he opened his logically apologetic mouth to say-

"I was like you"

You don't even know me.

"I know when I see one"

Then how are you so- public?

"Stop giving heed to what others say or think"

Easier said than done.

"There always is someone waiting for you"

As if I haven't been told that like a million times. As if I haven't pointedly lied about hope consistently.

He hands me a single red rose and bowed with lively blue eyes. With a smile, he walked away buttoning up his blazer.

How can he be like me when he was so-

I don't get to finish my thoughts as my phone rang, picking it up skipping a glance at the caller's id I press it by my ear.

"Hello?"

"Oh hello, sissy" I can sketch his annoying dimpled smile through his utterance.

"What do you want? Wait- why are you in my room?"

The line goes dead for a second.

"How do you know I am in your room" there was the grip of hesitation by him that had me grinning. All I had to do was try and lie my theory.

"Look around. I have cameras all over"

He shrieked. Then there was a train of shuffles and fallouts

"How could you. I could've been dancing around in my underwear. I thought I had the house to myself" he barked.

"I like to keep tabs on pests"

"You call me an insect? If so I'd rather be mothra or Rodan. The fire demon"

My face twists with disgust. Don't get me wrong, I love monster verse but my younger brother was addicted to them. He is fifteen if one wonders.

"Anyhow. When are you coming home?"

Scowling I look at the bright blue sky.

"Tomorrow" I sigh. I don't think I genuinely wish to return home. But-

"Great. Mail me the flight details. Dad got a call from Mr. Kim. Your suitor wishes to pick you up from the airport"

He then hung up. Leaving me to fend courage for myself. I do hate my brother. But sometimes he is the closest to a friend I have. So I call him back.

"What is it now?" He puckers sassily. A hint of a smile on his intonation.

"For real?" I ask balancing my excitement. But fail invariably.

"Stop freaking out Shin" he advises.

CHAPTER 2

S HIN

When I searched for an unfamiliar face among the area for arrivals. It dawned upon that every single person here was unknown to me. I had his profile somewhere crumpled and tucked among the countless drawers in my room. I took an oath to only award it a glance when there was an advancement from him.

Look where the stubbornness got me to.

When the clattering hall dispersed until only I and the haste newcomers remained after one full hour. I got up checking the details I had sent my brother for the umpteenth time. He could've forwarded me the man's number- or even better, the man could've called me himself. But something told me with the binging and dimming situation- that there was something that wasn't adding up.

Years of writing had marred me into an effortless observer. When you are the forgotten one hiding among the crowd you learn to listen and understand more. Interpret better. You just sit there waiting for your turn to speak and when it comes, you are terrified of what will come out.

I have so many colors. I wish I could let them out like everyone else. If not with everyone- might just get cozy enough with one to do it with.

I smile when a shiny black Tesla rolled and stopped by where I stood contemplating. The tinted window slides low- I bent to see a young man.

A bit too young.

"You are not twenty-six"

I know his age- but not his face?

"I am eighteen" the charming young lad grins, he's got the same jerk like dimple as my brothers.

"Who may you be?" I shove my hair behind. It's a pissed-off trait I grew up with. When I didn't know what to do, I claw at the frame of my hair and scratch it back.

The boy gingerly traumatized gulps.

I am fine with younger ones. They are like cubs. Tiny and harm-less.

Maybe I should just wait to grow old. When no one will ever have more experience to tell me off or affect me that way.

"I am junior. Lee has some work so I took his place. You are expected at home for dinner" he grins again. I don't blame him. If I had that kind of flashy teeth I would too.

"Lee? That's his name?" I shouldn't be asking that.

"You didn't know?" He then shakes his hair and ushers me to get it "please get in Miss Han. I apologize for the delay"

I don't think he meant it. If anything he looked as if he was caged with a serpent in the car and he was not prepared for such cause.

Or it could be my over analyzation.

His mobile pings, it was flat against the holder so the script basically flashed itself at my face.

I officially disown you from being my brother

The boy panicked and hurriedly attempted to vile it from me by bringing his elbow.

"Don't bother. I saw" I mumble.

"Lee is acceptable. He is a slightly-

"-against this marriage as of now"

"What? No! I mean yeah- But

I rendered him speechless. Why is it that it's either I don't speak but when I do- the others don't.

He took a deep breath then he lets it out. I saw the brand embossed on his leather jacket. I was wearing a looney tunes sock beneath my converse. I wasn't aware of it until the flight landed at the airport.

Which had me in half-

I gasped aloud.

"Miss Han. I swear it's nothing of the sort. Please stop feeling for it"

What?

"Oh no," I said blinking. "I did not happen to exclaim for that"

He frowns as I made myself smaller.

"Then what is it?"

Good question.

I looked down at my lap, my laptop bag in hand with all the essentials at least. That's apt for now. Then I looked at him with a faint scowl.

"I forgot my luggage at the airport"

Surprisingly he laughs, contagious as it was I joined his mirth. And soon we were driving by their residential pavement after some comfortable silence.

"Should I send someone to pick them up?" Too mature for an eighteen-year-old dude. I thought.

"I don't have that many things, to be honest. Not what I'll use here in hometown though"

He looks at me playfully, as if he was cooking up his imagination.

"It's my batwoman costume in the bag" he nods, knowing we both are just passing time here. None serious "I rob the city at night because I am not a born billionaire like Bruce Wayne. No, I am not an exotic pole dancer if that's what you are thinking" he nods, jutting has his chin out and nodded, playing along.

"I thought of drugs first"

When he kills the engine and presents me with a toothy smile, the knots in my chest numb. What a sweet boy. I haven't had such ease conversing in such a long long time. I could see my brother in him- but then he got out of the car and I realized he stood at almost six feet in height.

My brother would look like a drenched poodle next to him. I do too. What does he feed on?

Standing in front of the beautiful sea-facing house I let the sound of shore calm me.

"Was he planning on ditching me today?" Sighing I ask. He frowns down at me. Almost as if he can't figure me out. As if he wants to ask why I was doing this when I had a choice.

No woman deserves to be ditched or humiliated. My palms sweat, I flex my jittery fingers as I answer.

"What's your reason?" An awaited question.

"I do have a choice. But I am not brave enough to choose" I don't think I can ever make the first move.

"I don't understand" he scratched his brows.

"Neither do I" standing with my entire weight upon the ankles I insert my hands in the pocket "But if I walk away from this arrangement, your father will force him into another prospect. And if it turns out to be an equally powerful alliance, he will forever remain trapped in it"

His crease intensifies.

Understandable.

"He will have his freedom with me. And all I would ask him in return is his friendship. He can leave the day he doesn't want to pretend anymore"

His lips form an oh, but then as the realism of my utterance settles, his eyes go wide.

I should open a school. I am good with kids.

"You surprise me" as we step in, he removes his shoe by the racks, meanwhile I inspected the meager paparazzi strolling by the gates. Barricaded by the guards that had opened the slides for us. When I removed my shoes I was glad the junior Kim wasn't interested in knowing the theme of my sock. I stretched my toes. The rich maroon rug was like yarn to a kitten's claw. So posh and soft. My jetlag-infested lungs articulate a sigh.

"Mom is out and the last time I saw Dad and Lee, they both were arguing inside their study" he looks from left to right. With unease, he chuckled. He had no clue how to handle a guest. I don't too.

"What's your name?" I ask finally.

"Aaron. Aaron Kim" he says. I did take note. Most of their names are English. Even his.

"Thanks for the ride Aaron," I say grateful to have an insight from him.

"I must thank you for your patience and- and for what you are doing for him," he said retreating a step but he sounded authentic so I don't pry "take the first right up the stairs and then round to the administrative hall. You'll find the room"

"You aren't coming?" I piqued. A whiplash of apprehensiveness controls my emotions.

"No" he finishes, distancing further. "You see this jacket? It's his. He'll pounce on me if he knows I stole it" with that he was gone. With his scrambled echo reflecting the house. Taking the yield of my problems I saunter. East to west as Aaron had mapped it up for me. The compartment was huge, if it wasn't for the voices dishing out of the semi ajar room by the end of the corridor I stood in, I would've given up.

"YOU WILL DO AS I SAY" yelled the gruff, mortifying tone. It was faint- but the more steps are taken the brutal the screams were. What kind of old man has this much stamina in him?

"You are too loud. Where's your ear aid gramps?" I wasn't foreseeing an exhausted reply to it. But I hear it. Clear and crystal.

"He will do as his father commands it," adds another demanding man.

"How about I do what I want to" the youthful one again.

"Do what you want?" like punch an administrator when you should be hugging and making contacts with them?" the yelling and screaming intensifies as the sentence meets the end.

"For the love of God, It was just a shove. How was I supposed to know that he was anemic and would fall off the last two stairs? And he was the one who started it- what I did was in defense" he said as if he was putting out facts for his father for the hundredth wise. He probably was saying it for the time.

"It doesn't matter what the truth is. The public believes in media"

"WHY ARE YOU BOTH WHISPERING? SPEAK LIKE A MAN"

It wasn't surreptitious. The room beheld three generations under its roofs. And that's seldom a positive factor.

"HE MEETS THE GIRL AND MARRIES ONLY IF THEY FIT EACH OTHERS LIKES" I had to push my index inside my ear.

"My poor ears" can relate with him.

"You marry her even if she sells lab rats for a living" what?

I don't sell lab rats.

"I want to go back to the states" he recent hissing.

"There is nothing left for you there"

Tapping my legs I waited for more drama. Eavesdropping always led to a closure- but with this, it didn't. So when I heard the ruffles- angry movements I backed off. A little.

"Son. I am sorry. I didn't mean that" it was a ripe shame I detected when the father said it, but there was no response to it- instead the door flung open- so harsh that my skin welcomed the rush of air that came with the man who stood by the frame blocking the view inside.

As tall as his brother and as legitimately pissed as anyone who should be in his position, he stood there with a stony face when he saw an interruption in the hallway.

His brows were something I envied the second I saw him- he was breathtaking. But so was I. And So is everyone in their own way. He had healthy skin, a trained physique, and a black t-shirt on. If it wasn't for the yellow printed pajamas he wore- I would've taken him seriously. And there was also something else-

Right now the only thing that mattered was not letting my anxiety get the best of me. So I raise my hand and awkwardly waved with a smile.

He looks at me, from head to toe and it stops at the toe- he frowns, his lips twitched.

"I hate looney tunes" he embarks. When he looks up I hold his gaze. now frowning.

Then in a matter of fact tone, I replied with a narrowed gaze.

"You are wearing their limited edition pants"

A vapor of casual bitterness passed between us. And by the edgy arched brows of his- it was palpable that we aren't having the dinner together that I am here for.

"It doesn't change the fact that I hate it" his voice was- to simply put this- he sounds precise and masculine. The right touch and blend of bold and civil. Though the way he presented it as of now was disrespectful. But I see where he comes from.

I don't like looney tunes either. The sock was a birthday gift from Hwan, my brother.

But I am still mystified about why this man here was so adamant about proving his point.

None of us moved. He crossed his arms impatiently, frowning at his feet and then at me.

"I am not hungry. I'll leave" I say flicking my thumb behind my shoulder, trudging on that same damn spot thinking-

This is how I lose. I saw a flash of regret silhouette his features. But he accentuates them into a stoic nod.

Was I embarrassed?

Yes.

But was I angry and embarrassed?

A huge yes.

But both the emotions canceled each other out so I decided to leave when-

"YOU ARE NOT IN YOUR STRAIGHT MIND"

Oh to be the grandfather. Automatically, I kept my plan of walking away on the side and scrutinized the onset of thunders that came from the room.

"And you are not in your right state of ears" a pause "put this on father. I don't have a healthy heart for this"

The skin by the cheekbone of his went pale. The tip of his tongue grazed the inside of his front teeth in calculated frustration. He avoids my gaze, but the second it met, I know he had too many things in his mind.

"I know what he is like. He can't make a good decision. For the sake of god, he wanted to become a professional dishwasher when he was a kid" the love of his father for his beloved son seeped out. And with it- flowed revelations that no one asked for. But none protested.

But it was lawful. After Lee had deliberately insulted me, I deserve to bask in his infamy.

"You should go" he takes a quick step when I stop him with a hand gesture.

"No. I should know"

As I said it- the Granpa began. Making my haste decision to stay a minute more the best thing tonight.

"WHATS WRONG IN BECOMING A DISHWASHER. HE HAS GOT THE FACE OF A JANITOR. ALSO HE IS GOOD AT IT- HE IS THE ONE WHO CLEANS MY DENTURES EVERYDAY FOR ME"

Face of a janitor?

When he ran a hand through his face, pretending to be unaffected by it- I see it, he had it in him. Face of a great looking janitor. I mean, it's his dream- who am I to judge?

"You are accustomed to screaming aren't you father. Then listen, he is my son and I know him from his diaper days-

Every father knows their kids from there. But- exclaiming was fine too.

"AND I KNOW YOU FROM YOUR DIAPER DAYS"

"But with Lee everything was different"

"HE WAS JUST LIKE ANYOTHER KID. STOP USING HIS WEAKNES-

Then Lee was gone, he stormed out from the corridor muttering profanities like a sacred chant. Once he was gone, I let out a sigh-

The banter wasn't about to stop soon, And I was out right behind him as soon as I felt the personal issue jam in. He walked to right while I went left by the divider. He knew I was right out with him, probably that will let him know that I didn't cross the line.

He didn't acknowledged it. But it was apparent.

Slowly I tracked my way through- tired and hungry.

-so I pulled out a bar of granola from my bag and ate my way through the mansion pondering over the short information I had of him.

He is somewhere between man and a boy

It's what Dad had his personality concluded within.

And he couldn't be more true.

CHAPTER 3

SHIN

Tramping outside Boccalino's, a European amenity restaurant I practiced my walk. Diners who departed the eatery lent some unexplainable glances at my location.

Sauntering I waddled and took the chair that was kept by a wall, all green and grassy structure that camouflaged me with the night.

Dressed in a rich, thick green dress and black heels, hiding wasn't a hassle. But for how long?

He has been inside for about an hour now. I received his text asking me once for where I was-

I remember my reply evidently.

On the way, stuck in traffic.

I was outside.

Will be there soon. In fifteen minutes may be.

Ten seconds would top, if I want to go in. I could see his visage from the window if I could crane my neck ardently.

He seems to be focused on his mobile as if glaring the screen to its execution. But then he grinned- a full-blown smile with his aligned teeth on display. His eyes lit up, shone like two sets of diamonds reflecting an LED bulb.

And it was indeed the lights reflecting his orbs for the moment. So when he turned around, I ducked swearing. He didn't see me, I try to soothe my spirit.

When I assess his surrounding once more- I sighed in recourse.

After our strange encounter yesterday, where we met for a minute- held eye contact without a single pleasantry in line, cue our rudeness. It was today I received a message from his number- two days later.

'Can we meet today?'

No.

Not after he left me abandoned by the airport And furthermore in his own house.

Not until he apologizes for-

'When and where?'

Is it possible for one to hire a professional slapper who slaps sense into a person?

I can call my brother.

But he stands at the epitome of senselessness himself.

So here I was, looking sharp and hanging out around trees waiting till the valet isn't tempted by his conscience to call the cops on me. Or worst, confront me.

"I'll go in" I mumble when Lee spun around looking, running a hair through as he got up checking his watch with hard eyes, and sat down squinting.

Distinguished from yesterday was his attire, with a dress shirt and brown coat on- he complimented his age and profile. But when his face acquired the uninterested grimace when a gorgeous girl waved and swayed towards him- as if he recognized her but wanted to ignore was so on display that it was unsettling how soon his preference changed.

He was smiling, then pissed and now almost looked cunning.

He didn't budge when she gestured for a hug, he did smile at her creepily until she realized that he was mocking her smile and left with a huff.

As soon as she was out, he went back to checking his wrist.

Trembling I got up. Knowing someone's bad side only makes it harder. I only wanted to let him wait for the hours I wasted at the airport. But it's likely that he must've an ample of important commitments to sweep rather than me who didn't.

When I was welcomed by the doorkeeper, it was the last positive ray of my existence felt. Approaching the table, my gaze is light on him. Feathery enough so I can steal them the minute it commences to a mutated one.

The leather seat, the glass table, and air, everything was degrees warmer inside. I was freezing outside.

Also, he was hotter up close. This might also be the unscientific addition to why I was burning up.

Don't worry. It's just a janitor's face.

He inspects me for an interval, a proficient smile stretches his lips. Scarcely.

"I apologize for my behavior yesterday Miss Han" he lowers his head in indication "my personal problems are in no way an excuse to be rude with others"

He certainly had this memorized. But how can he deliver it so ably?

Assorted origin is blessed, aren't they?

But i- I spew facts. When I have to speak I say it without a filter. Because I have to say something and facts are what's lying there introductorily.

"Aren't I the core of your personal issues?"

There.

I see the blunt humor in his face. Was he not predicting that?

"It makes it easier that you are aware. Eavesdropping helps I guess" ouch. I discern the regret in him too. But it was too late.

"Here's what I feel about what should be done right" oh no, I know my face was straight as I start. Not giving away a brim of how much I am trying to be polite here "The grandfather must wear his aid, the father shouldn't yell at this age and the son should see to it if the doors are closed before they all sit for a night of commotion. One can stop a mouth from speaking. But not an ear from listening"

Clamor. Countless doubts and scenarios arise in my mind where this will become distressed soon.

By left I see him curl his fingers by the fork.

Is he going to stab me with it? He could be a psychopath. God! I don't even know him.

He jabs through the refreshment bakes and stuffs his mouth with it, chewing as he snorted.

"Aaron told me you were handful" he points the edge of the culinary at me, his tongue poking the inward of his cheek as he eased in his couch "he also notified me of your offer"

Thank you, Aaron. You made this susceptible. But how formal we are to each other so far, it's high key we stop pretending and accept that we are way young for such negotiation. I mean I can see his millennial traits while I am a gen z at it's edge.

"What are your reasons?"

Or not.

That was so straight to the principle that I froze for the moment.

I gulp. Sniffing as the waitress walks in handing over the menu. I smile at her, polished and happy for the distraction. I say thank you.

Then I busied myself among the categories it offered. There was a melodic throat-clearing demanding my attention.

"I haven't received the answer yet" it was surprising how sharp and balanced his utterance was. As if he wasn't the same man who had comic pajamas on a couple of days ago.

He was impeccably social and impatient. By how comfortable his tendencies were, it felt as if he is someone who chose a personality for himself.

When it's the traits that builts a person, but with people like him- they seem to make themselves. Uncontrollable, free spirited and optimistic. They are rare-

It's seldom I get to meet someone like him. But not an impossibility. They are the ones I am most envious of.

I don't look up. I wanted to shove the hair falling on my face back. But since I was being so crucially scrutinized. I bite my lips looking up.

"Guess for me" miming his tone I emphasized. So I can find a way out of this question.

He blinks, then smiles. There it was- as if a switch in him that goes off, like a free fall. He had beautiful lips, intense at the verge and soft in middle. A balance. Again.

He rubs his hands, excitedly preparing for it. His brow shot up-

"Revenge on an Ex?"

I nod sideways. If he is giving me an option I want to accept a cool lie.

"A family heritage in line?"

Clicked my tongue in denial.

"You have a scandal too?"

Haven't killed my brother accidentally yet. So...

"Not getting it am I?" He ponders, lost as the waitress visits again. To take order this wise.

"I will tell you one day. That is if you have taken upon the offer" I was proposing to him. Right? If not in the actual context I still was asking him to marry me.

He scratched his brow with the index that had his Louis Vuitton watch strapped. My eyes dwelled on its dial, the time read it was 9.17 pm.

Time will cease, you'll only regret it if you can use this moment.

I had to prompt myself for it as I poured my gaze into his. The nerves by my toes went cold, numbing me - yet my throat was parched as if I had ran a miles by the desert. I could dwell later but now- I had to do this,

"So tell me Mr. Kim" my toes curl as the unpredictable man watched me with a critical gaze. Waiting for me serve the sentence said. So I do it. Wooden and light, my voice for once was as stable as I wished for it to be -

"Will you marry me?"

Incredibly decisive, I said it. Though intense, He had a rare twinkling eye which is therapeutic. Even when seems so profound in thoughts it felt as if he wasn't judging you. He was simply amused and curious.

"I will," he says after what seems like an eternity, then ever so slowly a tension blooms on his face as he adds "I will marry you because I am being forced to"

Claiming the custody of my heart I sulk, out of energy. I can't seem to think of an occurrence. But then seem to know what he was asking of me-

"But I want the freedom to walk out of it the day I want to. An hour, a week a month and I don't think I'll even have to mention a year"

Immediately I found my lips moving, before I know I was laughing at how serious he was about it. Drained, I let the short laugh slip through the crack. He scowled, lips narrowed in a qualm.

"It's not funny. I don't know you- I still can't trust you. I may seem friendly. But I have my doubts, Miss Han-

" Call me Shin"

" Then call me Lee"

" Fine"

Not a problem since it's what I call him in my head.

" So where was I? Yes. I am skeptical that I can't understand why you are doing this. You probably know my weakness, my history-

I literally saw your face yesterday and I heard you confess that you punched a man with low immunity.

But I don't tell him that. It's rude. Unlike him- I am not rude. Not when I want to be nice.

"I understand. Trusting me mustn't be easy" I surmised. He rose his brows condoning. He develops a troubled aura. Eventually frustrated.

"Then why are you agreeing with all this. You may have chosen this for whatever your cause is- but please don't expect me to be faithful" it was a segment injected with annoyance.

He wasn't talking about his looney tunes pants, it was symbolism. A warning so that I won't dare trap him later.

"I can't tell you my reasons Lee" I sigh, my heels nervously taps against the marbled floor.

Lee.

Shaun Kim Lee.

Why does he has Lee attached after his name ends? According to the data he was born with the name Shaun Kim, Lee was an additive later when he got older.

Though I wasn't complaining. His name is easy to fit. Not strange in any way. Maybe because it's so common around.

Suddenly I was yanked back to the circumstance at disposal as sat straight- running a hand through his well styled hair.

"Fine then" he lets his hands fall and gets up, his jaw clenched and nerve ticking. But still monitored his actions to be less brash "Meet you at the altar then. Miss Han"

In imagination, I roll my eyes. In reality, I correct him.

"It's shin"

He had the audacity to roll his. I just shouldn't have held from exhibiting my distaste. Then-

He leaves. Like he did last night.

The food arrives. The sympathy in the eyes of the waitress was lovely, a woman supporting a woman. Skillfully she plates the edibles for me. I thank each of her with a smile. But once she was out of sight I felt my eyes throb with hurt. I cut the meat in half, shoving my hair back. Finally being myself.

I am fighting myself. Socializing too much against my comfort zone. Something people of my age are used to by now. But then, I could easy easily hide what I feel. So in many ways I do feel superior to them- I merely can't show it. That's all.

For a moment it's peaceful. I was savoring each bite. I am not scared of being alone, but of feeling lonely. Now that I know he was going to unite with me no matter what, I will take baby steps towards shaping our relationship into a friendship. I am his best shot- with others, it will be the messiest one. I won't bother him that much.

It's what I think.

But then-

Then a minute later he comes storming back, buttoning up his blazer. Everything that was fading about our encounter comes back storming eventually, it gets harder to swallow. He stands noticing that I was having my dinner, he appeared amused for a second, but then it was gone-

I wasn't planning on leaving without food. Nope.

But fortunately, he wasn't here for the food that I had already paid for. We aren't bonded officially yet for him to eat off my money. Since he wasn't here for sustenance-

-He was here for?

"I won't apologize for making you wait at the airport" he blurted, my mouth was full of chicken and sauce so I don't do much. I stare though. I think I am surprised, I know my eyes were smiling. But that didn't last for long when he leaned, with one of his hands on table and other by the head of my seat-

He was slightly close.

And he has clear skin and he smelled amazing . So I wasn't complaining about that either. But I did got tense when he spoke-

"You made me wait today by hanging out of this very restaurant for like an hour. So I reckon, we are equal now shin"

We hold the eye contact, I don't choke- but my conscience did. He revolved his gaze around the food and picking his side of fork he pins it through the piece of fish on my plate. Devouring the bite he flings the utensil upon the napkin and walks away.

Not once turning back to me. I watch him leave-

Then - when he was ultimately gone. Now Free of concern I head butt the table squealing until the waiter checked on me. I aimlessly thanked her for worrying and ignored the audience that watched me. I was a pro at ignorance. If I can't see- they are not there.

CHAPTER 4

SHIN

He lied.

He fabricated a lie when he said slash quoted that we would meet at the alter, because in a week Dad received an alarming call from the father Kim, suggesting a family lunch. which means they yearn to gather one full family together so that they could talk about me and him. This feels so soon, so real, and yet so weird. And Dad and Mom in a frenzy of fangirling over a political figure like Mr.Kim invited them to our house instead.

How beautiful is this scenario?

My sarcasm peaked soaring heights. And so did my patience. At eleven in the morning when I woke up to Hwan dragging my gaming consolers out of my wardrobe, I sat up screaming at the top of my lungs. My blood-related sibling, not that I have another one stared at me, his eyes wide as of a deer hitting a headlight. He then took off running.

"MOM BROUGHT THIS FOR BOTH OF US TO PLAY WITH"

crawling out in a half awakened state, I got out of my room. Cracking my knuckles as I got on my feet, he still wobbled around the stair ways.

"Mom got us so many things to share. BUT DID YOU LET ME HAVE IT?" I saw him miss two of his steps but I don't pause to pity. No one was here to rescue him. if Mom and Dad were here, they won't bother too.

"You are a grown-up woman, why can't you buy it" he doesn't holler this instant, but when I near the top of the stairway with him at the standing at the last one- he renews "be considerate, or else you will never become a friendly parental figure"

"You are not my child" I descend three steps while he hops to the ground. We circle each other like two blood thirsty hyenas. We were two blood thirty hyenas.

"Then I am not a priest" with that he attempted to bolt off, but I was quick to reach him, tackling him to the ground, I grabbed on the controller from his arm. But I forgot to acknowledge that he wasn't the slender, acne-prone and braces plagued kid anymore. So there wasn't much I could threaten him with.

Or else scratching his pimples always had him crying out in agony.

So in a second, I found a fistful of my hair imprisoned in his pudgy hands. I grabbed his ankles and soon we were a mess of bones, skull, and skin.

"Respect me. I am older" I grunted maniacally, I lost few strands of hair but it was worth it. I eventually had him in a vice clutch. I could perform a chokeslam, but I might end up with a broken hip if his weight was taken into consideration.

"Not in a million years" he grunted, dramatically croaking his voice. Dad walked in at the moment, when Hwan reached his hand out to a sleepy Dad, he received a hi-five. I grinned at his visage that left for the kitchen where I believe Mom was putting up the menu.

They were used to this, at least until we behaved in front of the guest nothing was a hassle. We as a family, cover-up good.

"Why did I have to be born in such a cruel household?" he lamented. Against my ethics, I smile- releasing him and collecting what was mine. Being myself around the family was stimulating. It's the only niche I fit in. And they probably are the only ones who know the real me. Not awkward me.

"You are getting good at self-defense I see. Though I was lenient on you" I don't roll my eyes in comprehensive manner, instead, I usually make a disgusted face. With my brows high and lips right- I convey my message.

"There wasn't a thing I wanted to defend"

"I wish I was the only son in this family"

"I could've been the only daughter if I had convinced Mom and Dad from-

My sentence was cut short as a couch pillow hits square on the side of my head, hwan smile slips as soon he gets attacked by one-too. Crawling and stumbling we ran up-we don't look behind to see who it was-

We just know.

Mom was pissed.

In the safety of my room, i steal a glimpse of the digital wall clock. It wasn't working so I had no idea of how late I was when I eventually got ready. Yes, I had my phone, but since I wanted to procrastinate- I dared my eyes to not look at it. So when Hwan gently knocked at the door- I got the message that our guests were home.

I opened the door to see him dressed in a decent dress shirt and trousers- I poked my skull out as he moved a little to the side confused.

"How do I look?" I whispered, vacating the door scantily.

"Like clown" he aggressively whispered back.

" A cute clown?"

This time he failed to club a genuine smile within.

"Yeah yeah," he waved pretending to be manlier. I did a small robotic twirl, very unhappy but attempting to be happy. I wanted to live my best life even if life has just been a plain loaf of bread to me. All I can do is choose the innards and spreads to enhance its flavors. Not letting it commence like a patient's diet.

"If you are done, let's go down," he says, annoyed "Mom must be ticking by now"

I make one last tour to my mirror, the peach illusion neck dress raved my cool blushy undertone. The coral makeup seems to hydrate my generally neutral features to something undeniably warm. I almost smiled at how good I looked with my tied-up hair.

But then I remembered what awaits me downstairs. A test. A test if I passed, I will be able to be one step nearer to my freedom. A release from my insecurities that I shouldn't even have.

We all are given a single life to flourish, and I was done being-

"Clown. No matter how hard you look- you are not-

As I walk out I smack his head hard. He tails behind rubbing the spot as we went down. Our parent had their back to us, while the family- when they said the whole family they had precisely meant it because it indeed was the entire family who sat in the middle.

When I requested my mind to provide me some aid in the said predicament, it shut off completely, and in emerged a word that my brain thought would help me-

it whispered sexily in through my cerebral cortex.

Footwear.

Yes, that's how random my wizarding geniusness was. I don't know what to do with the word so I smile as they welcomed me- the stunning mother Kim with open arms and a peck, the tough father Kim a pressed handshake, the Granpa Kim with thankfully a hearing aid gave a joyful pat on the shoulder, the big sister Kim- I wasn't aware of a sister but damn the breathtaking sister Kim hugged with a cold stare, the junior Kim winked and grinned while the most important Kim that I had ignored so far respectively bowed in acknowledgment with a subtle hard stare.

Though my family was dressed to perfection, it was evident that kims know how to carry a body with the fabric on. We were pretenders and they were natural. Still, it doesn't eliminate the validity that we live our lives caring less and loving more.

Nope. Not loving. Respectful and affectionate. That is if we cancel out the millions of fights we have in a week.

They had an authority among them, while we ruled our choices. Their body language says it all. Also the half-baked conversation I heard weeks ago.

"I hope it wasn't a bother finding the house" I get the question out, the way Mom watched me with a curt smile. I know I was on the right path.

"Oh no sweetie. The house is outstandingly elegant and the architectural scheme is so apparent that the chauffeur was quick to locate it. It beautiful" Mrs. Kim sings praises as I shift looking at my father who had a proud glint in his eyes as he gave me a told you so look.

When we had first brought and renovated the house, I convinced my family that our home was straight out of those murder mystery documentary shows in which a nanny murders the whole family because she wasn't given a raise.

Since that day- we never talked of how beautiful our glassy domicile was.

We lived in unsaid fear of mary poppins turning psycho. And we don't even have a nanny.

"It is, what Mother said" came a smooth batter like input of the sister Kim whose name-

"Sera. I am sera" she sips, her eyes warming up to the cold drink that service girl served us with.

"So Miss Han" began Mr. Kim. I wasn't fond of him so I let my eyes sweep over Lee- he seems to be much more invested at the three dollar painting I had mounted with a thousand dollar bracket framing it by the left wall to him.

"I must congratulate you and my son on making and believing in such a good prospect for the future. This is what I except from youth instead of.... We are elated to welcome you...I want to thank..."

I get it why Lee occupied himself with the portrait. His Dad- still thinks that he is a senator.

For a second our gaze intersects, and I felt the muffled smile on his face as he looked away. He was discreetly enjoying this.

Then so many questions were thrown on my way, I dodged it like a ninja who was ridden in paranoia but, still, a ninja so has to act up.

When Mom suggested we sit for lunch , I let out a staggering breath. So far both the parties had been phenomenal- throwing each other's success around like confetti. They had sectors of lands, private businesses, and political heritage. While my mother runs the nation's top two medical research centers- my Dad had his moment when he said he sells fortune cookies for a living. Yeah, I love my dad.

No. I adore my Dad. He is the best.

Love isn't real and it shouldn't be. It just an obsession that won't let you rest in peace.

Seated at the lunch table, with helpers swarming in and out prompting the delicacies as we are in cultural silence. With just some occasional talk of food and weather- it soon got awkward when Lee and I who sat beside became the center of attention. He was near- but his thoughts were so distant that his presence failed to capture my worries.

"So Lee" Dad started, his plate empty and the last bite nibbled as he patted his lips with a napkin.

"Yes sir" good to know he was listening.

"Where did you say you completed your schooling again?" Lee who had been minding his business like me, paused chewing on his mashed potato. Swallowing it he takes his time- not much fond of the topic was he?

"I graduated from Stuart, a private academy in Orlando. After that, I got into Brooklyn university"

My eyes were sharp to catch the short drop of conversation by his part and how he had been the quietest of all. I also don't miss the concerning gaze Mrs. Kim had on her son. Too infused by what was going on I totally was caught off guard when a similar question was thrown my way.

"Mrs. Han mentioned earlier that you were homeschooled, darling. But I don't see a reason why you wanted to stay isolated when there are qualified schools in our country for you to choose from" the pang that my chest felt at Mrs. Kim's doubts were physical. Concealing my abrupt difficulty to say something was getting on my nerves. It didn't help that Lee eventually tilted to look at me with a raised brow.

I felt a painful jab on my calf, Hwan chugged down his drink simultaneously as the second poke was felt. But before I could cover up Dad did it for me.

"We had many plans for her lessons, customized and certain languages that she interested in. But not a single educational institute in the city was so special to make my daughter feel satisfied" I know the tender guilt beneath his gleaming smile, the intention behind why Mom left for the kitchen to get wine when it was right in front of her was questionable- but Hwan and I know better. He managed the situation by-

"I once dislocated my shoulder while paragliding. Has anyone broken their bone before?"

And this is how I know we are blood-related. We don't know when and how to speak, but we do know how to reel out of it by our randomness. But when Lee randomly got up among the buzzing chatters no one gave heed. Not even when he offered me his hand-

"The hand is not for staring" I hear him say, when he twitches his fingers in a manner one uses to pet an animal I grab it. They were warm, really cozy. I go with him as he takes me out when we finally were by the backyard he lets it go. We trek through the enormous garden with him barely making an effort to do anything more. Walking next to him I had several questions lurking in dark. But I made a promise to myself that I won't speak until-

"Not much of a talker are you?"

He has no idea.

"What do you want me to say?" I stumble slightly, he doesn't move or attempt to steady me. With hands-on his pockets he for a second paused to amusedly stare at me as I wobbled by the dry dirt patch and gather my balance later.

I fancy wearing heels. Being quite flexible and having taken three year course as a gymnast- proportions with three to four inch heel had never been a problem. But today- it was more of the mental imbalance than any physical rhythm that staggered me.

"Don't you have questions?" his brows nipped, the stark sunlight falls on his face mercilessly.

So many questions.

But most importantly-

"Are you wearing sunscreen?" that was a question right? "It too sunny"

The voice around us visibly drops, I arc my palms against my forehead to clear my vision. Squinting I saw him narrow his eyes.

"I am not" he ultimately replies "are you?"

He asked me. I nod claiming yes.

"Let's go to the outhouse" this time I got ahead. I heard his steps fall next to me. When we got to the porch I smugly opened the door to my safe haven. It was the most artistic room in our estate. He hummed an appreciation. The white couch, vines of plants, the wooden swing, and slanted rooftop with cooling glasses- everything here screamed calm and peace.

That is until I ruined it by turning to him who now occupied a cot-

"Why are you here?" nope. Keep your tongue in check shin. "You said you'll meet me at the altar" too late.

Single of his brow perked, he chewed his lower lip in. It was pretty hot. Was he trying to be intimidating? Maybe or it could be dry chapped lips.

"I came, it's a sign that I am not mad" he draws out as if he was making a kid understand his theory. But no- I had my own,

"You don't understand. You ruined the aesthetic of such a good dialogue. Imagine us directly facing each other at the alter with no clue of how what we are thinking of it" I say, donning a stoic face. His goes stern too. He listened as if he cannot believe his ears. So when I couldn't hold it any longer and cracked up- did his eyes diluted into recognition. Surprisingly soon he was laughing with me.

"You are so problematic" he muses, settling in his breathing looking away shaking his head in disbelief.

"Well, that's because I aggressively ignore my problems until they go away. Turns out- in the end I just became one without realizing" I sigh, taking off my heels, noticing that I was wearing to different shoes of similar color.

Is this what my mind tried to warn me?

I was too deep staring at my shoes to notice that I had his full attention. Thankfully he speaks first, breaking the void filling the room.

"I am sorry about that night"

He said the same that night too.

"I know what you are thinking" he then caught his slip, he clicked his tongue " no, scratch that. I don't know what you are thinking. I can't. You are unpredictable"

I nod. Accepting the tag.

"I get that a lot" shrugging I wait.

He continues after he too noticed my shoes, he doesn't comment. Probably too much for him.

"You see. Since we are going to do this. I want to make it sincere"

What?

No. It wasn't in the plan.

He must've seen my ridiculed state as he lifted his arms in surrender.

"Not what you are thinking. But if we are going to fake it for the world- I want it to look real. Real enough to be on the covers of magazines and under my family's eagle eye" he licks his lower lip. Surely a dry skin. But that is not what's important.

"What can I do to be convincing?" My query lingers in the air. I watch him as he got up and walked towards me. He then sat next to me putting some decent space between us. He turned, this is the nearest we had ever been.

And his lips aren't chapped. They are simply pink now as a result of his toothy assaults.

"We can be friends" his voice was thick as if he was precarious of what he was suggesting. As if the thought itself was crazy. But I want to assure him that it's not. It serves as the plot of any cliche novel across the globe. So he wasn't alone.

"Friends?" It was lovely. Playing dumb. But no, the word was alien to me. And he was giving me what I'd wanted him to say.

Terrific.

"Yes. I think it'll make things easier for us. I am good with friendship" his smile accompanied by a smoldering one-shouldered shrug was cool. So cool. "I make a good friend"

I believed him. At that moment I don't have anything else to keep my faith in. Only if I had known that this friendship would be the start of so many others ships in making.

But no- I was naive as I grinned. I had this gorgeous dimpled smile that can melt chocolates. It doesn't melt him because the next thing he asks of me is just a tease.

"So where do you want to tie the knot shin?" He smirks, one of his shoe tipping to push the cot- it craddles us deliberately.

I thought of the list. My list of locations I've always wanted to visit. This wedding was my ticket to freedom. And I am going to do it my way.

"The sin city" I reveal with a twinkle in my eyes. His vanishes as he looked at me through side. His entire demeanor changed, as if had suggested something that I shouldn't have.

"Las Vegas?"

I nod once, afraid what has had him on edge.

"Why?"

I fish for a reason.

"The greater the wedding destination, the more the media speculate"

He is silent for few seconds. Then-

"You are smart" he asserted. Composing but yet apprehensive.

"I am Asian" I announce. For the sake of stereotype.

"I am Asian too" this seem to disperse the strangeness as he defended. But I had to enquire-

"You don't think you are smart?"

He gapes, I could map the lines of agitation in him. He was questioning himself and his existence.

Nothing was exchanged anymore. Not when my brother stormed in with the dessert platter and a creepy grin.

"I was dying out there with boredom, They drain me" he declared openly. As Aaron walked in behind him.

"It's no better. My brother is worse"

They both paused to look at an harmless us.

"Oh trust me, he sure can't beat my demonic sister"

Lee and I passively stared at the inconvenience. Then we turned to look at each other- a gloomy agreement looming among us. As if we silently were whispering.

Chapter 5

S HIN

The heart was on fire. My throat parched, it stung when I inhaled. The day came around quicker than I had anticipated. With the chaos that erupted after the announcement of the wedding, I hadn't been able to sit tight.

Not in my twenty-two years of life have I exerted my body until it shut off completely. One day I was at the dress trails and the next, I was in bed begging Mom to let me stay home.

But since I was her only girl and she can't pamper Hwan with the tiaras and heels, she kept coming back to me. In the midst of grappling situations that I kept wrestling with the past months. I did spare time to think of Lee.

And how he got the easier way out.

He can wear his office suit and no one would question him. But me? It was a met gala I prepared for.

When the hunt for the perfect menu, flowers, guest list, destination, and event flow was passed on, the stereotypical fear seeped in.

I carried it with me everywhere. Even when we reached the states. When I shower, when I eat, when I sleep. I think about all the things that could go wrong.

What if I trip on the way to the head altar?

What if I end up sneezing on his face?

What if I get like by him like before?

Damn those ifs.

But when the day revolves around, it all falls into place naturally. And now it was time-

Beneath the chapels dome Lee and I stood, his stance an embodiment of sunshine as he smiled handsomely when he saw me, pretending to rave me from head to toe-

What a darn good actor.

So now, as I finally stood with him opposite to me, successful so far- I go numb.

All I see are his eyes and that they are dark brown. Literally nothing special about it, but on his face it fits right. Oh so right and to be so complacent.

Lee and I were holding each other's hands, grateful that mine was covered in laced gloves. It's gross to let him know how my palms get cold and moist when I am nervous.

I hear the priest read out the vows. We were fooling the priest, we are not doing the death do us apart script here. We are fooling so many who came to wish us.

But Lee wasn't concerned about it, instead, he motioned at my lips with a discreet flick of his gaze and mouthed 'smile'

Shit.

What if there's something stuck in my teeth from the breakfast?

Kicking my overbearing voices aside I smile as per his needs. It goes on for a long time and soon Lee was permitted by the clergy person to kiss me.

I had completely forgotten about this part. By the off-guard look on his face for a second, I think he did too. So he gulps, leaning slowly- and it was the last slow thing he does.

He doesn't kiss.

He pecks.

He pecks me. The kiss that seals wedlock was compatible with the acceleration in which a pigeon picks their crumbs. But imagine that in slow motion taken with 4k DSLR. But yet so fast that I felt as if I was kissing a pigeon. A bird with soft lips. I don't mind, I got married. In Las Vegas. Wearing a thirty thousand dollar wedding gown from Ralph Lauren, where sera Kim was revealed to be director of the labels that runs Korean branch, I flaunted the laced curves in my mirrored reflection. But when it came to parading it for the guests who were awaiting my entry- I had thrown my entire weight at Dad's arms to drag me by the aisle.

My intuition told me that Mom was praying under her breath, even after the circle closed. Hoping I won't faint with all the eyes that were on me. I know I would've if I hadn't practiced what to be said for hundreds of times in my hotel room. So when I delivered it, it came out smooth, butter smooth, glossier than my waxed legs and suddenly it was over. To celebrate the success I skipped lunch. Gathering every ounce of me I throttled to the restroom where I stayed for half an hour while my now-husband ignited my phone with messages and calls.

If I was out they might ask me to do a speech, make a toast, and perhaps even expect me to narrate My life, dreams and aspirations so far- I was to pathetic for tha-

No.

I inwardly screamed, this is not how it should go. My parents deserve to know that I was living it all. I was doing this for myself- being selfish. Not residing or hiding anymore.

Authorizing my legs to move, I decide to go back. Reaching the door I slowly pull at the lever.

But When I peeked out, I let out a muffled scream when I saw Lee standing there- outrageously pissed. I've never seen him looking so predatorily, yet again I don't actually know him too. He had his arms crossed, leaning his tailored back by the secluded wall. His dress shoes tips and hair pushed aside. His lips twitched as mine went lax.

"You struggle with digestive issues?"

It's the first thing he spoke about since we got marital In status. How romantic.

"Nope"

"Then you must like the atmosphere of a washroom?"

"Certainly not"

He grunts to himself. I love replying to sarcasm, it's a trait that brings out the worst in people. And by people, I meant Hwan. So when Lee runs his hands contentious over his hairdo- I don't smile. Even if I felt the tugs I kept a straight face. Showing too many emotions to others is a vulnerability I can't afford. What if they think of me as an attention seeker?

"There are people who have been asking for us" he explains as if I wasn't aware of that. It's what I was striving to avoid "So can we like go over what we have to do in order to be-

"We met at a party in Manila a year ago, we met through our friends. We dated because we were single, but soon we fell in love with each other and before we knew it got serious. Our family apparently knew each other through their contacts which only made things easier for us. A month ago we decided to get married and then here we are"

The colors of his face wavered as he took them in. Then after a while, he slowly tipped his head in admission.

"Sounds satisfying"

"It's an average fake relationships cliche excuse"

He frowned confused. I sighed fatigued from the day's chores.

"I am a good storyteller. Now let's go, get this done with" I waved my hands in gestures.

It was strange, odd how comfortable I was getting with him around despite I hadn't seen him in like weeks. The lunch at our house was the last meet we were together. And the I dos were the initial words we directed at each other after our previous convention. It's been possible because how the number of times he apologized to me since we met.

For the hypocritical looney tunes insult to the blaming for his lack of trust in me which was, a bit dumb if you try to understand it. Or to have kissed me this morning as of now as we walked.

All I could think was-

He bites, but he betters.

But dear Lee. You don't have to be sorry about the kiss today- it was freaking mandatory. It almost felt as if he was sorry for himself but convincing otherwise.

Ouch.

Even if he didn't mentioned it verbally. He face said it all.

He took it upon himself to narrate in the essay. I latched to his arms and occasionally smiled, drizzling inputs here and there. And before I knew it was dark out. We were dancing now, he had his hand flat against my netted back while mine was on his chest.

His chest vibrated so much that I had to ask-

"Why aren't you picking up your phone?"

He had been avoiding the person on the other end of the line for about nine missed calls now.

"I can't"

"Why"

"They are from my friends"

"So?"

"They probably read of it, whatever this is through their notification bubble" his necks stern, lips pursing as if he was troubled by the thought of facing his mates.

I wish I could help him relax- but instead-

My heels accidentally steps on his shoes. For the third time tonight.

"God shin, watch your steps" he groans. He has a seductive groan, I note.

Unlike him. I don't apologize. Instead, I derail from his pain into something that might cause him more pain.

"They must be mad at you"

He glimpsed at me displeased.

"Thanks for making me feel better"

"You are welcome"

He pauses mid-track. Spinning me around i let him guide me into a quick lift. Next I was on my feet,

"Do you not understand sarcasm?" he was serious about his inquiry. It was a dim dance floor so I don't think my small twinge of smile was visible.

"I do. But I like to play dumb" he must not have been prepared for this type of uncommon craziness. Because he did stop everything for a second to-

"What does it give you?" he asks, taking my hands again. Gentle than before. But not exceeding a respectable space between us. What a gentleman.

I think of an answer.and that would be-

I feed on the opposition's frustration.

But what I admit is-

"It's fun"

His face morphs into a subtle confusion.

"How so?" With every word he says, the proximity transcends a quirky vibration to my arms. I shrug the sensation away as I started at him in all seriousness and explained-

"Try calling 911 and ask them what their emergency was"

His expressive outlines were modest initially , then the next thing I knew was his chest was resonating with laughter. A laugh which even made his eyes glassy. In between his humor he spoke-

"Smile. We should look real"

When I obeyed he laughed harder.

"Too creepy shin, a little less stretch maybe"

But as he kept snickering I found my false smile dissolve into a scarily genuine one. And soon we weren't pretending anymore. Diving deeper into the night we gave a hearty send-off to the visitors. Soon we began to scatter and Lee stood next to me whispering to himself.

"My spine hurts from the courtesy."

He was smiling brilliantly for the show still, as we wait for the valet to drive in his car.

"You are not even wearing a gown. This is as heavy as my ego" I admit as he chuckled still looking ahead when an electric blue audio rolls in. The four plain rings were hotter than my wedding ring that weighed my finger.

"Once I was appointed the role of an evil stepmother in a school play. I know what you are going through" he pinches the netted fabric of my dress and eyes it with pity.

"Why the evil stepmother?"

The valet hands him the keys.

"Why the most unpredictable question?"

I start to walk,

"No. Why though?"

He stops looking at me through his shoulder. The lights produced an angelic tinge over his outline.

"I am rich and was a brat. Enough reasons to make a good villain" he doesn't change positions, as if he awaits my response.

"Why the unpredictable answer?" This wise it was me who reciprocated. His shoulders squared slightly, buying him a second to think.

He checks his watch, I see the back of him tilt to do so, but he speaks simultaneously as he began to walk.

"You make it easy. You are odd shin and I am odd too"

He had a knack for using the person's name that he speaks to often. I have heard him mention my name five times in today itself.

I do not wait for a man to help me in, I gather the skirt which was one step away from becoming a floor mop, and dived into the passenger seat. Lee jogs to the driving and soon we were off on the road of a city where-

"Why is Vegas all about casinos and strip clubs in movies. It seems like a pretty normal city to me" I said pressing my palm flat upon the window as the luminous city waltz by.

"You have never been here?" I hear him ask. No emotions in them- neither curiosity. A mere small talk to suck the silence out.

"No. It's why i wanted to be here. A place to check off my list of places I want to see"

And also because you were trying to convince your father that you wanted to go back to states.

I confess the former, the latter kept for myself to dwell on, wondering why did his preferences even mattered to me. When I had asked Dad about where Lee used to live before he returned, It was quite strange to hear that it was vegas. I never pictured a person to have a permanent residence here. Not a person like Lee at least.

With the movement of the vehicle, my mind swivels back and forth, in and off the topic I wished to abide by .My neck cradles with the cars slithering momentum. He was a very fine driver. Making use of the last speed resort but never exceeding it, also the authentic choice of his car was drool-worthy in itself.

"You like it so far?" I was surprised he asked, even while looking so fargone.

"It's nice" I lie "it's different. And different is nice"

He hums with a sigh, approving my reasoning. It was effortless, so simple to talk to him. He doesn't know me, maybe this is how restorative it is to get therapy done. You can be yourself with a stranger who has nothing to do with you.

"You grew up in states" I was not a question "What was it like?"

He wheels the car with one hand, scratching his brow with the other with a nostalgic smile. His honest smile was reassuring to know he wasn't a picky presenter, he shows what he thinks. Unlike me.

"It was my best life. I grew fond of many people and developed passion for cars, failed tons of math tests and i- and I lived when I was here." listening to him was like a dense symphony, an incomplete melody by the way he ended the sentence. Leaving it as a past.

"Why did you left?" It slipped before I could stop myself. I cup my elbows anxiously.

He doesn't answer that. I let it go as I should. I slouch further as the tulle from the gown buffs up around me in fluff. I impersonated a cloud in cosplay. I tried to sit still, but soon my hands dug through my pockets- unfortunately, all that came out was the wrapper of cookies that I had finished this morning.

In hopes of something further in-depth I swoop in again.

"Is that- Is that a-

He traded his amused glances from me to the road ahead.

"A pocket?" I end for him " yeah I got it stitched. Comes handy"

He nodded, a satirical rise of his brow told me he was impressed. I was proud of my quick thinking as well. The night doesn't seem to end soon and neither does the road- in five minutes he entered a parking area that I was sure wasn't a residential region.

He then comes to a slow stop. My gaze picks up the large M ignited in yellow.

"I am hungry" he rubs his belly, staring at the joint with so much gratitude that I was enthralled for the time. He looked just so delicious. But you know what else was tasty? Chicken nuggets. So I grin.

"I am hungry too" I searched for my belly, to rub mine as he did. But I lost my arms somewhere within the meters of fabric. So i gave up.

"You skipped meal today so that you can admire the women's washroom. Wasn't expecting you to be full" he said undoing his seatbelt. Then he lifts his gaze to squint at me "Were you going to ditch me?"

I'd be a lie if I deny it. But his demeanor was salty, and it was powerful in a strange manner that leaves one paralyzed- my tongue goes thick not producing any statement at all.

"I may have be lenient on you so far. But I expect your full cooperation shin" I hadn't seen that coming. The razor-like shift in his utterance, like a command. Something that felt as if he wasn't apologetic like he usually is. So when he continued I listened religiously "I have had my way around people in past. I know how it's done- so I mean it. I don't take it easy when I am played at"

We both stare. None taking their gaze off of each other. Then he smiles humbly, slipping in as if he hadn't warned me with red lights going around. So when he got out, I took my time to collect myself.

Then finally when he hollers my name did I Rush out of the car hugging the useless frills to my chest. It was like carrying a life-sized stuff toy with me. I walk past him not sparing a glance.

He follows me by stepping on my skirt,

"Sorry" he sighs.

It Won't be a surprise if his first words as a kid were revealed to be "please forgive me for I have sinned"

But then, I just had witnessed him confess to have sinned and not give a dime about it.

So I kept the thoughts for later to ponder upon.

When we entered, our privacy was disrupted by eager eaters who saw us walk in. In a tux and gown, we did stand out. We went to the counter, Lee stood with his side leaned to the bar while I pointed my gloved index at the LED poster.

"Nuggets"

"Nuggets"

I snap my neck at him, Lee- who was looking at his phone raised his eyes to see me standing there like a child with my hand up to order my food.

He wants what I want.

"We have only one last serving left" at that, we both turn to look at the staff who was ogling at us in awe as she spoke "I advise you both can share-

"Get me the nuggets and the lady can have something else"

I still had my finger up. My lips gaped similar to that of a fish. Lee who so far had a resting glitch face mischievously smiled. I think I got his joke so I almost join him.

"Don't worry" he chuckles and I nod shaking my head "I am not heartless"

"I know"

"Good. I can spare half a bite for my wife for sure".

CHAPTER 6

S HIN

Dealing with my thoughts and sanity is a chore in itself. The racing impressions and reflections to every trivial thing that I find intriguing or detracting, restrains my energy. Exhausted just by doing nothing has been my metier. Most of the time I don't know what to say or do- or how to get my thoughts out.

Even as of now- it's clear in my head. The monologue- but there is a possibility that I would forget what I am even thinking about the next second to come. An hyperactivity- that's just confined to my mind. A person who knows that she is evidently cool inside her head- but a boring bundle of a verbal mess when she speaks.

No surprise that I gave up on the nuggets so easily. My spine is not even there in existence. Maybe it was some illusion that had me tranquilized around Lee so far. Because now- in my head- I was freaking out.

We have been silent for too long.

"You rented a penthouse?" My fingers tamper, clipping each other and drawing strings from the threaded satin. We stood out of the large glassy marbled door as Lee searched his pockets for the key card. I stood inches behind him,

"No. I bought this when I used to live here. But sera recently has been renovating it for us. She likes to supervise the needs" he pulls up the token and shoved it by the scanner.

Good thing he likes to shove entities too.

The machine bings and the clock ticks, he sighs in relief, probably with a far view of resting for the night. Couldn't say that for myself. He tilts sideways as he walks in- simultaneously listing-

"Our attires and essentials have already been shifted. Sera made sure that we-

He halted as soon as he stepped through the access hallway. I stopped abruptly beside him, bumping my shoulder accidentally. But that wasn't the concern that gripped us. The tension rippled with each breath I took-

What had us both in a spell, For a minute was the embellishment that covered every nook and corner of the apartment that did. Flowers, lights, and banners. It was a Christmas party in here for us. A sensual one, yet a reception.

But then again. That wasn't my concern as my eyes started to tear up.

"She outdid herself" Lee hesitantly scratched his head-turning. And when he saw me, his eyes went slight wide in an alarming motion "oh God, I am so sorry if you feel uncomfortable by this. I had no idea that-

"I am not uncomfortable" I sob, sniffing. I bet my face was flushed scarlet by now.

"Then what?" He takes a step near, trying to figure this out. Figure me out to precise with hands on his hips. I wish I could cry harder right then and there. I have had it all packed from the day-

"I am something else" I coughed, wiping the healing trails of tears. Pinching the bridge of my nose I struggled to mask my pain into nonchalance. But it was getting harder to breathe.

He looks at me, blank a second, and relaxed the next. Maybe I was doing a good of pretending to be fine and he-

"I get it. You are turned on" he scans his appartment, his lips curving "with such set up, I would too"

No.

Mission abort.

His mind wasn't working as well.

Gawking in pieces, I wait as my nose twitched. Then my lips formed an O. At last turning my side to him I bent down sneezing.

Then two more In a row.

By now the stock of tender hair were curtaining my face, no sooner than it, my mouth began blurting facts to the man who had no shame concluding his theories.

"I am allergic Lee" it was accompanied by another tiny sneeze "The flowers" wildly I gesture.

He looks around, a light coat of blush toning his cheeks. But the smile of his was nurturing as if he would have commented it even if he knew about my allergy . He was a bit on the naughtier side wasn't he?

"There were flowers at the wedding too" does he suspect that I am lying? Does he really think it's because I am horny?

One doesn't sneeze when they are craving it. I know that much.

My vision blurred at the Q and A. But I wander obediently.

"Those were fake. Mom made sure of it" crossing my arms, I hold my elbow as I peek at side. With my free hand, I cup the area by my nose and mouth to shield them from inhaling the fragrance.

"What do i do now?" I ask, wheezing softly. Hideous in expression.

He doesn't reply the instant, But the next thing he does was peculiar. He takes his blazer off and flings it by the chair near the kitchen counter. Undoing his cuffs he Rolls the sleeve of his white shirt and strides towards where I presume the kitchen was, a minute of clatters and the sounds of things falling and breaking later he came out with a vacuum cleaner and a mop in hold.

"What are you still doing here?" It was a scolding, "Go to changing room and get changed. I'll take care of it"

When I don't leave still- he blows air out. Exhaling with frustration he drops both the household equipment to the ground.

"I know I am going to be a vision as I flex while I clean" he dusts the imaginary crumbs off his shoulder, then his behavior got severe where he was glaring at me "But you can enjoy the show some other time. Now buzz off from here before you suffocate. I don't know how to perform a CPR"

Immediately I saunter off from his view owning to the seriousness of the moment. I go left with faith in my instinct.

"It's on right shin" I hear him scream faintly.

It would not be an issue to sleep in here, I mull with the option as I sat on the cherry red chaise chair in the middle of the walk-in wardrobe slash dresser cabin.

It had everything I need, and all I need is a ground to sleep. it stretched a good hundred square feet for me to use. But I don't think it will be taken lightly by Lee who has been going around the house with the awful vibrations of the machine for about an hour now.

Does he feel like accomplishing a sense of responsibility?

Why was he doing this anyway?

"It's over"

I blink, pausing to scroll my phone screen I look up. He was standing there by the door, not a fraction of him was out of shape. Though a sheen of exhaustion could be seen on the crown of his face nothing else was different.

He was fit.

Fit as a fiddle.

I got up, signing a thumb up for his duty. I can't trust my mouth tonight. I walked to him with my eyes on the two pink petals that sat on his matted hairline.

I pick it up for him and clap it out of my hand. Then I finally mount my courage to look at him. Like completely attentive of what he was behaving like-

Unfortunately, he had his gaze cast low- or specifically at my toned legs. He looked impressed and mildly in daze. Of course, he was a man- and by how at ease his attitude is, I bet he has adequate knowledge of courting girls.

He was too confident.

Yet I wasn't afraid of him. Not much. Not until now.

"Haven't seen legs before?" No. I should've kept quiet. But they were just legs, it won't hurt to talk about it. I try to reason my conscience that wearing shorts wasn't a bad idea. It's what I always have been wearing to bed for years now. Bailing tonight would mark the beginning of new a insecurity.

It was just skin.

I wait for him to say something.

My conscience kept providing the flash warnings, nonetheless, I was scraping trouble for myself.

He doesn't meet my stare shortly, he takes his time. Lethargic and slow, with a smirk he replies.

"Not like yours"

"Friends don't flirt"

Pathetic shin.

"How is noticing that your legs are unnaturally pale flirtatious?"

Unnaturally pale.

Don't let it affect you.

Don't.

Though I pick up the crack in his tone that was proof that he wasn't being serious about it, I have millions of other ways to convince myself that he couldn't have been more candid.

"You don't want to wake the wrong side of me"

Wrong side.

I don't mean the fighter part of me that'll protest or argue with him. He doesn't even realize what he is contributing to, that they were helping one evaporate the morsel of willpower they had worked on for months and years. Nobody could because it was us who was at fault.

"It's bad" I admit as jab my index at his buttoned chest with a tight-lipped smile. The kind I use with Hwan. And my family. It's a mystery how I was hoping him to understand.

"You can't. You are in debt. I saved your life by cleaning every inch of this place" he took a step closer, stamping one of his hand on the door frame that lined behind me "I keep doing more than what I had bargained for"

It was uncalled, the sudden rush of anger that brimmed in my eyes. And suddenly I was tearing up. His words weren't something that stung me. It was the fatigue, pent-up insecurities, and the consequence of what I had been doing so far that perched on me like rubble.

Though it was humorous to see him melt into slush, the afraid eyes did it for me as I pushed his arms aside.

"Shin, listen" he calls after me. I don't stop for him.

"Hey, I was just teasing you. Isn't it what friends do?"

I don't know. I don't have any.

"I am sorry girl" his hurried footsteps made my pace rapid, but when his fingers curled by my wrist did my body goes cold.

He comes and stands in front. I scowl harder. He smiles sheepishly.

"Your shorts caught me off guard. That was it" he asserted "you have nice legs. I swear"

It shouldn't affect me the way it did. I wasn't fetching for compliments-

I hate the blush I donned even if he was just trying to make me feel better. Twisting free from him I try to walk to the room, he runs and outdoes me as he blocks my path. Coming to stand in front.

"I was embarrassed okay. I got caught checking you out and I had to lie. You really are beautiful" he blurts, his tone bathed with so much dept and integrity that- goodness, I wasn't able to think straight. Gaping like a fish I frown-

He holds a hand up, motioning me to stay the way I was -

"You don't have to forgive me" he smiles, angling slightly lower to look at me in the eye "But remember, don't let anyone tell you how you look or should look"

My heart raced as if it was the organ that got the message the most. As if the heart was screaming at me to stop listening to my head. It wanted me to tell the man how grateful I was for what he said. To confess.

I don't do it though. I stood cemented in the same spot, unmoving and rigid as he winked playfully and walked away towards the room.

He lied when he said he failed in maths.

Because he was sharp, so accurate at calculating a humans emotion and relation that it got scarier as I realized that he had been reading me all along, playing the dumb character with a charming smile. He had me pierced with the probability-

Suddenly it wasn't so difficult to grasp the reason behind why I felt it was safe to be myself around him. Even if it was bare minimum. It was made possible because he kept wielding and morphing circumstances into what will keep me warm.

Maybe he was terrible with numbers. But he was adding me up sequentially. Wizarding his way into my head and for the sake of God-

We have just met for the third time in two months. Jerking the palpitating thoughts i jogged towards his previous direction. He stood in the middle his eyes narrowed at the bed-

His face gives everything that he wants to show. Fooling you into thinking that he is an open book when he plays the guide into opening yours.

I don't know if I should be thankful or frightened about this. But as long as he helps me with my head- I think I can manage. And stop right when it diverts it's ways into my heart-

Because my heart was weaker than my brain. And I don't think I can harbour a heartbreak even if I tend to not believe in love.

The rug was plush, my feet sinks into the sensation as I walk in-

The interior of the residence was ten times more dominant, be it each contrasting piece of art or the furniture that occupied the room was so in coordination. Sera knew what she was doing with this place. And so did Lee when he cleaned it.

"Which side of the bed you prefer?" I ask, we were adults, I think it's mature to share a master bedroom than to sleep on a couch or on the floor of an unfurnished room. Coming back and Remotely standing next to me he shrugs.

"The one you least prefer. I sleep anywhere. Also, it's way past my bedtime" he looks down at his watch, astonished.

It was quiet after that. Then-

"You follow a bedtime?"

He yawns nodding, closing his eyes while demonstrating. I moved and sat by the left corner dragging in the comforter up to my thighs. The bed was too big for the two of us. But I wasn't complaining- I want the space. We need the space.

Dimming the lights out he makes a quick trip to the washroom and when he came back he had a black t-shirt and white sweats on. Also, his eyes were drooping shut so when his head ultimately hits the pillow. He is dead asleep.

Like a sculpture, poised he was flat out cold with shallow breathes that indicated his mortality.

He has a bedtime. It shouldn't be a surprise, but to a girl like me who despite the exasperation I endured today laid there wide awake- it was envious to see a man sprawled out so briefly.

Soon I was basking in boredom, pressing my cheeks against the pillow I squint my gaze at him.

Poking the tip of his nose with my pinky, I dab at it to make sure he was asleep. When nothing happened I began-

"Lookit, the little baby. Cuddled in his cot right when the clock strikes" cooing, I roll my eyes. Striking over all the formalities we had so far.

If he was awake I would have punched myself in my mouth before deluding this out.

"Ah, look at those pretty eyes. Shut as if lids are glued by" I whisper aggressively, and then shriek out freaking when simultaneously he opened his eyes as the sentence expired. Starting directly at me.

The apology got stuck in my throat- as it should. But when he closed them back as if nothing happened, I froze out further.

That insufficient action of his splits my night further, seconds gathered to minutes and minutes to quarter of an hour- and it's when he sat up.

Sat up as if he was a puppet and there was an invisible tug in his chest that cause him to sit straight.

"What happened?" I mimic his position and shoved my hair back. Fumbling around I turned the lights on, it blinds me instantly - but I keep blinking to adjust my vision. "You need anything?"

I was desperate. I just want him to go back to sleep and let me swim in my thoughts alone. But he was there- swinging in between. Confusing me.

He was staring at his lap. His pupils far gone- as if he was lost among constellations.

"What do you want Lee?" I whisper, afraid if he still thought I was a segment of his nightmare or whatever on earth that is going in with him.

"Koalas"

What?

"What?"

He shakes his head like a whiny puppy, his hair fluffs up in consonance with his bustle.

"Koalas belong in a shopping cart" he grumbles softly, his voice induced with slumber and fatigue. He doesn't look up, he reaches his and out and fists up the comforter, tugging it to his chest he shuts his eyes with glee.

"They belong in jungle Lee. Not shopping cart"

I.....don't know what I was doing. But I was doing it.

But as he kept caressing the balled up duvet by his chest, nestling it as if soothing a baby- or a baby koala in this case- it wasn't arduous to figure out the cause.

Stifling a smile I roll my lower lip in. Slowly getting it. Understanding it.

"I must hug a bear" he was- he sounded convinced. Inspired even.

Padding my palms I search for my phone. This was too good to be true. But darn the phone that died the moment I tried opening it.

Does this happen everyday?

He was in bliss, with heavy lids almost sealed and a smile so alive.

"Aren't bears dangerous?"

Though I bet he can't hear me or know about his surroundings, I randomly kept adding my insight into it.

Only if everyone in the world owned this habit, it will be a lot easier for us socially awkward to feel less lonely at night.

"I can buy a bear if I want" he was-determined. There was a tense frown marking his commitment. So when he blindly searched for something I tried to stop him from slapping himself awake.

That will be a loss of free entertainment. But when he caught on to my nook, he tugged me forward. And before I know I was engulfed into the biggest and warmest of hugs ever known to mankind.

"Must also hug a koala"

I feel his chin dig on top of my crown. Panicking I tried to unleash my body when he dropped back to bed. Taking me down with him.

He was so damn strong that even after multiple trials I failed, as the time passed I gave up. Exhausted I wait for him to shift so I could sneak out, but his steady heartbeat, right beneath where my ears rested kept hypnotizing me hauntingly. And suddenly, I was dozing out.

CHAPTER 7

S HIN

If laziness were to be embodied into a picture, the evening we woke up to would be it.

We don't know how the morning surpassed because when we woke up the sun was at its peak, getting ready to set. Lee walked out the room half-dazed as I was out in the living area with my phone in the clutch-

"I am ordering pizza, you fine with it?" I ask, scrolling through the app for the options.

"Yeah" hoarse he yawned, a sign of awakeness "I like pineapples on top though"

Don't judge.

Grunting under my breath I wanted to spare him the deprecating glance because I believed in opinions. But I failed-

He had a fat smile awaiting me. How was he so happy? Is that how people who like pineapple on pizza looks? So surreal?

Even if so- I won't have it even if there was a gun pointed at my head to carry out the offense. The violation of breaching a law. A law where cheese was contaminated by something so-so-

"It's okay. I get that look often" he cracks his knuckles and styles his hair "it's three-thirty? we were asleep for so long?" He mumbles checking his phone then he checks me.

Not we. He was. I woke up at intervals where I found us tangled together, so to avoid facing the embarrassment I forced myself back to sleep so he can wake up first and I can pretend to sleep still.

We could have avoided it smoothly, but he had to wake up first and nudge me awake, mentioning that I was sleeping in his bicep and how it was cutting out his blood flow.

He could've pushed me, punched me. But he had to make a PowerPoint context out of it to describe my skulls weight on him. How long was he awake before he decided that I should know about him clotting because he unconsciously decided that I was a koala and wanted to hug me in his sleep.

Which inspired meThat I should perhaps quit being nice to him if he was going to treat me like one of his dudes. Not girls, but dudes. So I ordered myself a few more treats and one small pizza for him.

While we sat to eat, and as I kept opening the boxes his smile fell.

"What are you having?" He asked, quizzical.

Inspecting each of the cartons I pick them.

"Cheeseburger, bagels, coke, and a banoffee pie. Oh yeah, a bag of onion rings as well" listing, I smugly bite on, each at a time.

"You'll be able to eat all that?" Should I consider that to be sexist?

"Mmmm"

"Great" disappointed he eats his pizza as I scrunch my nose, chewing. He rolls his eyes at the visible revulsion from me. However, we don't. still in silence, it felt as if he wasn't accustomed to a quiescent atmosphere.

"I think I've learned rnd my lesson" he cleared his throat.

Booting and rebooting my social techniques I tilt my head with incoherent regard.

"And what would that be?" It comes out scratchy, any introvert's nightmare when they speak when not wishing of a conversation at all. I soothe my throat by sipping on water. It was gentlemanly of him to wait as I compiled.

He slides the box of pizza aside and interlaces his fingers togeather. Sitting straighter. Sharper

What was he negotiating?

"I should've shared the nuggets with you"

Oh heavens.

No.

He can't.

It'll thrust me into reconciling my deeds. Into overthinking each and every conversation to see if I had been bad to him. Or should I quote a 'bitch'.

Although I wouldn't have done him any harm, I can convince my mind to trick itself- I believe I can be a criminal with no crime in record.

"No, you shouldn't" I press.

He watched me stoically, nodding sideways. Declining my advice.

"I don't know what I was thinking, but I was extremely hungry and-

"You are bluffing, you sh-

"It happens. Type one diabetic for years and yet I give into the cravings"

The minutes that followed were empty. None of us spoke until I realized he was waiting for me to ascend.

So I ask.

"You are diabetic?"

That wasn't a necessity. But I can overthink about it at night how I had asked him an apparent question when he had it revealed precisely.

He smiles, and he should smile less- it's frustrating how he is so easy on eyes and in personality, it makes me forge my temperament to the likes of his.

"Why do you think I am so sweet?" He wiggles his brows, I dislike his lenience more by the second "I've had it since I was thirteen so it isn't a big deal. I am used to it by now"

Used to it?

He was.

I wasn't.

As I gnawed at my lips stressing, in a flash his demeanor morphed and he waved furiously.

"Quite the pity"

"I am not pitying you"

"Then what's that I see in your face?" His tone went a notch deep, it the first wise it happened. A intonation that indicated he solemnly disliked being pitied.

With Wit. I begged my innate vocabularies for it. And it provided me with

"Beauty?"

With risk I held his stare, his blatant nothingness crumbles and he, with much contemplation, took my admission into account.

"So, you are not sympathizing with me?" He reminded me I played with the skeletal bracelet that hung by my wrist beneath the table "is it because I didn't share the nuggets?"

He- was, he was unbelievable.

"You are manipulating me" arguing I cemented my notion, the home shoes tapping restlessly by the floor where he can't see.

"I am not. You are just different than other girls. It surprises me"

Oh, here it goes.

"I am like every other girl Lee. It's the strategy of how we express our emotions that's diverse" emphasizing I fought against stereotyping sexism. But what I failed to expect was-

"How you defend a gender is what makes you unusual, I think it's fine to be rare. I am not like many men out there- but I am happy how I turned out" when he sat back relaxed and tore through the pizza- I know what he meant. He depicts what he deciphered.

"Fine"

I announce.

"What for?" He plays innocent by batting his lashes, though the mischief Dripped in his utterance.

"Is this all for some bagels?" Cupping my elbow I affirmed. "The compliments?"

He eyed the bag with fondness, then he traded his glances around his options. Finally, he grins, it even excites me to punch thyself in the face as he confides-

"Bagels and onion rings"

If the phrase actively functional was a person, it would be Lee. In the meager period of half an evening with him under the roof, I subconsciously took into account that he just can't sit still when he had nothing to do or somewhere to be.

He could swing by and explore the world out there- but when asked, he gloomily mumbled something about paparazzi and how they will expect him to be with or be seen with his new bride instead of alone customizing sugar and gluten-free candies out there.

He tapped his legs as he watched me smash my keyboard accompanied by a stony aura.

"What are you doing?" A keyboard smash appeared on Mac's screen as I got deflected by him.

"Typing?"

"Why is that a question?"

I thought of it, it logically shouldn't have been dubious. But my lack of corelating with given query was too obvious for him. He oddly was smart to notice it.

"I don't know" I shrug. He sighed- it was positive. As if he was tired of me but he understood.

"You are an exclusive kind of introvert" he played with the paperweight on the study table, on who's the chair he sat- "it will be easier if you open up a little. I don't mind a new friend. I never mind a new addition"

He tossed the pebble, catching once and repeating beside. But then, the vital segment of his utterance enticed my hearing.

I don't mind a new friend.

He had brought this up during the initial family dinner as well. Was he so sure that we could connect the manner an ally does?

"We can't force a friendship to happen" wisely I jut my chin out, I believe I have a better understanding of human emotions and relationships than he does. A writer- unknowingly has the ability to know how the lineage works. It's how they bond with their readers because they were once a reader too. So when I saw him smirk, impressed. I continued. "It'll happen if it's meant to be"

Then my blood rushes everywhere, in nooks and corners as I burn up with the heat of verbally illustrating my point across to a man who seem to know what to do every time we speak when I honestly don't.

I breathe. He sits there still flinging that damn stationery statically. Then finally says-

"Woah"

He drawls it out like a toddler who has seen iron man accustom his iron suit for the first time.

I see why Dad addressed him as a man slash boy. He reduces his personality to fit just about anything.

"You have a smart and psychological mind. You should give a shot at writing- become a scriptwriter or something" he suggests. I nod. But then-

Wait!

"Lee"

His name suits him. Neat and alluring. I won't admit it ever to his face though.

"Yes?" He balmed his enthusiasm on me as I crossed my arms, shutting the laptop for the night.

"What's your profession?" He blinks, but the passiveness was absent when he rocked slowly in the swivel chair.

"You don't know?" Why was he so surprised?

"You work for your father, its the default I assumed"

His brows shot up, not in rapid gesture. But as if it amused him.

"I do work for him, but I used to practice a different domain. It didn't work out though" he turned his back to me by making a quarter circle with the chair. The dip in his emotion was minor- but it was there. So when he sneakily turned again with a butt hurt dramatization. I arched my own brow.

"So you married me without even making a trip to google?"

Seriously this man is not getting it. Why was he least bit offend- ed when he knew that this was a deal-

"What do you know about me?" Throwing it at him I puckered my lips smugly. Watching the confidence dim out in his face. He drops the page stopper on the metal flask and scooted in one clean swipe. Until our knees were inches apart.

"You are the princess of your family. Until you weren't. you were forced to carry out a family legacy so you were thrown into this alliance business so our parents could feed off each other's revenues"

It must disturbs me, or worse I should feel humiliated of how low his imaginations worked on. I won't blame him since I was twenty-two and not most under my age manages to succeed in their career as I did. But even I was mere a Google search away.

I should be offended. But no. The way he was so assured of it- I felt the ounce of laugh bubble through my chest until I was giggling, mockingly.

"I am right aren't I?" He winks, his eyes shining perkily. I roll my eyes and wave at him.

"You are dramatic" I sniffed, containing the mirth "What genre of books do you read to even assemble such fantasy?"

I wasn't expecting him to answer it. But he does-

"I took an oath to never read after I read an awful one" looking low at his lap as if recalling a trauma, he spits out the sentence with so much malice that I had to know more.

"What book was it?" Spreading the nonchalance card I pry. But I was not prepared for what came next.

"Oh trust me. Your noble and naive heart won't take the amount of bloodshed and betrayals" he starts off hauntingly "The writer calls itself Elixir. Let's call it- it because whoever it is, is a monster. The hardcopy was retailing like a hot cake in the market and I had to know what the commotion was all about. I was left angry and bitter for the days to come after I finished it"

If to be monitored by a blood pulse electricon, I bet mine would be shooting higher than then average bar.

Elixir?

Monster?

Did he just call me a monster?

"But I bet there was something about it that people liked. I mean you told me yourself that it was a charting one" Pathetically I soothe the wound my pride was cut through with as he snorts despisingly.

"The book is an art though. Perfectly crafted characters and crammed with an intense, fierce plot. But what's the use- it's like the author hates her creation. Killing them all as if it won't affect the readers" each stab, with each criticism I was stabbed till my self-esteem and bravery was a pool of useless muck on the ground. For the final product, I ask in a small detached voice. With a hope that he was considerate-

"What will you advice the writer with if you ever got to meet her?"

He doesn't notice the her that I slipped in. But glad he was a balanced feminist as he sneered evilly at the thought- I swallowed my dignity.

"I won't tell- I'll threaten to shave its eyebrows off and force it to change the ending so that everyone gets to live a happily ever after"

That's it?

My trembling lips almost forms a smile when-

"After the changes are made, I'll shave the brows anyway. It deserves it"

CHAPTER 8

S HIN

The title credits rolled by the vast theatrical screen, the lights in the room dimmed out with the High defined curve frame being the sole source of glare that was luminous. Initially, it was unduly bright, but as minutes passed with my thoughts getting sucked by the plot of the movie- I got lost in it.

The room was packed with the audience, some confused some frustrated, and rare, extraordinarily talented ones sat there with their proficiency enjoying the brain burner that Christopher Nolan had presented us with. Quarter in the movie- I pull a notebook out from my backpack and clicked at the butt of my pen.

I felt a knock in my wrist after fifteen minutes-

Shifting my ponytail to the obtainable shoulder I look at the side, I see Lee staring dead at my notes.

"I want a paper too" he whispers, his wavering eyes trading from mine to the pages. I raise my brow smugly, slouching on the plush cinema chair with folded arms.

"I thought you liked challenging yourself when I had asked you prepare for this" he changes course, glaring at the action scene that breached the natural laws of physics and yet it was a possibility. So we had to know how he made it work.

"I underestimated this" he shakes his head in dismay as if his pride was wounded by it "I never use to compile for my exams- but they seldom caused such frustration. Why would you even want to watch this?"

Leaning, I undo the strap of my heels and crossed my legs, jotting down another crucial hint as a faint smile played by my lips. It was this morning had I fetched an online ticket to watch Tenet, as an avid admirer of Nolan's masterpiece I know what I was reserving for. But for the misery of lee which he brought onto himself was his shortcoming.

I randomly had asked him during the breakfast, with much vigor I had mumbled-

"I am going out to watch tenet this evening. Want to join?"

Anticipating a denial, I munched on my cereal as the worst was over. But-

"Are you asking me on a date?" swallowing the food, I watched him grin cheekily. He was having fun collecting my tongue-tied moments. When I don't reply he goes on to add "friends go on dates all the time. Of course, I want to go"

I exhale, disliking the idea of even asking him to go out with me. But as a responsible Nolan enthusiast, I had warned him for what he was getting into-i had read the reviews and even I don't think I was prepared. But he was pretentious and arrogant, quoting that it's a movie and I am being too harsh about it.

Fast forward half an hour into it- he was eating his words in bitter reality.

"I have met this man at a party. He isn't as complicated in-person" Lee mutters, grabbing a fistful of popcorn kernels while I sat there staring at him with saucers for eyes.

"What do you mean by you have met him? Pattinson?"

He looks at me as if he felt ridiculed at my sudden yelling whispers.

"No. The Nolan guy" he corrects me. He rectifies me as if it was common for him to meet-

"You are speaking of the Christopher Nolan?"

First, there was a frown, then it was a calm realization and conclusively the smirk settled on his face.

"One of my friends is an A-list director and I sometimes tag along with him to film festivals. So- yeah. I think I met him. More than once maybe" he steals his gaze working me up further, he rips a page from the note and pulls out his pen from the rugged maroon jacket he wore atop of his black t-shirt.

Even as he pretended to be decisive, he had the wicked glint. He liked how envious I was. I sighed aloud- enough for him to hear and not rattle the viewers. With the rapidly adapting panorama, the hue upon us kept flickering. But he looked good with every color that rained on him.

"A man who wears looney tunes for pants got lucky" shrugging I tried to focus, but both our interest that once dwelled on the plot was long gone.

"Those weren't mine. It was Aarons" he defended serenely "he took my clothes so I had to steal his"

The sibling drama. I recall Hwans text this morning- it was of my face photoshopped into the body of a chimp.

"Hwan does that that too" I mused, missing that idiot for no apparent reason.

The grunts from the protagonist who took hits filled the silence. Then-

"He steals your clothes?"

It takes me a jiffy to get what he was worried about. Then I was a bubbling out-

"Oh- I, no- we mostly fight about the last piece of cake, him borrowing my charger and not returning them, stupid stuff like that" scratching my arms I scrunch my nose at the memories, getting carried away- failing to stop right there as I - " I am glad he is boy, I sleep tight knowing my Victorias secret collection are safe"

The actions sequences intensity as the leads grunts was a full-blown scream as I finished- he was a bit late from distracting me from the blunder, wasn't he?

I bury my face by brisking into the bulletins I had up so far- it made zero sense after what I had said since half a minute had lapsed by, I began entertaining if the revelation was luckily camouflaged by the sounds from -

"Victoria's secret huh?"

Shit.

"Nice choice"

The rest of the movie was absorbed through my peripheral vision, the baby hairs contouring my face from him was sufficient - but after a duration, my hair became a nuisance, since I forgot to spray them this morning, they had their free will to sprawl out no matter how fiercely I tried to part them. I kept propelling it occasionally not realizing that I had an audience.

"You should pin it up" Lee denotes, the snacks we streamed in went extinct an hour ago, we somehow managed to chug it in by the first ten minutes. So he sat there- empty of any movements.

"I don't have one at me now," I told blowing at a strand of hair from my perception.

A minute passed, then in a sudden move, the pen was yanked from my clutch. Perplexed I looked up at lee as he separated the cap from its body. He then discards the pen by its previous slot, that will be my hand. I watch him create some expanse, a tiny space between the cap and its holding clip. Soon I felt his fingers comb my layers to the side- a cool metallic touch of the clip made by his hack finally clamps through my scalp as he fastens it. He shifts to inspect his job and nods in approval.

"I used to have bangs in high school" he closes his eye in dramatization "it was hassle"

I look away as soon as he opened them.

"Looks like you just got through all the struggles I go through" I state recalling how he had admitted about the gown he wore in a play. But strangely, as he answered- It felt as if he was answering in various encrypted decrees to all the unshared story between us.

"Not all. Not All of it"

We were strolling around by the pavement, the metropolis hummed with life at the peak hour. The city hoisted so many colors at once that failed to contrast each other. They vaguely fought for dominance. Just as crazy as to how the stories we usually hear from this station.

Busy roads, shouting groups, bass from a shabby-looking club, and every meter that we passed felt like an onset of someone's tale who has been here- here for short while and never forever.

Which reminds me that I don't have a forever to complete my script. I had a deadline and I was lagging behind. So much that even if I had been out tonight my mind was reeling into the mess that I strived to sought out.

"I cannot believe I was able to estimate the plot. I am proud of myself" Lee announces, his hands in his pocket as we walked. He had this fat glint of mirth in his gaze as he craned his neck to peek at the crown of a plaza tower. "What about you?"

Thanks to you. I think I only recall the title of the movie.

"I was close as well" I lie through my teeth.

He smirks starting down at me, soon he nudges me in the shoulder with his as I lazily dragged my steps.

"It's okay if you feel dumb. I can explain it to you" if it was physically feasible to scratch the mischief from his tone and posture- I would be doing it on repeat. "They look uncomfortable"

I stir around to see what he proclaimed, but he tapped at the top of my head so I was staring down at my own feet.

Oh.

"I like wearing them" I smile, wiggling my toes "I am comfortable wearing them"

He frowns in disbelief.

"That's- you are probably the only girl who ever said that" he breathed, a heavy breath as he brackets the back of his neck with his palms. He has been doing it more than a normal in quotient. Breathing ragged as if he was physically exerting even though if we just walked "Do you also like wearing two different shoes in a pair?"

It was not present. The dip of his general persona was discernible. He looked tense and uneasy.

"I don't know how that happened. The nervousness I guess" he doesn't look at me in the eyes like he always does. Rolling his lips in, he nods distracted- and I think I can second guess what it was. "Lee, you want to sit somewhere"

"Hm?" dazed and clueless he tilts, I don't pause - before I can create a niche that I could throw my courage into- I grab the nook of his jacket and tug at him. He follows me as I motion him to sit by the street bench. He does it without a question.

"I think you should check your blood levels" I purpose.

He jerks his head with a smile, the one with drained energy. The one that flunked to reach his eyes. He doesn't speak but proceeds to take out the strip canister and the monitor from the blazer. When the test kit almost slips through his clutch-i don't think. I snatch it from him when I saw how much his fingers were trembling.

"When was the last time you had it monitored," I ask pinching the top of his index and clicking the needle at his skin. Drawing a drop of blood. I looked up when he doesn't answer. He was watching me with an unreadable expression. "When was it Lee?" I try again.

His gaze wavered as if he was fighting his thoughts out.

"Two days ago?"

What?

Wasn't he type 1?

"You do know that you must check on it at least twice a day?" I was way more pissed than I should be "Are you trying to kill yourself?"

He had the guts to chuckle. But when the numbers popped in- I wish I could flick his lips with a spatula. This wasn't a reason to smile-

"It's been a while since it got that high" he smiles at the deadly glare I was diverting at him. But he heaved as if it was fumbling through.

"Please tell me you got your shot on you" I sighed, he blinks nodding. Patting his jacket and thankfully producing out the insulin pen. I lean without a thought- but he takes it away from my reach. His smile dropping avidly.

"I will do it. Thanks" with that he angles to the side, lifting two inch of his shirt by his waist and he pricked the skin below his rib cage. Injecting the contents.

Once he was done he searched for the trash can, I offer to do it for him.

"You know I am fine right" it wasn't annoyed in nature. Mere practical. "I can walk"

"You can. But you don't have to. It takes time for the blood to stabilize at your level" spreading out facts that he probably knows I take the disposable syringe that he willingly let's go by renouncing his grip on it.

When I come back and take my seat he seems to be drowned in his world. With arms folded and gaze craned by his lap he remained passive.

"How do you know so much about this?" Breezy and lucid, he asks starting ahead at the relaxed roadway.

Is this what he was thinking?

"Well- I um-

Since he told me of it yesterday I spent half the night research-ing articles after articles on type 1 diabetics as he kept narrating about how he would like to eat a cuisine made of water in his sleep.

What even goes on in his dreams? I was explicitly curious.

"My mother. She is a doctor. So I snoop around her memos and books sometimes" can he see through my lies? I hope not. I can fool a mass with my pretense, but he seem to extract words and sentences out of me that leads me astray.

His brows squeezed in as if he was pretending to accept the notion.

"Yeah, right" he nods "isn't she a gynecologist?"

I desperately wanted to decrease the idea of it. I was dying for a different conversation.

"Yes she is" I smile, the false one "she has been ranked at the top this year by the Forbes Korean issue"

"That's great" he adds, expanding the topic furthermore, he doesn't let my mind rest or worry- he reaches to me from the crack and extras my original persona. It scared me. "What else you learned from her?

What I learned?

Oh, nothing at all.

She use to kick me out of her office in a ninja fashion because I was a troubled kid who was so adamant to know where babies came from. Since she told me that she helps the parents bring babies into this world- literally., I used to think of her as the key to answer the universe.

Since I can't confide to him of that, I did the other thing-

That is creating a larger pit of what the hell are you blurting out shin?

"I realized the she is best in what she does" I could've stopped, but was I thinking? No. Was I going to do something about it? Absolutely not. "If you ever plan to have a baby, bring your wife to Mom. She actually has published this pregnancy chart which sa-

I smack my fist softly by my forehead in imagination, in reality, I sat straighter cutting my own words off-

"Forget about it. Forget that I ever did anything"

Time ticked,

It was half a minute -

Half a minute When my lips twitched, I had no alibi, when I heard him snort- my chuckle was next on lane. When none of us could hold it together our laughter sprouts. From the low hum of disbelief to a full blown tremor. We weren't even looking at each other.

We seem to agree that he has understands it by now. And I was scarily comfortable with it.

"ADHD" I say when my voice stabled enough. Meeting his warm gaze I shrug smiling. If a month ago if anyone had told me that i'd be sitting beside a man, married to him in a busy night of Las Vegas, confessing him of my disorder with little to no hesitation- I would have mentally gagged because of how impossible and unnerving the scenario was. Even in a foresight.

But fate knows how to play it's card. So when he brings pulls out the cap from my hair that I had abandoned because of the forgetfulness that comes free while dealing with attention behavioural conditions.

"It's cute" he winks, playing with clipper.

"Not when it's accompanied with social anxiety" I pout, rolling my eyes.

He observes quietly, not like a therapist. But simply curious.

"Where do you think it gets hard for you?" I don't miss the slight concern in his attitude. He shouldn't be. It's what I was running away from. And also- and also-

"I speak my mind, sometimes the things that I shouldn't be saying out loud included. My mind races in a multiple directions, hopping from one interest to another, so as I speak. I don't worry about the consequences, I am not even aware that I am doing it. But once I am done-" pausing I notice that I had been tapping my legs restlessly, another unconscious trait. So I try to halt and resumed "- then I tend to go through the mistake in mind. It doesn't stop at times, my mind doesn't stop when I ask him to"

I hook my thumbs through strap of my backpack since the silence between us after what I had disclosed got to me , he slides- eliminating the the good feet of distance that we sat in. But our frame doesn't exceed the limit- I can feel his proximity, but can't sense it materially.

He ridges his body lower since I was no way near bold enough to look up at him. He was smiling.

That darn friendly smile that had a promising language of it's own.

"You don't have to do that with me" he Says, the stubby, minuscule of hesitant gestures of mine melts off. Into the night and onto a boulder of hope "I believe in diversity. I think I can get where you are coming from"

"I know" I admit, even if it was the blush I felt that was heating up my cheeks. I could care less. As if the validation wasn't enough- he went on to explain how severe he was about his phrase.

"No. You must know" he ushered, the tense film in his stare rapidly evaporates- opening a window to a playful one "You can walk around the house in your victorias secret lingerie and I wont judge. I won't even bat an eye-

He wasn't Hwan, neither was he anywhere near being a part of my family. But he was growing into a person closest to me apart from the group I grew up with. So when I stomp at his feet hard.

CHAPTER 9

L EE

Cursed with a default face that radiates chronic tenderness and a cheerful ambience- I attract every kind of crowd that I don't want to be with. For years I had people coming over with prospects and fooleries, thinking of me as someone who they believed they could walk over. Without a consequence in vision.

I pity them.

I do.

The world is always prepared for the one who is complex and dire in personality. But never for the one who has it all in control. Never for the one who can do both. So when I entered Only Hour, a base nightclub by the second floor of the cosmopolitan skyscraper that I was easily more familiar than my original hometown. I see the heads turn, considerations lure and intentions tumble. I have been here almost every other day during my three years of living in vegas.

Not the club- but what was beyond this building and with who operates it. my stint here was at the twenty-seventh tier, but here I was. In a bar, by the counter- judging the frenzy. The very trait that I pledge to avoid, had thought me a lesson. When the misfortunes and cunning strategies of people I used to work with and for stabbed me in the gut did I learn.

I fell.

Scraped my skin until it bled. I wasn't naïve- but the hostile atmosphere and people were just extra careful. Maybe If I was as unforgiving and smart as my friends are, I might I've seen it all going down. At twenty-two, I was giving up everything I had worked for. Four years ago- under the roof of this building, I had killed my dreams. Knowing that none of it was my fault.

Four years ago-

I begged. My pleads had resonated the walls of their cabin where they were asking me to quit. To forget everything when being on tracks, under gear is all I had known since the day I first had taken on the wheels as a teen. Even before that- I broke rules, hired a private trainer, did my research- obtained my NASCAR license. Began my journey in a youth racing league when I was fifteen.

I had won.

From then, year after year- I had no fusion to look back. I was at the top of my career, a rage among the logistics. Want and need of the sponsors and investors.

Investors-

I was faithful to one- had been to him since the beginning. But when his personal stocks and shares collapsed, he used me to spring his position into the hub again. He paid for a racing collision- In agreement with the investor of the only competitor I considered by the field.

Nicholas Moreno.

He sold the race. I would've forgiven him. After all it was only a race.

But what none of us knew what how vile they had been with their tactics. It even made me laugh at how cleverly it was executed. From manipulating the agency to landing me in hospital for half a month, publishing the cover story to deeming me unfit for the sports because of my health. The national committee apologized to me for baring me with a reason that I had no control over.

I didn't cause the accident.

I didn't ask for this.

My opponent could've asked me and I would've given him years of win. Would have refused to even participate in his trials. But this- this was insanity. You can't ruin a man for your pleasure. I wouldn't have understood because I am young and pathetic. Aren't I?

It's why I had been laying through the sleepless nights pondering upon where I went wrong.

When I couldn't find the answer, I locked myself up refusing to come out to my friends who- fruitlessly were camping out around the house. honestly- I wouldn't know what I might have done without them. At the time I had realized that – I had made friends with people from all walks of life.

Clarissa Blakewall was a lawyer who threatened me to stop being a wuss and leave it up to her and her celebrity prosecutor of a father. While Alex and his Wife Elzina white, who I had never- ever addressed by her real name- opting to call her chingu since she Is the only friend I had who had a friendly face were considering buying and crushing the stakes of my ex sponsor. Trust me- they don't bluff when they consider such crazy antics. When they mention it- they know they are capable of doing it.

Hailey Howard was an actress and media personality- she sensibly argued with Edmund Sargent- the hotshot director and her ex-boyfriend that they should give me some space. To which Edmund had told her off by mentioning that the only space he needs is from her. she complained to me about her ex for an hour later that day.

It kept my mind off of stuff so I welcomed it. In a week they had me up In spirits. Or it's what I pretended to be in. They tried to stay in turns.

Clarissa and Hailey lounged for three days in a row. Their sole purpose was getting me back on my feet. Food, proteins, and diet supplements- they had taken the role of two mothers. Elzina had a son to take care of so she parted with a warm comforting hug- But left her husband behind.

Alex White- if there's anything one should know about him- is that he is, he is a stone that occasionally laughs and speaks. But he is there- right behind, hovering above, watching and loving us. His first night with me- he walks into my room with his pillows and duvet thrown across his shoulder.

Then he takes a seat on the vacant side, looking through his shoulder, frowning.

"What are you so happy about?" he grunts, he hates it when I grin. I personally feel as if he mostly doesn't know what to do with me. do I scare him? I mean, I'd be an honor to affect the aura of the mighty Alexander White. A guy can wonder.

"Why are you here?" I raise a quick brow " In my room"

His gaze coils in disinterest as he lays down. I turned to my side, my head propped by my hand.

"You know- you are the most perverted among us three. But I don't think anyone will ever believe that" he brings his hand behind him. So his head rests on it.

"Perks of being an Asian" I smirk. I have never seen him look so disgusted. I was curious why the students of Stuarts were so scared of us all. Though we were popular and shit- there was nothing much exotic about us. We were a bunch of idiots whose life had always been spiralling off the vast.

Just like anyone else. But then- we also were toxic in some ways- because not understanding why they feared is also a sign that we seldom were afraid of anything.

"You should've gone along with Chingu," I say- the humor in my tone vanishing into air.

"I should have"

"Yeah"

"In dreams"

One can't tell Alex White what to do. Except- surely with the exception of Elzina, none can tame him.

"You can sleep in the other room buddy" I promote, switching the lights off "You already are doing too much. All I could do I advise you to get a good sleep night"

He had a powerful snort- it made me feel stupid even if it was a fair point across.

"Can't have you bruising more of that pretty face with your night adventures" he mutters sleepily. Knocking myself out earlier than others had been habitual- I wasn't used to staying up awake after my scheduled bedtime. so when I realized that Alex was zoning off, it dawned on me finally that why do people keep complaining of the stress tampering with their sleep.

Like an owl I had my eyes wide, staring at the ceiling-

"So you think my face is pretty" I had to keep him awake. Something dark was trying to get to me and can't let that happen.

"Pretty lame. Yeah"

I wasn't disappointed that I asked. But his mind seems to waver off- so when he speaks, I wasn't anticipating it.

"Why do you sleepwalk?"

Was he serious?

"Alex" I pause- "You can't just ask a person why they sleepwalk. They walk in their sleep and they don't know why or how. It's how it functions. If I knew why I wouldn't be participating in a midnight cardio"

Surprisingly even in the dullness, I was able to suspect his smile- did he? Was he?

Since when did Alexander White began to joke around? But I was glad he was capable- because it helped. Sort of.

When Edmund turned in to fill the last week of our deal, is when my guard kept crumbling despite my will to pull the last week of my stay in here. I couldn't live here like this- and if they knew what I was going to do, they might try to change my decision. But not Edmund, he knows me the best.

We use to share a dorm room. He knew how to wake me up in rank with the stages of the slumber I was in. Be it splashing me with a glass of water or simply slapping me into reality. Literally. When it happened I never question him. we would nod at each other and go back to bed. He would assure my father about my failing grades when the results came in and would pull out three tickets to a movie the second he'd hung up. Alex will be dragged by his collar. He was on leaner and slightly shorter on scale than us. with Edmund soaring the built of a hunk- it wasn't a chore. Though I was almost as tall as Edmund with lean but muscular body- I could never dream of putting up a physical fight with him like how Alex desired to.

Edmund is like a big brother I never had. I don't even know what or how I must fill in the role because I haven't been much around my family. Aaron was my younger brother- but it's all I know.

"I know what you are planning to do. I saw you packing your bags last night" Edmund throws a dipping smile at me as he prepared to leave. I don't reply to him the instant- watching him fasten his shoulder bag. But after an acute silence, I say-

"I need a break" the muscles in my throat tightens as if it does not want to allow the lie.

"All I can hope is it's just a break" Edmund pats my shoulder, engulfing me into a hug. I needed this so I return it. Grateful "Remember. We will always be waiting. No matter what"

Nothing echoed after he was gone.

It was cold- the apartment seems to host me and yet once Edmund left. It seems to bore a void. As if I wasn't there despite still standing in the middle of it. I sat by the couch- alone, physically and mentally. I let my head fall on my hand – the numb veil I had on dispersing as a sob left my body.

Is this how it ends here.

Crying felt good- it washed the chaos that I had up bottled for two months. They were cleansing it off- but the stain, it still was too fresh. There was nothing here left for me to fight for.

I need a break?

How honest was I?

Pretty honest!

I came back. but I wasn't here to fight, it will be a shame to proceed with a fight that I know I will already be winning. I rather was here to tear this place into pieces until it's stripped to ashes.

As I sipped on my diet coke, smirking at the ginger who had been hitting on me since the moment I stepped in. Though I hadn't shown any kind of sign or ushered her advancement- yet she was there, getting fooled because of my face.

The music luckily wasn't as ear-shattering as it usually uses to be. Since it wasn't weekend the club seem to harbor a decent amount of party-goers. Something that Clarissa will appreciate. I wonder if this was shin's scene? No matter how tastefully I try- I can't picture her dancing. But rather cooped up in her own world sitting by the secluded corner with the most random questions regarding the crowd seem to be her way. I won't lie- watching her react to anything, in general, is entertaining.

When I first saw her standing there in the corridor, awkward but with the brave front- I hadn't given heed about her or her appearance. When you are dying for a way out from a forced marriage, you quit thinking straight. I had been rude to her, but when she raised her small but tall nose as if to match my complete strature- defending her looney tunes sock and putting me back to my place did I began to think rationally.

I wasn't the only one being forced into a marriage perhaps.

I had thought.

But the next time we met- she had made it clear. She wanted to marry me for unknown reasons. The one that I still attempt to claw through her little slips. But no- none of them helped. Her little slips? It doesn't do me good, when she confessed about her struggles, I didn't know what to say-

I had it in my doubts. She was too interesting, but with such a quirky personality came its challenges. I wish she believed that I meant every word of what I had said last night,

Not the lingerie part.

No not that.

Alex wasn't lying. I wish I had a filter. But then again, I loved how she reacted to it.

Loved? what the hell am I saying?

When the ginger, dressed in high shorts and string top came to stand beside me with a sultry smile did I own up to what I had been doing. Smiling at my thoughts while unconsciously blemishing out mixed signals to a girl who I don't want anything to do with.

"Hey," her lips were full. So when she smiled I had to stare at them. I smirked though I didn't want to "You are new here" she says nearing, her red manicured nails brush against my arms.

"I am" I lie. Shifting so I was completely facing her.

"Temporary?"

My eye shrunk in an elongated wink as if I was reminiscing.

"I don't know" I shrug, stretching my lips into a million-dollar smile. "You are gorgeous" a quick flirt doesn't harm anyone.

She bites her lower lip, her fake lashe seems to fan more as she steps closer.

"You aren't so bad yourself" she whispers, snaking her arm through my neck she pulls me- I lead so she could speak in my ear. Her perfume was giving me a headache "So what are you doing tonight?"

And this is where I decide to draw the line. I massage my neck in order to stroke her hold off of me. With what I presume is with twinkling eyes I declare-

"My favorite K-pop band is having a comeback. I plan on streaming the single"

The channeling she had up decomposed, but she springs up her hope and tried one more of her shot. I was impressed by her persistence.

"What about tomorrow?"

Of course, I had an answer for that.

"Me and my friends have selected a few of the trending group tiktoks. I am going to make that. I am so excited" she stumbled with her drinks, probably blinded by my grin as she walked away after a ridiculed see you around later then.

Tik tok- my friends and I? why am I such a genius?

Tilting my wrist I glance at the time. it had been half an hour since the meeting was scheduled. He must be waiting- sweating out at my absence. Cameron blaze, the man who sold me to save himself from bankruptcy.

A month ago when I had dialed an early morning call to Clarissa she had been just out of a renowned national case hearing. When I asked her to direct and reopen the case for me, she had it divert to her father.

The Ian Blakewall.

And with the name- defeat wasn't an option.

So when I received an urgent call from Cameron. I had stared dead at the screen, at his name with so much hate that it surprised me of what I was capable of. My unforgiving voice had agreed to his pleads- he begged me to meet him. I accepted. So now I lounged by the bar mere tiers down to his office.

I gestured at the bartender- he waddled with multiple bottles he carried that he had been stocking up.

"Can I take a selfie with you?" he was tongue-tied for the second, but the young lad soon nodded happily. Dumping the drinks he wiped his palms by his uniform. When we posed, I made sure the neon sign of the title-only hour was captured by the image.

Uploading it on Instagram I slipped my phone into the pocket, cracking my knuckles I got up buttoning my suit. As I map my journey to the exit I calculate the time it'll take for Cameron and his staffs to understand that I had been right under their wing as they sat there haunted because of my absence or how many minutes it's going to take him to run across the bar trying to seek me.

I don't care though. As I walk to the parking lot- pressing the keys to unlock my car. I heard my name being called from behind. It was feminine- and so familiar that I regret knowing who she was even before I turned to look.

"Lee"

No. I am in no mood to see her or have this coincidence take wheel. But then again- Maddison worked for Cameron. Isn't it how she became my assistance in the first place?

She looked not a day older than how she used to. the same long blonde hair. Sunkissed skin and deceiving noble eyes. The difference today is I don't long to see them smile at me or heal me. she was a con- always there for money and fame. There to use me like how they all did.

"How are you?" it was strange how I wasn't angry or a least bit hurt to see her. In oppose to it I felt an alien annoyance creep through as I smiled. She frowned, did she really thought I would change just because I cannot do what I want anymore?

"So much better," I say, I felt as if I owe her the answer. She made me question my loyalty after she dumped me for Nicholas. And today- I am a better man with a purpose. when she doesn't continue the chain i move to leave when-

"I am sorry"

Faking an astonishment I nod. My gaze must have had been too sharp on her as she stole hers. The guilt wasn't doing it to me. she could have had her fairy tale- she just failed to understand my impact. With or without a career. I was powerful.

Her and Cameron. They did this to themselves. They chose the wrong person.

"Don't be Maddison" I open the door, but then I looked at her – I have no semblance of why I did it. But from my pocket, I pulled my wedding ring out and slipped it by my finger as she watched me, a shadow of appalled awareness. I do it as if I was proud of it- and I don't know why. But I know it wasn't an exhibit for Maddison or anyone else "I was way out of your league. I am glad you did what you did. It helped me realize my place and worth"

Not once with the appetite to look back, I got into my car, driving into the lane as I without a will or onset was reminded of my past and present. After what happened last night with my diabetic levels I had been cautious, I did check my vitals today and it had been at its healthiest. Then why was my heart so erratic?

Was I falling sick?

It couldn't be.

It took me twenty minutes to get to the penthouse, I park my car acting out to get home faster than I could've. I text shin to check if she was home because when I woke up- I saw a yellow poster atop of her pillow.

I will be back soon.

That's it!

Against my ethics I was frustrated. She may look younger- but she was twenty-two. She could be there out doing whatever she wanted- but this note was too short to of a note to humble me up. what does she take me for? She was my responsibility while we are here and she-

Are you home now?

I type on my phone with my nose flaring up. she wasn't there when I left in the evening- is that her early?

Yes and no. I am at the park.

Park- the customized yard for the residents in the structure. That was at the posterior annex of the building. Bribing my mind I walk to where she supposedly was hanging out. I spot her a minute into the garden, she sat with her back resting on a tree- the golden lights creating a mild hue around her as he frowned at the screen on her lap. What does she keep doing in it? It doesn't feel that pleasant by her expressions. But she is mostly there glaring or staring coldly at the monitor most of the day as she typed.

I swear I once saw her smother the keyboard with a smash and cunning smile.

She had her raven black hair curled and wore a maroon dress with a white cropped jacket. Her signature heels sat beside her as had her bare, stocking-clad feet propped up in a picnic pillow.

Where had she- why is she dressed up?

But my monotone contemplations decipher when I felt a movement by the bushes- it was pitch black at where I stood and I sensed a presence. When I saw the visage- I don't wait. In three-step I was fisting, a gather of the man's shirt- rocking him out of his hiding spot. Startled he shrieks as I motion him with my index to my lips- warning him to shut his mouth.

I know this guy too well- though he was a nuisance I always thought I had a much more important job to tend to. But today, he crossed the line. It wasn't me he was spying on.

Paparazzi, media, stalker, call it what you want but when I yank the camera out of him and shove him to the side, he doesn't stop me as I scroll through. they were images of shin from now, some from last night of us. further from Korea.

"Please –Please sir. Don't-

I lift one of my hands, not enough to heed a look at him but to halt his disgusting stutters. Clicking open the data slot, I pluck the reel card out and drop it to the ground. With the heel of my shoe, I crush it to my satisfaction. When I look at him, he was still there. as if he was too afraid to even move from there.

Good.

"I don't want to see you again" I throw the camera at him, flocking and trembling he caught it with frantic nods. But I wasn't done yet- also, I wasn't done understanding where the depth of my promise was leading me to- but I say it without a flounder-

"And if I see you around the girl, I'll make sure you aren't seen again"

CHAPTER 10

S HIN

Life doesn't revolve around and over a person. But the world you make does. It rotates and fluctuates back and forth to the leaps and moods of hence mind. So there must be an explanation for why I go stark blank at the question-

How did you come up with this fantasy world?

From who or where is the protagonist's character is inspired from?

Or the most anticipated ones that asked me at the book signing event since my three-day trial en route had been-

Please give us a hint about the last investment in the trilogy?

Hint?

Do I know what I am doing with the supernatural world that I created? Do I want to ruin it in the midst of a war?

Do I want to keep my lovable characters alive?

Is there even a way to save them when I had established no euphoric hole for them to get out of their mishaps?

I go through the same crisis as my readers- because so far, I have no clue what the hell I am doing with it. Similar to how the two previous books in sequence went through. It worked out at the finale- because as a cliffhanger, I would kill most of them for the sake of an honorary death.

But since I received a specific criticism from someone that I shouldn't be bothered about. My capabilities to roast my rulings had been electrified. I can't seem to write a single line without his face scolding or swearing at my decisions in conscience.

"It's a surprise" I smile at the seventeen-year-old girl, she squirmed giggling as I collected her books and flicked my wrist by the pages as I signed.

"You are amazing. Do you even know that?" She chips as I shook my head mentally. Begging her through my eyes to understand.

This might not be the case after the last in series is released. So don't pressurize me more than I already am.

"I am so lucky that you chose las vegas For your tour in States. I couldn't believe my eyes when it was announced" she heaves breathing, for a moment I thought she might end up kissing me if I moved slightly towards her.

"I am still shocked I agreed to this" I mutter under my breath so only I could hear it.

"You said something Elixir?" She blinks as I frantically gestured no. Why was I doing this? I haven't done such an act even in my own hometown. But why here?

What changed?

People?

Atmosphere?

My common sense?

Probably the last since I know that the time I get away from my home and with the companionship of Lee as an excuse is the only duration I have to treat my fears. With a small list of tasks to accomplish i-

I- I want to take a trip to the aquarium and get myself a pet fish. Which reminds me that I had been gaping, impersonating the vertebrate I was thinking of.

"Thank you for the love. Please look forward to the climax" compelling it out I attend to her as she romped to my side and requested a selfie.

When she vacated, the boy behind in line came forward. He had a wide smile and high cheekbones, making his face look older than he must be. His curly hair was perfectly trimmed in symmetry. Like bob ross- which suddenly had me in a grip.

What should I be doing first?

Buy a fish or lure some acrylics and learn to paint?

Such a tough verdict to make. So I ask him one good question-

"Is this for your girlfriend?"

It plummets, his smile. Shit. Why do I keep assuming that most of my readers to be girls or some violent teenagers. He looked old- but not more than twenty.

"I don't have a girlfriend" he doesn't bother to hide his dismay. But he shrugs clicking his tongue- "But I dream of finding someone like Inara oneday"

Inara?

She is the one who plays the lead. He dreams? What kind of dream are they? Are they rated r? Is it-

No- focus shin. Focus.

When I sign his copy, He divulged into a much subjective issue. He seems to keep an eye on the events I go through.

"Congratulation on your marriage Elixir. I have been waiting for you to post the lucky man's image. The last post from you was of a half baked shrimp you failed to cook"

Don't take me wrong.

When I say the one who has read my book doesn't contribute to my difficulty and apprehension was because they felt like family since they had already decided to love and support what I do. In return, I try to be as courageous and deserving despite my choices.

But when I say family, I wasn't foreseeing to meet someone who seems to have my posts memorized.

"Soon. I'll do it soon"

Our face is all over Korea though- he could type it right away and find Lee out. But-

"It's fine. I saw. Since you won't reveal him, I looked it up. He is good, but you are more beautiful" he says with a sincere glimmer in his orbs. So I wrap up his posters and offer him a cupcake.

"Best of luck kid. It was pleasant meeting you" his smile drops again as he walks off murmuring how he was merely two years younger than me and certainly that must not constitute a kid.

So I was right. He was twenty.

The next was a forty-three-year mom of four who was the most normal one so far. Then there was a punk boyfriend who wanted me to sign a book to surprise her girlfriend. But the one he gave me was an erotica despite the large banner beside me that had the name and the cover mentioning credits. He somehow was here with the wrong one.

He stunned me through his shaved head and brow piercings, so I signed it without a question.

"You don't look like someone who writes these" he drums his fingers lightly at the hardcopy. His stench-infected odor if cigarettes hits me as equally as his stature. His muscle stood out through his sleeveless vest.

"Don't go on my face"

Go home.

"It was nice meeting you" I conclude it abruptly in a small voice as he frowns leaving. Exhaling a breath of relief I grabbed a brownie and took a bite, dried of energy.

Since I have been on it for two hours I had forgotten completely of where, what, and how I landed here. When I received the invitation from one of the leading literature communities in the States I had accepted it.

I had been to a different region two days ago too. Since Lee had been asleep I decided to write him a note before I left. But I wasn't sure as to where he had been since I was back at penthouse by evening with him gone. When he came back late at night- there was a brittle transition in his behavior.

He talked less and stayed less. Was out most of the time and when he came he went straight to bed taking his shoes off. In the morning he ordered us breakfast and tried to attempt at small talks, but his mind seemed to waver at a different dimension because he wouldn't realize if I answered him or not.

From what I could gather- he wasn't pissed, neither was he distant. He was just- being less Lee. And when a person is less of himself it's a consecutive result of chronic stress.

It wasn't my crisis so I made an effort to not think thickly of it. But name or blame it on curiosity or the enigmatic indications from him, he roamed in my thoughts even when I had left him alone there this morning as well.

I forgot to write him the note too. It was already 4 in the evening so I took my phone out to check on him. But when I switched it ON did I come across the six miss calls and one precise text of his awaiting me leisurely. They were as follow-

Don't you think a note like before would have done the job?

Snorting with annoyance I cross my legs under the table, one of my heels digs through the plush carpet as I typed.

I forgot. And you should not worry. i can take care of myself.

There was no reply for a while. I decided to take a break since it was wee hours of options given to me. I wasn't done for the day- but I can rest for a moment. The book club was under the wing of a luxury mall so when I craved some tacos I got up dusting my beige halter neck dress and adjusted my headband.

When I passed through the security check by the food court I was painfully made aware of the attention I received. For most- I was a stranger to them. But when I garnered some heated glances from men and boys, I couldn't help but squirm with worry. I know I looked good. It had been my focal point to dress and appear as appealing as I could for the event. But now- I think I was too early to put myself in such an uncalled spotlight.

So I make half a circle as my stomach drops. The appetite suddenly a past decoy. I wasn't hungry anymore- so when I grabbed my coffee from the counter of Starbucks, an order that I had up by the nearest station I was by - I tried to scruff my way out as soon as I could.

Big mistake.

In haste, I ceased to operate, outperforming my patience as I collided with the first person that entered through the door. The iced drink lathers by my wrist and hand, but the majority of the dark brown liquid soaks through the unfortunate man's clear white hoodie who collided against me.

"Fuck" I whisper. He still in trance had his gaze low. When he looked up tilting is when I finally saw his face. His hair was trimmed in fauxhawk undercut was light Auburn in colour. He had sharp features that complimented his olive skin-

And when he saw me with those odd blue eyes-

I know they weren't his real eye color. But they did wonders with his five o clock shadow that finished up his face.

"It's okay"

It was him who said that. Probably since I hadn't uttered a word or looked away from him after I had cursed.

"It's not" I mumble with my trembling hands coming up to pat his shirt. But before I could do it- I retreat them away "Let me buy you a new shirt. Please"

This is how it's done. I was dying inside with the number of eyes on us- but when he smirks inserting his hands inside his jeans pocket, inclining. Melting further in embarrassment I derail with my mouth slightly agape and my eyes fatigued from thinking too hard.

"What's your name?" he says as we switch to the side so others could pass by and the staff could clean the mess I cultivated.

Why wasn't I gone when he said it was fine?

Why was I here?

Yes. Manner. Stupid Asian manners.

"Please. Let me repay" I plead.

His gaze rises in amusement. For some unfathomable reason, I disliked the attitude he regarded me with. Me and my body- I wasn't comfortable.

"That's a unique name. Please let me repay?"

I force out a chuckle. As awkward as it came I did a slight bow at him.

"Forgive me. I am extremely sorry. I wasn't looking where I was going" with last resort I took a step back to leave since he said it was fine. It's what he expects from me. Right? To just go.

A bad omen vibes through us when he straightened up frowning.

"Actually. You can give me your number and name. So I could link you to the designer who customized this shirt for me. You can repay me through her" he must've smelled the hesitation in me- but all I could smell among us was the aroma of coffee I had sprayed on him. So despite my mind screaming at me to not do it and settle it with money- I refuted. Selecting my card from my sling bag I hand it to him. He reads through them as I stood there like a student whose test papers were corrected through.

"Han shin young," he says it as if he was tasting my name on his lips. I nod playing at the strap of my purse. He extends his hand with a murky glint in his eyes. I take it for the shake as he puts a name to his face-

"Nicholas Moreno"

Exhausted I take my seat. The golden fluorescents upon the ceiling panel were committed to where I sat. For a couple of minutes, I pondered upon the blunder. Though I desperately wished to balance it out. I secretly aspired the I don't get his call.

So when my mobile rang with a text indication. My heart raced with scenarios.

They weren't pleasant.

Where are you?

It was Lee. I exhale smiling. I had never been so happy about his name lighting up in fonts by the screen.

I replied to him with my present destination.

When can I pick you up?

Squinting I read the message twice to see if I was bluffing. So when I honestly answered him- his reaction was perceptible.

"Three hours later? What are you planning to do there? Mop the floors?

What was he so pressed about? I don't text him again for two huge reasons.

One: Because I was being unprofessional while on a work that has promised me of a big fat cheque.

Two: Because I heard I heard my name being called. No, screamed with respect from the doorway as a security guard attempted to keep a man at bay. A very, very familiar man.

"MISS HAN SHIN YOUNG" he hollers " I DONT HAVE THE PASS. BUT TELL HIM WE KNOW EACH OTHER"

Almost slipping through my seat I crane my wide eyed gaze to look at him. I know him. I was sure he was the man I met at the conference in Manila two months ago.

Fisher?

Fixer?

"ITS ALDO FISCHER. REMEMBER?" There was it. The one with a witch wife. As he struggled to free himself from the guard's clutches I contemplate to let him be. But since he was attracting attention I motion for the security to let him go.

And soon we found ourselves seated facing each other.

"I heard you got married" he speeds the starters, chugging the glass of water I gave him "Congratulations"

I don't say anything. I merely watch him- waiting for him to earn up to the matter.

"I wish for you both to have a successful marriage," he says warming his jaws with the dab of a hanky. He was nervous as heck. So like me. I guess he wasn't lying when he said he could understand.

"How is your wife?" It was a router. To make him know that I wasn't bitter about what had happened "And kids"

He goes tight for a second, then chuckled. A sad glint in his tone as he adjusted the loose strap of his watch.

"She filed for a divorce two weeks ago" he surges as I sat there sympathizing with him in mask. In reality, I wasn't so shocked by it. With the suffocation the woman was- I was surprised it had worked for so long. But when Fischer spoke again. I knew why. "She also wants the custody of both the girls"

Kids.

I see why Fischer stayed.

"But we are not here to talk about my misfortunes. But of a prospect" he undertook an involuntary pride. As if to convince me.

"Not happening. I am not selling the script" when I say it with a straight face, his entire demeanor falls into a mush.

"Please" he cries out of frustration "It will save me my job"

Rolling the pencil on the table I refused to look up at him so I could avoid being ushered into a guilt trip.

"There are better works your director can adapt from" I provide with my small, but detailed voice.

"You think I haven't tried that. He is obsessed with this project and I am a hamster that he is willing to sacrifice"

This leads me to a question.

"Why are you a hamster?" I inspect as his frustration dissolves.

"Why not?" He still had a thoughtful look on his face. He hadn't given it an impression.

"You can be a goat or a panda" I was stalling now.

"Probably because I get so scared easily. No, look. Hamster fits me and I -

He stops short. Then he glares at me or it's what I think he does.

"You are trying to seize me off the track" he accuses me as I smile in worry. What happened after that was pure chaos. He got up with a villainous glance and walked around me. Then he dropped down to my feet, grabbing my ankle,creating a scene. It took him two guards and a promise of consideration from me to take him out.

After that, the last three hours flew by with my mind and body occupied. When I was out into the main shopping hall I exhaled a loud sigh with my hands cupped by my knees as I crouched breathing.

Having skipped lunch and now standing at the peak hours of dinner time, I spot a lone vending machine by the right. With a vulnerable walk, I reach through my bag and pushed in the money for a pack of smarties and a nutrition bar, I expect it to roll down the disc tray as it always does.

But nothing comes out as I stare at the opening, waiting for it to answer me. Going as far as to tap the side of the storage I do my best to represent a composed ambiance. But when a converse clad leg from behind kicks at the base of the machine with sheer force do I jump shrieking.

With a hand to my heart, I turn to notice Lee who stood there as if he just didn't kick a private property. He looked unamused and ably I bothered, clothed in a simple long-sleeved t-shirt, khaki pants, and an additive baseball cap.

He looks at me through the side, his signature grin nonexistent. Missing since two days in a row now.

"You shouldn't kick something that gives you food" as I said it. I know it's not what I should be confiding to a person who was here for the sole requirement of taking me home.

"Similar to how one shouldn't leave a person uninformed when they share the same roof" he presses at the buttons with his voice as pressed with the pressure he was pressing at.

"I should have" admitting I rise a brow " But I forgot. Isn't it the same way how you sometimes leave the house too?"

He halts his repairing mechanisms as he shifts, the bright glow from the vending machine casts a luminous around us. The illumination that can reveal the blackheads that you don't even have. His nose, still looked glassy and clean. But they were high and sharp tonight. Angry even.

"It's different"

"It's sexist"

"You don't know this city like I do"

When I punch at the button harshly I know I was exhilarating my pent-up emotions that I should be sleeping off.

"You don't know me like I do" I couldn't recognize my voice as it lacked any kind of uncertainty. It felt as if it was raw with the truth. With Lee, in a week I wasn't holding my guard anymore. So when he grabs my wrist and makes me look at him. I hate how skillfully he could read me.

"Maybe I don't know you. But you are a defenseless girl in a new place- I am just trying to take care of you" his voice softens as i steal my gaze from his overwhelming ones.

"Seoul wasn't any better" I mumble to myself. The forbidden days resurfacing.

"You said something?" he lets go of my hands as I tap, defeated by the useless metal box that ate my money.

"I said I don't want to be taken care of"

when I say that I am unethical when it comes to redeeming my adamant attitude. I mean it. Perhaps if I had lacked a drawback in my temperament that keeps me grounded. I would've been the typical mean girl that everyone hates.

But Lee had an experimental answer to that. He moves my hands away from the buttons.

"Sometimes stubbornness needs to be treated with care" he lifts his palms up to the metallic glass frame "You have to gently stroke and caress them. Make them understand that you mean no harm" he does the very thing he says. Brushes the back of his fingers lightly by it.

Then he smirks. The kind that wasn't offensive or troubling. But casually intimidating.

"And at last, you got to smack some sense so they are surprised and give you what you want"

There was a sound of him swatting it carefully.

And just like that the engine vibrates and out slips the contents I had been yearning for. With a stoic posture I grab the treats, aware of the easy smile he now had after having made his point.

A point where he necessarily wasn't talking about an outrageous vending machine.

CHAPTER 11

S HIN
 Can't be seen. I know even if someone came in, they won't be able to see me. It's not their eyes deceiving, neither was I hiding. But I know I was an illusion in a segment of the past. Yet it felt so real and eerie. The room, the stench, the emotions.

The scratchy grey concrete scrapes, as if the slow, haunting steps that I was advancing with were walking over a bed of shattered glass. When I let my gaze stretch across the floor- I see it. The shreds of broken ceramics. The rays from the stripped ventilation help the room into a patterned gleam, the moonlight only made the atmosphere worse.

When I heard the groan of a young girl in pain, from a corner that I cannot see- her withering visage finally adjusts to the likes of my vision as I battle to look through. In a soaring leap, it all comes back to me. Like tumbling boulders of Jenga as the freezing night engulfs me. I hug myself- the dress and fancy heels that I wore weren't a shield from the room that lacked a heater.

But I know I was the future- I know I am the future so my heart went out for the girl in a bloodied t-shirt. She was young- not more than eleven. Half in and out of consciousness, she wills her eyes to plead. They were staring right at me. Through me. I couldn't even cry for her. How long has she been here for?

I look around in search of an escape. when I see the rusty door- I couldn't move. I don't move because I know it was locked. I know we both were trapped. So I make my way to her- crouch with a knee to the ground. It takes the young girl a complete minute to hoist herself up, her hair matted by her side, impeded with dried blood. Her russet brown eyes are afraid- her chapped lips parts as she whispered-

"It's cold" a frosty smoke wavers by her utterance as if justifying the truth.

"I know" my voice doesn't crack like hers. But it's the most I could do.

"I am hungry" a sob hikes her up.

I close my eyes- as her soft cries resonate. I don't open them to look at my younger self. But when the lock ticks- I feel every little junction of the fear bite through me.

When I open my eyes, I am gasping for air. Gaping around me for something to grab, to find a defense when a hand bleakly hold mine down.

"Shin. Its me. Lee" I hear him aiming to ensure me as I struggled to get away from his touch "Its just me" he repeats it again. Much slower this wise. And it's when I fall back to the seat- staring up at the leather interior of his car as a pulsing headache complains through me.

"What happened?" sulking I rub my temples, choking the thoughts away as I always do, it has became a habit by now. But not him. The piercing gaze of Lee flips my insides.

"You fell asleep" he narrates it cautiously, removing and discarding his cap by the glove box as he runs his hand across his hair to nap it up "And I think you had a nightmare. Just a bad dream I guess"

It wasn't a dream. But I was glad it was for now.

"Are you okay?" he should quit with the subtle regards, it will only make it irk me into blaming myself for letting the three days ruin the eleven years of my life. I was here to rectify and fix it alone. I was here to stop letting others do it for me. and with Lee- It wasn't possible. He was too considerate.

"Should we go see a doctor?"

Jostling the hair out of my face I snap to side. He was already analyzing me with his counterfeiting eyes. So when I vent- he barely reacted to it.

"You said so, it was just a dream. Can you stop treating me like a kid?"

He nods after a hefty silence. Still glossed with frustration that he shouldn't be a part of- I unlock the door and got out only to shuffle. Back and forth I turn, anyone would be standing out in a colossal arena while they had retired from the vehicle comprehending for it to be the place one has been residing in would do it too.

Soon I hear him leave the car. I don't question until he comes and stands next to me. The air was merciful in nature- the blend of humidity and moistening night only adds to the perfect composition to a track's atmosphere. I could stand here the whole night and not get bored. That is if my mind would let me.

"What is this?"

Playing with my finger I ferment my voice to remain nonchalant. But the traitorous excitement seeps through, as I suspected- Lee was stifling a smile knowingly even before I gave up pretending.

"You said that I don't know you the way you do. And it's true. Since we barely make an effort- I decided to let you know what I do to get rid of my thoughts" he stares ahead at the empty bleachers, his eyes shone with pride that seems to light him up.

"You race?"

He scrunched his nose playfully. His lips forming a smile.

"I used to. Was a professional formula one driver once" he preached his right arm up, resting it by the top of his black car so he was looking at me "I was later deemed unfit? It's why I returned to Korea"

The environment remained the same. He made it seem as if he hasn't just revealed his misfortunes to me. His positivity inspired me- but was he the same man he shows inside out? This speculation still lingered in the form of a question to which I can't seek an answer to. Not when he is doing more than he needs to keep me functioning.

"I am sorry" as I say it, he stands up pushing his body from the car.

"You don't have to be" he describes it like the words were crisp in his mouth. Awaiting the predictable response from me "I don't like to dwell on the past. And tonight- neither should you"

I skim through his physical language like a page from a book. A quick glance to see what he meant. But when he draws out his car keys and lifts my hand. I know what he wanted me to do.

"Focus on speed. I love how it feels to fly through the tracks" his maneuvering gaze is a hostage. So I listen to him. obediently "I want to know how it will be for you"

My emotions jumbled into a compounding ideology. When the keys got dumped into my palms- my lips curls into a smile that wasn't a result of practiced generator. I didn't even grasp the image of my reaction until I felt the need to stop doing it.

"I love your car" I nod, enclosing the keys into my fist as he lifts his brows jerking his head towards his Audi.

"You should see my collection someday?" he says backing up, paving a way so that I could reach the driver's side.

"A collection" I state slipping in with a nod.

"I anticipated you to be surprised by it. Impressed even" he leans so that his chin rested upon the open doors frame, he was grinning wide. I flop into the seat to look at him, also to cherish the feel of basking in such domain.

"A face not necessarily be the window to a personality. One can have the face of an angel and may work for a hitman. You never know"

"So you work for a hitman?"

"What?" But soon I got what he did with my prompt. Dismissing the odd feel of warmth at his wink I roll my eyes "I am. I kill people"

And it wasn't completely a lie.

Later his features contort into the one of complex deep thinking.

"So what you are saying is I don't look like a rac-

"Absolutely. I am shocked. But since I wasn't stiff to ideas- I can accept it with respect" I don't know why I keep cutting him off. But I was too hyper and actively in need to test this drive. I wanted him to let me concentrate.

But-

I look at him in time to witness his lip in a pucker. Then he pouts with cold sad eyes- dramatizing as he walks across and takes the passenger seat. He licks his lips while rolling his sleeve by the elbow. His pout was now gone, but the slight swell of his lips remained.

Even when he wasn't distracting me. I still wasn't focussed.

"Seatbelt" he orders. I slide the band down immediately. He asks me to press on the gas- the engine purrs to life, seductively. The tracks were empty- not a single livelihood to be seen at farthest of the vicinity. So when I start- I go smooth.

A lap later- I had read through the path enough to increase my speed.

"You doing good sweetie" he cheers, holding the bar for support since he was a plus and was a victim of inertia. I roll my eyes at his mockery- I work hard to maintain the balance of the vehicle with no jerky movements. Because as Lee had quoted thrice until now-

"Remember. Smoother is-

"-Faster"

When I picked up the final speed, I let go of the instructions and let my body go numb with the thrill. I laugh out, a peal of laughter that I had forgotten was a piece of me. It pummelled through me tonight. I wasn't loitering into fitful nuisance - the momentum that kept pushing me to limits had me caged in a euphoria that I couldn't understand. I don't want it to understand. So when it was

time for me to stop- I tone down the speed to an average, then I do the one thing that Lee probably hadn't expected me to since he- since he decently shouted-

"What are you doing?"

I removed my right foot from the throttle sharply, it causes an automatic transmission – a break with the right foot. I steer the wheel sharply in the direction I desired for it to- pulling the brake I held on to the safe button as the seething screech echoes, reels through. The car spins to a halt after the model skid.

When I lift my head, with my right hand curled dead on the wheel- I see the tracks through the curtain of my hair layering my face. Grinning I turn to look at Lee-

"It's been a long time since I did that" I heave, but when I saw Lee staring out with jaws clenched I decided to cease perking up. "You okay. Lee?"

"Do I look okay?" he undid his seat belt and cleared his throat. "I didn't know you could do that"

Instantly my smile was back, his were still absent. But I don't pry at it. I was feeling too light and up high in the abyss for me to marvel about his.

"Dad. He taught me. He had this spare car that he'd let me trash around with"

As I reach out and grab my sling, so that I could have my treats that I suddenly remembered about- I heard him mumble- not high- nor low. But enough for me to listen.

"I am never getting fooled by someone's face. ever"

The damp grass wasn't wet with vapor. Cooling enough for sensation, but not so greasy to imprint any unwanted pattern in your clothes. So when Lee said he wanted to relax his spine before he drives us back to the penthouse – I inferred that bleachers were off-limits. He seems to agree with me as we made our way to the acres of wide-spreading grass bed- the lights here temporarily flickered to life as it's sensors selects our presence. My vision relied on the soft faint glow from them.

There were seats by the intervals, but I loved the feel of clean grass on my skin so I plopped to the ground. Lee followed the suit without a blink.

The sky was dull and gloomy, with no stars in sight. Not mandatory for them to make a moment better. They can do whatever they want. However, they want- but aren't they still a part of a constellation that moves in a circle? Like us. like all of us.

As I had been ogling at the basic night, I felt his gaze on me. He simultaneously starts to speak as I looked at him.

"Why Vegas?" he sat with his legs crossed in front of him, both his palms lay flat. Pushing his shoulder up. while I sat idly with the pack of sugar bites nestled by my lap.

It doesn't set me off, his query. It coursed through me that it was the third time he was asking me the same question. I don't lie today.

"When I first came to meet you, you were attempting to convince your Dad to let you go" biting my lower lip I search through the bag to find my preferred flavor "I was told that you use to live here. since I haven't been to vegas- I decided to kill two stones with a bird"

When I found the orange charm, I pop it in. As I chewed looking around- I realized I was still being watched at.

"Two birds with a stone"

Faltering my index to gratify his correction, I nod.

"Hope for whatever reason you are here for its commencing by"

When there was a regulative silence that proceeded after what I had asked- confused I dust my hands and snap my fingers by his face. He doesn't blink even at that, letting his gaze fall to by the patch of marble square with water sprayer he breathes. His demeanor fluctuates faster than I could say his name. From happy, shock to acutely passive. As of now- I cannot know what goes within him even if I project through. He has to say it himself- there was no other option.

"It is in progress" he makes circles with his pinky "What about yours. How has it been so far?"

Like a crackling cassette, the incidents rewinds in sequence. With a pained sigh, I grumble.

Terrible.

But I lie. Like always.

"I haven't been able to do the things that I wanted to yet. But the week wasn't void of anything less interesting than it should be" I sounded so convincing or maybe I was believing in what I was remarking.

A heavy gust of wind sweeps through, fluttering our clothes, hair and caressing our skin. I close my eyes momentarily to sink in the feels. And also to avoid the dust that could get into them.

"What things?'

There wasn't a completive second wasted. I tell him without hesitation- the mystery of how I was able to do so will always remain a mystery. Maybe it was the air or it could be the development in me. But he was the most trustworthy element I had at my disposal so-

"I have this list of tasks that I would like to do before we part ways" enjoying two more bites I swallow them before continuing "of course. It always depends on you for when to do that. When you decide to end the marriage, I'll go back"

The way he regarded me with perplexion as if he was fighting something crucial was strange. He had the tensed outlook similar to that of Hwan when we bickered. But contrary to it- Lee kept it to himself, probably settling to ask something else instead.

"What kind of task?" his tone differed, it was precise and laced with brooding curiosity.

"Nothing interesting" I try to wave him off. But-

"No. you have to tell me. I want to be a part of this"

I pause hogging up when he certainly was considering to be there for me. I place the bag aside and smiled at him. He doesn't mimic me like I want him to.

"You must have a better place to be than tag along with me"

"I don't"

"That's t a lie. You have friends here"

"They will kill me if I showed up now after having avoided them for weeks" he arcs his brows as if challenging me. Weaving on to how placid and dedicated I was to keep him at bay.

"Talk to them. They'll understand" by the present, I was requesting him. making it quite pathetically obvious as a slow smirk marks his features.

"No. you have to understand that It's fruitless to distract me. I am helping you complete the list of tasks. You like it or not" with that he tries to reach for the candies. Tried because as soon as I regarded the advancement I hurl the packet back to me. He grabs the empty air instead.

"What's your level?"

He humours the question as if to dodge it away, his eyes fighting a smile. It was detoxifying to watch him shake his head befittingly. Taking me for a fool.

"I checked. I can have that" he gestures with his chin jutted out.

"Level Lee"

With that- there was an onset of stares that lasted until none of us vouched away from.

"Borderline. But still manageable" I squeal as his voice rose an octave high by the end as he launched his arms to grab the smarties from me. Soon I was crawling away-

"Take the granola bar- it's much healthier for you" I piqued when his fingers grab my ankles, he was too swift with motions. And to strong for my physique.

"No- I need those" his arms snakes through my waist, In reflex I react fast, curving my hands across the last few that were left, I cram it into my mouth right when he spins me around. I seal my lips shut landing on my back as he grabs my wrist lifting it above my head.

He goes stiff when he realizes what I had done. He cups my cheeks, his thumb pressing down my chin in disbelief.

But that wasn't the only thing we got aware of. When the heat from our proximity slowly began to make it's presence felt. With our bodies tangled up upon the grass and his conscious weight on me did we went inflexible. As if we both couldn't move or think. Or at least mine didn't.

Thankfully, Lee flings himself off. Rolling to side as I sat up choking after having swallowed the confections.

"It's getting late. We should leave" he suggests as I nod, holding in another fit of cough to be polite.

But no matter what I did. The shift of something puzzling seem to have taken home in between us this night, because it was the initial time It had been an complete hour with a person who was able to keep my attention glued to him and his antics.

As for him-

He was doing it again. His occasional. The beginning of him being less Lee like.

But it was a tad bit severe.

Who am I kidding! It was a lot severe.

CHAPTER 12

L^{EE}

Last night presumably was the first in the week where I was awake as shin slept. I fought to not skim through her visage while she was at it. Losing, as I compiled to side with my arm cushioning my head. The most comfortable position I could find to browse her- it wedged the room into a state of tranquility. Her peaceful stature, the one that wasn't so keen on stealing her expressive gaze away from me whenever they caught me staring at her.

Why had I been fascinated by her tonight? It had been a lingering thought that has been contributing to my brisk awakeness was constant. I had a counterclaim to justify my actions.

That would be my lack of relationships during past years that had deprive me of-

She fits so perfectly in my embrace.

As i thought I was wrestling for an essence of artificially colored and morbidly preserved pack of candy. I realized I was paving a way to my doom because Soon the smarties didn't appear as delicious as her soft pink lips that contorted into a pout.

To put it this way- I had been impressed by the details she cloaked while she dressed or walked or the way she carried herself despite the hundreds of distractions she embroils in a moment- but I had been too diligent to accept that I was slowly, but surely getting attracted to her.

Like the pieces of the jigsaw, every single image of her fixes into a finished product. The mental pictures that I didn't even know I had- clubbed together to remind me that- I was messing this up.

The cold shower in the morning didn't aid either. My head wasn't empty of her. Her ash brown hair that she seldom styled in a wave ignited with a golden spectrum whenever the sunlight touched her as she moved, It was an imagery that was vivid as a day. Also something I didn't know I had observed about her, I was yearning to know how it will be like to have my hand buried in them. She had a thin waist, I know because I had held her by it last night. They were on repeat. Every feel of it despite the way I had held her did not even had an intention behind it.

I just wanted the stupid candy. But here I was-

There were more than a couple of ideas that latched into my undignified aspirations. I had always been show and not tell kind of man. I could show her- but the ethical and moral part of me was so disgusted by what I was contemplating to offer a girl who was classically off-limits for such an absurd proposal.

I can't taint someone so pure just because I can't have control over my physical needs. It was pathetic. So shameful-

So I shove a spoonful of cereal into my mouth- chewing on it roughly as she sat opposite to me by the kitchen counter- a skipped seat in front so I could see through the side. She woke up earlier than me- she did have a good night's sleep. Unlike me.

It explains why she was done with her breakfast ages ago and now had some kind of notes scrawled all across. Her mac book was open, her newly delivered goldfish swarm around in a jar- that too was present by the top. she had a scented candle lit among them. Why does she even need that when she herself smells so divine?

I must drown myself in the fishbowl.

"What are you doing?" slicing the soggy broth into half I ask. A conversation does disperse the brewing awkwardness.

"I am editing" she heaves a sigh and her hair does that fluttering thing again. But I keep my phase.

"You are an editor?" there was an unrequired surprise in my tone, I wasn't perspective of her to have a job. Let alone an editor. She spins the pencil, weaving it in and out of her sleek fingers. Her eyes were hesitant before she nods in short.

"I write articles and stuffs" she drawls out as I give her an easy smile. It looked like she wasn't fond of whatever she had been up to. It was evident as she kept scattering her concentration from the pages to the lone fish. Every damn time with a sad sigh.

Soon I was joining her in liberation. With stacks of documents piled in, I was emulating her. They were sent by my father- it came in this morning. Apparently I was only allotted a week's day off to enjoy the bliss of my married life with the girl who sat across.

The very girl who was watched with an astonishment and amusement combined.

"Your family owns a casino here?"

I don't bother to hide my vanity, flipping the file close I lean back.

"I am breaking it down though. An affluent hotel sounds much more reputable for the family's reputation" I shrug as if it wasn't a big deal. But it was- I had been working my ass off to get this project done.

"So- you are like an heir or something?" she cracks her knuckles in detective fashion, for the moment I forgot where we are and where I should be looking at so I stared at the fish. "Since your older sister chose a different career"

"Yeah- yeah, something like that" scratching my brow, which was a habit that frictions when I was nervous- which was rare in regular. But I was doing it today, regardless of wanting to or not "I would dump it on Aaron any day- but he takes half a day to decide if he wants to have peanut butter or chocolate spread on his bread. So Dad has to do with the best shot he got"

It was silent then, unwillingly I lift my defeated gaze to look at her. she had her lips mashed and an intellectual contemplative impression going on as she peered at her memos.

"I understand" she separates her thumb and index- gathering the tress of hair by her shoulder. She grows them up, revealing her porcelain neck – her off-shoulder top was a bonus. She tied her hair in a bun- I hooked my thumb and undid the top two buttons of my polo to hydrate.

"It's hot" she exclaims fanning her exposed skin with a frown, her eyes glancing at the sunny morning from the ceiling window.

I look down at the stocks report, biting the inside of my cheeks.

"It is. It unbearably is"

It wasn't the sole thing that kept driving me crazy, the one aspect that wasn't hot- but still was making me go nuts was her deliberation. If it wasn't for her suggestion, Dad would have never let me come back to this city- and neither would have I been able to heal the forgotten wounds with the traitors roaming free without a conscience. If they could do it to me- it could happen to anyone, I am privileged. But not everyone is. To abuse power for the one who had done it in the past is a dish served on the same platter.

And shin doesn't even know that she is preparing the cuisine with me.

So I cannot let her be.

"Don't celebrate that I have given up on what you said last night," I say, striking off the useless spectators with a red highlighter, "You will tell me the tasks and I will share it with you"

When she received my attention- there was not much to be differentiated between the fish and herself. Though there was an additive scowl with the gaping mouth- she was about to say something when the bell rang. I motion her to sit tight as I got up to receive the door. The penthouse was vast and had an immense decorative interior, more than I would like. When I quote sera outdid herself, I mean every single word. It doesn't feel like I am walking in my own house. With a large chandelier to the indoor pool room, it now hosted a gym room and a subdivided gaming parlour. Even as reach the door- I still was inches deep into recollecting the changes done here, too preoccupied to notice the person on the other end until I had entirely torn the door open.

Was it late to shut it on his face?

"Who is it?" the soft, curious voice of shin reaches me from behind. but the warning bell shrills as I backed a step away. My heart didn't hammer- but bones sure we're worried.

"Edmund?"

It comes off sloppy- and rightfully horrified. Neat but terrified.

"Lee!" he takes a step inside- I retreat one more.

"Edmund" this echoed as if I was scrapping at a negotiation. We can take buddy.

"Lee?" he did not want to talk.

An approximative of ten-second passed. And then we were all over-

"We are adults now. we can sit and talk through this" I scream running as he chased me down the hall.

"We are talking through" he jumps through the couch nearing, as I circled the chaise lounge- he looked bigger than before, also probably because I hadn't seen him in person for two years. He has changed so muc-" I prefer to talk with my fist"

Nope- he hasn't changed.

He was a fatheristic anomaly, but the industry screwed with his saintliness and little by little, he became this- this inked dude with the patience of an apple. He turns sour in minutes if left open.

I left him clueless for a week. So when I was tackled into the sofa with his fingers crushing my collars, I croaked.

"You weigh like a cow" he lifts me up with my shirt as I grab at his wrist, it was of no use- but I was acting out.

"You had a cow on top of you?" he wheezed tiredly after the active hunt.

"No" I whisper grinning "But if I had, I bet It'll be as heavy as you"

He did punch me then. A temporarily bruising one which I know there was no escape from because it's when Edmund resumed to behave In likes of a normal citizen. And a friend. Massaging my cheekbone I sat up once he got off me. His tattoo sleeve was veiled by his black leather jacket and his checkered shirt was as creased as mine.

"You could have avoided this?" he says, gaining his breaths. Running a hand through his brunette cluster. His shadowed beard may intimidate others. But I know he has it because Hailey hates it on him. He was still the golden president of Stuart beneath the rugged outlook. "I am probably the most forgiving one. Elzina wanted me to carry a baseball bat along so I could-

He swallows his sentence as his gaze lands on shin. The poor girl who had to witness this on a blissful Sunday morning for no reason, she stood cemented by the floor near where we were a while ago. Edmunds's neck snaps at my direction and I snuggle into the fuzzy couch with a smile.

He gradually seems to realize that with news of marriage printed across tabloids comes a wife.

"Did I just scarred my first impression?" he mouths, its barely a whisper. I nod as he got on his feet immediately. Shin forces an uncertain smile- slowly walking to us when Edmund dusted his jacket , scooping the last pride into a bucket as shin bowed.

Internally I groan at how courteous she was.

Edmund who had his hand extended- copies her right when she brings her out to reach him. They do this twice before they got a hold of it.

"It's a pleasure to finally meet you Shin Young" Edmund's intonation had been the deepest among us all, while mine falls more on the intense side and Alex to the cold and passive ones. So to watch the six feet two inches of him look down so tenderly at the small shin little shin and then at me was like getting an approval from a mother.

Even my mother doesn't do that.

"You know my name?" it morphes into a genuine happiness as Edmund shrugs.

"Of course I do. I memorized the name and face the day I found out about the wedding through the fan page of Lee on Instagram"

"You follow my fan page?"

"You have a fan page?"

We three were not on the same page. Wait- we weren't on the same book either. So I was flashing out my commercially acclaimed teeth after Shin's alter ego emerged at a crucial moment.

"Wait-" she inspects Edmunds's face, her nervousness vanishing in strips, "I think I know you"

Edmund flexes his posture, throwing a smug smile at me. he doesn't know Shin yet- so as he turned to her, she was there with the conspiracy plot twist.

"You are Hailey Howards Ex aren't you?"

She makes me so proud.

Bewildered Edmund merely blinks politely as I doubled over a fit of silent laughter. Shin softly gasp,

"I am so sorry. That's so disrespectful of me" she angles her head in guilt " Ex or not- I know you are a famous director. It's just I love her movies and- I shouldn't even be saying this and i-

"It's okay" the way Edmund tried to calm her down only cause my mirth to reciprocate. With my fist to mouth, I let my gaze stay crinkled at them "I like to be reminded of my past mistakes. It grounds me"

After he got innocently roasted by shin, he offered us that we sit and have a chat. Shin was quiet as usual- after she had confessed of her social phobia, it was the first wise I saw her interact with someone else other than me. A person she did not know or met. Yet she sat there so strong and composed- probably too busy tracking her thoughts. I wish I could help her, If only she was as transparent as Edmunds's punch to tell me exactly how it feels or just what she needs.

As for Edmund- he was here because of work. Had been since three days- he filled me in with everything that had taken place in Orlando so far- and It made me comprehend how terribly I miss them all. In the middle of the narration, another bell tings- cutting his words as Edmund got up. Shin was sipping on a carton of Australian hazelnut and choco milk that Edmund had brought for us. we finished it a while ago- but since shin looks like a slow drinker, she still had the straw preached between her lips. She wasn't even drinking.

"You don't like it?" I ask in the absence of Edmund "You can give it to me if you don't"

She releases the straw and looks at me, her lidded eyes wide like a doll. She was a doll.

Shut up Lee!

"It's not that" she bites her lower lip in all seriousness "It's just that, I am lactose intolerant and i-

Two footsteps ascends and we both look at its owner- the person who was tailing with multiple luggage bags behind Edmund wasn't a stranger. it was me who fetched Aldo Fischer his job- how or why, was a difficult question to answer. But I had nothing against this harmless dude. Contrary to it I pity at how harsh Edmund is to him.

Mr. Fischers face lights up as soon as he sees me, but when it falls on the shin, a loud shuffle of bags tackling down his shoulders fills the void. He points at shin, unhurriedly with susceptible gaze and utters one acknowledging word-

"You"

For her answer- shin chokes. She wasn't even drinking but lifts her index asking for a minute. We give her that. She uses it to clear her throat- her eyes rigid on Mr. Fischer.

"You both know each other?" a confused Edmund trades his gaze by both of them. I do too- what was it that we are not seeing?

I had never seen shin volunteer to reply so fast. She picks herself up with an unyielding smile and grabbed Mr.Fischers hand as if in welcome. Mr. Fischer still stood there- his eyes held the melancholy that wasn't adding up with shins chirpy addressing.

"We- actually met at a church nearby"

To which I had to ask with a suspicious arc of the brow.

"You went to a church?"

To which Edmund had to know-

"There is a church nearby?"

CHAPTER 13

S HIN

It wasn't fair.

The fate toyed with me, not that it had drizzled it's unyielding lucky charms on me ever since I was a kid. I still wanted it to behave since It already had done its worst. So when I saw Fischer walk in- my prosecutions were more of a reflex and lucidly not the result of a shock. When I shook his hand, which was a bone-crushing message disguised and forwarded through the gesture- he knew to keep his mouth sealed.

But I don't reckon it was as convincing to Lee, since he would would scan us both to see how much of a stranger we were to be enough to believe that we were acquainted in church.

My exclusive empathy towards Fischer was the occasional smile I kept darting his way, reminding him to smile and quit acting so sloppy. He sat there as if I he swallowed a lemon and had it struck up his throat. sad and bitter.

I am sorry Fischer. But I have my reasons.

Fischer and I were the quietest among us four, Fischer's was understandable- mine was a habit. But to see the face of a celebrity that I often came across as I flipped through the glossy pages of Harper Bazar or rolling stone affected me more than it should. Probably because it took me a mere minute to put the two and two together.

He was the director. He was the one.

And he was looking at Lee with such adoration and smile that it made me sick. Lee was equally smitten to see his friend there that he has probably has forgotten to check me out since an hour. I was not a fool- I know he had been up onto it since this morning. Can't blame him either- cause I was no better.

His thoughts have been flailing my mind ever since last night- I even dreamt of him seated on a Ferrari in traditional hanbok with paparazzi clicking his pictures as he happily posed. He was famous- I searched for him before I went to bed. I wasn't left dis-appointed- he looked ravishing in his racing gears, those images popped up sooner than the articles. I had scrolled through it for an unnecessary fifteen minutes till he walked out of the washroom. His hair damp from the shower as he towel-dried his hair.

Trained in his reflection, he styled his strands for bed. In an automatism I found my fingers combing my own tress. Who was I attempting to impress? For the sake of sanity, I wake up with a bird's nest. Every. Single. Day.

But when you had a specimen like a Lee around, you uncon-sciously froth to take care of one's own appearance. Today I real-ized Lee had a perfect back, broad and lean. His arms get a slight rise of veins when he is stressing a hold onto something. His gaze is always bold on you and he never, like ever shy's away from staring. He doesn't glance- he stares. Hard and impulsive.

Also, he got the perfect set of abs to end his beauty saga. How do I know? He apparently had done a session of a photo shoot for his marshalls campaign. It was for Calvin Klein's jeans- he only wore jeans in that. The search educated me more than what I had bargained for.

So I had to purchase my long-listed, and awaited goldfish the next morning. I haven't named her yet, but she keeps fermenting me. I desire to be like her, a careless freak In a bowl moving in circles, but happy.

How do I presume for her to be happy?

I don't know- I plainly assume it. Isn't how we all interpret things and make them work?

If one looks good.

They must feel good.

It's how I go through my life. Providing them a false variation of me. It works.

Work reminds me of how Edmund Sargent, god bless the surname itself that resounds as if he is a knight from the renaissance. He was here for a quick segment of his movie, but he also announced that he wanted to treat us both before he leaves for a tribal island on the east coast where the further extension of the shoot was scheduled.

Lee's face fell like a puppy whose favorite toy was chewed up by a toddler. And when we finally were at the pastry parlor that Edmund drove us to- He took Lee to the counter, Fischer and I occupied a booth that had a crystal vision of the elegantly large, all-white bakery that smelled of cocoa and money. The place we lounged had a wall staked up entirely of one-way glass so we could catch a glimpse of the city outside. Also- did I mention we were at the topmost floor of one of the largest towers In Nevada?

From where I was positioned- the sun set that I saw from up here, played a game of hide and seek among the buildings. It was surreal. The sun was orange in hue- the color of my gold fish, same in spectrum. I wonder if she feels my absence. And that's how I ruin a moment-

I could've admired the ball of fire. But no, I had a fish to compare it with.

"I feel like a third wheel," I say picking a roasted almond from the square wood plate that had been there is welcome. Crushing the shell texture between my molars I watch as Edmund pats Lee on his shoulder, They both laughed presumably sharing a joke while they dictated the flavors to the staff. I cannot hear them, but their energy was filtering the quiescent atmosphere.

"You are the fourth. I had always been the third" I look back a Fischer smirking. We both were cowards so we compliment each other.

"So that's the director huh?" motioning my thumb I smile, he melts in-seat stretching his creamy woolen jacket, covering his chest. The bitter twist of his lips returning in full score.

"So you are the wife huh?"

It wasn't a battle of squirming anymore as he shot up suddenly, his cunning grin was harmless- I stared right back at him.

"I can blow the cover in an instant. I have an upper hand. It looks as if Lee has no idea about who you are, or else Mr. Sargent would have personally contacted you. Why use me?" he snaps his fingers, my bracelets crinkle as I rest my elbow by the tabletop. It was cold, so I take it take it down.

"Doing that won't get you anywhere" manipulation wasn't my forte, but when it came to such appraisal- anybody in my place would act the same. So I continue "You'll lose your promotion"

He crossed his arms, his chest puffs up, his nose flares as if to deny- then he frowns, and his body deflates when my statement got to him.

"M-My promotion?" he bellowed in murmur, his eyes spans up as I grabbed more almonds to keep my heart in check. What am I doing? Will I be able to take such a step? "You will agree to it?" he expressed in awe. Swallowing the nutritive I offer my demand.

"I need time" I freeze the second I told that, the burden of what could happen falls on me as I blink it off. Stabilizing my voice I stare at him "I will sell it, but now- there is something that I have to take care of. But before I do it. Buy me time- don't let him find out that it's me"

As I speak of him, I shift to spot them still with their claws deep in the showcase. Like two kids elated to make the best of coin and food. Lee, as if scenting my stare turned to look at me. He waved, signaling me to join him. It was terrible already that I was reaping flustered by his sole presence. I was happy were I was, Fischer and my almonds. The sun was tipping us a farewell and the store lights seem to lethargically bath in a warm yellow hue.

Lee scowls when I don't do much, except stare. Keen on the need of moment I mouth, 'go on. I am fine', as soon as I suspect him trying to walk over here.

He halts perplexed, but he moves to the barrier, providing a window to the pleasantries.

'Which one?'

By now we read lips as we communicated.

'Anyone'

'You sure?'

'Totally'

"How do you know that Mr. Sargent doesn't know about you already?" startled at Fischer's remarks, I run a hand down my face. I had momentarily forgotten about the plus one until he spoke. I refrain from facing Fisher that instant as Lee tilts his head in concern.

Wasn't of use was it to keep telling him that he shouldn't be babysitting me always, it seems to trigger a more complicated response from him. I shake my head with a lighthearted assurance- then I look at the old man, nattily.

"He wasn't pouncing at me to get a contract signed like you were Fischer"

He seem to evaluate it with a deep crease crowing him.

"You are smart"

"It's common sense"

"I probably lack that" he admits, then- "Fischer? Seriously? I am thirty-three"

Avoiding his gaze I scrunch my nose. Did that slip?

"It's what I address you in the head. Besides- I am not in Korea and you would never have understood our cultural honorifics. So...

"You can call me that. It's refreshing. I hate my name honestly" he shudders, ultimately plunging into the bowl of dry fruits. It's the rule- eat as much amount of free food as you can.

"I would too. If I was named Aldo" I snort- he snorts. We mutually decided we had ugly snorts so we were quiet for a while. Then piece by piece it juggled us both and our onset of displeasure was so in sync that it scared us.

"Ah, it can't be true-

"How can you-

-of all the girls-

-of all the directors-

-Lee married you?"

-it is a friend of Lee"

We were back to normal when Lee and Edmund joined us, I scooted my body into the smallest corner as soon as Lee sat next to me. The wide sofa wasn't enough to maintain a distance from him, he was burning me up. He rose his brow in notion.

"I am ashamed of Lee" Edmund politely looks at me. My anxiety strikes again- how can Lee have such influential friends? How can I have such an influential husband like Lee. Why was I even here?

Yes- I did this to myself.

"Edmund- you are overreacting" Lee interrupts as Edmund was about to proceed. Edmund awards him a disgusted snort.

"I am not. A man that doesn't know his wife's preference is a shame on earth" as he recites, Lee slides a brownie delight my way with his disapproving gaze on Edmund. Fischer had no call in this, by the time I dug through my first bite he was halfway done with his strawberry tart. "I Know Aldo's likes by now"

Lee sighed, nodding. His gaze hooded as he took the scolding in. but mentally I could feel his naked frustration. I wasn't the only one hiding secrets, was I?

The texture of liquid mousse and cake elopes my tongue as I closed my eyes in ecstasy.

"It is so good" I whispered.

"Is it?" Lee was quick to ask in relief. I nod, no wonder why Edmund and Lee explained that they were a regular here. In fact Edmund had reserved the whole parlor for the evening and had gluten-free desserts customized for Lee. He was the happiest I ever saw- with three full servings on his platter.

By now- Fischer and I weren't so skeptical of tagging and wheeling around these two birdies, because as the day commences, it's the food that matters. They shared some old, inside jokes which went above our head- but it's the lineage of so many new names that they brought up that gave me an insight into the past life of Lee. He must've been such a dedicated social butterfly. There were so many of his friends mentioned in a span of fifteen minutes that I lost count after three.

I was the opposite of him in every sense with an ability to block my own family if It got too much to bear while he might end up opening the doors for thieves to get in so he can befriend them for his entertainment. A person who wasn't transparent, but opaque- foreshadowing everything so one could always come back for more. It was him.

"You said you are staying for a couple more days" Lee diverts it at Edmund, not once making Edmund garner a conversation at me. He replied for me- it was amusing and moving to know he was distracting his friend so I won't be pressured into speaking against my comfort.

Dwelling into it will only swerve my spiraling allurement towards him. so I focus on the cake and conversation and not on his subtle meticulous efforts to aid me. I don't want and want it at the same time.

I bet none of the leading feminist community out there would ever desire a spineless feminist like me who won't stand up for herself, but also would not like to borrow someone's spine when in need- which makes me appreciate the spine structure of Lee. It's beautiful. Perfect even. Wasn't infested by text neck or shaggy posture- he had a runway figure that-

"I have to meet someone before I go-" Edmund paused, he had an intimidating jawline which made the one on Lee look delicate. Though they both were of the same age, Edmund seem to have aged more than Lee, similar to me, I still have ten percent of my baby fat left on my cheeks. "-I have to convince a writer to let me turn her work into a motion picture"

Both Fischer and I locked our gaze for two good seconds, then we resumed eating. My appetite vanished in a clockwise direction as the conversation between the two friends unfolded.

"You are already off on a new project? I thought you were packed for two years" Edmund takes a moment to reply, I hear them with my eyes cast on the saucy dessert. I can't look up- not now.

"I do- but I can't lose this opportunity to anyone else" he dips his utensils and sat up, I don't inspect his top though "I tried sending Aldo to meet her. Twice. But that stubborn woman rejected my proposal, unbelievable isn't it?"

Lee nods sideways, a bit lagging. Even disinterested. But then-

"She calls herself Elixir. But isn't she a mortal like us all? From where does all such attitude comes from? I swear if I met –

Lee drops his spoon on the table. It falls with a clink followed by silence.

"What did you say her name was?"

Pause

"Elixir"

Acute pause

"Her name?" ridiculously stretched pause "Elixir is a girl?" he exclaimed with hurt clouding his voice. The disbelief so evident as if this was the betrayal he wasn't anticipating. My heart began to go out for him, but then u remembered why he hates me so much. He loathes Elixir with passion.

"You know her? you read her work?" Edmund, probably immune to such reactions resumed eating "Its astonishing to know how one can create such art and yet have shitty personality"

Fischer had his gaze glued to the glass window. He was staring at a far distance, his soul a mix of peace and prosperity as if he was levitating inwardly, embarkingng to make himself feel invisible. Contrary to him, I was charring with animosity.

"No- what's to be panicked about is how a girl can invest such monstrosity" I had no clue from where I found the butter knife to butcher the contents of my plate. I wish I could promise that I wasn't imagining a face while I was at it "Be careful when you meet her. She seems evil"

Like his friend, Edmund was to quick to acknowledge Lee.

"I will" he then looks at a meditating Fischer "He has been like that since he met her. Don't worry buddy" he goes as far as to place a hand on his shoulder. Fischer doesn't budge or turn to look at Edmund. "-she can't say no to me. I am a Sargent, send me her details I'll personally-

"-We should go now" Fischer rattles the top as he ascends in the speed of a light. His breaths were hard, his eyes narrowed and pleading. He pushes Edmund to the side as he makes his way out.

since we all were done – Lee collectively decides that it was indeed time to leave. But Edmund had more remarks to be coined my way-

"I wish we had more time in our hands to get to know each other. My apologies that this idiot kept me occupied. If I find time- I will swing by the penthouse" his smile was easy- mine wasn't. I couldn't stomach one after having heard my praise in such aligned and steep narration. Hesitantly, he tipped and looked away when my placid gaze became too disturbing. In the elevator I stood in front- they were behind me with fFisher abandoning us all as he took stairs. He quoted it as for digestion. I bet it wasn't.

"Is shin young Alright?" I could see their reflection on the mirrored elevator door. So can they see me? even with my back to them, I could see them staring down at the top of my fuming skull.

"It's shin" I blurt. My voice void of sweet artificiality.

"Is shin alright?"

Why on earth will he whisper to Lee when we were inside a box thirty-seven story above the ground?

I was right here.

"I don't know" Lee replies in the same tone. But he also had to tame his curiosity in such severe moment-

"Aren't your heels taller than usual?"

"Yes" grunting I glare at the lowering number in the digital board. The number ten in neon red was calming my nerves. I was almost there.

"Why will you wear something so sharp? Does it hurt?"

Enough-

I can't take the criticism anymore. The next thing might be them asking me why I breathe the wrong way.

Spinning around I stared at them. Dividedly. Sniffing I coiled my fingers into a ball.

"No" I watch Lee regard me sparkingly. Edmund was understandably confused " No- my ankles don't hurt. And I had to wear them so I don't look like a freaking chicken nugget among two roasted beef legs"

A ring echoes.

More light pours in as the door slides open.

Turing, I walk away. But not before I heard Edmund and Lee simultaneously whisper talk among themselves-

"Poor girl, she must be so upset to-

"Did she just called us-

-have a husband who is not aware-

-roasted beef legs?"

- of her favorite flavour"

So...?

CHAPTER 14

S HIN

The woman's slap was reassuring, her palms weren't as calloused or merciless as the man's punch. I preferred her mode of torture to the other one. I was starving, the woman was against the idea. But lost to him. An hour more, I don't think I can keep my concious awakened.

My head falls to the side with half of my body hunching with the momentum. Her hand weaves through my hair and I was yanked back- I face him. I should've known. She never touched my hair. Shabby, tall, and grouchy since the day I had opened my eyes. I can't even recognize how many hours it had been since they took me in a hostage.

I focus on the split, thick brown scar running down his side, from his temple to the ear lobe. His cropped hair damp with grease and dirt, he smelled of burnt coal.

"Listen here kid" he growls, a chill elopes my battered body at the raging threat, if listening was an emotion- I was doing my best to not let him think otherwise. I listened obediently "It's either your mother listens to us, or you die here"

When my mouth thirsted to swallow the fear before I could free my words out, I couldn't. They were parched. So dry that I couldn't feel the texture of my tongue. My gaze darts to the woman- unlike him, she resembled a person one would pass through the street.

Her eyes were always alert, though she kicked and thrashed me around right before each call they made to Mom so I could beg and cry as I spoke. She wasn't as cruel with the pressure she used. I looked at her for solace. My eyes hazing with each blink.

She crossed her arms, looking away. she often did that when the man was around me. Ignored initially, but later stopped him at the right time from damaging me beyond repair,

But tonight it was fruitless, it was as if I was rooting to find a pearl among a bucket of muck.

I breathed through my parted lips, the blocked nostrils too tight as a result of the constant mental breakdowns I was having.

"She won't do it" my voice trembled, an octave higher than me "What you are asking for is too big"

Abruptly I am pushed to the side, he screams in frustration as my temple hits the concrete. Soon my visions weren't vague, but blacking out altogether. For the first time, I took notice of the lady fighting with the man-

"This won't do" it came from far away, her terrified voice scream-ing in shock as a hand presses against the side of my head, probably to curtail the blood flow. I feel the touch, I hear the sounds. But they slip away the hastier I tried to keep my conscience alive "This kid is not the one we are here to kill"

I wanted to hear, know more of what they had in store for me. To believe that my mother will choose me over her duty.

But I know- even if she choose to do it, our life will be worse than what these two could do to me.

So I slept through it.

Slept through it similar to how I sleep through every good thing that could have happened to me.

My trainers spring against the ground as I ran, the sole bit my toes uncomfortably since the sneakers were new. I ran with the speed, propelling my stamina in a quest to vacate my mind. It was six-thirty in the morning, and the park had infrequent joggers minding their own business. With my hoodie up in order to avoid any social interactions, I fling my priority into planning my day.

I had my calendar full of what I must be doing today. But when I received a call from the alleged designer that the coffee guy had implemented me off- I realized I had entirely forgotten about him too. I can't even recall his name until the woman herself had brought it up.

"Mr. Moreno had us see to it. any time today will be fine with Belinda, we already have his tailoring measure-

Nicholas Moreno.

My insides groaned at how stupid I was. I had gambled with the impression that I will turn into a new leaf today when I was a grown-up tree that lacked photosynthesisim. It certainly was too late. Wheezing I slowed on the track, bent with my hands on my knees gasping for air. I glare at the path ahead of me, and in two minutes I was running again.

Again and away from regrets, mistakes, and traumas. The morning had been cloudier than what the weather had suggested, I can't even jog in peace. Hicking up the pace, harder and faster I comprehensively began to envy Lee as I skim over the events from yesterday.

Even with a shattered dream, he had a life where he had ample reasons he could live for. A story that he could proceed with. A life that he could look forward to. I don't see or speculate mine to be like his. Resting by a tree, I let my head fall to my hand as i skids into a seating position. No matter how much I resisted the tears kept coming. My body fell weaker as I bawled my eyes out in the secluded corner. The strong façade I had up melts, my sanity acts as a diplomatic wax that can't survive a temperature. A coward. A stupid girl who sleeps only to wake up without hope.

As I cried, I even forgot what I was crying about. When the drizzling rain pelts, I cross my leg and hug it to my chest. Miles away from home- wondering what my family was up to. It's not been that long- but I miss them. The rain was soft by where I sat, the trees behaved as a loose ceiling while the view I had was of a heavy downpour. The smell of earthy musk whiffs pasts with the slight sprinkle of rain spraying on my face. The wind was in frenzy.

The sudden onset of rain steered the park clear of runners and walkers. I- perhaps was the only one who sat there drenching without care. I got up, unzipping the hoodie, taking it off completely so I was left in a black tank top and grey yoga pants. The sky was grey, the clouds still hid the sun beneath. But I was done hiding- I have cried enough for a week to last. Stepping on the mainland I look up at the sky- they fall on me. eEach drop on my skin as they healed me for the moment. The absence of pain can't be a permanence, but the key is to treasure the little relief you conjure in between.

The splatters of water hitting metal sheets and the jostle of leaves fights for dominance, I smile sadly at the thought of such natural chaos, It was beautiful, the melody of them in dispute - when I open my eyes, I see something equally fascinating – I see him.

Lee.

Farby the lane as our eyes met. His were on mine- though far, I could make out his explorative gaze on me with a glance. He had his brows furrowed, his clothes drenched similar to mine. The shirt that he wore to bed last night stuck to him like a second skin. We don't do anything else- we just stare. Without words, without an interruptive movement from either of us.

I couldn't look away. It felt as if I had no control over what I wanted to do. When he neared- his steps turning quicker as he strides, I blinked rapidly to lose the water weighing my lashes down.

"What are you doing?" he hisses gritting his teeth, pushing his wet hair back. With an exposed forehead and angry stare he brought the top of his knuckles and flicked the top of my forehead "You want to get sick or what?"

Rubbing the spot with disbelief I gawked at him.

"What a hypocrite! You are here soaked in rain too. Where's the umbrella huh?" I raise my knuckles to return his favor. But he was fast as he grabbed my wrist- ducking right in time.

"Oh yeah? If it wasn't for you I wouldn't even be here. I woke up without you using me as a make-shift pillow. I freaked and came here looking for you. You even didn't had your phone on you" he bursts, his anyious eyes pinning me for a few seconds. Finally he shakes his head like a puppy, droplets of water falls on me as I flinched. It sets me back upright.

"I don't use you as a pillow" I shout, cutting through the lies he was knitting. "I would never do that. I coul-

"Then why do I find us tangled by the sheets early in morning every day? I have been helping you go back to your side of the bed at sharp seven so we could avoid the awkward confrontations. Now I even clock an alarm to carry out the deed. I wake up to detach us"

When he said deed, he made sure to flash his pearly white teeth sassily. It irked me. He probably wanted me to be moved by it-

"It's too early for this" I sigh, despising the burns on my cheek. He was four years older than me, yet he was so immature. why can't he just let things pass? Why was he giving my heart such a difficult time?

"It's also too early for so many things between us. but I am holding back aren't I?" he grunts with a snappy jerk, he then regards me through the side- the darts from the sky calms as the sun sluggishly yawns through. "Let's go, I have no clue of how to take care of a sick girl. I barely could look after myself. We can't have you catching a cold or flu"

Ouch.

"I can take care-

"Of yourself. I know. but what if it gets bad- what if it affects your digestive juices and you start puking. I can't run around with bowl so you coul-

Whining I stomp off, he follows me grinning as we drag soaked shoes through the reception, then the elevator. At least the penthouse. Once in I move in the direction of our room to clean up- but his call halts me-

"Hey shin"

Biting my lips to store my bursting irritation in, I turn around.

"Now what?" the tip of my nose bumps into his buttoned chest as I stumble, I regain my startled self as he supports me by the arm. I wasn't prepared to face him so close by, so with a wide-spanned gaze, I look at him questioningly. His search mine, thoroughly. As if he was flipping the pages that were scripted with something he couldn't read. I won't let him. He can't know.

Neither can he cross the line I have drawn between us. It's poisonous enough for both of us, it will be the beginning of a story that possibly will be left incomplete.

"You cried?" his utterance couldn't be more fragile. And these signs couldn't alert me more. They were enough for me to yank my hand back. But his hold only got stronger.

"I wasn't"

"Your eyes are swollen, nose pink. Don't lie to me"

"I did not. It might be falling ill or something" seething a silent breath in at the unprepared crack in my reply that only ironed his creasing doubts. He slants as he looked at me- challengingly. That was the last straw, with my might I attempt to shove him off- but he pulled me to him. His vice arms embraced me into a hug so tight that I momentarily swooned within. His words vibrates through him, I could feel the touch of them as it transcends from him to me.

"My language of comfort had always been this" his palms cups the back of my head as my cheek cushions against his wet damp shirt "You can hold me, hug me, or talk to me when it gets hard for you. Okay?"

It was pathetic what I did in succession. It shouldn't be this way- he shouldn't be acting out the way he is. He was the ticket to my temporary freedom, he wasn't supposed to trek his position into someone important. But when I hugged him- returning everything that he was making me feel then was a mistake.

A mistake that will leave us hurting if we didn't stop.

It's not a past.

It's not the present.

But a future that was bigger than us both. But I was clenching on to him with a vulnerability that he thinks he could heal. If only he knew that anything that had happened or anything thing that I am so far has nothing to do with what might happen next.

CHAPTER 15

When you don't think.

You do the unthinkable.

For instance, When Lee took an eternity to retire from the wash-room, with a tense knuckle I knocked at the door. When I failed to receive a reply- I scream over and over. Shouting his humble name to get him out. After I showered, he had immediately sauntered off to kick start the day. he vanished since then. He wasn't a long shower taker, contrary to the popular belief that handsome beings take a herculean time to pamper themselves. Lee and I were abnormally easy with our routines.

But not today.

Though the bathroom with high floor jacuzzi, a chair, and an LED monitor was to die far. We seldom utilized any of it. So far at least. But today- I heard the stereo rage through what was behind the wall. The bass beats bounced faintly as I touched the door.

"LEE"

No answer.

"SHAUN KIM LEE"

The noise increased drastically.

"PLEASE THROW THE BAG OF MAKEUP AT MY FACE AND KINDLY RESUME WHAT YOU ARE DOING"

The music didn't perish, but thankfully the door got yanked open. I collect myself from lurching forward as I had been dramatically leaning by the plank of wood to get my message across. But what I wasn't doing was- a decent job of keeping my mouth shut as he stood there with an untied bathrobe. The steamy abs exposed for an uncalled reason. His belted trouser hung by the hip line. I don't glance at his face immediately- mistake to not be made as such in future must be noted. Because Lee was as unforgiving as he is in norms. They must be very little fibs that he could tease me about later. I can't afford more.

"That's a good physique right there" craning my neck I muster an appreciative nod. I can't let him know I was affected- not a least bit. His lips quirk into a vague smirk. He raised a remote above his head, when he pressed at a button. The music stops.

"How do I know this is a façade?" he pokes my left cheek with his index "They are turning red"

Swatting his hand I walk in, the giant mirror by the sink provides me an access to track him- he arrived and stood behind me. A goofy grin nurturing his humor. Accidently I glance in the forbidden path once more. Gaining a chuckle and shake of the head from him. When I pick the bag of makeup to take it along-

"If you leave now, you are only going to prove me right. You are flustered aren't you?"

For a moment, our gaze lock through the reflection. He then ambles to the seater next to the steamer- tying the white towel robe he sat down with his side facing me, All while a dusty smile plays across his lips. His policies were self-centered but seldom came across as conceited. If anything, he seems to pledge with facts more than forcing an opinion. He was never wrong.

When he allowed me to use him for comfort, he didn't know or needed to know what it was about. He only wanted to be the cure for a disease he doesn't know. But his prescription couldn't be any more inclined.

Groping through the tubes of lipsticks through the pouch I select my usual coral peach tone for the day. The sun was off its leash, as if the rainy episode never happened. It was wildly radiant. And my full-sleeved cotton top and skinny jeans weren't a summery wear. But since I was running out of sunscreen – I can't let my sensitive skin fight without armor.

As I applied the thick, long-lasting tint on my lips. Lee began to bombard me with questions so obvious that I paused for a second.

"You are going out?"

No Lee, I want to look good so I can be home so that I could compose a song with my fish.

"Yes" caressing my lips with my finger to smear the color in even, I internally scream at how I got caught checking Lee out twice in a minute. Hormones thrilled with the imagery of provocative thoughts that I kept bashing away. But I continue to speak as he had his gaze highlighted at what I have to say "There is this guy-

"Ah a guy"

"Will you let me finish?" my heart raced with how soon his outlines soured in distaste. He wasn't the same person the second a flicker of ambiguous emotion struck through him. He lowered his head, inspecting his palms- it was better that way. To not have him in the vicinity.

"Isn't it always starts with a guy?" it was cold- and raw. I wasn't naïve to know how our marriage was going. I could end this by lying to him. Today it's an attraction. But tomorrow it could be more if left untreated. But I don't do it. I was pathetically so selfish, the with a clumsy smile I don't venture twice before steering his doubts away. But he beats me to it.

"It always begins with a guy"

He was unbelievable.

"I spilled coffee on his designer clothes so now I have to repay him to do so- he wants me to meet his fashion coordinator. I know it's stupid. But he insisted" I exhale applying a coat of mascara on my lashes "I don't want to go. But I feel guilty"

Not yet recovered from his own theories he nudged his nose stonily in the air.

"Don't go then"

"What?"

"I'll go instead of you. I will buy him some flowers and take him on a date. I'll creep him out to the point he won't use such cheap tactics to lure an innocent girl in" with each letter added, he stood up slowly. His stare shone with consideration. He wasn't bluffing, was he?

"Innocent girl? You think I don't know what he is doing?" I jump as he passed by, shrugging off the robe with his back to me. He reached for the navy blue t-shirt that he had it hung by the bar line. He pulls it through him, he turns around once he got through the sleeve- I throw my entire focus towards applying my eyeliner. I don't wing it through the first try like usual.

"So you are still going?" it was accusative.

"Yes" was I squeaking?

"Fine" he sighs, shifting beside me to style his hair. He stared at me from above with a furrowed brow, and suddenly he nudged me hard using his hip. Stumbling a couple of steps to the side I grunt. Pretending to be stable. "I am coming with you"

"It's my respo-

"Did I stutter Shin?" he was morphing into a molten dark choco-late. Bitter for the tongue but good for health. So I swallow my pride as he employed the black blazer to compliment his outfit as I brush my hair. The heat from the bath he had in prior was respirating through the room still.

How hot was his temperature preference?

It also smelled like him. There wasn't an apt fragrance that defined him. But it reminds me of forest and sunset. He smells and felt warm. But also strong. Firm, but nothing that is too heavy on you.

"Okay then. Let's help this grown-up man find his fit" I tap at my cheeks to get the daytime serum in when my wrist gets grabbed and my hand gets shaken like a twig in front of my face.

"Where's the ring?" he asks, his eyes trained tiredly on my finger.

"In the bag" with the freehand I fish through it and present it to him. He snatched it from me and slipped it in with a angry nose scrunch.

"This" he announced "-this ring is an anti-pervert exposure. Wear it even when you are home"

Stifling a weak laugh I nod.

"I don't think the man is a pervert" I admit as he released me with a chuckle. He leaves me with a lingering statement to ponder upon.

"You also probably think that I am not one either"

Cracking my spine I pout squinting/once he was out of vision, flexing my shoulders in intervals. Wondering if Lee knows that it's not just them. Or him. Girls can be one too. Because I sure as hell am.

It was five hours ago.

But it doesn't seem like it.

The clock strikes twelve- the longer and shorter hands meet sharply by the grandiose clock. I wrap my thoughts around the fact that it wasn't much, the amount of period that had passed since I was at the private park. Rethinking and cursing at the choices I made. It almost felt like the memory was a ghost- unreal until the moment Lee came into the picture.

My fingers tear through my hair as I looked at him scoff his plate of waffles, brooding as I blinked in self-pity. He was flirty, outgoing, and comically positive in nature. He probably was behaving in such a way since he is chained to me because of our legal bonding. With my elbow propped on the table of I hop where Lee pulled over to grab his breakfast- I lick my lips in anticipation.

But nothing came out.

"Say it. Even if it's an insult. I won't mind" he forks a piece of pineapple as he speaks. He doesn't lookup. I was that obvious when I was with him. But when I start- I got distracted by the necessity. So I tell him.

"We should get some shrimps and fish. I do think I can survive on frozen food and take outs anymore" he stared at me through his lashes, chewing slowly.

"I can't cook"

He confessed.

"Me neither"

There was no shame in it. so I drum my nails across the screen of my phone that I had it place on the side.

"We can learn. It's healthy"

He sniffs nodding, a hesitative touch to it. Almost as if he was having a war flashback. But then he directed his butter knife at me- his brow arced artistically. The sun rays kissed his face lovingly, like a liquification from an angel's halo. Then I realized that it was the lights reflecting from the metal beams that were framing the window panel. He wasn't a Disney prince for him to-

What was I doing?

Yes, I was staring at him.

"Let's go back to square one. What were you going to ask me before your grocery chart served as an alibi?" uncapping the small bottle of water I drink it with a nonchalant shrug, by then I was done he still was awaiting my response.

"Know that you can't escape this" his confidence riled me meticulously. So I offer him another fill.

"Why do you call yourself Lee? Isn't your official name just Shaun Kim. You were born with it" as I say it- it took me a while to grasp the depth of it. Why had I not thought of it before? Why was I asking him this in the form of an excuse when this does seem strange? Shaun Kim- does that mean his original name is Shaun?

It cloaks his face- like a glove. I stare at him in surprise. But he was answering me with a smile, so I shift my jaw upright.

"It's a long story, but to be brief" he wipes the corner of his mouth with a napkin, his orbs turns hazel under the bright invasion. He was a sunshine himself- so there wasn't much harm a sun could do to him. He didn't seem bothered though. "I was sent here when I was in seventh grade. I studied at a private boarding school because after Dad became a senator the family's security became the priority. Since I was quite weak in studies, Dad was against the idea of homeschooling me. So they made me pack my bags and suddenly I was flying miles away from home"

I cannot move or think of anything to say. I merely listen without an interruption. His words comb through me as my chest condensed. My heart heavy on me. His family wasn't safe- ever. I recall the morning when I had turned the T.V with a bag of chips on my lap. The news flashed with a cropped image of the senator and how he got kidnapped on the night of his son's eighteenth birthday party in the U.K. Apparently he was brought back to safety after three to four hours of severe FBI operation.

Son's birthday?

Was it Lee?

As I yearned to know deeper, I remember how Mom ran in to my room. The day was vivid in memory of how She had seized the remote- switching it shut. As a mother, kidnapping and abduction or even the thought of it wasn't a farce- her eyes frightened by the thought of anything identical triggering her daughter with discomfort. She had been through the trauma once. I don't think she was capable of it again.

It's useless to pretend as if you are undefeated. Nothing much remains the same. The victims gather new perspectives. We can't help but see the world in a different light. If a person survives, they lose faith in humanity. They begin to search for the cracks that renders one evil. Trust- the promise that comes with the term becomes a hollow lie. Then you learn new fears. The ones that weren't there.

It was funny, really. I got abducted after my school hours. I had carried the trophy I won in an interschool oration competition. It was the last sermon where I had smiled on stage- ecstatic to speak in front of so many people from the various stage of life. The last day I held the mic with the joy of recognizing how I want to be heard. As of now- I can't even hear myself clearly. It's noisy in there.

But today- as I sat here with Lee. It wasn't the same. I felt safe when he was around, like how I feel with my family . It again, shouldn't be this way. As for the feel of it, it was understandable since we both were grown-ups and physically it was impossible to not sense the pull. It was better to acknowledge our shameless philosophies than to open a door for something worse. I can't let the emotions get to me. Not with him. Not with anyone.

But here I was, nipping at his utterance religiously. I was so lost in it that had to remind myself to get my shit together.

"You regret leaving Seoul?" I caress my wrist nervously, he breathes a smile.

"It's odd. I don't" he leans slightly as if he wanted me to hear this "When I was fifteen, I was taller for my age. using my mother's surname Lee as an alternate identity I would sneak out to partake in illegal street racing. I wouldn't have been able to do that with guards flocking around in Korea now would I?"

"You began your career with street racing?" I ask, my excitement frizzing despite my try to obstruct them "Is that how you got your name?"

He lifts one of his shoulders with a smug jerk.

"When I won consistently with people older than me- I thrived with the idea of gearing into the professional world. where speed was a language that everyone spoke. But not everything is permanent in showbiz is it?"

We don't exchange anything after that, it was futile. He doesn't need me to tell him how he should feel- he knows what to do. So exiting the eatery we got into his car, when the engine purrs – igniting the car with a low hiss, I turn to him with a wide intake of breath.

"You can help me complete the tasks"

In his seat I watch him transcend from poised to wonder. And finally, he blooms into a grinning mess.

"What changed?"

Chewing on my lower lip I recount. What changed?. Maybe at times it was wise to let the water flow casually. Barricading them will only cause it to rage a tide that was meant to be calm.

To dumb it down.

Pushing this away might repel us with a whiplash we weren't prepared for. And also it was just fair that-

"It's fair after you keep answering me everything I ask if you"

A countable three seconds passes between my reasoning and his rejoinder.

"How many are there?" he dives into it, throwing away a moment where I could regain.

"Ten"

"Shoot" he guns it at me using his accessible hand while he wheels with the other. I nod, digging my heels into the mat. With a soft voice, I let it go-

"I want to get chased by that police"

He chuckled, glancing at me as if what I said was adorable . It was the same as Hwans when he comes across any Godzilla franchise for the tenth time. My brother thinks giant nuclear monsters are cute. I worry for his love life.

"That's funny," he remarks "Now the real one" he gestures with an authoritative tone. But-

"It is real. I want to be in a police chase. It doesn't have to be serious- but I want them to tail behind me" the image was so alluring in my head that I was soon supporting a fat grin. Unfortunately, his were gone. "I also want to visit an escape room. the haunted kind. Then I want to try some disgusting insects, they can be fried with spices though, so I don't puke. Also, I want to punch someone deserving. I have it practiced on my brother – so I do know how to pack one good-

"Shin"

"Yeah"

There was a short dose of silence followed by that. Then he brought the car in reverse- as he was driving into a free lane he looked at me through side-

"Is there something that's normal among the list?" then his lids thins in suggestive note "Like kissing in rain or falling asleep under a starry sky?"

Rolling my eyes with a sly smile I snuggle in my position.

"I do. I want to get a tattoo. Learn to ride a horse, Visit an island. Buy my own car and to participate in a public event" I tick them

on the empty air , the lazy smile Lee had was an imitation of mine "Are those normal enough?"

"Very" we entered the gates of a large brick studio. Lee and I got out- soon we walking side by side. As we enter, I postly prepared to let a hefty hole invade my savings. It was huge- I let my gaze sweep through the ghastly interior. Lee had his hands inside his pockets, his forehead creasing. Was he getting bored? Is he regretting-

"They were only nine"

Forget the paranoia.

"What was?"

He regards me acquisitively, his lips twitching.

"You said there were ten things you wanted to do. But you only mentioned nine. You thought I wouldn't notice?" my body goes cold inside my clothes as I pretend to be unbothered. I wasn't speculating he would wink it in so soon. I didn't even think that he would take this into account as seriously as he is doing it now. The last of it- was just for me. I don't want anyone to know- but the time was running out. I don't know if I'll be able to outrun them. I can't crawl- at this rate I was bound to fail.

So when a staff clad in a pencil skirt and pastel green shirt walked to me with her hips swaying in class, I instantly move to glance at Lee. He was still frowning and had his gaze welded on her. But when I connected the line I acknowledged how it wasn't the hips he was so keen on- but a bouquet of flowers that she was carrying with her.

"Miss Han?" she asks.

"Uh-yes" I clear my unprepared throat.

Her lips were glossier than the black epoxy flooring that we stood on, she spoke offering me the souvenir-

"Sir will arrive soon. He sent these flowers as an apology for the wait"

I don't receive it. In fact- it never comes my way. Lee paws at it, snatching and stepping away in few quick motions. He smiles at the girl- the polished mannerism with spearing purpose in the wake.

"Mrs. Kim is actually allergic to flowers. So I'll just keep this somewhere" with that he simply flung it across the nearest couch a couple feet from us. The exclusive shock on the girl's face was evident so I had to help her.

"I am Miss Han. That's my husband. We recently got married and stuff" her smile stuttered and succumbed as she nods. she advised us to sit while she went to grab some drinks for us. she didn't return.

"That was rude of you?"

He plops next to me, adjusting his shirt by stretching it through his hem.

"You care?"

I think of it thoroughly.

"No. Not really. But I should feel bad shouldn't I?"

He clicks his tongue. He smirks scrutinizing me avidly, my mouth dries out at how hectic it was to be merely looked at by him.

"You aren't as sympathizing as I thought you were," he says, his voice acquired a dark edge that was first for me.

Your friend, his assistant and you think I am a bitch. And you don't even know that the bitch you think of a bitch is just me being a bitch. No surprise there- I don't have a friend. I scared them away with my wit and nervous blunders. So no- I am not sympathetic. I don't even feel sorry for myself.

Our gaze poured into each other, peculiarly, the time slowed down while I studied him. It was beautiful to be a part of such a still moment until

-Until a mystique sound of the camera going off caused us both to tear our sight off of each other and gawk at the direction of a man dressed in pure denim. He had his hair up in a bun and yellow ray bans hung by the v of his neckline. He removed the camera from his face and smiled politely.

"I am sorry. But the moment you both were sharing by then, begged to be captured. I'll send them to you- trust me you'll be thankful"

Lee wasn't as lost as I was- he was up in instant-

"I know you"

The man smiled, raising the camera.

"We had collaborated for a session once. You said you want to be called Lee. Am I right?"

They were an old acquaintance, let me repeat they were. His name was Samuel Krigen, and he was here to do his job. But the subject who was to be shot here was struck somewhere and samuel was running around the studio to kill the time. one thing led to another and soon Lee wished to know if I had ever had a photo taken by a professional. Like the monument of honesty I was- I confessed the truth. And that's how I found myself seated in a cherry red chaise lounge, with an artist adding some finishing touches to my makeup. The ring light flicks on as I was addressed to pose for the folio.

Lee stood behind the photographer as I glared at him. I had no clue of what to be done. Was anyone even going to direct me?

"It's not for the passport sweetie"Lee ushers me, the grin can't fool me now. he was enjoying this more than he should. For the same of God I was here because of him "Relax"

He mouths the last word. The weight doest leave my shoulder. I look around for some inspiration- there were large posters of gorgeous models contorting their bodies into an aesthetic positions. I take in the one where a ginger dressed in a loose fit had her ankles tipped in an acute angle.

Before I could bail on it- I removed my shoes. Kicking it aside. I check the flexibility of my skinny jeans- since it was of a popular brand it didn't disappoint me. I do a split first- I think I heard a gasp from the cute makeup artist I had hovering above me. I grab my ankle with my gaze hot on the photo of the model. My muscle and bone allows me to mold my body like hers. Despite years of quitting the gym class, I maintained my contortive moves so that I could hit and kick Hwan from angles he least expects me to.

Weirdly- I was using it today. I tilt my face to look at the photographer. He wasn't behind the lens anymore- his mouth was wide open – his teeth on show. Barely was he hiding his thoughts. Plunging into the feels I skip from looking at Lee as the flash goes off. Then another- then more.

Samuel kept cheering me up and encouraging me. constantly reminding me how good they were coming out. But my ears never came across the good job sweetie from the man I want to hear it from. After ten minutes of various elusive poses. I blink rapidly, adjusting to the normal lights after bearing the glaring assault.

I smile when I see Lee- he had his arms crossed, he stood in the same place he was before. But the grin and soft, playful stares seem to have died down amidst the darkness that shadowed him once the shoot had begun. Did the change of lightings affect him as well?

"You okay?" I ask, was he feeling down? "Do you want to sit somewhere? should I get you something?" I look around so I could fetch him water- has he even been taking care of himself? as I saw a booth I try to move- but I felt him pull me back. Hold me in from loitering off.

"I am fine" he didn't sound fine. His voice was deeper than usual- when he breathes it comes of ragged. I would have missed it if I wasn't so sure how he is in general.

"You aren't lying are you?" he moves his head to the side, implying a no. I sigh- but abruptly I realized what had happened. I chirp- never in million years would I have behaved so childishly. But I was excited to be validated "How was i? are they any good?"

For few seconds he doesn't spill anything. He only watched me. Was he trying to build the anticipation? If so, then it worked. When he said it. I believed him.

"It was perfect"

He steps near, I wait for him to say something more. But he veers in a path that seem be expressive in itself. More than what a phrase could convey. The commotion around us subsides into a plain silence. At least for me it does. I cannot hear anything else other the beats of my heart that rushed to my ears. He wasn't suffocating me. Neither was he invading a voluntary space. But still my course of thoughts went haywire by how intense he was staring at and through me.

His lips parts to say something. I don't hear it since the minute got fractured by a girls voice.

"Miss Han"

His clutch leaves me, suddenly it was cold. He blinks retreating, halting when he hears the girl announce-

"Mr. Moreno has arrived"

Chapter 16

LEE

"Sorry for keeping you, Miss Han"

Though I had my back to the man, the familiar voice ignited a stream of memories that weren't pleasant in existence. It was twisting and loathsome that my intellect decided to completely ignore the prospect of such a coincidence to occur. But even in a city that's infested with sin, there were only a few assholes it harbored. And a Moreno with that cynical touch in utterance could only be the prick himself.

So I turn around, my surface a blank canvas with mobility to change according to what the scoundrel has to offer. It was curative to witness the color drain from his face. He probably wasn't friendly with the idea of a reunion. With his company and agency backing and cleaning up his trash- he doesn't know how to get through the shards of glass left behind when he shattered a man career.

"Lee?"

He has changed. Something in him has- not in ferocity. But beneath his hide, he didn't look so good. Then it hits me. Of course, it wasn't well for him. I knew it the moment Clarissa called me today, We had enough evidence to carry out the prosecution.

"Nicholas. Nice to see you man" I smile, of all the images I could link him with- I remember one where he stood with Madison with his filthy hand on her waist. In the middle of my house was it where I found them, she went with him the day I needed to be held and comforted the most. But it wasn't that which seem to boil my blood- it's the thought of what he might have planned if I wasn't here with Shin. He wasn't touching her or even next to her- but I was going crazy just by the thought of it. It wasn't making sense. So I fucking smile at him. It's worse for me to do it through a façade. It's when I am the most unforgiving. "Still the same. Missed me?"

He doesn't answer at the moment. I don't expect him to- all I wanted now was to get shin out of here. I felt her presence next to me, but I don't want to look at her. after the shoot and what I went through it- I don't think it was safe for her to interest my attention so soon.

"How are you?" he asks, his discomfort morphs into a forced nonchalance. Mine doesn't. it boosts me to walk slightly towards him, confront him personally. But shin was a still at an arms reach- I make sure of it.

"I am as fine as I could be. But what about you? " I glance at my watch wishing the time would move promptly. I hate his mere existence. I look up with my light eyes, training it on him so it could wrench him more. "I don't think you could say the same"

In a spur of a second, his gaze speared into a glare. But they were afraid in corners. It was relaxing.

"Why are you back?" his voice was an octave above a whisper, "I thought you had an empire to take care of"

I closed my eyes with a chuckle, I detest how I was finding this so entertaining. He didn't share the same sentiment though.

"I didn't come here alone" I reach behind and coiled my fingers by Shin's wrist. She had a small one- and by the number of times I had held her by it- I bet I could blindly sketch them on a sheet despite my zero experience in the field. I bring it up so her ring was on display "My wife wanted to get married here"

We have been using the marriage card more often than I would like. But it didn't feel wrong.

There was a silence. But it wasn't Moreno who had to add something.

"Lee" shin whispers, leaning a bit by me "It's the wrong hand"

Taking it to notice, I say-

"Show the other"

Obediently she does as I drop her ringless one. She waves of- as if she was desperate to escape the situation too. Good. I prefer it this way. When Morenos demeanor soured the least, I know he was playing it casually.

"What are you trying to imply Lee" he smirks, the arrogance brutally fake on him. "The girl ruined my shirt, I asked to be repaid. What's the catch that I am not getting here?"

In an odd move I threw a quick glance at shin. Her nose twitched with a short crease clipping between her brows. She too thinks it's ridiculous. Who wouldn't- people get paid by money and not being guilt-tripped into a shopping date to fulfil some measly motives.

"Same old Moreno" I know it was the last jab, there wasn't much he could say or do after this. Though I wish I could do this other way with shin not around. "Always after someone who is taken or committed. Like a dog, tailing around anyone who you pass by"

I wish I could've left right then- but the son of a gun still had it in him-

"Madison did chose me. A dog over a pup" his smirk was petty, I wasn't sadly smiling anymore. His words did get to me as pathetic as it was, I itched to bash his skull against a wall. Pup? He thinks I looked like a puppy?

My jaw numbs from the hideous clenching, flipping my wallet I trace out my card. I hand it to the girl who received us initially, she looked at it as if I was holding a glass of blood out for her. but takes It nevertheless.

"Extract the money enough to pay for the highest attire at price" then as an afterthought I scratch my brow with my index "You know what? make it two" with a deceptive glance at his way I grab shin's hand again. Interlacing our fingers as I start to walk- but when we were about to cross path with him, I look to the side. "Bid them wisely in some kind of auction in future" I place a supportive hand at his shoulder, he tensed at that. He wasn't immune, was he? So I grit it down his range "You are going to need the money to survive"

My steps were bold, even when I was free from the suffocative studio- I still held my head high up. When we stood next to the car, I wasn't so sure. A constellation of anger and frustration soon drizzled over me. and then I know I wanted to change into a curve before I go off. Shin probably wasn't awaiting a snappy outrage as she flinched when I shifted to look at her, abruptly.

I took a deep breath. Exhaling it through my lips I calmly spanned my arms towards the direction where we came from.

"Shin" I used a tone that one does to make a child understand the tribe "You just can't go out alone to meet a man with a face like that"

The air blows her hair into her face, she tucks them behind her ears with her gaze narrowing.

"You mean that I shouldn't go alone to meet a man whose personality you already knew but it just began to fit his face as he revealed his true colors and now you think everyone with a similar structure or shape is a jerk?"

That tied my tongue in complication. She wasn't wrong. Hell- she couldn't be more precise. What am I to do with her? She was a living box of Pandora for me, the more I know of her- the harder it gets to stay away. A little bundle of trouble she was for me. That's all.

Like the candies, to crave but can't have.

Can't have- but it still has been causing these blunders which leave me conducting a pep talk inside my head for hours in the bathroom. Hug me and hold me whenever you need me?

What was I high on when I permitted her to do such a thing? It got so frustrating to the point where I was pulling my hair out.

Why do I want to protect her so bad?

What was I even protecting her from? If this keeps going on- she might be needing protection from me instead.

"Who is he?" there she goes. Tearing me open further. But I was too late to throw this off the bush.

"He use to be a rival in tracks" her lips part, but she restrains herself from prying. I don't stop though. She can know- it's nothing

I ever tried to hide. It wasn't my fault for it to be ashamed of "Four years ago when I got into an accident, it wasn't because of my negligence. But it happened because it was meant to happen"

She blinks, Once. Twice. By the third they spanned with realization. Then she lets out a stream of curse in our national language. It was adorable. So I cursed at my conscience.

"You were framed by that- that- ?" she was fighting her own words now, her shoulders raised, her thin frame shifts in brakes. She looks through my shoulder at the glass door "You were so rude in there"

Immediately I frown- I believe I wasn't- But-

"You insulted dogs by addressing him as one"

The vexed atmosphere dissolved because when I heard my own laugh even before I knew I was doing it, it's when you know that you are entirely off the hook-

-but it also meant that I accidentally was getting chained by something else. Or rather someone.

By the time we drove around, it was a peak hour for lunch enthusiasts. We decided to wait in line when the restaurant which Shin and I randomly sighted by was full. It was a buffet hub, and the aroma of grilled meat and tangy sauce overtook the other equally enticing flavors that I could taste just by its smell. Shin seems to contribute with my thoughts as her gaze kept switching by the vessels upon the stove top. Preplanning what and how to have it all without throwing up.

They weren't any reservations we could make or bribe the old woman with who seems to run the homey East Asian restaurant. She was strict with the rules. Since it was on a first come first serve basis, we waited outside.

Shin produced out a tube of sunscreen from her satchel- rewinding me to the moment she had asked me if I was wearing any SPF serum. It was in her backyard- almost three months ago. I'd be a lie if I say I hadn't thought of her during the period that passed between our agreement and marriage. Though we never met- she crossed my mind more often than I delighted. Regrettably, it was always connected to deviate my sense of paranoia. I was betrayed once- I couldn't risk it again.

But my worry was futile.

Each minute with her- I regret ditching her the whole time.

So the least I could do was apply a coat of sunscreen as we stood, despite a layer that I previously had on. She was relieved. As for the lunch- we didn't speak. There wasn't a thing to, the food and our actions spoke for us. Each time when we praised a starter- it was conveyed by us serving it upon the other's plate and ushering to try it since our mouths were full.

She seems to enjoy the seafood better compared to the rest. When we got out I was a pound heavier and for a petite girl like shin, she did her best. She- was her best. It was five in the evening and Shin scrolled over her grocery note summarized on her phone. And soon we were surfing through the aisles of the convenience.

"Oh this is embarrassing" she mutters sitting cross-legged, tugged in a shopping cart as I wheeled. "I can walk, it's not that bad"

Rolling my eyes I softly hit my knuckle by her round head.

"Why didn't you tell me before. Your ankle is swollen" I sigh turning right, she leans sideways and slides a red baseball cap. She wears it to conceal herself. Smart move.

"Exaggeration right there. Its just red- not-

She halts when I drop a tray of shrimp wrapped in a saran on her lap. She inspects it like a child would with their toy. But she wasn't one- so it was totally childish of her to be walking around in a distorted shoe. Apparently my haste to get us out of the clothing store caused an inch of her heel to chip off. I wouldn't have known if I hadn't caught her grimacing with the steps when she thought I wasn't looking at her.

We did get new shoes. A comfortable converse. But there was no way she was walking with that tiny red foot of hers. size six feet- they were pretty small compared to mine. Despite the tantrums, it was easy to pick her up- The cart was big enough for her.

"We need vegetables" there was a mounted mirror in front of us, I wasn't able to see her eyes because of the cap- but did envisioned the pout with which she pointed once she found it. I had never seen someone look so happy in a venture to purchase peas and onions. But there she was-

For how long has she been craving for a home cooked meal?

"People are like vegetables. they each have a quality that complements a human nature"

I- wasn't expecting the debut of a Shinian philosophy. But did she ever turned out as my expectations? This was a waste of my energy. So I smile at her- a dignified one.

"Please explain me teacher" sarcastically I press my palms together- as if praying to a monk. My utterance was a mix of I am pissed off at you for not telling me about your leg earlier

-and

Please go on, I really want to know what you have to say.

But she's doesn't care, she dived into the sea of doctrines right away.

"Turnips, Radishes and Broccoli" Deep into this, her eye elucidates a strange passion "They are the least favorite ones into society. The Moreno guy falls in this category. Disliked, unwanted, and bitter-bland. An exception to few spices they don't go well with anything else. Harvested only for the bare population that prefers them"

I chew on my bottom lip, trying to not admit how relatable it was. But then-

"What about me? What am I?"

Her eyes graze the bed of various greens, It puts me into a state of unease. I don't want to be spinach.

"A carrot"

Thank heavens, it–

"You are like a bunny"

Wait- what?

"Have you seen yourself?" it wasn't a defense, my smile was for real this wise. She was as close to a rabbit as far as anyone across the vicinity. I refuse to be called a puppy and a bunny in a day.

"Yeah- don't go on me now. I don't know why I said that either" her nose flared as she picks a bag of carrots "You are sweet like these, crunchy and hard in texture, but vibrant and sweet within. Aren't you?"

I hum with my thoughts circling on their own. Erring to hold it in- I ask-

"What do mean by crunchy and hard?" chuckling I clutch the bar, pushing forward, not anticipating an answer.

"Oh- that's because I saw your abs today. First hand. They were firm- just like-

She didn't render me speechless. She couldn't even if she tried to. Because I was a man of many words. But she somehow jumbled it down to make me think of one single term despite my fierce struggle to create a sentence. Even within my head, all I could exclaim was-

Fuck.

To help us both out of the situation, I played it cool. I wasn't cool.

"What about you?"

"hm?"

"What's your vegetable?"

She rubs her hands sluggishly, embracing her knees to her chest as the contents kept invading her space. She stared ahead.

"I am a potato"

I nod in respect.

"Why do you think you are a potato?"

My interviewing abilities skyrockets with her. I do ask her questions with an interest in knowing her more. Basics may be- but it's a start. But I know that I want to get there- a silent wish to know what caused her to break down this morning. Why was she here? Why did she want to get married to a stranger? Why is she-

Yes there were many whys

But I yearned to know why she thinks of herself to be a potato tonight? The rest could wait until she was comfortable.

"It's mostly a dish served by edge that no one notices until they want to enhance the taste of something that's utterly boring. Potato is never a main, but neither completely abandoned from the circle. It's just-there"

My grasp on the hilt squeezed, I had no head start to do any but uselessly confess-

"But I like a potato"

And she had the apt response for it.

"That's you being a carrot"

Half an hour into the stroll we were done- she stood next to me by the billing counter when I nudge her elbow with mine to alter her attention from staring at the small twelve by twelve decorative pillows to me.

"What's on ten?"

She frowns as if she couldn't get me. Did she take me for a fool? She shouldn't- I wouldn't let her. My aggressively sharp brow raise gains me a sigh from her. The clicks of the scanner reading the bar codes breaks through us in short whiles.

"You might have counted it wrong"

"I am bad at estimations. Not counting"

"I forgot what it was"

"Nothing truer has ever been said" then I blurt a fact that brought out the fraction of Shin I never saw- yet "You need me to complete them. So better hurry"

She chuckled, running a hand through her hair in disbelief. She was a feminist- I was one too. I am identified my mother's surname for a reason. It was a tribute. I knew it will influence Shin- but what I didn't perceive was impulsive outcome of it from her. She grabbed the pillow- the size of an infant and dumped it into the billing pile.

"I can get done with them in ten days If I want" she didn't even look at me- It was so much fun to watch her fume with fervor "I want to drive today" I don't think- with a smile I slip the key into her outstretched palm.

I may be- shouldn't have.

Twenty minutes later I was clutching my chest with my ears ringing with the siren from a cop's vehicle that was chasing us. We were speeding.

Shin was speeding.

And the terrifying aspect was her being happy about it. With my breathing forgotten and hands fastened on the dashboard- I kept navigating her. I had to clear my throat twice since it kept clogging because of how alarmed I was. she drove at residents pace we left- the streets were lighting up with the early night falling in. It went loyal until she brought her phone out to check the route with least traffic- and as soon as she spotted a cop on duty, the car ignited with an acceleration that threw us back.

I wasn't prepared.

She was.

So far it's been three minutes into the action and I was – undeniably enjoying whatever this was. On minute four she entered another avenue- slowing it down- then she stopped entirely.

Then she was crawling over the passenger seat, my seat. Over me.

"What are you doing?" I ask breathing. Heavily.

She faced me, fisting the material of my blazer and tugging it.

"Throw yourself at the driver's seat. I wanted the chase, but I can't go to prison"

The screech of another vehicle inverting surrounds us, there was no way we are getting out of this. So I responsibly ask-

"Why?"

She shoves me, in a reflex I vacate so she could take my spot. And I - was she throwing me under the bus?

"Don't worry. You are only there because you can't get pregnant"

With that she grabs the pillow she procured from the mart, shoving it inside her top she turns in time when we heard a knock by the window. I roll it down, the young official In uniform, aided with a Bluetooth headset leaned with a sturdy face to inspect me.

He opens his mouth when-

-A scream cuts through. It was shin- she had her hand placed above her enlarged cosplay of a belly while the other one masked her face. She doesn't stop there, as a falsetto she inserts a sob with another pitiful scream.

The horrified cop steps away, speaking into his mic-

"Sir it's a lady in labor"

He was probably heeded an order- because with a bow he motioned his arm frantically, imploring us to hurry.

I drive-

Half a minute into the road I look at her, she glimpsed between her fingers. She uncovers her face and removes the pillow, hugging it to her chest. With a relaxed smile, she closed her eyes resting her head on the pad.

I smile with her. A sense of calm washes over me as I refused to reject and deny something that I have been doing for a while.

An acceptance of the degree I was falling at. I know I was falling way faster than I could keep up.

Faster than I could catch my breath.

Faster than anything that had ever happened to me that was so beautiful.

CHAPTER 17

S HIN

The floor could be lava. Because I- Han Shin-young didn't care a dime because i levitated, high up without a band of worry clipping my legs shackled to the ground. With the car chase- I had initiated the list. I took the reins and acted out of impulse- finished a task and didn't get arrested. Even if I did, I had faith in Lee and his connections. He was loaded- he was at the rack of hierarchy that could be used to extinguish any kind of crime that's committed.

Not that I would do anything as such But it's reassuring to have a backup. That night- the range of sleep that welcomed me was a treasuring one. When my mind and body fell upon the matters , I sank into it. As if it was made out of clouds instead compressed cotton. I had a smile on my face when I closed my eyes, the haziness wasn't there while I tried to fall asleep, half awake into the night I felt a tight tug by my waist. And in a smooth sliding motion, my back was heatedly flat against the chest of Lee.

"I know satin curtains are like our siblings"

With a wink, I open my eyes to decrypt the code. It was futile, he speaks the language of ancient Gods in his sleep.

"But Shin is softer than satin" he groans, a melancholic depth in it. As for me, I gawked in a force that caused a tick by my jaw. Since when was I an ingredient of his archaic text? Flinching, I shuffled to scramble his arm from me, in reflex, he crushed a portion of my shirt with a low lament.

"Lee should ask curtain for her skincare routine" With wide eyes, I stared at the wall opposite to me, I prayed for strength and prosperity. One of his long legs coils mine into a tangled mess. And soon his morning's confessions tumbled over me, or should I say lies.

We don't wake up like this because of me.

And he must be aware of his habits. There was no other way to it.

He was deliberately dumping it on me.

This actualization only riled me up into coercing my manners into kicking him to his corner of the bed. He coughed, rolling to the other side- Releasing me as I exhaled with all my might. But with luck on air for me that night, he didn't depart from the bed to take his usual little stroll. Four days ago, I discovered him experimenting to get past through the bathroom, the doors were close- and he wasn't aiming his take on telekinesis. But to a sole audience like me, It was a scene out of conjuring, it did scare me to the bones.

I had the lights on the whole time after I had him tucked in.

Two days ago he sat by the dresser and stared at the ground while he suggested that wasps and fruits are the same things and why no one should fear watermelons. I assembled a tray of drink and a bowl of popcorns to enjoy while he was at it, I did record him though.

To agree that the film of whatever that made us strangers in the past was sterile by now. After I had shared some of the most fascinating moments in my life with him so far, it was safe to say that he was now a member of my real world. A place where I am myself. Where the roof, walls, and windows are people who accept me as I am. Where I wasn't afraid to be seen or spoken to. Or be listened.

As for the feelings I thought I was fighting with?

I recognized that Lee grew up in a western world, his ideologies and view of how he sees and deciphers it must be different. Reckless even. He must have had many relationships in past, with girls and women who were capable in many ways than me. He can have anyone he wished for. Isn't that a reason why our marriage is bound to be temporary? As long as it's just me and my possibly developing unrequited emotions, and not his. it was fine. I could always tell my heart to shut up and it'll.

He is a great friend though-

I would never admit it to him.

Madison- it was the name Moreno had uttered. The spark of fury that lived and died within seconds on his eyes wasn't so fast enough to evade me. she could be his ex, she could still be his something if it was enough to poison his ever happy smile even for a minute. I don't intend to find out because divulging deeper would only open him more to me, and the bounteous it gets the further damage it could do to my heart.

I am contended to befriending his surface. I can't risk reaching his soul.

And so I throw my mind into concluding the final drafts for the next four days. Latching myself in the gaming room I only came out to cook meals that were instant. The poor shrimps froze within the refrigerator momentarily. Lee wasn't home either- with his hotel project and its construction modifications nearing a deadline, he was always out dressed in a three-piece suit and a distressed face. But he rang me up every three or four hours to check on me and my food intake.

I aimed to assure him that I would never cook the shrimp or japchae without him since he paid for the grocery. By his end of the line, I only received a silence, and when he spoke there was always a hint of a smile in his voice.

By the weekend I had the first rough edition packed and sent to the editor. I spent an hour bawling my eyes out as I realized how the trilogy that I had initially begun in my room as a sixteen-year-old scrawny kid with running nose and pigtails, ended with me sitting in the middle of a multi-million dollar penthouse in Las vegas six years later.

I bestowed the lead characters with a happy ending, they deserved it after the turmoil I had put them through. I hope when Lee finds it out, he might hate Elixir a little less than he already does. With that, I wait for the draft to get polished, edited, and printed in a month, the editor tolerates me because I pay her twice the price to have it done quickly since I seldom submit the chapters on time. which reminded me of my duelist again.

I can't afford to procrastinate.

So on the morning was the weekend, I wake up Lee with a surprise breakfast for him decorated on a portable desk. Meals on bed gets the job done, always. He sat up with his bed hair angry on his face, a contrast to how elated he was to be served as a prince. He indeed was a knight for me today.

"You like it?" I chirp when I said I was ardently getting comfortable around and with him. I meant it. It oddly seems to throw him off guard every single time as he stared passively at me with dazed eyes.

"Who wouldn't?" he grins inhaling the aroma with a cute sound that he produced from the back of his throat. With the same throat the causes the unintentionally seductive groans when things don't go well for him at work "You trying on what here missy?" he wiggled his brows as I took a seat on the bed facing him. I rub my hands with an ecstatic smile.

"I am trying to get you to help me"

A single brow arcs this while.

"And what would that be?" he drawls out slipping his fingers through the hand of the large porcelain coffee mug. I scoot near him. it was weekend, he could- I want him to-

"You are going to help me buy my own car today"

He had the mug slanted as he siped, his eyes conveyed how he was on to this idea already. It shone with an impressive indication.

"What do I get in return?" he asks suggestively, even biting his lips to get the joke across. Instead of blushing or wasting time I fork the seasoned watermelon and shoved it into his mouth.

"You are already having it"

He might have majored in a flirtationship. But I had my share of character analyzation done to justify the characters of my book. My google search history was a dark place that can put an FBI termination to shame. I saw it coming. But what Lee hadn't mastered yet was my ability to buy a car that just wasn't an ordinary SUV. I directed him to a dealership showroom for Aston Martin, I bet he had numerous questions lingering by the tip of his tongue by the time we arrived.

I must be unsettling when I promised him that it was with the money I save because of my job.

"What kind of editor gets paid so much?" he mused as I flipped through the pages of the document after having denied any auto financial loan or monthly interest to the staff who helped us. "It almost makes me want to be one"

He wasn't wrong though, even with my career exploding off with the young adult fantasy peaking the charts- I had made more money with my smart investments than in one had pay. Doubling and tripling my net worth because I had my parents to guide me with the premature fame I received. As a result, I signed into the contract. Officially making a two hundred thousand dollar vehicle as mine. It was sleek, it was metallic, it was mine. And I wouldn't change a wire or seat about it. It screamed at me.

"You don't sell drugs do you?" his theories doesn't fog his excitement. Surrounded by cars, he was like a kid on Christmas. But with a conscience. I touch the smooth hood of what will be mine tomorrow after it gets delivered . But Lee was touching analogies that soared through me, it had me in a fit of giggles.

"Sometimes, I have a meth lab in my basement. I make them myself"

He still takes a minute to recover from the sarcasm I keep constantly employing on him.

When we walked out to the fresh gust of air, the grin we wore was hopeless. We had been inside for three hours detonating what and how we wanted it. Now when it was done, the wind was lighter- the sky, brighter and us- so much happier.

"I never had this much fun after I had purchased my first"

I shake my head to scatter the wilding hair from my face.

"You are happy because I am happy" I reason.

"And why do you think that is?" I felt his gaze on me, I don't return it. Because I had to make things straight and with him looking at me like that, it won't feel real to my tongue. And that won't be fair to him.

"Because that's what friends do" beating the twitch of my hand, I shove them into the pocket of my jeans "- they celebrate the success and give you a shoulder to cry on when they fail. Isn't it why you permitted me to use you as a strength when I have a hard time?"

The wave of silence with the noise of wheels rolling down the road got dense. He didn't break the chain of it- but when he did-

"What if a person Is prepared to give their all instead of just strength? Does that count as friendship too?" there wasn't a trace of Lee when he spoke, the words weren't cut into soft edges with his subtle forgiving nature. It tears through, bold and cocky. Arrogant even. For the first time, he acted like a person one stereotypes of his caliber to be.

I don't answer him with the fear of ruining it further.

And my lack of an answer was a claim in itself.

The next morning, I got educated about two things that necessarily wasn't a first hand warning.

One was- Lee doesn't ignore you when he is mad.

Two- he makes you wish that you were ignored by him.

So when i woke up with a breakfast on the bed, It wasn't friendly. It was simply breakfast on the bed with him exploiting Kanye west on the stereo with a volume that should be illegal in the mornings. With each bite it took, he reciprocated his debt. Then he texted me to get ready to receive the car. I was right in front of him in the living room as I got the message.

I went for a striped jumpsuit instead of a dress, to which I was awarded with a verbal jab.

"Less application of sunscreen today I guess"

Nobody, none in twenty-two years of my existence had so harmlessly tried to get back at me. But the moment he said it, his nonchalant eyes admitted the embarrassment with a silent nod. But the absence of his smile churned me every time I looked at him expecting him to be lively. But it was temporary- he will get over it. He has to.

I implored for the old Lee to redeem and the day hadn't even completed it's cycle yet.

Lee was harmless, I religiously belived-

No, he wasn't,

Because when he made me drive to where his friend Edmund and his assistant resided, I was eating down my modesty towards him . He used me as a chauffeur to meet his friend, But when Edmund and Fischer walked towards us with their summer clothes on, I ushered Lee to spill.

"What is going on?" I ask drumming my fingers by the steering in nervousness.

With a lazy stare, he turns to me, his friend and Fischer still had a colossal yard to pass through.

"Edmund wanted to learn about marine life for his new project" he states playing with the strap of his watch, his features fighting a cunning smile "We are going to an aquarium"

My mouth opens and closes in accord, not able to grasp where and how I fall into the equation. He navigated me through it though-

"Since you are my friend, I want to treat you how I treat one authentically. I drag them into shit that isn't for them, If I want them to drive around, I make them. I honestly don't take care or protect them because they are just friends until it's really necessary. I always have their back though- but I don't indicate it often"

We held our stares, I gulp in some moisture as the thread of what he implied knitted into a crystal elucidation. Friend or foe, Lee was loyal to both the affairs. I had seen him with Moreno, so with Edmund. But what he narrated now was diligence,

Forcing a friendship into our equation won't do me good.

It was a warning.

If I was his real friend, I won't be second-guessing this outing.

But before I could gather the courage to advocate my thoughts, the door to the passenger sear from both the sides simultaneous clicks open.

"You got a new one?" the lack of surprise in Edmunds's voice was palpable. When Lee revealed he had a collection, he meant it. He took me to the private basement, 3 to the ground. There were seven. Each breathtaking than the other, convertible, roadsters, and classic, he could live off of them if he decided to quit making money.

I went to the right man for advice- but he wronged me when he was friend-zoned.

So he doesn't whirl the conversation to him like he did last wise. Letting me fend for what I had done, Edmund awaited a response from us so I craned through my shoulder with a polite smile.

"It's mine actually"

Edmund was kind, with a pleasant smile he comments.

"Gorgeous. Lee and you are match made in heaven"

Unfortunately, he only steered the cold awkwardness between Lee and I into a wider pit. Sighing I drove us to the said aquarium. Astoundingly once I entered the world of marine creatures trapped in a glass case, despite my distaste towards the treatment of animals in a cage I found it attention-grabbing. I hated it, but since I relate with these mammals more than the ones that walked on earth, I surfed through the trivia plates that instructed us about the specimen on display.

Lee and Fischer were the quietest of us four. Though Edmund wasn't vocal, his enthusiasm shone with how crucially he scanned each of them with thick glass tight on his nose. Fischer was beside him jotting down in his I pad as Edmund dictated his discoveries and ideas. The corridor was a pulsing pattern of bluish-green hue created by the underwater luminous.

The massive transitions among us were making my movements denser. As if I was wearing a spandex suit that was two sizes smaller for me. So I shift to face Lee simultaneously as his phone goes off. He doesn't spare me a glance,

"I have to take this" he mumbled, looking at the Id "You go ahead, it'll take me a while"

The temperature in the room dropped after he was gone, hugging myself I follow them, at a point, I found Edmund beside me with his hands inside the pocket of his hoodie. He had the hood up to cloak his face, probably to disguise it from anyone who could recognize him.

It still feels unreal, to have a celebrity like him enacting normal stuffs. Fischer was a couple of feet away from us- crafting Q and A with a marine guide.

As for me and Edmund, we traded occasional, defined, and formal smiles whenever our gaze intersected. The adult dolphin modeled twice for us, I swear I saw the disappointment in his face when he came for the third round and saw us both.

A visible pity towards the lack of social skill. A fish could do better. The dolphin - was like Lee.

Luckily- it was Edmund who finally broke the barrier-

"Heard you like fish" he says with a his dimple popping up, it was a bonus on his chiseled jawline. How can Hailey Howard dump such a snack?

But soon I retaliate, it wasn't what I should be concerned of. The fact that Edmund knows my love for fish is what should signal me with red lights. What else does Lee share?

"Yeah, I love seafood" I reply with my ears heating up. Was Lee done with his revenge? What was taking him so long? he could have left me alone, I ace with the prospect of living and roaming in solitude.

Edmund chuckled with due respect, also he looked uneasy for someone who was a public person. Did I say something wrong?

"I was told that you have a pet fish. I think I got confused-

"I do have a pet goldfish"

"Oh you do?" the discomfort was so apparent that I took a moment to refer to what might be rendering him astray. Inwardly I sigh in understanding. With a small, guilty smile I tilt my head with a shrug.

"It's strange you see. I like them both ways. And a pet and as a food" with genuine palm to my heart I confess my sins "I wrap their tank with a towel if I am feasting on their family next to them"

He went stern a second, but when the fulfilling corner of his eyes crinkled- I knew it wasn't going to be as inconvenient with him like a while ago. His laugh followed as I accompanied him with an easy smile.

"How do you know about that?" I enquire as the dolphin fluttered its tail for encouragement.

"Lee called to know what I had planned for today" I don't miss the tenderness in his tone that he had for Lee, "He said he wanted to join along, he was sure that you'll like it"

I was gritting my jaw by the time he said it. And since he seems to witness the sloppy transformation in my mood, he continued.

"Fight?"

Is it one?

"I don't know"

Not that I was entirely blind. Edmund Sargent was a master of artistic direction who taught professionals to act. He knows an emotion when he sees one.

"I am generally a good conversation keeper. But you being the wife of Lee, I don't know what to ask or say. None of us here in the states knew that he was dating, let alone his plans for the wedding" I snort as he shrugged with a single shoulder. He was witty and grounded. Mature with the right phrase to gain a person's trust formally.

So I get it out.

"We didn't date" Creating the loophole, I fill them with the present assurance. I smile at him as he took it in, it mustn't have been difficult for him to digest the fact. He wasn't invited to the wedding for a reason- but before he could worry I resume "It's complicated. But where we are now, it rocky but nothing that can't be rectified. We are fine"

Are we though?

When I presumed Edmund to have the tendency to put anxiety at ease- I infer it. Because he proved me next by dispersing the atmosphere into something that we both were accustomed to.

"I used to be his roommate" he raises his brows with a humorous glint.

A chuckle escapes my lips with a slow onset of a grin.

"How do you sleep at night?"

Well, at last, I was acknowledged by someone who's past is my present.

"I don't" I pause to gather my schedule "I sleep at two after I get him back to bed. I find myself making videos of him debating why fruits aren't a lethal war weapon"

Locking my lips in a thin line, I stifle my laugh, unlike Edmund who was having a party inside his head. Because he had his back to a frowning Lee who jogged up to us, perhaps a million questions were running down his lane- but his pissed gesture of hitting Edmund at the back of the head only ailed my pain. Edmund didn't budge, he rolled his eyes letting let in.

"Why does I feel like you both are backstabbing me?"

Batting my lashes I answer for us,

"That's because we were"

Narrowing his gaze he shuffles, filling the space next to me. I hold my chin up. I watch Edmund shake his head as he walked away to join Fischer.

"So you are going around making friends now huh?" the step he ascended soared with intimidation, with my blood reaching my neck in haste I force my composure from crumbling. In spite of the proximity, he always limits it to environments protocol. It worries me of going back home with him where he doesn't have to give heed to his conscience. The thought hadn't crossed my mind until today. Until now.

"Only if my other friend wasn't so stubborn. I wouldn't have to be so hell-bent on proving him wrong. A friendship is equally beautiful you see"

Mistakes upon mistakes. It's what I've been doing because I am desperate to stop him. I hadn't seen his quirky smile in a day, it was clogging my brain cells. I don't even have many at this point.

"What if the said friend proves her wrong?"

My breath staggered at the vice confidence in his tone.

"Tell me shin" he takes a step further, I look around to see that we were alone now. Not that it had anyone else other than us before-but with Edmund and Fischer gone from the section, Lee wasn't having it. I take a step back when he leans with his face just an inch away from mine. "if I prove her wrong-

my toes curl inside my shoes, his voice felt like a touch on the skin. Sinfully intense and cruel for anyone who tried to resist them.

-will she let me have it my way?"

With how he framed it, it scarcely was said in terms of an option. There wasn't an option that he gave me- with how frantic my heart was behaving. He knew he wasn't losing. Not at this rate.

CHAPTER 18

S HIN

"Lee- since when did you turn into an escape room enthusiast?" Edmund enquired as we stood outside the Hollywood studious. The large font illuminated the purpose we were here for. Lee steals his gaze away from Edmund as Fischer clamps his finger by the necktie, stretching it loose with a moist face. "You never came with us to a common one, let alone the one with the haunted theme"

With a combined effort I keep my eyes trained on the door ahead. I haven't been to one because I haven't had a chance, but Lee has voluntarily passed such opportunities because-

"The last time I remember, this kind of activity freaks you out" Edmund's voice was a blend of amusement and excitement. A visual errand to notice the hesitative texture of Lee and Fischer was enough to tell the tale, they weren't cut out for this. But Lee had it schemed, the aquarium was just an en route.

Lee makes a disagreeing sound with a hand to his waist.

"People change buddy. I am not the eighteen-year-old boy you used to know"

Edmund irons his creases into a deeper stage of understanding.

"A year ago you supported my debut as a paranormal movie director, you made me stay online because you couldn't fall asleep after you watched th-

"It was a sick movie"

"-trailer Lee. You didn't watch the movie. It was trailer"

Lee closed his eyes, as if he stood in solitary with his rupturing pride. His wounded self-esteem was hilarious to me. So when I got scolded, my smile only grew in size.

"Why is it funny you?" he cocks his head, his tongue poking the inside of his cheek "It was based on a true story and our family house had a history of a supernatural presence, I was making sure to live through a night"

That provoked me into maintaining the stance in order to infuriate him.

Edmunds was first to enter the swiveling gate, then a grunting Fischer stomps off- vanishing into the Raven-black overcast. Lee stood by me with a hand out for me to hold, a prolific determination shadowed him.

"Stay here if it's not your scene" the suggestion was met with a profound frown, I replayed what I had said to make sure it wasn't as ridiculous as what Lee was trying to make of it.

"You believe Edmund?" he snorts as it was my turn to scowl "I pretended to be scared so Edmund could have a reassuring review before the release of his film. He was constantly irrational about it since it was his debut, but my dramatics saved him from the baseless anxiety"

A series of sensations erupts by the pit of my stomach, it wasn't fair for a man to be so perfect when I battled with a fate that kept dragging me ten-step away the moment I took one towards him. It freaking hurt to fight the truth.

"But- but you also avoided such activities-

"Most of them were related to calculations, it was to preserve my dignity" he winks at me, snaking his arm by my shoulder he stared ahead "You do the smart work. I'll protect you from zombies or whatever the hell that's inside" he says with a skeptic twitch of his lips.

He wasn't lying, because once in- he guarded me from the jump scares with his tactics. He wasn't as immune to them as he implied, but neither did he lose his cool like Fischer and Edmund. The corridors and room we walked through had bloodied walls, props that were disgusting to look at with chopped dummies, and some real actors in prosthetics. They flung themselves at us when we expected the least. From the fireplace as we looked for the clue, behind the couch, from above the ceiling? They were everywhere.

Edmund threw Fischer around with occasional expletives, he protected himself countless times by sacrificing his assistant. By now I highly doubted that Edmund had any right to make fun of Lee when it came to this genre. Because unlike him, Lee had a selective coping mechanism. It was to get mad at any zombie or butchered actor that paid him a visit.

"YOU HAVE NO MORALS SCARING A DIABETIC MAN LIKE THAT"

"FINE THAT WAS COOL, NOW GO AWAY"

"ALDO STOP SCREAMING"

Were his go to's

But Edmund embraced a terrified Fischer only to push him into a chamber of nightmares once he couldn't find a way out.

"What kind of an escape room is this" Edmund grunts as I held on to a fist of the shirt Lee had on, he lost his jacket during the first stage of chaos. How it was possible? it's a mystery. I have been concealed behind him in silence for so long that I doubt anyone other than us knew that a girl accompanied these three fellows in.

"The scariest one according to survey in the US" breathed Lee, a pain in his utterance. Then in the dark, he tried to feel my presence.

"You okay?"

Was I?

"I think so"

With the little light through the phone flash Edmund flags it around with wonder.

"Where is Aldo?" he inquires, to which Aldo gripes from behind.

"Don't bring the light here, my pants came loose. I am trying to wear them back"

Edmund killed the torch in respect to his fallen and forced knight. But soon we were looking for the clues, I unlatched myself from Lee looking around individually- as I wander around I bump into a wall. On a concentrated note- I realized it wasn't, in fact a wall. But a large and tall marble pillar.

"Shin" I hear Lee summon me "Stop walking into walls and come here"

Obediently with a harsh blush, I enlist to where they all had huddled by a pool table. Edmund had a ball which he tossed at me with a sheepish smile, scratching the back of his head.

"There's an equation in that" Lee taps at the said variables "Now do the Asian magic"

I look at him, and then at the rest two. Then realizing how hope-less they were I pick my mobile out and punched in the numbers for an answer. I flick the screen at Lee whose lips formed an O, they collectively decided that they were not functioning under pressure. It was the stress meddling with the sanity apparently.

I would like to quote otherwise if I had a chance. But I was polite, so I don't say much.

The number took us to an asylum room where we had a family of zombies waiting for us to touch our feet as they swarm by the floors. Edmund in adrenaline punched one in the face when it tried to slither across his neck. And worriedly I had snatched someone's wig because I had one silky cluster coiled in my hand.

The room gave us another clue, which led us to more adventures where we puzzled the separated words into a phrase when we got to the final room. It was-

Surprise me with what you say and you all will live

Edmund puckered his lips in frustration, the thirst to escape was getting to us all now. But as soon as Edmund read the script the room falls into pitch-black darkness, the lights burn out and an AI announcement spears through.

"The use of technologies for illumination is prohibited at the final round"

When I had wished for a walk through a thrilling game night, I hadn't foreseen the desperate outcome it could cause me. I was dying to be set free from here. Especially when the bold dose of air was shot at us from every nook and corner, the one we imagine to befall on the day of doom weighs us down. The floor rattles throwing us slightly off-balance, I got on one of my knees as Lee was beside me, always holding my hands. But a hand hits my head, it stayed buried in my hair as Fischer screams.

He hollered helplessly.

"MY HAND IS STUCK IN A WIG" I shake my head like a puppy to get him off "THERE IS A ZOMBIE IN HERE"

I grab his wrist tightly with a metallic grunt.

"That. is. my. Hair. Fischer" I don't raise my voice like these three men. Apparently I discovered that my coping mechanism was dying inside a little rather than damaging my vocal cords or expanding my lungs just because I can.

He shrieked as if the fact terrified him more than the zombie. In a dancing room, Edmund was first to realize we need to do something to get out of here.

"Surprise her" he commanded.

"What?" Lee replied uselessly.

"The clue was to surprise whatever the hell it is. So say something"

We stayed mum for a moment. Then Fischer decided to go first.

"I hate my wife"

A loud covens laugh echoes as nitrogen water gets sprayed on us. Nothing else happens.

"I am a celebrity" Edmund offers. The screeching mockery of a laugh kept increasing manifold.

The earthquake intensifies with Lee joining the force.

"The earth is round"

With each piercing laugh of hers, the tension in me fusions. So when I try my shot- I do it with passion and flow.

"Fucking Die Bitch"

It stops.

Everything stops. None made a sound, I could hear the beats of my heart make amends with the relieving night light the floods the room once the shutters gradually rolls up to an outside world. There were staffs waiting for us with towels and trophies, cheering us as we walked out as if we were some kind of wounded war heroes. Not Fischer, he crawled out on his fours until Edmund went back and supported him to his feet.

We survived for an hour,

So when I craved ice creams to celebrate, the others leaped in agreement. Must be their throat that burned because of how pretentious they were. When we stood by the stall is when we broke out into a fit of laughter-

The feminine mix of my giggles got drowned by their masculine howls. Which also reminded me of the lack of female support in my life. With the exception of my mother and short acquaintance that lived through sera Kim when we surfed for the wedding dress- I had no other woman around me. With the chic manner, I dress and live, it did trick people into speculating that I belong to a feministic circle. When the reality was-

"I don't get paid enough for this" Fischer began cracking up in the middle, I hadn't seen him smile so wide until now. His once gelled hair was a league of its own at present, it stood out into directions that challenged a couple of laws in physics. Edmund and Lee had wrinkles in their clothes, apart from that they looked fine, the jacket that Lee wore when he went in, was never found. For me- my hair got styled by Lee with his skillful hands. He remarked that he had a psychic hunch that the neighboring birds were plotting to lay their eggs on it.

But when they brought the reason for our escape up- it flushed off any last resort I had to maintain my clean record.

"To think of it. It wasn't only the witch that got surprised by that" Edmund teased the topic as I throw my concentration into inspecting the flavor I wanted. Lee was next on line- I felt my head being fondled with a pat- I refused to look at them.

"Who knew our little Shin was capable of something so severe. She saves our lives"

The snort that erupted from Fischer nips me up, especially when he housed a space beside me with an offer once Lee and Edmund strolled away to get something else to go along.

"I don't get paid enough" he mumbled, taking a bite from his cone. I mimic his, the creamy taste of cookie dough makes me smile. So do Fischers' catastrophes.

"What do you want me to do about it?" the railing cushioned our backs, he rests his elbows on them perking up at the rotation of the ferris wheel.

"You can fill the gap. Since I am keeping your identity a secret and buying you the time you asked for" I arc my brow, I pretended to search my sling- then pulled out a finger for him for an answer, he chuckled. But then, I was kind at heart- or I do try to be. Since I know he was struggling with a stinky divorce- I ask

"How much?"

The reply wasn't instantaneous.

"It's a lot. Are you sure?"

"Tell me before I change my mind"

"Forgive me for what happened at Manila"

He doesn't pause to let me intervene, he carries on with a rough self malice not once ripping his eyes from what he had been looking at.

"I knew how my wife would've reacted. I let it happen in front of my kids. I made you go through it because I wanted the last push, a reason to finally call it quits with her. To know and witness why I can't stay in a toxic marriage" he blows out air with a sad smile. The man was breaking down slowly in front of me- not crying or in hysterics. But he is breaking it into segments, letting me know how he used me. "I must have been professional, I guess- the things you keep putting me through. I deserve it"

Chuckling in disbelief I move my hair, it curtains me when the breeze stroked us. The ice cream wasn't as sweet as it was before since Fischer had paid for it.

"I- have no words"

Suddenly the guilt I usually sensed when it came to him, bids a farewell. I hadn't ever been known for a forgiving nature. Shaking my head in denial- I watch him nod in acceptance. Not when I had trusted him, not when I had fought through my fears to open a door for friendship. If he had done his part virtuously, he would have been in a better place. Promoted even.

He leaves me to be once Edmund and Lee return, Lee jogs to where I stood. Fischer kept Edmund busy with work, his posture fatigued and worn down-

"We are visiting the island" is what Lee declares as soon as he comes to a halt, a strand of his hair falls on his forehead loosely. Arching my back from the support I stood straight, my eyes lighting up. Again because of this man.

"Why? Whe- How?" he smirks motioning his thumb at his friend who was on phone. A flock of girls by him who had probably recognized him as they ogled at the sight.

"He's leaving for Santa Catalina. An island near California to check the location in two days" he blurts as if he couldn't keep up with the words with how fast his thoughts were running. "We are at four. With six more to go"

Each thread in me knots into a complexity I couldn't undo. With not enough strength to speak I merely watch him as the surrounding bursts with zeal. But with him, it was a different world in its entirety. I was slowing down in it- where my heart raced, skipped, and confronted me to be fair with her. But I played along as if nothing changed between us. Betraying my own self.

"Thanks for today," I say as a beam of light from rides reflects him. But they weren't brighter than his aura or his livelihood.

"I have to go now," he says scanning the throng of carnival fans through which he has to walk through. His chest deflates but the stare was still hot on me when he looked at me "I have to finish the paperwork tonight if we have to leave for the vacation. Edmund will take the cab too, so drive home safely. Don't stop or go around alone by yourself. Call me if anything even feels wrong. Okay?"

I nod frantically hoping he would just stride away, but his gaze flickers at the cone of ice cream longingly as he couldn't have it as a whole.

"Can I have a bite?" one of his lids narrows into a plead. Immediately I raise it up to him so that he could have the untouched side. But he twists my wrist gently and feasts through the portion where I have previously eaten through.

"Tastes heavenly" the quivering smirk and pouring gaze had me caged. Even when he was gone I stood there until I couldn't sense my nose because of the rare cold night. I did drove through. alone with my fingers trembling at my stupidity.

How stupid was I to let things get this far?

When the phone rang, I dropped it to the ground. Stopping the car by the side I got out with my phone. Calling my mother who had previously rang me up. With tears on the brink, I speak- my voice was a contrast to how I looked in person.

"Mom. How are you?"

In a snap, I receive a high pitch response that was a result of my unconscious mistake.

"Oh, you don't ask your aging mother how she is after you had called her a week ago young lady" she couldn't be more pissed than she was, so with a blink I push the heel of my palm to smudge the wetness in my lashes as I leaned by the hood of the car. It was a friendly neighborhood with residential housing that you seen in an average Hollywood movie. With trees, houses, and a sidewalk.

"Please forgive this child of yours. She has been a brat" I could feel her smile bloom through, God, I miss her so much.

"How is my baby doing?" she asks, her voice was like a warm cup of coffee in a freezing eve. "Is my son-in-law treating her right?"

Flipping through the past fifteen days, I let out a staggering breath. When I don't reply to her the instant- she pans through me in seconds.

"Is something wrong Shin?" there she was, the real mother of mine without the lighthearted armor she had it donned. She was a warrior disguised as a queen. "Do I need to have a talk with this boy?"

Smiling at the sky I sniff, finally trusting my voice again.

"He treats me too well Mom" I confess. Just a little too well than I want him to.

The was silence by her side. The serenity made me feel as if she was beside me by the moment.

"Are you happy?" the fear, I sense it.

"More than you probably think"

More than I should be.

"Then why-" I could hear her confusion developing. If only she knew- if only I could tell her "Then what is it that's bothering you?"

Chapter 19

S HIN

    The drying wounds weren't the ones to scar me. If I were to escape today, I would heal in no time. For an eleven-year-old girl, I was stronger than how I was seen by the others. Isn't it why I had shoved my five-year-old brother to the concreate when I was abducted after school? It was my responsibility to pick Hwan from his elementary class- but wasn't trading myself to save him a bigger one? I did good, didn't I?

    But why was I regretting it into the night? I've stopped crying out for help, I wasn't losing hope. I was finally giving in to my fears. I yearn It was all I had to go through. The blows and starvation. But when the drunken man stumbled in with wobbly legs and a crooked smile, I realized that I hadn't known the real fear at all.

    The curdling stench of cheap beer hits me when he crouched in front. I scrambled into the wall, curling into a small mass, praying that he couldn't see me if I did so. But when he touched my arm, it wasn't the contact with cuts that burns me. It was something else. I shiver, I was afraid- I hated every breath that I took within the moment his dirty hand reached my neck. He wasn't trying to kill me-

I wish he did at the minute.

I was young, but I knew it was a bad touch. I froze when he leaned in, his nails digs by my collar bone. My world became blurry mess, I couldn't speak, breathe or think until there was a loud scream. When I was yanked to my feet by the woman- I glance at the shards of glass scattered by the unconscious man. Half of the bottle with which the woman who had whacked him with was still in her clutch. For a second I think she was going to stab me with it.

But she drags me out, she dips a towel into a bowl of lukewarm water, and runs it across my face and arms. But I still feel his touch on me- I squirm. I don't cry or plead. She saved me before I he could do anything to me- but did she save me from what a maze my life will become after this?

She could've been late, even a few minutes would have been enough. She was aware of that because her eyes were afraid, sad and regrets flooded them when she cleaned my wounds. They don't matter now did they,

The bowl of water turns scarlet as she squeezed the towel into them. she took me to my home, outside the gates, she heeds me a warning. It sounds like a request.

"You don't utter a thing. Understand"

I don't reply, she doesn't stay back to make sure I'll keep my lips sealed. She runs off, I walk to the front gate- my battered body winced with each step I took. I think I rang the bell- I think it's what I do before I passed out.

I woke up in my room, IVs taped in, monitors beeping off, Mom holding my hand with tears streaming down her cheeks, Dad next to her holding his in to stay strong for me. Despite my hazy vision I smile for them- I was happy to see them. I cried while I smiled.

In few days, as I recovered I had officials dressed in informal clothes with a wrapped teddy bear come visit me. They were here for interrogation, they kept it short- subtle, threading on a thin line to not trigger any wrong memories since my Mom was right beside me.

It was short because I lie-

"I don't remember much"

They don't believe me.

"They did it for ransom I guess, I heard them discussing about money few times" it was quizzical how small my voice was, the sooner these men entered the room, my stomach churned with anxiety that I wasn't familiar with. My palms began to sweat. My heart hammered. I didn't feel like myself anymore.

And that would be the birth of my chronic social anxiety. A fear that I'll learn to host through the years.

"It's strange, I did not receive any calls for it" my Mom adds, her voice filled with rage. My head pulsed with an ache as if a nail was being pelted to it. she must have so many questions lingering, higher with each hour she saw the baseless marks of abuse on her daughter's skin. She was a mother, she would have done anything for me. she would have even killed the senator that was admitted at her center, because that what they had asked of me.

The death of a minister by the hands of my mother in exchange for her child. But they never made the effort to make an early move.

They wanted to keep me there for a week before they rang my mother up. The more the days, the higher the apprehension.

I knew the cause, a dark history that redeemed. No one else did.

"You sure dear- there is nothing else you remember," they ask with a surreptitious request on his face. As if he knew it was a lie. He was trained for this.

I think back to it all, every second of it plays like a film that you have watched countless times. I hold the person's stare, it would be the last time I would be bold enough to lie because if I testify a truth today, they might dig out more since it involves a possible threat to a high-ranking official. They may even forget that I was a child when it came to interrogation.

I can't let them know what happened and what could've happened. So with my cowardice winning the race, I say it-

"I don't. There is nothing else I remember that could be helpful"

When I quote that I am an unforgiving person, I may be lying to my honest traits for the sake of betterment. Because it's what I want to be. Bold, strong, and someone who is untouchable. For years I had learned to live in comfort where I was my only solace. But with the onset of vulnerable psychological weaknesses - my family wielded me into a golden cage. They may not show in my vicinity- but I always was by theirs. Hwan acted like my older brother at times, I wasn't made to move off from my family house, and despite my love for fashion I never was able to pursue a career in it- since it involved a hound of interactions, I settled to ignore my ambitions and kept throwing myself into the community library where human interactions was a forbidden rule in itself. Book gave me another gateway to leave my surroundings behind. I got sucked into the world of words and their sheer elegance, it gradually became a medicine that kept my mind in one place.

It was free therapy and I liked free stuff.

Soon I found myself scribbling the paragraphs of how I would end up writing a book if I ever were to. I began to compose what I wanted to read- the original publishing happened because I had enough money from my Christmas and birthday party to secretly fund my first edition. I never thought I would ever be republishing the copies. I just strived to receive at least two or three reviews from the readers to see what they think of it. Let alone millions.

As for its present success- it's a history and mystery combined. I am an accidental author who still craves victorias secrets and ralph Lauren. If everything had gone well, I see myself in the position of sera Kim. Not that I am grateful, what I have is more than what I had bargained for. But can't a person have more than one hobby or interest?

Sera Kim- she is the daughter of ex-senator. So is Lee. I had forgiven their lineage long ago. Funny how I woke up and decided to forgive someone who has clue about a girl like me who probably saved the senator's life. My heart was clean of any dirt for them, if not- I would've never agreed to marry Lee.

Lee-

He was my ticket to freedom. He was supposed to. Now-I wasn't just married to him, I was falling for him. Slightly better than my devotion for heels and I accepted it last night. With a night where he wasn't there beside me, I utilized it to organize a set of if's and what if's.

While I distinguished the what if's, I began to wonder if I could be selfish this wise. To test if it was safe to play with steam and not the fire itself. To see if I gave in to the instincts, would it disappear on time before i-

The lock softly clicks open and I immediately shut my eyes, feigning a sleep. He came in late after work- he was street smart, so was he a major fluff. He was a combination of many things that was woven beautifully. So when such man adjusted the duvet on me and caressed my head gently before moving to the washroom to fresh up for the night. I lose it once he was gone-

I can't do this.

I wanted to be selfish. I wanted him. I have been a ghost of my past for so long that now realizing that I am indeed a woman who had emotions subpar her insecurity was shocking in a sense. He doesn't sleep in the bed that night- he took the couch which confused me.

But the one day we had in the middle before we were supposed to join Edmund in his cruise trip to Catalina, I cracked the code. When either path ends with me hurt, I might as well run along with the one where I wasn't being a wimp. I tried to find Lee the next night, he wasn't in here. so I check the surveillance footage by the screen near the gym. I found him in his garage, the picture of a tiny Lee digging through what appeared was a toolbox.

The private garage was a car gallery. It was a luxury museum for his collections, and by how he simply refers it as his basement was an insult to the marvel the core was. With walls covered in dark leather and glassy rich black flooring that would cost an average person, his kidneys weren't just a basement. It was an art that he likes to be humble about. When I first went there- I wasn't able to make my mind up if I genuinely relish the penthouse more to the underground room.

When his mobile rang with a memo flashing across his screen by the kitchen counter I reach for it.

The reminder read Dose Two, which wasn't a hassle to understand. It was his insulin. I highly doubt that with his phone left here he remembers that it was time for it. So I pick up his pen from his side of the night table where he usually has it tossed, as I jog my way down I collect some snacks just in case if he gets hungry after the shot. My legs tap restlessly as the elevator descends. The passcode to the gallery was the same as that of the penthouse-so I highly doubt my procrastination was a result of me forgetting and confusing the numbers.

It was Lee- he shouldn't be making me this nervous.

The flat panels separate when the egress slides open to reveal the thin and dim lines of lights that what the sole golden spectrum among the complete black interior of the area that it covers, I knew it was too late to call it quits. I walk in, absorbing the eccentric magnificence of it as if it was my first time here. If one met Lee a couple of times in their lives and were given a blind tour of this place without revealing the identity of the man who possessed it, the idea of something like this to be the likes or preference of Lee would never, ever cross their mind.

It was different than him,

With power and intimidation painted in walls and fragrance, one may think that it won't fit Lee in here.

But they couldn't be more wrong. Because this was his scene, I say it because I see it. He stood there by one of his seven cars, a gray Lamborghini to precise. The hood popped up as he leaned to inspect the complex wires maimed by the engine. His arms rested on either side of the thin frame, the sleeve of his black shirt rolled up.

"What brings you here?" he doesn't look up, but there was a glitch of a sly smile in his voice as he concentrated on the task at hand. I chose to go with the facts.

"You left your phone up there"

"And?"

Jerking my neck with the ounce of courage I had loitering some-where I walk to him, he brings his thumb to caress his lower lip with a frown, with his other hand still pressed by the mouth of the vehicle. Why won't he look at me?

"It's time for your shot" I sigh inwardly at the lower register, I keep sounding fragile even if I was prepared. What I wasn't prepared was for Lee to snap, he shifts- grabbing the hood and closing it with a force that wasn't so compact. Turning, he tilts his head as he regarded me.

With an oversized maroon shirt and white shorts beneath- I looked like a Christmas party thrown in the midst of an dungeon execution. his orbs stains in a flicker of darkness as he meets my gaze.

"Do it"

With a bruised intelligence I blurt out a-

"What?"

He raised two of his fingers and tapped his left shoulder.

"Give me my shot" he dictates starting to unbutton the top of his shirt as I hurriedly dump the snacks by the leather couch. When I return to him he sat by the edge of his car- slant enough for support. But not completely seated. He watched me, he was like the one alpha hawk upset with his prey.

My cold fingers gets a hold of his collar, when I slide it by his shoulder until his lower buttons that still held the shirt together bands the hem by his beicep, I settled to inject him with what I have. It was a lot more than necessary. I do it with his gaze on me all while as I struggled to keep my sanity at bay.

I breath when once it was done. He wasn't having it. It was as if he woke up and decided today was the one where he was obligated to dismantle my peace with his alter persona. I don't know him this way, I don't know what to say to him when he wasn't himself.

But this was also him. This is him too.

"Why are you here?" it was low but modulated and controlled. Sharp even.

"Why are you ignoring me? you even slept on the couch last night" it comes out brittle, and what came out of me wasn't logical. Not a sensible question to ask a man who was cold and mad. He was a broken refrigerator.

He exhales a breathy laugh, it catches mine.

"You really have to ask that after I have been so obvious with my feelings Shin?" he stalks forward, stopping after two full steps when I stumbled one back. the nonchalances crack through, the sleek anger and hurt veers in his eyes. But almost as if his gears changed, he smirks through them "You can't expect me to sleep through the night when you are right beside me. I don't think I should be explaining a why of it"

He was ardent, I wasn't. My knees were weak and my heart hadn't been weaker. But when he says it- I let him.

"I like you shin" his exposed chest span heaves in relief, he had been keeping it inside him for so long "I wasn't ready for this to happen, but you have no right to coerce me into thinking otherwise"

The silence that emerged after him was a pleasant one.

"Then don't think otherwise" I say, my nails squeezing into my palms. His lips parts, the tip of his tongue touches the inner bridge of his teeth, his eyes melting with the slow reach of meaning behind what I had said. "But remember that there isn't much I could give you- you might even

I don't get to finish my words as they were cut short but how quick and smooth his movements were, for a second I was alone and the next, his lips were on mine, soft and merciful in the beginning as his vigorous arms circled my waist. Not letting me fall, not letting me stand. It was him who dominated the entirety of it. It felt as if the air, room, gravity- all were employed by this new side of Lee that I doubt many knew of.

It wasn't my voice that moans when he feasts into my lower lip, biting it with a smile as he lifts me, no sooner than it, he placed me against the hood of his car he was previously working on. I recall him mentioning that it was his first the last time we were here. The thin summer shirt I wore seldom concealed me as he explored me in the midst of the ferocious kiss. His lios were soft, his intentions weren't. He wasn't civil anymore. Though it wasn't a bare touch it still ignited a train of fire in me. He curves my body, completely molding me into his. When he breaks the kiss he still holds me that way,

Regaining the lost oxygen was a reflex, but turning back from what just happened wasn't.

He watched me with so much care and intensity that I forgot my name at the moment. He runs a hand through my hair, a slow smile forming by the corners.his orbs, diluted. He shifts to give me enough space to recover. But then his gaze ran over my probably swollen lips in what I think is concern, He runs his thumb along with my lower one as I flinch. My skin was ridiculously sensitive. Though I wasn't bleeding, I could sense a tiny cut in there- when I smile swatting his hands off, looking away because I was admittedly feeling shy. He dared to shamelessly add fire to the fuel.

"And this is just a percentage of the reason for why I can't sleep in the same bed as you until you are ready"

CHAPTER 20

L EE

The knife cuts through the skin shell, one sleek motion and it wilts through in middle- undressing the shrimp. The youtube tutorial suggested it to be done with light pressure. I don't think I have it in me, to be gentle with anything- one look at shin's lip, the red siren goes off inferring that I should keep my distance from her, It's a requirement so that I don't end up scaring her away. So I stood a collective six inches away from the tabletop counter where she sat on, her legs crossed and cozily tucked as she operated on a frozen shrimp.

I was hovering above her, for moral comfort as she administered the ingredients. The present image of a butchered sea creature proves to be the most adequate one to keep me from reimaging the kind of kiss that I didn't know I had it in me. Like a starved soul, that I undoubtedly was- had pounced on her the moment she dropped the curtain of courtesy that remarked that type of relationship we had.

The reign of what it actually meant registered with the trails of shiver she reacted with every little touch of mine. Not that I could put it into words of what I felt then, it was what I had never felt before. I was high, I was low. Her lips were cold and soft – warming up to mine until it almost was feverish in temperature. To the popular belief that I smile a lot that I do it for the sake of a disposition and identity, in the time of true ecstasy- I turn into this confusedly drenched excuse of a man that doesn't know how to keep his mouth in check.

Filter?

Do I know how it works?

With others it was different- the girls I dated in past were either older or were the same age as me. But shin- she was four good years younger to me. At that age, I don't think I knew what I wanted to do the next day with my life, let alone get on in a serious relationship with a said wife. Our charts were already a messed version in itself. Where we were two individuals in a legal marriage testing their take on dating.

I can't afford to race our journey like I usually do with things. If I wanted to run, I might just crawl instead. Because my face and bilingual ability were the only Korean thing about me. And yeah, the two-year military enlistment I completed for the last years counts the most. It probably was the addition among the reason why I had forgotten how fragile girls are. But I can't deny that shin's fragility was a tad bit on the amusing side. She was sensitive to the sun, to flowers, to touches that were overwhelming on her. She doesn't complain- but I try to be safe whenever I hold her, to make sure I am not leaving temporary marks on her. Even if it were only for a couple of minutes- I keep myself from being the cause of her discomfort.

Can't guarantee how long I will last though-

Because shin might be younger than me, but she has her priorities straight. Most of what she does or says are signs of maturity in itself. She may have had a standard Asian childhood, But she probably grew up with her own ideologies that made her different among all the other proposals I declined.

They were four girls I met prior to her. The awkward dinner silence was the common thing I made sure we had among us. Embellished and bandaged for the occasion they sat there with embarrassment that I caused them as they tried to shove a conversation down my throat. Again- they were older and some same as me. From reputed families and heritage backgrounds. I disliked what I had to do in order to secure my freedom. But I did it anyway.

A forced arranged marriage wasn't my scene.

But then she stumbled in with her peculiar nervous gestures and a tempting proposal. The same girl who months later managed a car chase and dodge a prison scene on her own was the one who probably waited outside the restaurant for half the hour to tame her anxiety when I first met her.

Which could say much for itself. I don't know much about her- not even a snippet of what she does about me. Much of my private life could be used as a textual subject in Korea with the amount of media attention we get. With my sister being a celebrity designer and my brother joining an agency to pursue his career as an idol was a bonus.

"This was easier than I thought" she blinks, soaring her spine as she marinated the shrimp with the canned sauce that she had brought along. Her synthetic gloved hands were red from spices when she moved her head to get the hair off her face, In an instant, I was there to hold it for her. "I think I get naturally good at whatever I do"

"I don't doubt it" fascinated I gather her hair, braiding it as best as I could into a bun. It was messy- but it did the job. I watched her confidence deflate the second I got near her. It was toxic to say I liked how vulnerable she gets around me- but since I knew the moment I hit a distraction, she'll be herself. Feisty, witty, and insanely sarcastic. She had been that way since we naively had decided to befriend each other. Her true colors began to incite the house with her presence.

"Mister Lee" she sighs, wiping her face with her forearms as I nod behind her back even though she can't see me "Is there any work you plan on doing or supervising the job Is all you want to do. You were the one who suggested we make the dinner at home tonight"

Instead of answering I hug her from behind,

Dinner at home? Those darn shrimps saved me from initiating another kiss that I had no control over, Bet I would have prompted it by the garage if I hadn't come up with the lie that I was hungry.

For poor shin, the said dinner was an armor she wasn't aware of.

"But I like watching you do it" I rest my chin on her shoulder, she squirms but held on to her customs. Her inner feminist won to our proximity as approximate of ten minutes later I was chopping onions with Shin examining me with swimming goggles on. I was given none. So I wiped my happy tears. She still sat at the table with a wide smile.

"I like watching you do this too" she cheerfully pats my shoulder in an act of encouragement "You are chopping them, right sweetie"

Sweetie.

Isn't that my choice of syllable to annoy her? So many elements were switching tonight, I could barely keep up with my thoughts and her. I stare at her through the peripheral . This wise, I was serious with my utterance.

"What made you change your mind?"

She plucks the spring greens from the basket-

"What change?" –playing it dumb like always.

"You know what I mean?"

She takes off the gear once I slide the contents from my cutting boards to the previously steaming broth in the pan as shin asks me to. Once she fits the lid, I wait for her. The aroma from fresh and grounded herbs fills the kitchen- the three-step ramen was the final décor to the enticing flavor dancing In air.

But- I want her to answer first. I won't eat or let her eat until she answers me.

So once I plate the food for us both and refused to pass them to her so she could dive in with her anticipating chopstick- the curve of her lips falls in dejection.

"It's like you understand the code, but won't cooperate" with my eyes smugly closed I tap my chopstick by the ledge of the fine china. "I am interested to know why you accepted me today"

Compromising to the comfort of her seat, she shifts in them. Her cheeks dusting in pink as she threw me a quick glance.

"I realized that I was trying to fix a wall that wasn't even there" her lips forms an unconscious pout, her gaze falls to the deserted chopsticks "But who could have thought that the Lee I was attracted to would blackmail me with me with something as sacred as a food for-

I slide it to her before I could say or think of it. Or let her finish.

That little vixen knows how to use the card while I was here scraping on delusions.

A grin flourished, a complete natural one as she dug through the edibles. She gasped the moment she chewed on it.

"I am a fucking chef" she exclaimed, but choked the sooner she realized what she had said. The amused smile that I had wasn't new- in fact the first time her versatile vocabulary surprised me was in the escape room. It probably was the day when I stopped looking at her with a stereotype. "Forget I said that, expletives does not go well with my pretty face-" sipping on water she waves at me- it was hard to keep myself from fueling her blush further, but since I wanted her to savor her food in peace I nod in humor.

But when I took my bite in, I realized why she was so confident about it. It was fucking good.

"This-" I chew fast to get it out "This- is delicious"

Her excited giggles earn a soft chuckle from me. she brings her phone out to take a snap of the food. Then she scrolls through her screen, so I intervene to ask-

"What's your ID on Instagram?"

She breaks her contact from the mobile, dropping it by her side with quick ignoring glances.

"We should finish first- its getting cold," she thinks she dodged the progression. But I had my intentions tracked down. If not all- I will get her to open up with what she had consent with. So while we ate, we managed a two-fold conversation. Formal at the beginning since I got to know that she had once aspired to become a fashion modulator.

Now that she said it, I could sense the passion similar to what sera have in regards to style and setting. When sera got promoted to the position of director- it was one of the proudest movements for our family. One- because she chose to do whatever the hell she wanted to, and Two- the most annoyingly reckless elder daughter finally achieved a milestone that we secretly thought she would lose because of how temperamental and egoistic her attitude was.

But Shin- she looked and felt like someone that could belong there.

"Fabrics, colors, and how it's shaped tells a story too. The world of art is closely connected, it's just an artist's vision that brings it to life" with a shrug she removes her hands from the table, done with dinner. But not with talk.

"So why didn't you do it. Become one I mean" my curiosity wasn't harsh- I knew what I wanted my whole life, I lived and enjoyed every second of the days I was at it. I wish I could understand the why of her-

She plays with the rim of the glass with a smile, I don't take my eyes off her. I don't think I would desire to look anywhere else while she was there, breathtakingly gorgeous and subtly dressed in a comfy large shirt that barely covered her upper thighs.

Everyday struggles of a decent man.

"If I chased my dreams, I would have still given up after" she cuts through before I could join "I don't feel comfortable around people I don't know. It took me years to get to where I am here today, but working atmosphere especially in a place like that. I would have been eaten alive" a shrug and that easy smile attempted to soothe me. But it promoted my existing need-

I needed to know what happened for her to elevate such fears, But since it hasn't even been a night of us together. I hold in, placing it among the hundreds more I have- it wasn't easy though.

So we plunge into something different. And with shin and her power to just ignore the stressful previous episode in a minute, it wasn't a chore to forget mine with her. Another habit of her that makes her adorable.

A woman now, child the next.

"So you were in military for the last two years?" my shoulders procured in stance at how shocked she was about it, but then she goes on to add "No wonder your abs are so steely"

That was general praise in her tone. Glad I chose to do the service since I could have used my condition to pass the enlistment. I did it to get away from the scrutinizing radar of media- But who would've thought It could be something that would- well since I had scarred her with my creative innuendos so far, I let one slip this while too-

"Not that you know how it feels. I have never been touched by you"

Her gaze searched my face calmly. She took a sip from her wine.

"I know a good one when I see one" a salute is thrown my way with two of her fingers. She was tipsy, but sane. She was the balance of Shin that was not shy at the moment and regret later. She will excuse this in the morning so now I smile in with a brewing frustration.

It took me her statement to realize that she might have had relationships in past as well. Did he have abs too? Was it as good as mine? Did she touched-

"I should try punching you in the face"

I tilt my humble face in subject with the serenity she was executing, I have stopped reacting to her and bargained to settle with a welcoming smile. She drains me, in a good way. In a very good way.

"And why would that be?"

She was soon by my side, squinting as she fists her arm.

"I want to see how quick your reflexes are" she bats her lashes, silently asking for permission. This comes after I had admitted that I was a black belt holder in taekwondo. It wasn't a lie though- I could choke slam a giant Edmund if I want, I just don't do it.

Angling my jaw I nod-

"Go ahead"

Half an hour later- she wheezed grinning. It was the initial punch she had filed by my ribs after countless tries. When she failed to get five across, she begged me to teach her the basics. I wouldn't have accepted if it wasn't for her antics.

"I want to learn them for self-defense. Don't you want me to be safe and-

And yeah- that's how we ended up in the gaming room where the space was wide, and her shirt was off. She had a tank top underneath- though.

Conceiving that she wouldn't be able to hurt me for all the good reasons, I taught her the minor tricks which she used on me to double-check. Her excuse was, it had been a month since she hit her brother, which makes me wonder at the kind of sibling bond she has-

"oh about that- we sometimes end up in ER" she mumbles, though I sensed the sarcasm I still was paranoid, I regard her as she twisted her body in stance and high kicked into the air. Her hand to eye coordination was something to die for- literally. She is small, but fast. And with flexibility at her disposal, I doubt she lost a fight with her brother.

Which again was worrisome.

"What do you both fight about?" she heaves a breath, turning to me with her hair falling around her bare shoulder. A thin layer of sweat glistens by her neck as she nibbled on her lip-

"It's a long story" she offers.

"we've got time, don't we?" my brow arcs as I fall into the couch, sitting with my arm around the header. She nods shifting to get to the shirt- I pull her to my lap in the immediate junction. A soft gasp leaves her as I fasten her to me. My arm locked by her waist as she stared with her big doe eyes. Despite the struggle to get my breathing in check, I assure her-

"Don't worry. I won't do anything" recognizing my own voice became a mystery, too low, too deep. I don't know what I was saying or was frantic to say- but I draw back the silky strands of her hair that framed half of her face with my thumb. The feel of her on me was enough for me, as for the transfixed gaze I had her pinned with- I don't know how long I did it until I used my voice again. "I-I just want to know your story. Nothing else"

It's her who tears her eyes from me. as always. A smile follows me as she blinks in a haze. Not as confident as before was she?

But she speaks, narrates doing her best to decapitate the tension in the room. The room which once housed LAN and gaming streams with a batches of hormonal dudes under its roof, now hosted two people who were in deep denial of the palpitating emotions. But it was better this way. I can't afford to rush and nor to trigger her with it. Heck, I don't think it ever was a physical attraction that led me to this. She was more than that, way more intense and real.

Because I was learning her- with each word she spoke, I found them sinking into me. I was memorizing every little detail that came with her- her likes, dislikes, views, and aspirations. I liked everything about it, her smile, her laugh, her clueless scowls, her cunning remarks, her quirky digs, and the fact that she could pack a punch. And when invested in her talks- I realized why,

"We were taught to save the pocket money given to us for anything said luxury we wanted to buy. My parents raised me and Hwan like any other average household. We do our own laundry, make our bed, buy stuffs with our savings. But as soon as I turned eighteen and my allowance got expanded-" she sighs in dramatic despair "Hwan had to snoop in. He would take just about anything from me without asking. So that's how our house mostly began to resemble a war ruin. Even now- I bet he is in my room instead of his, he likes my gaming set up and I also believe he is using my Nintendo switch-

"Wait" I raise my hand sitting straighter-

"What?" perplexed she asks scanning her surrounding. But it was her again.

"You play?"

Slowly she turns to throw me a sweet- sweet smile.

"What do you think I do here when you are gone?" she gestures her index, circling at the parlor top.

A crack of code, we knew what it meant. As an avid gamer- the challenge was hot on heels and couple of hours later we were on the floor with me attempting to not break the controller into two and her collecting my misery with a cheeky smile and occasional chicken flap dance. It was her victory move.

"I am so polite" she muses with a hand to her heart If it were anyone else, they'd be rubbing it on their opponents face" she leans, she had her maroon shirt on. she must've sneaked into it when I was getting my ass kicked by her. She was a pro gamer- someone my older mates from tracks will worship if they'd ever know of her. Not that I'll ever let that happen.

"Why is there a pole here?"

She leans her side by the pole, the ceiling to floor pillar that was there for decorative purpose. But it was indeed an odd placement.

"I question that since day one" Imitating her, I side with the foot of the couch. The energy running low from all that happened tonight. But still as an afterthought, I add "You can dance on it. Flexible ones have it easy don't they?"

She covers her fluster with a snort.

"It's a curse too. I end up kicking myself sometimes"

What was this girl?

I don't know. because then she winked at me-

"You want me to dance for you?" she says simultaneously inspecting the pole for strength. I sat there gaping with useless air that came out of my mouth, she grinned back with mischief "But you have to work more on that, I have to like you a little more for me to put on a show for you"

Pursing my lips I rig my jaws to let her have her moment.

"So you like me less now?" I draw out, craning my neck to stare at the higher ceiling from where I could spot the entrance of our room by floor one.

"If I did, I wouldn't have been loving every bit of conversation that we have once you are asleep"

A part of my soul leaves me, I close my eyes with a smile. I have been waiting for this-

"What did I do?" I ask with a tilt, the cold blue light from the still monitor casts a glow on her as stifles her smile in.

"That's a secret between and my sleeping beauty. Can't share" her lids droops as the day's fatigue gets to her, a tiny yawn follows my observation. I call her over-

"Come here"

"What?" she blinks her sleep-induced gaze as I motion at my lap.

"Sleep"

Hesitant at first, she does crawl over and snuggled once in. With her head on my lap I comb her hair gently until she dozed off, which was in less then a minute . For the rest half of the hour, I was on the phone flipping through the mails and sorting out what needed to be cleared before we leave for the island tomorrow. Once done I carried her to our room.

She was angelic even when she wasn't doing anything.

I take the couch with no sleep on near sight. Not when I had a million thoughts scattered around. Not simple when most of them suddenly seem to welcome Shin in them. With how dangerously fast it was changing for me- I only feared a reality where I might crash into a dead end.

Only if I had known that it was real.

Not my emotions. But the fear.

CHAPTER 21

S HIN

The passenger cruise was huge. Big enough for me to get lost on as I strolled about. And- it's what happened. My little exploration led me to the main deck. My floral summer dress fought the wind. The hair wasn't an exception. Not that I call it getting lost- it was my strategic maneuver to get to the deck. With lone time for self after what had happened last night- I use it as a gateway where I could finally let the happiness settle in. A smile cracks through as I drank in the sight, endless bed of the blue ocean and the clear sky that met them, I could taste the salt in my lips. The sun was bright but cold here- almost as if she wasn't in a pursuit to bother me when I had ultimately begun to let my guard down.

As if she wasn't keen on teasing me once I stopped hiding from it. Or covering.

With Lee, it was different. It wasn't about revealing a part of me to him. But knowing and freeing one that I had knowingly choked and slammed within me. He makes me selfish- no matter how long it will last for us, but as of present, I want to be the one for him. He makes me happy, happier than I have ever doubted with my boundaries on line. I want to stay this way as long as it lasts-

It might be unfair to him. but I want this, because eventually, after years and years of failed practice it took me a boy to keep my mind on track. I wasn't dispersing inside my own brain anymore because his thoughts and smile have me in a trace. He has me occupied. Even with him not here- It still was him in me.

The refreshing atmosphere wakes me, my eyes squint with a crinkle of a smile, and then I almost got thrown to the floor with someone ramming their cow-like body at my back. With the last vision, I checked there was only the harmless ol me here to be, when I spun around to witness the cause I soured faster than a curdling milk.

"Fischer" I stare at the one who skillfully seems to wrestle his way into becoming the bane of my existence "If you use your eyes, you'll notice that there's room for hundreds more here" I even use my outstretched hand to justify my point. He- didn't take that into account, because I got hugged by him with a tremble. My bowl-like head got forcefully jammed into his chest as he cried dramatically-

"Please save me" he sniffs, his nose by my shoulder- was he getting his snot on me? Because I have been tricked by this same act by Hwan and- no-no, Hwan is fifteen. Fischer was-

"I am not captain marvel, the only thing I can save for you is your future kids. That is only if you get off me now"

He is experienced, I hadn't held back with him since day one of our encounters. So he takes me seriously like he should and does the job. Nodding and stood there awaiting a signal from me.

"Shoot" I was kind so yeah-

"My sister is here with her boyfriend. I invited them for a holiday since I don't get to meet her often" he rolls his lips in as if expecting me to understand the dire situation which was?

"So what? you want me to cook for them?"

He catches on with my sarcasm and something else. That would be my lack of knowledge.

"Lee will kill me the moment he gets to know of it. He may look kind- but he is not that kind you know"

He chuckles with desperation evident in his voice, when he realized how clueless I was- he sighs.

"Madison Fischer is my sister. Lee is her Ex"

My impression of a lifeless stone must have been too realistic for him as he shook me out of trance to add-

"That is not the main concern here shin, it's her boyfriend. If Lee has ever hated a person in his life it's him- it's-

"Nicholas Moreno," I say it slowly, but through the whizzing wind, he hears it as Fischer nods. Each one lagging in speed. At first, I stare- then I glare. Then I hit his arm hard because -

"Does dating douchebag and Bitches run in family?" I was furious at the thought of how this can ruin our stay. The passenger cruise was a guide package- the seven-day host for the cruisers with resorts, cottage, party, and activities all coiled in one place. So ignoring the other campers was an impossibility. Suddenly I itched to go find Lee and lock him up somewhere. Can I do that?

"Well, she dated your husband too. You think he is one-

"Oh, she never deserved him" I wave the thought off. Lee did tell me about the unhealthy relationship he had with a girl who cheated on him with Moreno once. It doesn't take a genius to connect the dots. But I can't seem to avoid the meager knot in my tummy. As if it was worried for the events to come henceforth. "Where is Lee?" I ask scrolling over the contacts.

"Searching for me I guess" Fischer croaks scrunching his nose. My gaze snaps to him.

"He knows?"

Fischer nods again.

"Yeah. Mr. Sargent told him. he is pissed. I got informed"

I sighed closing my eyes, recalling how excited Lee was about this. Probably even more than me. But when I heard a footstep join in and Fischer jump off behind me, using me as a shield - I knew who to expect. Lee stood there, his gaze dangerously zeroed on a spooked Fischer. Lee was in his formals, navy blue polo with rolled sleeves and black jeans. He even wore dress shoes. Edmund in his shorts and coconut print shirt regarded Lee with the same judgment as I did when I saw him walk in for the Lunch a while ago. Apparently, he was too into the vacation that he forgot to get himself some clothes for the occasion.

In actuality, he and I had been too invested in our shrimps, taekwondo class, gaming, and decapitating sexual tension in the room to work on his wardrobe. They went on to discuss how one of their friends called Alex might have gone as far as to hire a stylist on the ship for the sake of impression. They agreed to it in seriousness, they said it has happened before. I stopped questioning the type of friends he has because each time, I feel like it's some kind of alien that's being mentioned.

Then I thought back to the time when I drank a whole bottle of ketchup so Hwan could have none. I have no right to be the judge here, do I?

"You seriously are going to use her for this?" Lee rakes Fischer with an unamused shake of the head. And it was the hottest thing I had seen since I woke up. Before it was the sip of soda he had after he ate his lunch- that was twenty-five minutes ago.

"She is the sweetest" Fischer exclaims as I look at him through my shoulder "Please. Be on my side for today" he whispers as I blink back at Lee who rolled his eyes, pursing his twitching lips. There he was, the Ever forgiving Lee. I squint my eyes with a shrug- asking him to let go of it. When Lee sighs through I double pat at Fischer-

"Buzz off now before he throws you out of the ship"

High on freedom, he jogs off into the farthest route from Lee. As we both watch him disappear into the corner. Lee walked and stood next to me with his hands shoved inside his pocket and a distant look in his eyes.

"How did you know I was planning to throw him into the water?"

I yelp at the acute deliberation In his tone. But I resolved to a snort-

"You won't do that, besides-

"We can send a manual, calling it an accident. I don't think this ocean graph has sharks in them. He would have survived"

Lee doesn't have a demographic. His mood rises and falls unlike a constant. He details his thoughts and is bare with what he thinks- it's easier to understand and read him, but with it- comes the precautionless twists and cliffhangers.

"I heard what happened" he doesn't react but watched me with curious dark eyes. I gulp in to moisten my throat because what I was about to do requires a certain form of bravery, to dissipate his paranoia and dissolve his cold worry. I have to play the hot one here. So I take a step near him, his gaze dilutes further. His features not as nonchalant- when I hold his side and tilt my face with a reassuring smile, I trace the stress in his neck. Good. I wasn't the only one with a dessert in my mouth "It doesn't matter Lee. as long as we have a room together, I really don't care who or what loiters outside"

In broad daylight, in a public domain I was here seducing a man into forgetting the aspects that were ruining his trip, but when my arms rise to circle his neck, on my tiptoes as he leans slightly to me in reflex- I realized it wasn't my doing either. I don't know why I cannot stop- but neither did I want to stop. By heavens, this was spiraling out of control.

I kiss his jaw slowly, my fingers curl by his arm. They tense under my touch as I move to tease, kissing the area just below his ears. So Close, I hear his sharp intake-but he speaks through.

"I won't let it mess this. I promise" he angles, proving me the access. He maintains a hazy smile with his husky and predictably affected utterance. Just about when he holds me and moves to claim my lips- a loud fit of cough interrupts us. The sound was familiar- so I attempt to rip off from Lee. He keeps me pinned with his eyes closed in frustration.

"Who died Edmund? " he grunts, turning his head to look at his friend, pissed and nobly clenching on to patience. "You could have coughed at the other side of the boat"

To which it was my duty to rectify-

"It's a ship"

Lee- wasn't impressed given to our situation.

Edmund awkwardly clears his nasalling voice to smile sheepish-ly at us, I kept trying to push the clutch of Lee from me which was futile, so I gave up. I returned Edmund the presumably distressed smile.

"I just came around looking for you" he murmured, confused. Then Lee decided to spice things up for Edmund with his advice.

"Yeah? How about you go back and let me have a moment with my wife here? or better you go find someone to date or beg Hailey to take you back." ouch-

Edmund's eyes widened, But then he childishly signed a finger at Lee.

"How is reminding me that I am single an insult?" he slurs, his lisps apparent. Was he drunk? I looked at a grinning Lee. He winks for an answer- I sigh in relief smiling for real once as Edmund tore his fingers through his hair. He was like a baby throwing tantrums at his brother "I am twenty-six, not sixty-two. I am happy for now with you"

Lee released me only to throw his arm around my shoulder in a casual fashion.

"I am your friend, I can't do what a girlfriend can do"

Edmund thinks of it crucially, and a with low whisper he announced.

"Don't make me miss Hailey than I already do"

My knees give out at the adorableness of it. I gawk in awe as Lee awards me a look of disbelief.

"That's the cutest thing I've ever seen" I blurt as Edmund smiled through his blurring eyes.

"Thank you Shin" he tips his head, then he looks around in inspection "Please continue what you were up to. And yes, get to the room if you take this further- I don't want Lee to catch col-

"Edmund"

"Yes Lee"

"Go. You need sleep"

The episode with Edmund sucks the proceedings from us, so two hours later when we reached the port Edmund made every existing effort known to the universe to avoid an eye contact with me. After his little nap he comes out rejenuvated, the hangover was something he dealt inside, because from out, he was brimming with a mission. The one where he pretended I didn't exist- also I was on the shorter side so the only action he had to do was to not look down.

Lee was enjoying it in his own world. My cheeks were in flames every time I tried to have a normal conversation with Lee, he seems to know exactly what I was trying to do or had tried to do. It was early in the night when we got off- the travel from arrivals to the cottage resort was twenty minutes. The only time I strayed away was when the beauty of the organic rising sea line emerged into view. The feel of beach sand beneath my flip-flops, the skyline that met the plateaus gave the night a vintage touch. The people, the season, and the lanterns hanging by the wires above us, it all fits in right. It was Perfect. It was Beautiful.

Then I swerve to look at Lee, who had his gaze on me. For how long had he been staring? I don't know. But to see that he stood out with his apparel and aura enough for others to ogle at him but him to be transfixed on me was pleasantly warming. Like being wrapped in a blanket on a freezing night.

"What are you thinking?" he leans down to whisper in my ears as more join in the crew. I think I spotted Moreno afar, a bit too far for me to be sure. But since I had to answer Lee-

"How many people do you think died because of a coconut falling to their head?"

His smiles drop, he retains his position as an uninvited member gives his input.

"I won't mind if one falls on me now" Fischer forces in between me and Lee with both his shoulders perched with mint green duffles, front and back. With jute hat lidding his skull and determination in his stance- I don't take him seriously.

"One fifty each year" comes another intervention, from Edmund this wise. He looked up from his phone with an apologetic smile. "It says apparently one fifty people die because of coconut falling to their head"

Four of us, as if puppet on strings look up to inspect if we are in a safer zone. We weren't.

"I don't feel safe anymore" Lee declared "Thanks Shin"

Before I could take his gratefulness into account a contagiously energetic man walks towards us with a boy carrying a mountain of lavender garlands next to him.

"Oh, my lovelies, welcome welcome to one of the most visited hectares in Catalina. Where we had built and nurtured each and every little detail to radiate love, romance, friendship, and beauty. You come here to us with trust and leave with memories that will make you believe in paradise-

He helps Edmund into the garland first and then, at Lee.

"Oh my look at all these beauties, especially you my dear-

He smiles at me lifting mine up when-

"She is allergic to flow-

He puts them on me anyway with a toothy grin, he was- Latina. He was gorgeous so I don't mind. But-

"Don't worry young man. These are fake- our guests and the health of lovely ladies as such is our responsibility. You okay my love?" he askes me as I nod with a blush. The man was charming and as soon as he left-

"Here take this too" another garland lands on me as I roll my eyes at Lee- "Don't you think you attract too much attention?" he muses.

"You think?" I bat my lashes as Edmund mumbled about how it he was disturbed by our comstant flirting. Everything was a big mess tonight- none of us were ourselves. But isn't it the point of leaving behind what you know for a week of exploration? But Edmund seems to be having an existential crisis while Lee was having a jealous breakdown. As for Fischer-

The man skipped a garland for him since he was surrounded by bags on either side. so I took mine and made him have it. His smile was everything. I felt like a proud mother- which reminds me that I had my fish inside a basket, safe and protected. I brought her here with me in case I decided to wake up and cut off contacts with humans.

Soon each group was scattered with a guide who took us to the lobby, the entire place was made of wood, bright beach lights hung from the ceiling as we waited for our keys from the reception. But there was a loud cry which made us turn around with curiosity-

It was a girl who had her hand cupped by her mouth in excla-mation. The people surrounding her fell silent to see what had her at the moment. she was looking at us-

"Woah, she recognized me even in this shirt and hoodie?" Ed-mund wondered with a smile.

"What makes you think its you" Lee squared his shoulder "I used to be pretty famous during my time too-

I stood there quiet as they both flexed to welcome the supposed fan, but the more I looked the more it felt as if she was-

She ran towards us as I gasp shuffling around- looking at Lee and then at Edmund who stared confused when the young girl basically grabbed my hand into hers-

No.

This can't be happening right now.

Don't Americas believe that all asians look the same?

Does she think I am hwasa? Or park shin hye?

"You are my inspiration" she cries, literally. Her eyes waters as I nod at her with a pained and enforced smile. It was too late. "I don't know what to say. I carry your books all around, it has the most special place in my heart and mind"

In this scenario, there was nothing else that could go wrong. So it finally happens as she goes-

"Please sign my copy Elixir. I am your fan"

CHAPTER 22

L EE

Nothing appears to faze me from sulking. Every morning I wake up in my hometown with a sense of alienation. As if I didn't belong to both the worlds, I seem to be losing my cause along with my sanity. And I only have to thank myself for that- at twenty-two I was a hopeless cause. So I ditched the day's office schedule and walked out from a meeting, not that I had any clue as to what was being presented to me. A workaholic father, monotonous staffs, and robotic application of trust on me wasn't something I had in mind when I agreed to let it come my way.

Sipping on the bitter coffee at a book café nearby I frowned at the avid readers, this place was more depressing than the office- but since drinks were good I let it slide. But as minutes passed with me suckling on the straw with further observation netting my way- I skipped my gaze to each desk where most of them seem to have their nose buried inside one particular book with black and orange spine, the title that I squint to read was futile but it was embossed in lavish calligraphy. I could make that one out.

I would be lying if I hadn't come across the book before, this café has been my go-to since a month- My socializing skills had been declining profusely because of how choppy my Korean has become after having spent most of my growth years in states, most of the time I miss on the honorifics which doesn't end well with the elders. I also at times mix up the languages and fail to use the apt term across. Since this café was basically a book store camouflaged as a food hub, it provided me the silence and peace I craved so diligently.

I have seen the peculiar book circulating countless wise- with it I also witnessed the changing colors on the said reader's faces. It resembled of a war flashback, it was entertaining to see how serious they were about a stupid book. How moving could it be? No matter what it is- it still was fiction. I wouldn't know because I have never been one to find out. But today- I found myself hovering over the racks of this glassy library in search for the copy-

I found none.

They were all gone - sold like a hot cake. My curiosity twisted me into coercing a nerdy high schooler into handing me over the paperback he had- for thrice the price of a hardcopy. Luckily the student was greedy, so I came back to my cosy corner to discover what the literary commotion was all about, but before I flipped it open my gaze fell upon the name of the author, strangely not the title- but the author.

Elixir.

My first instinct was to realize how stunning the name was- the serum for eternal life. With such positivity radiating from a writer's name, I dived into the introduction. Reading the opening-

It was nothing like I had imagined.

There is nothing ever more pacifying than waking up to a morning of assassination-

And from that line to the nine at night- I had digested half of the crazy world in there. I got out when I was told the café was closing in for the day. I stayed up the night and googled upon the next in series by the dawn.

I growled In agony when the stats informed placidly that it will take a year more. I re-read the book thrice during the period, each time I did so, I discovered the unconditional depth and symbolism it withheld. It was a work of genius, though I won't admit It was the female lead with her insecurities and social phobias that had me. She was beautifully crafted into a character to be brave inside but a calculated explosion out. Inara was my first fictional crush at the age of twenty-three-

Pathetic- but nobody will ever know.

And it was because of her I came to recognize of the struggles that comes with a specific disorder. Soon I found myself trying to control my anger towards the vulnerable staff who I suspected of retaining low self-esteem. I always saw the little part of Inara in them. But never the entire.

Because Inara was a mess. She was a foul mouth, she had worlds inside her head where she served as a warrior- she was feisty. Her small contribution always led to bigger outcomes while she secretly enjoyed the chaos she caused with an innocent smile.

It was impossible to meet someone like her in real life. I knew it and so I waited for the sequel to come out patiently. Cursing the Elixir once in a while to pick his lazy ass up and get done with it under his review graph.

Though I loved the characters, my passion was to hate the author. The knack for killing his own creation without a second thought seems to be his forte- he doesn't seem to spare one good thing in a person's life. At one point I even wrote a page long mail to approach him with an offer to not kill Mathews, my other favorite character who I revised by the cunning pattern, I knew my man was going to be the next sacrificial goat.

I held back respecting the artist.

He died in the next book.

Elixir was a grim reaper. No one likes grim reaper. Not me. Not anyone.

Yes, I have a personal vendetta against someone I'll never meet. But at least I had a fictional Inara alive with me- that chances of meeting someone like her was low, but for now, I was relieved that she was alive though not in the substantial universe.

She apparently did existed in the real world.

Her name was Shin and she was more Inara than Inara herself. It was like the fantasy where you couldn't understand a thing, I- at times dream in Spanish with subtitles written on the floor for me to understand the concept. But with Shin- it was stranger. Every little thing she did, ate, spoke or looked was just a replica of a damn fictional girl who she didn't even know of.

Or that's what I thought.

The battered copy that she signed with her slight trembling hands was the same. It was the first edition. I knew it because I have it. But what I didn't know, and was blind to an actual fact was how good was she at cursively signing a book under the tag of Elixir because I personally believed that this was a part of those bizarre dreams I have where I try to conduct on meeting on satin curtains and fight for the rights on koalas maternity holidays.

The girl hugged Shin, shin hugs her back. For some reason, Edmund looked at shin with the tendency of how a congressman looks at a republican who has two heads instead of one. As seconds kept ticking by, I was frowning harder. Wondering why was I hell-bent on convincing a reality to be an illusion.

When shin turned around staring at her shoes- I still was caught up in the things that weren't adding up.

"I'll be back in a few" she exhales taking a slow step back, I don't follow her but when Edmund takes one ahead she takes off running. The exit was near so it doesn't take her long to vanish. Edmund rooted in the ground turns to me with a big fat grin- sarcastic grin to precise.

"What was that?" he asks smiling through the damage. Fischer perhaps was the only one who looked stable among us as he came and stood in the middle, sipping in a bottle of chocolate milk. He squints his gaze by where Shin left-

"Not what. But who" he nods with a drained chuckle " That was Elixir"

It was silence a second.

Then Edmund and I shared a look of slow panic that seeped in.

Then we took off- only two steps in and we were tumbling down to the floor in a tangle of human limbs.

"What the hell Edmund, get off me" I grunt wheezing, trying to get the man who grabbed my collar among the fiasco, shaking me up.

"Shin is Elixir? Why didn't you tell me?" he whisper yells as I yanked his-

"My wife is Elixir. Why wasn't I told?" by now we both complied with our execution in manly grunts, our eyes filled with the flashbacks of why she might have kept this from us. He runs a hand through his face pushing me aside- though the visitors scattered to their dorms and cottage- there still lingered few who glanced alternatively at two men on the ground battling a crisis. I glared at them. It worked they scrambled away.

"I called her a monster" I muse lifelessly as Edmund rested his back by the reception desk. "Technically I called Elixir a monster" I reasoned.

"I went for her personality-" he stops short and glares at Fischer who sat on a trailer case looking down at us. Literally "What's your excuse?"

Fischer smiled.

He had none.

"You knew?" Edmund exclaimed aggressively "Of course you did, you met her in manila –

"-And at her book signing event, and then multiple times with you guys. She wanted to keep this a secret for some reason. She threatened me to not sell the script if I revealed her identity"

This affects Edmund radically as he got up on his feet, he wobbled as he did so- I emerge his suit dusting my shirt as I stared at the trail she left from. Where was she? Not that I would have known how to act with her here, I just wanted to know why she hid this from me despite I think I knew the answer for it.

"Shin is not capable of something like a threat" it sounded more like a self-assurance than fact as I frowned at Edmund's faith. I arc a brow.

"She certainly is" when I say it, his first instinct was to shrug it off in nonchalance.

"Believes the man who didn't know that shin was-

"Inara is inspired from her. They both are the same- and you know how inara functions. Now equate it with Shin"

Edmund's mouths open in defense when Fischer steps in-

"She hasn't forgiven me about something that happened in Malta to this date. She empathizes with me but won't think twice before deciding to kick me out if the need arises" he narrates it as if it was a morning news and not something that would make us curious.

"What happened in Malta?"

Fischer's chugs his milk away,

"You could ask her that"

If that wasn't enough pressure on me, Edmund cupped my face roughly. Making me look at him ,

"You can do this. Be the best man ever- sweep her off her feet and enchant her with your charms-

Disgusted I claw at his leech-like fingers. The desperation of a director working under his father was hazardous to have around. But since he was my friend I remind him-

"I am not an actor. I don't need a direction"

Psychotically he folded my ears with a grin.

"I can count on you. you'll set things right. Plummet at her feet and apologize from me-

"I attempted that. It didn't work" interrupted Fischer which bare-ly wavered Edmund's spirits.

"Do it anyways- she'll have to let her guard down if-

Was I planning on that? On an apology? Absolutely not. Because I felt the raw hurt and anger in me that I had been keeping at bay since I had Fischer and Edmund around me. the self-doubt was strong as I was considering if I was ever good enough for her. She was gone the moment this accident exposed her- it might have been the constant baseless complaint from me that had her hiding things around.

After Edmund realized how far gone I was, he sympathized to my relief and gave me a useless pat on the back. So soon I was alone to dwell in my thoughts, once I got to my room with our belongings- I sighed taking a seat at the edge of the bed. The room was big- the wooden flooring was a noisy nuisance, the minimalist interior only made the misery apparent. It had a kind king-sized bed with dark sheets and some fresh plants in- nothing else.

Playing with my travel case I spin it, the wheels smoothly changes the axis whenever moved in a clockwise motion. The large glass window on right was closed, but transparent in nature. The view of the adjoining garden and pond was a breathtaking sight. I wait for Shin to come back comprehending how blindly I had been in love with her traits for years even before I knew she existed.

In a matter of seconds, as now I know who she was, everything made sense. The mystery that came with how intensely I was falling for her fell into place. I couldn't help but smile with anger at the thought- why did I ever not tried to get to know her better?

Did I give her too much space? Does she speculate that I wasn't serious about her? Of us?

The low knock on the door escalates my heart. It had never experienced such malfunctions in my life- so when she stepped in her innocent little summer dress and white Nike air force, looking as if she just came out of a conference with angels and fairies, I strived to remind myself that I was supposed to confront her and not- and not –

Forget it.

She closes the door behind her, her gaze brushing mine as she mostly trained them on my shoes. Of course, she was more interested in them- they weren't so bold on her as my stare was.

Her neck tilts, like every damn time before she attempts to gather some courage – she does that. Not a single move of her has ever escaped my vision. Never once since I met her. hHer lips parts, she tries to hold my gaze, but nothing comes out.

So I help her out. By making it worse.

"I don't know what to say Shin. All I am going to do is stare until you say something" crossing my arm I regard her as she hugged a teddy bear to her chest. Why does she have a stuffed toy with her?

"I won't be able to speak if you look at me like that"

"Do you want me to look away?"

"Yes"

"I won't"

The clutch on the bear visibly sews as I watch her fight the jitters, her gaze soon goes stiff. When no room given, Shin adapts in her own way. She fears, but refused to fear the fear itself. One of the most celebrated quotes from her book.

"I always believed it won't be much of a need to share our personal life with someone who will always be a temporary stop in my life" I didn't like how true that was, but isn't it how we started our journey? "But then you criticized how vile and unjustified my themes were-

She glances at me but hurries into her sentence as if she knew I was bracing to interrupt her. I honestly was.

-by then, I think I already in a way had been feeling these unknown emotions for you and as much as I hated it, I thought revealing it would only tamper with the image you had of me. I was afraid that you'll see me in a different light and not as the same girl that you developed feelings for"

By now she had the brown tanned bear glided towards her front and hugged it to her, the crease she had was almost as if she was mad at me. And I was mad for her.

After the long silence, I glance sideways in a gesture.

"Come here," I say,

"I won't" I blink at her in amusement, she sighs walking over. Even she paused a bit at how ridiculously loud the wood planks were "I am going to sit here because my legs ache- it has nothing to do with your comman-

"Who said you are going to sit there?" before she could react I pull her down, hoisting her so her knees were positioned on either side of me- resting on the bed. She gasps staring wide at me- with the hand that wasn't fastening her I stick the bear aside. Pulling her closer to me in one go, I trace her back- watching her fight my touch as the fingers skim her soft skin was beautiful. She holds onto my shoulder when I duck in- kissing her collar bone while my palms cups the back of her neck as I course lower.

This is what she tried this afternoon to distract me-

It was only fair we continued and I return the favor. But I was losing it- Her fragrance eloped me- the warmth burns me. Begs me to unleash the barriers I have kept so far. It just wasn't fair that she could play me so easily while I was losing in my own game.

"Why do you have that?" I ask kissing my way back up, fisting her hair gently I bring our lips closer, brushing them but never meeting them. Her eyes were closed as she speaks, breathy.

"To compensate- I wanted you to think that I was still cute"

Then I was kissing her. With all I have and with all my need I kiss her. I press her harder against my chest- she was addicting, and in that moment I wanted to be the selfish man who craved to live in her thoughts, to be the source of her everything. To be the one to wake up in the morning beside and spend the night with. The one with who she could share her day and laugh away the worries. The one who was hers.

Because she was mine and nothing could stop me from keeping it this way.

When I break the kiss. We both were out of breath. But that doesn't stop me from dropping her into the bed and leaning down to her- with time to spare I lift her chin by curling my fingers down it. she swallows as I smile at her-

"I want you to fall for me more" brushing my thumb against her jaw I don't let her cut through, I can't do this with her lingering doubts regarding relationship. Not when It feels like I was manipulating her with lust. I want her to understand the sincerity of my confessions. So I look at her with other plans in mind- "Since I am giving you more time, I still have to avenge the secrets you kept from me"

"Wait- it wasn't a secret" she defended as I nod sarcastically "You could've googled me like how i-

Confused she tried to get up I push her back and began to attack her with tickles. Her laugh was contagious. And so was everything that she is.

CHAPTER 23

S HIN
The first four days fly by. Each one categorized with the zest it was packed with, not just me and Lee- the moments were designed and crafted by the intervention of a devastated movie maker whose only aim for the given week was to shower me with praises and purchase the commodities to lure me into a business contract, and as for his assistant , Fischer was the one who carried out the assignment for him.

Flowers, chocolates, and random tributes were something I have been waking up to-

I get paid, pampered, and spoiled by three men. For work, for forgiveness, and for affection.

"If an ancient goddess were to have ever lived on earth, she must have looked like Shin" this was the ice breaker that Edmund spewed on the day after we met after he got aware of who I was. The torment was naked in his eyes, but he managed a charming smile. Right then- I deduced that he could walk on any lengths to have his endeavor accomplished. I liked his professionalism- it's something I lacked profusely.

But this, extra credit done by his friend didn't go well on Lee-

"Can you not do that" he frowned at Edmund who sassily jerked his head at the said beloved friend. His tropically aesthetic pink-sleeved shirt with its half sleeve provided an easy access to peer at the tattoos that covered his forearm. They were gorgeous- just like him. Pity that lee was still in his formals as we stood in the corridor where we accidentally met before the breakfast-

Not that I believe it's an accident.

"Do what?" mused Edmund.

"Compliment her so much. I am not as articulative as you- I will end up looking bland in impression if you keep this up. And I can't have that" I sucked in an awe as I gawked at him with glittering eyes, he gazed at me with it equally. And then-

"It's fine Lee- you show me better" I pat his cheek once when his smile drops and I realized with a whiplash. You can't take an attention deficit out of a person. But neither can they avoid the blush that's a result of the aftermath. These two friends were painfully savage. They were frank to the junction where they had to remind each other to tone it low because I was around.

But little did they know the kind of surprise I can surprise myself with. Them too.

So when Lee- with a shy smile purposed the we should leave for the horse riding classes, I don't question him. Edmund and Fischer probably thought we were two horny people escaping a situation. But we weren't. Lee indeed had booked us the three-day rehearsal by the outskirts of the isle. The grassy field was vast and had one lone coordinator. He was the same Mexican dude from the resort-

The garland man with artificial flowers so that the one with allergy reactions won't get sick.

He was vocal- kept speaking and monitoring without a break. He was superficially nice and that benefited me with the anxiety I had before meeting my tutor. The only job I had to do was pursue his instructions and smile with a nod. Since I had stretchable jeans and a t-shirt with a rough brown jacket on, the sole thing he helped me gear upon was the elbow and knee pads with a helmet. The leather gloves were a bonus- when I turned with my hands to hips at Lee, I couldn't help but roll my eyes at how clouded he was with jealousy.

"How do I look?" I grin to ease his nerves "Hot? Badass? Lara cro-

"A kitten. You look like a kitten"

Arresting a giggle within, I flutter at him.

"You are such a ray of sunshine"

Ruffling his hair, I land a brisk peck on his cheeks and resumed with the lessons. It took twenty minutes to stack the basics while Lee was on his white horse just deliberately circling around while it grazed the grass. In intervals, he ingrained his time to drill holes across the trainers skull. He'd proceeded to scratch his horse once he receives a signal from me to be sure I was comfortable.

A wink, a nod, and a slight tilt from me. He would smile before lifting off.

The change in him was evident, though it was slight it still was obvious. He knows who I am- and with it came the pressure of how relatable I was with the main character of something I created. He was linking the plots that he hasn't heard from me- but had read. When I had it published- I was naïve, there were contaminations with the flow of what I wrote, but at the end of the day – despite my tries to conceal it, it still was me in it. It wasn't an unconscious move- but my own decision to keep it that way. A person who met me and understood a part of me, for them the book was an alley to strip me off. Barer than I could be on my own skin. Almost as if they could touch my soul.

And Lee was clever enough to connect it. Maybe he was disputing them- but he wasn't the one to turn blind on it. I know It won't be long before I have to answer him.

But it wasn't today or tonight. So we spent the entire day discovering the island piece by piece which somehow ended up with me teaching Lee a few hacks on how to bargain at a local shop. I value money and the labels I buy from. It was ironic- but when wasn't I weird.

"So you buy things from smaller stalls so they could profit out of it?" he asks as we hustle in the humid weather through the lane with tents ,an open aisle of handcrafted culinary sets and mineral ornaments. So far Lee seems to be enjoying his quick buys. A jute wallet, sunglasses, and an ashtray which he found cute though he doesn't smoke.

"I like the designer clothes I buy, but it doesn't mean I neglect the simplicity that comes with these outlets. They are homemade, weaved without a prejudice, for anyone who wants to buy them. They don't do it with a configuration or with an artistic view in mind- and these pieces feel humane to me"

I leave ahead only to find him standing behind with the paper bags and a skeptical look.

"What happened? Why are you giving me such a questioning look?" I ask shielding my vision from the evening sun with my forearms. He seems to have a faint smile by how he closed on as he spoke.

"I am not. It just- I was looking at my answer"

On day two Lee aspired to celebrate my progress with the riding lessons by inviting Edmund and Fischer to lunch. He ordered me a plate of various insects and worms-

What was I thinking when I wrote the task? I have no clue- and so did Edmund and Fischer. So they smiled uncertainly at Lee who squinted at them. That got me additional judgemental looks than I ever had- from the waitress and from anyone who sat by my vicinity.

But how fidgety Lee was, it appeared as if he was the one going to do it. why was he nervous? It's me- I got myself here.

"Don't worry shin. I think you'll look smart if you do it" Edmund encouraged me, I raised a brow at him and the six feet something man realized it wasn't a time to piss me off. Not when I had cuisine of little fried insects on my platter.

"I am smart. Even if I eat this or not"

I heard a snort from Lee and once he received a glare he pretended as if it didn't happen. Of all the days he could have chosen- why today?

"I don't want to do this-" I sigh as a confused Lee frowned at me until I add "-alone"

I point a butter knife at Fischer who was silently lamenting in disgust of what he thought was bout to happen.

"I want Fischer to join me"

And so the twist led with him declining the offer.

"I have irritable bowel syndrome, my stomach may-

"I'll sell the script and demand a promotion for you. also you'll be forgiven"

He was sacrificed by his boss in less than a minute with Lee administrating my decision with why I shouldn't forgive him. I did tell him about what had happened, and let's say- Lee is hot when he gets angry. So the session began with our nose scrunched, and ended up with a passive face where we both agreed on-

"They taste like almonds"

Fischer nods with wonder as he mouths in one more- probably to actually savor the flavor.

"Roasted to precise"

Then it was a quest to get Lee and Edmund to try tasting it. They weren't in a shape to receive such psychological trauma, they were ready to throw hands and legs at Fischer- but It was me with the script again, so Edmund lost his morals. As for Lee- I only had to whisper to him how he'll sleep on the couch that night to get him to try it.

But honestly- we did it so Fischer and I weren't the only disgusting ones. Once out, four of us rushed to grab a brush, paste, and some mint gums. Mentally I paid homage to the urns of creatures that Bear Grylls digested for the sake of survival. Lee looked like he was formulating to turn into a vegan any day. He looked sick- but a kiss from me melted it away. The make-out sessions might have gone a little further that night as he stopped himself right after his hands skimmed under my skirt-

But I still had a hickey under my collar bone, and it was something he looked so proud of every time my shirt shifts through. Day three was when he got in the horse with me- I could say by now I don't feel the requirement of a mentor, I could be one myself. So when Lee got behind me holding onto the reins I leaned on him sighing – he guides us into a lazy forest stroll.

The smell of wet earth and rustle of trees dance in the air- and in such tenor, Lee asked me something that he seems to be really curious of-

"What would I have been if Elixir was inspired by me?"

It was as if Elixir was the third person among us- whenever he praised, specified a quote, he mentioned it as if she wasn't me. I played along since it was fun to.

I crane my neck to look at him, but then stared ahead with a goofy smile.

"The main leads best friend who sucks at math"

There was a crackle of pride as he snickered sarcastically. But then I go on to balm his wound-

"I might have liked the character a tad bit more as I wrote him, probably given him the contemporary spin-off he most certainly deserves" I arch to stretch my spine as he scoops me up to him, I yelp in surprise as he nuzzled by my neck smiling.

"I would like that" my breathing hitches as he utters broodingly "Besides, Elixir's narrative of intimacy does give me the hints of how my girl likes it. Do you think she'll make my spin-off a bit on the bolder side? I won't mind that"

There was nothing to differentiate between my brain and a cup of jelly. They were one thing that was uselessly inside my skull which contributed zero vocabularies to my baseless stuttering. And just like that suddenly all the fantasies I had while writing those scenes with an angry blush on my virgin self didn't appear to be fantasy at all.

Little would have I known how terribly It might land me years later into a situation that even the horse sympathized about. Lee knows me inside out- and it was hard to breathe now. So I focus on it and let him have his moment. He got what he wants- I was furiously flustered.

"What's the ten shin?"

I close my eyes simply with no way to answer that- the list, it was coming to an end and so was the patience that Lee had bestowed on me. But I can't – not when It could ruin everything. Temporarily or not- I want to be loved by him and love him the way he does.

Love-

I must be going crazy to have such faith in a stupidity. But it wasn't- I was in love with the boy who I met four months ago- heard him screaming at his grandfather to seam his hearing aid in. The same jerk who ditched me at the airport and the dinner.

The one who helped me complete my wishes, the one to touch me with the scrutiny that didn't have me coiling in memories of the past. To have me at the moment where I wasn't slipping into fear when he was near- he puts me at ease, he makes it easy for me to live and breath.

I want you to fall for me more.

It's what he was waiting for when there wasn't more I could love him with.

But my love comes with a falsehood where I can't promise him a future where he won't get hurt. So I fall into silence and he again lets me be. I hate how understanding he is in norms with what he can't achieve.

If only I had known that his wrath emerges in his vulnerability- only if I had known I would be the cause to break him down to his worsts. He slept on the couch without a word exchanged between us tonight, but the good night kiss on my forehead lingered still as I tried to knock my senses into tranquility.

Shoving the comforter away I sat up with my hands trembling. This wasn't going to be okay- I don't have a way out of this. It was sweating, my head hammered with pain, and my body numbed with each pulsing rhythm of my heart.

I looked at Lee to see him completely into the night. The faint illumination from the pond behind the glass screen was the only source of light- but I was plunging into the darkness inside. The walls suffocated me as if ganging up . I withered into a ball.

I deserve to be happy.

It's okay if I felt like I was using Lee for this.

I just want to be fucking selfish for once- is that too much to ask?

Gritting my teeth in anger I slip on in a pastel cardigan and made my way to the beach- since the resort was built upon one- the sea line was simply a backyard for it- I sat there on the bed of sand facing the waves and inhaling the sunken air until my head cleared out. The weakness from my racing thoughts still hovered proactively, but it got better with the passing minutes. A shadow falls upon me as I turn to look at this beautiful girl who smiled at me-

"You mind if I sit beside?"

I do.

"Absolutely not" thought I had a spine grown somewhere living with Lee?

She does what she proclaimed. We sit in silence with the rush of crashing waves cocooning us until she looks at me- I recede her gaze with an awkward smile. her eyes were stunning green-almost emerald.Curly ash hair framed her small face softly. Her features were sharp but feminine- she wore a pink maxi dress with a mandarin collar and bell sleeve. In the middle of the night, I sat there feeling underdressed despite my pajamas and cardigan being the universally prescribed garment for night.

"I couldn't sleep" she looks up at the stars, I follow her suit "What about you?"

"Same" my voice comes out distant- but my mind was wheeling into the vehicle that was me. Finally.

"It's a beautiful night. Isn't it?" it was rhetorical- in my impression, it wasn't, the night was too soon. It marks another end of a beautiful day- "I am Madison" she says when I don't agree to her pretense.

I look at her with my face naked of anything. she smiles nevertheless-

"I know who you are. And now that I told my name you must have figured out who I am" her tone was sweet, it lacked the malice or bitterness that I had her acquitted within my imagination, so when I unconsciously watched with no spare words to offer- her brows pulled down with confusion "I am sorry to ask- but are you okay?"

With an intake, I nod-

"I am"

She licks her lips and nods unassured.

"I probably would've acted this way if it was someone else other than you. so yeah- that's my normal" I blurt as a slow relief cracks through her. It was genuine- I was desperate in search of a girl who cheated on Lee, but couldn't succeed.

"You are adorable" she says as I frown with my might.

"I hear that a lot. Asian stereotype and shit" clenching my fist into a paw I tip my head at my lap "Sorry about that"

She chuckles as I pout mildly while I played with the hem of my top when-

"I know you have this image of me. Probably tarnished beyond what I could do to change it. And this vacation was a horrible coincidence- But I am making sure to steer clear of your path. I am not going to be the bad girl here. I promise"

She had the shine in her eyes and life in her voice. She looked older, maybe same age as Lee or slightly younger. Her confidence was something I began to envy the second she opened her mouth- she didn't stammer or stutter, she gleamed with every minor move she made- perhaps this is what Lee liked about her.

"I am not adorable" I state as if declining to accept her previous compliment as she watched me in wait "I can be a whole circus if I want"

I don't know why but I let out a short laugh along with her. I don't know what her intentions were but she didn't have a knife on her- so I let her be in my moment.

"I see he chose the right one"

He did not.

"He is the happiest I had ever seen him when he is with you. I wasn't stalking. I swear" she said fixing the neck of her dress.

I squint my gaze with a twitch of my lips, her friendly demeanor rubbing off on me.

"After all the positivity you are pouring my way, even though I am just a stranger to you- I feel obliged to give you a piece of my mind" I don't let her sink into a worry as I smiled "You are like a French fry"

She gapes as I smirked to just rile her up –

"Don't worry. You are like the meme- Tall, Blonde and Gorgeous"

For a second I think she was offended, but then her features morphs as she gets the gen z humor in spark and that's how we felt empowered in the night as two women who seem to have kept their past aside. She sat there reciting various things she had tried in the island so far as I listened attentively- when we decided to part ways after she received a call from her boyfriend, I got up first dusting my pants. Since she was in a dress I offered her my hand. she flinched with a hiss his when I clutched her elbows-

"Are you okay?"

She was sharply soon with a reply- perhaps too sharp for me to believe.

"I am" she pales as she hurries to assure me- but then her gaze hooks onto something behind me as her frantic gestures ceased. I whirled to face Lee who watched us with a polluted emotion. It was nothing and many things at the same time, and none were favorable.

"Lee" she addressed with a nod, with no reciprocation from him Madison took her to leave after a formal it was nice meeting you on my way. With her retiring, I strode to Lee who had apparent reasons to be here-

"I couldn't sleep"

He wasn't here for excuses

"You could've woken me up"

"I wanted to be alone and out"

"Alone and out? Maddison was with you"

Frustrated at how I was hurting him i whisper with my staggering and useless alibis. The other things he didn't strife to know- but a simple truth.

"She came in later. I don't have to answer you everything now do I?" no- no no shin, this was destructive from so many edges- the glassy wall tumbles through his façade as clenched his jaw-

"You'll answer me everything Shin. I'll wait no matter how long it takes" he said with a courage that I know will diffuse soon, I blink in my tears as I pass through him to get back to the room. He doesn't stop me- but this night slapped me with a proficiency that there wasn't a destined pace for things to change- for it to break. But mending was a process that could last till one's last breath.

And I can't curse that upon Lee.

I love him too much for that.

CHAPTER 24

L EE

Physical activities keep one in shape, It's a prosperous lifestyle that everyone should adopt to their routine. Pushups, lifting weights, or running on a mill- these are indoor exercises that don't benefit you with what an outdoor venture can. Cycling is the best in my opinion, you receive the vitamins from sun, oxygen from air and beauty from nature as you do it. So as I biked over the lane scattered with blossoming trees with thriving flowers on either side as I mentally claimed how much I was dedicated to my fitness mantras.

Surely it's what I was peddling for, it has nothing to do with getting away from a girl who has been successfully stirring off the acute anger that I thought I had towards her. I had freaked out when I woke up in the middle of the night having stubbed my little toe by a plant stand- I don't know why, I was on my feet while I slept- but I did manage to spot the empty side of the bed. When I realized she wasn't having a reception inside the washroom I went out in search of her-

I did find her on the beach as I had suspected- but with someone, I didn't.

Least bothered about the presence of Madison, I had my eyes on Shin. All I could think of was the change in her behavior after I asked her of the last wish- it wasn't obscure anymore. She was hiding it from me with all her might. Despite my generous effort, I found the hurt creep in, a frustration that wasn't necessarily directed at her but myself. Conceivably I wasn't doing enough to gain her trust- but then she was there hovering beside me on her knees as I woke up in the morning.

In her paw sleeved shirt and loosely braided hair, she blinked clutching the teddy to her chest-

That darn teddy and that precious face-

I swallowed the startled gasp as I sulked rolling on the couch, the comforter I had spread on me drifts deserted with a ruffle. Resting my cheek on my folded arm I raise a brow-

"I shouldn't have behaved the way I did last night"

My eyes fall to her lips, they were rosier than ever. Almost red. I bet she had been gnawing on them with anticipation before I woke up. One look at her wide eyes and I know I am not wrong. If only I could run a hand through her soft waves- but I can't, for once I redeem into the stoic person that'll teach her to not mess with me. Not when I am firmly possessive of her.

"I am stupid"

Squinting my eyes, I sat up. Her gaze latched on to the tiniest adjustments I made to myself like a puppy that's been denied to play with.

"That you are" I mutter under my breath as she scoffed at how promptly I approved it. But I wasn't lying- she was stupid enough

to reckon that I was willingly acting this out when I had to hold every fiber of my body from not cuddling the life out of her. and maybe more. Certainly more.

She then pulls her up to the sofa and filed into space where I had been laying a while ago. Pushing the mountain of blanket aside she scoots to me.

"Fine. Now that we both agree. You can go back to being the normal Lee right?" I jump up and away from her when she carries her hand up to link with mine because I have zero resistance and innumerable ways by which I'll break through the mask I had now.

"It's getting late, I need to shower" I announce as I move towards the washroom, her scream got mixed with the splatter of water as I open the tap -

"We are on vacation for god sake. What are we late for?"

That was a delayed reaction, and I hummed a melody as I washed my hair because I was contended. I regretted being so happy when I came out because she had now changed into a checkered shorts and a lacey crop top. Her hair hurled into a high ponytail providing the perfect access to her neck.

It was obvious.

It was a freaking thirst trap.

So I throw a towel at myself as I angrily dried my hair.

"You know what? I am in love with this outfit. It accentuates my body in the right places. I can't wait to go out wearing this"

She must be kidding me-

But then again- she was her own person. She can wear anything she wants out as long as I am not around to chokeslam any man who even bats their eye her way. I exercised breathing trying to not stray my gaze longer at her bare waist.

Forgive her and let this go. May be its time-

Demanded the devil in me.

You know what? shin should be made aware of how much her efforts are paying off. Its her birthright to seduce her man.

The angel was no better. Cracking my knuckles I turned around and grabbed my jacket- I scowled at her passionately as she scrunched her nose in confusion.

"Fitness Is important" I quote out of thin air- and with that, I was gone from her vision. I speed out like a leaf blower blowing the leaves in an autumn ground. It wasn't an unpleasant verdict that I made in the spur of seconds. But as I pedaled across on the lone route with cool sun shades on- I heard the rings of bell resonate around me. A figure cycling on a smaller bike reaches next to me.

"What a beautiful day" she exclaims melodiously as I lost my balance- staggering for a while I correct my position as I remove the glasses to lament with a grimace. Shin grins at me, our momentum the same as the wheels roll through. thankfully she had her previous large shirt on top of her crop - but that isn't the case here. how is she-

"I have a tracker pinned on you?"

"What?"

"Kidding. I just followed you" shrugging she winks at me, my face must have given off the vibe of horror I was feeling, she uses it to her advantage "I'll keep stalking you until you forgive me"

"Do it- I like being stalked"

It was a miracle that she doesn't think of me as a psychopath by now. She stayed glued to me the entire journey.

I ride ahead as we both fall into a moment of calming silence. The sky wasn't stark visibility here with the trees veiling what's spread above- when we reached a river stream fifteen minutes into our activity- we found ourselves sitting on a smooth surface. On top of the moisty rock I couldn't help but admire the symphony of it.

Shin had been awfully quiet since she came into the picture that I morbidly felt guilty to have been so stubborn with her. My lips part to end the play but she beats me to it-

"I was abducted when I was eleven"

It was factually presented, lack of sensitivity in the utterance had me wondering if my pretended nonchalance had to do anything with what she was saying. Was she forcing it out? I don't stop her. I couldn't with how desperate I was. so I turn to watch her, her as she stared into the expanse with a faint smile. With her wrist atop of the closed knees, she played with the wedding band.

"It was in the evening, after I had won in an inter-school oration championship" a pause is all she takes before she dives in "They kept me for three days, those days passed with the pace of a snail. I was starved and abused enough to let me consciously feel it. I always wished to pass out then. It was better that way"

Patient-

Is that how I must have looked as I listened, as I clashed with the hurricane of emotions that groped me at the moment. My heart raced with anger at the cruel fate of hers. Of a girl whose story wasn't just so different than Innaras- it's what I had dreaded to not to be true. I yearned for it to be the fiction it was- but her words were indecisively raw with its veins connecting to reality.

It wasn't remorse or pity that I felt towards a world that failed her, it was pure anger and nothing else.

"How did you get out?" I grab her hands that were freezing, tightly grasping onto them- I only asked something that might help her remember the relief she had when was free.

"There- there was this woman whose guilt helped me. She took me to my home, but threatened me with warnings-" she stops right there as I frown once I felt that she was trying to slip away from me. I press at our breaching hold with my gaze spearing on her-

"Then what happened?" I assume I know what, but I don't want to believe it "Please tell me they fucking got caught"

She steals her gaze from me, her eyes were glassy as light reflects through them.

"Shin" I whisper. It wasn't disbelief – it was the torture that came with the knowledge that those people were out there living their lives while an innocent girl struggled with the demons that they infested on her. Those fucking parasites-

"I didn't know what else to do. I dropped out from school, refused to go out or trust anyone, I had never held a microphone since then- It use to take me an hour of a pep talk before I was able to order a portion of food from the menu. But I learned to live through- I became monotonous with a life that I planned. Even with a sentence that I spoke- I wasn't irrational, I was just scared of anyone who looked at my way. But then you came along." She paused to chuckle as if in dismay "You knew what you wanted in life, while I married you to fight through my insecurities. You told me that I had none. When you began to praise them- I started to believe that my flaws are what made me amazing. You were my first friend apart from my family. You are my cure and I can't lose you Lee. I can't afford that" my mouth dropped open, it was turbulence that passed through me as this beautiful girl watched me with tears in her eyes, her voice deep but soft- hoarse with all the things she said- she meant.

"shut up" she complained as I wiped her tears.

"I didn't say anything" finally clamming my jaw I watched her carefully as a smile threatened to breakthrough me.

"Your face says it all" even her sniffles were lovely, she wasn't lying when she said I even praise the things that she deems to be flaws. Everything about her was perfect.

"Please" cupping her face I made her look at me. "Don't cry"

She blinked rapidly, gulping it with a pursed lip.

"I can't stop" she sniffs again as I wipe another trail of her tears with my sleeve "Actually I can't stop crying-"

She sobs hysterically which had my heart falling low until-

"-I have this terrible toothache since I woke up this morning" then she gazes into my perplexed but resurrecting eyes as she whispers "- it's getting worse by the minute"

If there's one thing that you should be -is to be prepared -when it comes to shin, we could be healing from tenure in a moment and next it was a rush to the dental clinic. In the chaos, I borrowed the SUV that Edmund had rented in which he drives through the existing portfolios for his station sites. He was quick to throw the keys at my face and sympathized with shin. Apparently he knows that real pain that comes with an infected gum. I don't- I had a smile that was commercial-worthy.

Even in her groans, she explained that her gums and molars are healthy- Except that she has had this ingrown wisdom tooth that she was supposed to have surgically removed ages ago. But she was just too scared and it was showings its signs now.

"It's fine. We can have it extracted today" supportive of the assignment I offer as she was quick to deny.

"I can't"

In the waiting room I casually ask like any normal person in my place.

"Why?" then I precisely extend my question "Why will you not have it removed when you are literally trembling with pain now" its a statement of scolding. She gritted her teeth and stretched her lips with a sizzle. Her legs restlessly tap as I watched with concern.

"I am not good with anesthetics"

Honestly, I don't get it on my first time. So she blurts. Dumbing it down for me.

"It works like drug or alcohol on me"

There was a pause- she groans when a smile flickers within me.

"That's it?"

"I want to cry so bad"

"You already did"

"Lee" she squeals.

"Shin" I had to imitate her.

"It's fair play, Edmund told me you have my night adventures recorded in your phone" I was useless at a time like this, so I attempt to distract her from it. By irking her further? Is this even how it's done?

"That snake" to compliment her words, she hissed. Her utterance Is a blend of moans and an aspiring parseltongue. She was fierce when in pain. So so feisty. I wasn't complaining- in fact, it was such a sight. Wait-What was I thinking?

Turns out that with so many revelations and outcomes I wasn't thinking straight. So when the dentist kept her on observation for two hours through which she slept as result of the induced medication and later that evening when they sedated her for the extraction, I went through a series of completion that changed the course of everything I had up so far.

I let it rest for now as I was allowed to take her back to our room. But this was a different state of shin that I received when the nurse helped her to me. Her right cheek was mildly swollen and her steps lagged. She seems to ground deep into a discovery that only she knew of.

So when I took her hand- the nurse lovingly gazed at shin and patted her head. I suspected that something was wrong. She then turned to me with a warm glint in her eyes.

"Take care of this sweet sweet girl"

I watched them both with equal attention, they seem to have contrasting emotions housed in them as once the nurse was gone I opened my mouth to ask Shin if she was feeling fine but-

"She has better breasts than mine" it was the second wise my jaw fell open, I looked around at the surprised patients and their companions. Hurriedly I assist her walk as she narrates her disbelief when we reached the car. "They are just so-" she gulps in through the numbness in her tongue- her lisps were an entirely different story. She was like a toddler learning her pronunciations "-So prominent. Lee-

She looks up at me with her eyes widening in shock- I was even failing to fetch the keys because I- cannot- think- straight- with- her- like- this.

"Yes Shin-" I breathe as I elevate her into the seat.

"Shin? Who is shin?" she sniffles as I nod rolling my lips in. It was eight at night, it took an entire day for them to fix her and return me a version of her which will probably be the cause of my death tonight. I close the door and got to the other side. I explain when I settled it-

"It's you. You are Shin"

Since I don't start the car right away, she goes mum. A series of questions running through her eyes.

"I am-" she points at herself furiously, but still her movements were lazy "I am?- my parents named me after a leggy part?"

It made sense- oddly it did as I let out a breathy laugh slamming my palm against the steering wheel.

"No wonder my breast aren't exceptional"

She stretched her tops hemline to peer inside, dunking her face inside her shirt - deaf to my mournful groan. She looks up with a small smile.

"But I like them the way they are"

I couldn't hold it in so I nod at her, encouraging her about it became an instant passion.

"I like them too" I comment as her eyes wells up with tears. Her lips quiver as I respectfully look at her.

"You do?" she squeaks as I bite the tip of my tongue.

"Not that I have met them personally. I still find them –

"You are so kind" she whispers cutting me off "Let me tie your shoelace"

In reflex, I grab her shoulder to her from exerting as she bends on her seat.

"No need. I can do it myself" I ensure her as she watched me with hurt clogging in "Why do you want to do it anyway?"

Seriously Lee? you are asking a drugged person why she wants to-

"I have a shoe tying kink?"

Choking with no intention of breathing soon. She waits patiently for me to reboot. Once I do I bring my wrist together to demonstrate her-

"You mean tied hands?"

she nods sideways with confusion.

"They don't sound bad. But I really want to tie your shoes"

And that's how I let her do it- I undid my laces so she could actually have something to work with. It took her three minutes and thirteen seconds to get the knot done. Yes, I counted. As I drove as she recited on her paranoia so far she skillfully concluded that the dentist took her tongue out instead of a tooth. She cried again when I told her that I can't spot her tongue when she opened her mouth for me to check in. she was back to normal- that is normal in her stage when she realized that she can always attach an artificial tongue in place. she sounded so sure and smart that I thought of searching the internet for such a possibility.

She was asleep by the time we reached the cottage.

I don't go out,

Within the vehicle I don't know for how long I watch her form, she was bundled up with her legs tucked by her arms and face angled to side in a comforting nook. For days I had waited for her to let me in- now that she did- even if just a morsel of it, I still was the useless man who could do nothing because it all laid in the past.

But today, I can't hide from the surge I felt among the chaos.

I can't see a future without her.

I don't want a future where it wasn't her with me.

If she needs me, I need her more. And I can't keep this to myself anymore. Once in I couldn't sleep- if it was her who was an owl yesterday- it was mine as of present. So I walk out like a kid in search of the last piece of the puzzle that could comfort him. I found myself in the adjoining pond by the yard- from here I could still see her through the glass. She was peaceful tonight.

She earned it since she took mine.

Under the dim light and bearing a dull headache I scrolled through my contacts- my legs dipped into the water by the ankles as I paused at chingu-

Elzina Winston- she was the little sister I never had, despite her merely being a couple of months younger than me. And she is perhaps the only one who won't judge me for ringing her up into the night- Alex judges people enough to even out her lack of it. With a smile, I dial on to her-

I had previously apologized to them a week ago- they were understanding enough which probably was the result of their general knowledge on how Asian politics and public image marketing works. So when the phone gets picked up from the other side and her groggy but curious voice fills in-

I smile at the titillating bed for pools.

I don't let her fetch as I checked on Shin- I moderately whisper scream at on phone to get my point across-

"Chingu, I am in love with my wife? Can you believe that?"

I scrunch my nose up with a sigh- my lungs were finally able to function through as she politely goes-

"That's really surprising"

Oh yeah? Shin and Elzinas sarcasm are almost alike- they can have a rap battle with the fiery banter they spit. There were some shuffles as I seamlessly continued my intervention with a raised brow-

"What do I do now?"

There was even more shuffling as I picked up two cold masculine words from her husband before the line went dead-

"Tell her"

It's what he said.

Tell her-

And the scary part was- there was nothing wrong in it. But it was when I realized that Shin still hasn't accepted me the way I want her to. There still was something that's not adding up-

-somthing that I can't seem to grasp.

-Something that she is not letting me see.

CHAPTER 25

S HIN

There was no use in making a fuss. He won't reveal the details of what happened after I got drugged. His charitable response so far was to smirk at me while ignoring my sulking dignity. By the attitude he had been such a tease lately, there wasn't an argument left in me. I know I did or said something that can backfire on me if I don't get to treat it before it erupts out of nowhere.

But Lee was stubborn. More than I was. So it wasn't a fair play. For two days I had been taken well care of, I felt like a princess by how my tooth extraction turned out. I received food on my bed, piggyback rides during the beach strolls, a customized padded suit, and a backpack embossed with my name on it when we went on a trekking tour. The mountain excursion which had Lee and me in envy as we watched Edmund fleetingly scamper over the rocky surface as if he was gliding through a skating rink. Transcending swiftly through one corner to other, sometimes pausing to look down at us literally with disgust and pity.

But we looked down at Fisher who with an aging man probably in his sixties, struggled a couple of meters behind us. Lee and I broadcasted the judgment from Edmund further to him. It made us perceive our stamina better, even if it was just illusion. But it was worth it- the view had us in a trance as four of us stood at the peak while the mountains covered the sun that sank beneath. The last trace of light was the golden spectrum scattered by the sky that slowly diminished with its source gone. This island gifted me with memories that I couldn't have made if it wasn't with Lee beside me. And oddly, Edmund and Fischer too had joined into the cause. They were my friends- even if I liked it or not, its what Edmund had announced after a toast at the bar last night.

"And it has nothing to do with you agreeing to the terms of contract tonight," he said with a grin as Lee picked my glass of liquor in exchange for a chocolate milk carton with a straw tucked in. For how long has been carrying them for me?

Since I can't have alcohol with the antibiotics I was taking for my wound to heal- he proclaimed himself to be in charge of my diet, sleep, and how to not kiss me as my jaw was still sensitive. Since Lee gets carried off in those predatorily smooches – it takes him just a consenting touch from me to jump from gentle to demanding in a second. So he often joked about how I should just relax during the calm before the storm since doesn't get to kiss me now.

I like to think that he jokes.

He doesn't.

So when he hugged me from behind after the sun was bleak, I merely wanted to bask in the feels of it. But Edmund turned with my eyes growing wide as we both simultaneously blurted-

"Casper deserves to be killed here"

Lee's chin slipped from my shoulder as Edmund and I couldn't help out a grin. We hi-fived at the great analogy we did- of course, it had been like this for the past two days. Visiting an island was my wish because of the imagery of such a nation that I had often used in the book- it was all based on research and I had never been to one in person. So I always craved to experience what I wrote.

For Edmund- he was here even before he knew of me to do the same. To bring a written narrative on screen. To give it life. It baffles me how fate works. What bothers me more was how confident these people were.

He was out here in search of locations when I hadn't sold the script yet. This kind of dedication requires - power?

Edmund during his policies looks like he would even get a gun to one's head to get the job done. But instead of shooting- he would tickle them till they gave in with it.

But by how they keep mentioning their friend Alexander- generally addressed as Alex- I bet he was someone who might actually consider pulling the trigger.

That dude was strange.

As for Lee-

It's his knowing smiles and laid-back persona that scares me more than his possible anger. He acts ordinary with extraordinary thoughts lurking within him. You see what he thinks, but you aren't prepared for how he might react to it.

He forgives you too much until you are indebted to his kindness. But he knows those debts- and he looks like he is just waiting for the right time to vice them back. It's not modest of how he plays, but I like how he spoils me. So during our last day, I persuaded him to join the associative gaming event hosted by the resort community for any housing members who would like to participate.

Since it was for couples and Edmund was so into sports- It took me a suggestive note.

"If you don't want to come, I will go with Edmund"

It was a genius move because Lee was here next to me with a tennis racket clutched in hand and a neon green ball on the other. Our first competitors were native couples from arizona in their mid-thirties. They were sweet and chill anout what was to come their way- which was nothing much since we Lee had the spirit of a geriatric mammoth.

"I don't feel good about this" he grumbled. Bouncing the ball to the floor with the racket. In his white-sleeved shirt and rolled-up sleeve, he could distract any woman he wanted across the hall. But he was distracting me the most- a player who must be focusing on her game rather than him. So I look ahead-

"I have a very good omen upon your new jeans. You'll do good"

He was quiet for a moment, contemplating why an educated girl like me would say something like that. I cross-stretch my ponytail, fastening it up. Since everyone was busy completing the various assignments to reach the finals- I wasn't palpitating with nervousness- I can tackle the two opponents. I know I can-

"That's similar to how my maths tutor used to motivate me before the exam" there was a nostalgic hint in his utterance, I look back at him to see a playful smile "I failed them anyways"

I adjusted my shirt and the band of my red skirt that were tighter by the waist but flared into a pleated frill- I looked hard into him with an alarm.

"I don't lose" I whisper- he blinks with a heave.

"Fine- I will lose for us both"

Turns out- we weren't bad players - in the first round we won. Ten minutes into it- we were screaming, plotting, and strategically winning the game. The second was a tough call but we won that too- then came Edmund and Fischer-

We don't question them since Lee had a conclusive idea of how they got in-

Fischer looked traumatized as Edmund winked at him snicker-ing.

"I swear he used to be the golden boy that every parent wished their daughter would end up with" Lee puckered his lips frown-ing at the slight PDA Edmund was throwing at Fischer so the ambassadors won't suspect the authenticity of their unity "Then Hollywood happened"

The laugh that bubbled into my stomach died when I realized there wasn't a way we could beat Edmund. He was athletic- he knew what he was doing- he was a man winning the duel- we lost the round three. But not entirely.

Since I was the queen of memory games, I took the reins of it. It was a nuisance when we saw Madison and Moreno among the other surfers- Madison smiled at me but it didn't quite reach her eyes when we passed each other. In contrast to it I felt Morenos gaze on us on multiple exchanges that made my concentration go haywire with what I was doing.

Lee was persistent that we quit everything and just leave.

But I didn't want to. I have been running away from enough things to add more timidity from me into the pit of things I am shameful of. I only had to deny the offer for him to understand what I was fighting through-

Edmund and Fischer made it to the finals along with us and the other two. Madison and Moreno were one among them. The last task was a VR battle- and one look at Lee told me that he was scorching into a competitive stance.

"I don't want to lose to them," I tell him as I wear my gears on- he helps the glasses into my eyes and straps the belt that crowns my head. Though I can't see- I hear the determination surging in him.

"Neither do I" then I feel his hand cup my face as I stood blind with my hands lax on either side clasping on to the controllers. He was kissing me, his hold light and feathery- it wasn't short or long. There weren't many movements in them- but were careful and sweet.

When I hear his voice again, I realize that he had just kissed me in a room where there weren't just us two. But many many more- but I don't sense the eyes on me- not when I was blind as a bat to what was happening around me.

"Are you okay?" he asks as in nod-

"Yes" I even stretch my lips and jam my teeth to make the point " Absolutely. My jaw Is fine too"

I listen to his chuckle as I realized that he craftily had done it in a manner where I wouldn't feel the burden of watchers on me yet experience a diverse display of affection which showed he wasn't going to hide his feelings from coming out. To me or in front of all.

"Let's get them all" he hypes me up when I couldn't respond with the energy he suddenly seems to broil with. But I play as if I had my rent due the next week- even when Moreno and we were standardizing in the winning streaks- we managed to breakthrough winning the last round. In sound cheers that erupted from around, I rip off the VR box from my face and turn throwing my arms around a laughing Lee. His chest vibrates with the mirth as he lifts me in a circle, his wrap on me firms as I smile when he puts me on my feet. A series of awes and exclamations whirls from the crowd- but it didn't matter- we were eloped with a bond that made anything else matter less. At the moment he was the most important person to me and nothing else mattered anymore.

They held a bash after the dinner, we were awarded a cup and a framed certificate. Lee commented that he felt like a student again- I jotted it in my mind to memorize how I felt the same, after a very very long time. As I was lazily stirring the dessert in my plate- the event coordinator poked his head between. Startled I let go of my fork as it fell on the tabletop with a tick.

He again was the same Mexican who ailed me with horse riding lessons. So his goofy behavior was normality among us two, so when he grinned and congratulated me on the win with a dimple – I smiled with a nod.

Soon there was a hand by his chest sliding him aside like a curtain.

"Thank you for wishing us on our win" clipped Lee with hard eyes. Nothing uncommon- again.

The coordinator brushed off Lee with an awkward nod- but proceeded to extend a card towards me.

"This ID belongs to Maddison Fischer- she seems to have dropped it during the games" I take it from him as he continued "Can you please return this back to her- the number is 209, its just on the right of the-

"We can't" my neck snaps to Lee as he sips on his wine, for once I was glad that his cold stare wasn't diverted at me. He slowly looks at me as if challenging me to say or do otherwise. Or more like a warning. I gulp in, stuck with my conscience as I look at the man- only to see him with his palms open-

I don't return the card-

"I will give it to her"

My toes curl as I refused to look at Lee. The man sighs in relief.

"Thank you so much. I wouldn't have asked if your condo wasn't close by theirs. Our staffs are packed for the night- you are such a savior my dear"

I smile then, but as soon as he was gone, so with him did my courage.

"You don't have to come-

"I never said I will"

My thumb grazes the blade of the card with her picture in a box. She was Maddison- but she looked younger- happier in it.

"It's not like you still have lingering feelings for her" I look up regretting instantly of what I had said. His face was blank as a virgin paper. "I am sorry"

He stares at me for a good time, he got up looking sideways, his jaws clamped. But when he finally gazed back at me they weren't so sober- his eyes. They shone with emotions that were complicated but so candid.

"I like everything about you shin, but I don't" he licks his lips as I anticipate "-I don't like how you never fight for me"

The guilt clings to me, it morbidly shafts its roots into with every step I took as we walked towards the corridor. I scout for reasons that I could unearth as an excuse- but it was too late. Tonight he was accounting for the balance we had so far- he was aware that how he has to contaminate a memory to serve things right. But I was a double-edged sword that could lance through him no matter what part of me he tried to hold me back with- if only I could go back and-

"I will wait here. Come soon" he leans his side by the intersection, even now forcing a small smile to put me at respite. I don't say anything but recruit to the passive cause I was here for. I stood in front of the brown door practicing internally if I should just fling it if Moreno opened the door. But to my dismay- there was a faint scream followed by a sharp churn of glass breaking. My voice clogs in me as the faint shouts of abuse resounds. They were faint because of how noise-proof the structure was. At first, I decide to knock at the door- but ended up slamming my fist at it. When there wasn't an answer I hit on the bell frantically enough for Lee to come running-

From right I saw the janitor jog in, searching for the brash knocks I was rendering on the door. But before he could open his mouth I speak up-

"I suspect abuse- do you have the key?" he gawks confused but some slow grasp onto the situation surfaces- but he wasn't quick until Lee pressed through the bell multiple times. His angry fist bangs through.

"MADISON- OPEN THE DOOR" he screams, the janitor fumbles through the phone and reads me the emergency code for the room. Lee was on it before I could do anything- he tears the door open as I stiffened at the scene unfolding. Lee was quick to push Moreno away along with the bottle of liquor he had raised above Madison, who battered on the floor sat there curled up. A large bruise ran

down her side, her lower lip was coated with blood, the dress worn were torn from edges and stained- her sobs and cry for help were much clear now that the door was open.

"Call the cops" I find myself instructing the janitor as I watched Lee wrap a blanket around Maddison as she embraced him, burying her face into his neck as he said something to her while making comforting circles on her back. But I don't wait- one look at Moreno and I freaking lose it. He stood there drunk- his eyes mad and red at Lee and Madison.

He tried to make a move unknown to Lee who was busy helping Madison. Storming in I push him back – he stumbled into the monitor unit as his eyes divert to mine. I see him- I see the man in Moreno- that filthy monster resurfacing tonight in a different place and body. But the same soul. But tonight I wasn't afraid.

I don't think I was this angry at someone ever.

"Don't even fucking look at them" I whisper gritting my teeth, my lips tremble with rage as I raise a finger at him.

"I will," he says, his salivating hiss was as inhumane as him. "I will ruin him the way he ruined me"

For some reason, all I could hear was madisons cries and Lee shouting at me to get out of the room. But no- I had to hold a conversation with a drunk filth to be able to breathe tonight.

"Ruined you? you deserve to rot- you are deranged and pretentions. And you'll die alone counting your sins" it was a piece of my mind, it brought peace to me once it was out for him to dwell once he was in his sense.

By now Lee implored me to just go- I look back to see him holding onto Madison, trying to keep her awake as she was losing consciousness. He was torn between the two situations- but I want to let him know that it was fine. He can aid Madison. I don't need his help now- not when I was standing up for one-

Moreno smirks as the resort's medics barge it. I don't look back to inspect the commotion. Not when I saw the knowing glint in his dangerous eyes.

"You are saving a man who married you as a subject for media" his hysterics crawls over my skin as I frown "I know everything about him Han Shin Young. He and people he is close to-you are defending a man who doesn't even know you well"

My throat was parched with my strength giving up. For a second it got dizzy as I blink in to focus-

"What do you mean?" I couldn't recognize my voice- it wasn't vulnerable- but confused and upset with how cruel it was.

He laughs maniacally as the room fell into silence once they took Madison out. I felt the rigid hold of Lee on my wrist tugging me back with a warning that I can't seem to register. I can't hear him as I twist my arm to free myself-

"What do you mean?" I shout at Moreno as he looks at me with a tilt of his head.

"If that man truly loved you, he won't be celebrating a vacation here if he knew that you-

I don't let him complete as I punch him. Despite the hit, he recovers fast to launch at me. But I got pulled in an instant with Lee shielding me as he grabs the collar from Moreno shirt-

"Don't. Even" Lee growls as the officers swarm in, he shoves Moreno towards them as they immediately bind him in cuffs. Cemented I watch them arrest him away-

Flinching to the attempt of Lee who tried to pacify me by taking a step- I raise my hand gesturing him to stop.

I was asking him to stop when everything in me begged to be embraced and comforted.

But I don't want it from him.

I don't want to get used to him.

But it wasn't a choice with him when he didn't gave a dime for what I was asking from him as I got draped by his arms. I sink into him with the voices silencing in me.

And with that I fall into a deeper stage of debt.

CHAPTER 26

The splash of cold water pacifies me. Repeating it thrice I stare at my reflection- tucking the wet matted hair behind my ears to see my pathetic face moist with despair. Securing the tap I let my hair free of the braid - using fingers to massage my scalp I attempt to appease the ache. Each memory of what had happened an hour ago gripes me into an essence of alienation.

Hugging myself into a smaller entity I stepped back to simply watch the girl in the mirror. If exhaustion had a face, she would be it. Her cheeks were flushed pink with how fast her mind was racing- her petite body donned with blacktop and skirt, they were there to put on a show- her eyes, they conceivably were the most impressive trait of hers. They were hooded, hazel, and expressive when they desired to.

They also were happier and prettier when she had been hell-bent on ignoring the reality she comes with.

Fatigued, I sigh jerking my head to get the thoughts out. Owing up to the mistake I did was the only solution to it- swabbing with the rolled-up towel on the basket, I fling it across once I was dry enough. Walking out i spot Lee on his mobile, seated by the edge of the bed, changed into a fresh light blue shirt. The older one had Madisons blood on them.

He looks up as soon as he senses my stare on him. I know I wasn't giving him a thing away as I imitated a stone at the moment. Never had my emotions ever been stonier than this- They were rigid, strong, and finally building up the wall between us than I should have done ages ago.

Only if he had let me be.

"How is she?" I ask, not allowing his dense stare to bother me. He takes his time to articulate a reply.

"Aldo is with her. She is fine" I secretly hoped to detect some kind of rage and concern when he spoke of Madison. But the way his entire focus was directed to and at me- I hated it. I despised the steps that had us here. breaking this chain was a necessity- and to do it, I want him to hate me. But I was so harmless in his view that no matter what I did- he would probably see through my lies.

So I stood there as he got up and walked over. He doesn't say a word- silently he tugs my hand to inspect the redness on my knuckles. I severely wish it did something to Moreno- it was the strongest punch I could pack. By the end of my brutal prayers – a soft sigh from Lee alerts me.

His thumb brushes my knuckles as he holds my gaze-

"Why didn't you leave when I asked you to?" it was a question, but the tone was rhetorical so I don't answer him. But it doesn't suffice there- not with how sharp his eyes got when I ignored him "What's wrong?"

The weather was unconditionally cold, with temperature decreasing as the night ascends. Snatching my hand from him ,I hugged myself again. I needed to quit the dependence I have on him. His smile, his voice, his care- I had gotten used to it. But habits that has been learned could be erased.

But was he a habit?

Breathing isn't a habit. And for me- Lee was no less. He was my necessity – he was something I've searched for and dreamt in my barren fantasy.

"When are we leaving tomorrow?"

The formality in my utterance didn't faze him, as if he knew I would behave in such this way. He always knew of a junction that will be harsh to go through. But not when.

Neither did I.

"By four. We also have to leave for Seoul in three days" he angles slightly to watch me, perplexed I frown at how It had completely skipped my mind- the Korean reception that takes place by the end of this week. A ceremony that will have us united for the sake of media and sorcerers. The reason this all began.

"So we reach our goal soon" I blurt, the frozen letters seeping off me without hesitation.

"What goal?"

Serious and persuasive. He was daring me to say it. I do it anyways-

"Your profile will steer clear. You will be free to do anything with your life once the conference takes place" with a prompt I lift my gaze to meet his. He rakes my face for the slip- I watch the anger cloud his eyes as he takes a step further. I retreat one with my hands falling to my side.

"Is this all a fucking game to you?" he seethes as I bite the inside of my lip.

Not a past- it's my future.

"If so-" he yanks me, wrapping my frame into a furious hold "-then you chose the wrong person for it"

His cologne twists my sanity into a mashed complication. He was like the warmest place I could find in the coldest night- so when he kisses me- I try to fight him off by a hand to his chest. But he scarcely budged as he slams me briskly against the wall- breathing down my neck- leaving a trail of wet kisses as he grabs my wrist, raising them above my head. Fastening me to his likes.

"Lee- don't" I force out the whisper as he arches my body to him. kissing me again to cut off the protest as I melt in. He doesn't even have to fight for dominance as I felt his finger grazed the inside of my thighs, sliding it up and down-

"You were saying something babe?" his husky utterance after he breaks the kiss was a cunning act. He knew what he was doing me- he was erasing the reasons that were there to erase him from my life. I couldn't do it- speak on his demands as he draws the hem of my shirt from the skirt. His fingers and palm squeezed my waist as he worked his way inside my top. "You want me to stop?"

He breaths.

"I- I, Lee" mine was no better. My words morphed into a moan as he explored me in nooks that I didn't have control over.

It was the audacity of his – his smirk that curled against my shoulder. He undid the top buttons of my shirt in quick moves. I closed my eyes when he picks me up, effortlessly. My legs wrap around him as he gets us to bed-

He leans with his gaze piercing onto mine, laying me on the soft matters as he moves the stray strands of hair from my face.

"You are beautiful," he says with his finger tracing over the lace of my undershirt- but his eyes never for once leaves mine, yet they seem to have memorized each and every detail of me- they were wild, they ere dark. Yet so gentle and raw with passion "I feel like my heart Is going to explode"

I raise my hand to his face- feeling the dampness of his hair from the shower he took and his heated skin on my palms-

"Mine too" I crane myself to kiss him, but he was all over me in a second. Shedding off the layers that separated us. Into the darkness, I felt him bite onto my shoulder as I gasped, with a knowing glint that followed he projected me on his discovery.

"You like that don't you?"

It was probably the only movement in the night where my hyperactivity gave in as I ramble-

"I don't know, maybe-" he frowns with the slow realization "-it's not something I experienced before"

He paused every little thing to look at me with his lips parted- I look away timid and shy from the combination hunger and shock that painted him. His fingers curl by the back of my neck, tilting me as he kissed me softly for the first time since this escalated.

"I don't know what to do with the surprise you are," he says, as I was pushed deeper into the sheets and a state of ecstasy as he whispered "I love you"

A breath hitched in my throat, he fists my hair in an abrupt surprise as he whispered in my ears,

"I don't think I've loved anyone the way I love you, and I promise to show you just how much"

I don't get to dwell

His nails sank into my skin by the small of my back, and suddenly it dawns on me. It reminds me furiously of why I wasn't able to resist him or his touch when I had my mind made and staked with excuses to end whatever had us in a bind.

It wasn't just any touch that's gone when he isn't with you. It was a poetry that possess you with its roots reaching far into your soul-making you an addict. I couldn't resist because he was writing himself on my skin and the scary thing was- I don't think I will ever be able to wash him away.

Not tomorrow, Not forever.

It was a lost battle- so I let him win.

CHAPTER 27

L EE

The light from the day spills in, it felt new . The morning. Like waking up to a day that was bound to be different than every other in past. The night was cold, but it morphed through and into a bearably humid dawn. I sat there with my back napping against the head of the bed in a plain white t-shirt and black tracks, my head in intervals butted against the board as I stared ahead.

Ahead because she was still peacefully asleep beside me. Her body encased in my shirt from last night- sizes bigger on her. I can't even spot her fingers by how long the sleeves were, only the tips. she slept on her side with the comforter spread up to her waist. Her silky strands fell upon her cheek as the dark hair intensified her pale skin.

And suddenly I remember how flushed and pink they were last night. Not that I had to remember something which never left my mind. But overwhelmed at what had happened I sat there with my hand tearing up my hair.

I certainly had underestimated my feelings for her. Whatever I do- doesn't feel enough with her. I want to touch her more, hold her tighter. Be the reason behind that smile and hear that quirky laugh of hers that she uses when she feels evil. I want to look into those confusedly eccentric eyes and tell her how she was wrecking my world and everything I had worked on for. But I know how the night happened-

And what she was about to do before I fused to my last resort.

I was in a mere quest to shut her up with a kiss. But then I forgot what I was kissing those velvet like lips for as my greed took over. Most of our clothes from the night still camped by the side – and I wouldn't change a thing about it.

I watched her with my heart pounding by my ribs, I could trace a small smile on my lips as she stirred with her fingers curling into paws. Her eyes flutter open slowly to the assault of a bright room. Then they stop on mine.

"Good morning" I wish as she subtly avoids a reply with a quick nod. "Is everything okay?-Are you-are you hurt?"

It doesn't feel good. The hunch of something sinking in me by how hers were so void. She hoists herself up and speaks for the initial wise-

"I- I have to use the restroom"

With that, she ripped off the sheets from her- the shirt covered her upper thighs like a short dress. I began to pace across the room desperately ceasing my thoughzts from biting into a conclusion. But when she came out she looked more watchful and alert. The front of her tress was damp with water- probably a result of her splashing herself awake.

She consciously fixes her stare on me- not saying or implying at a snippet of what's going on in her head. But I know it doesn't seem to be doing me a favor. So I grab her hand and walk us to the porch. I make her sit by the cot chair. Bottling up my perfecting patience and throwing it aside I face her, our knees grazed as I took her hands in mine with a stern gaze.

"What happened? Look at me"

She deliberately doesn't. So I make her. I don't care at this point if I was startling her. I can't recite the concerns I have for her when they are clouded by my suspicions. Vile and ridiculous suspicions.

"I think I've waited enough shin- I want you to-

"Last night was a mistake"

I don't breathe- I don't let her breathe.

"No. It wasn't"

My hold on her fastens in hopes of her taking her words back. But she swallows in. With each second the determination of her brews hotter. Until they simmered me into a man that was breaking into one with sanding edges.

"Is it because I confessed to you?" it was a forced tenderness in my voice, I could execute the true anger that soared in me – not when she looked unapologetically fragile while doing this "You don't have to return them now. Heck, you don't have to love me today Or in a year. Take your time- but just- just stop thinking of us as a mistake"

Her lips tremble but her words didn't.

"I am sorry" she shakes her head, snatching her hands from me. Her eyes go soft- and I hate it. I hate those eyes at the moment. The empathy it came with.

"Don't do this to me"

I don't beg. I just say. Say it out loud for her to hear- for her to listen. But that was it- it's the last breath i waste on convincing her. My jaw tensed as I nod once – an inquisitive chuckle leaves me.

"I can look into every little detail about your past and the present shin" I see the light dim in her, I bet mine was painted with humoring rage "-Just like how Moreno probably knows about you. I have enough power to not just know but also to destroy. But I never did anything as such because I wanted and waited to gain your trust in me"

This wise her demeanor deceives her restraint as she squints agitated.

"You had my trust and companionship as much as I was willing to. And I am glad you didn't cross the line we had- I also believe you won't invade my privacy still"

An electric silence befalls the yard as I find myself smiling at that. My patience crumbled to ashes at her strange trust in me. But she couldn't be more wrong. She doesn't know the Lee I could be because I never let her see it. The lee was unforgiving- the man despite finding Madison in such condition didn't feel the resent or remorse towards because he was too preoccupied with his contempt to accumulate general humanity.

I was worried for her survival.

But I wouldn't care if she healed later or not.

I don't do much when I get hurt. I walk away and let them be or bleed without a thought. Then what's different with shin? Where is the toxic nonchalance I want to show her instead of my vulnerability? Perhaps because deep down I still believed she was lying to me. It's my truth against her lie.

"You trust me way too much for a person with whom you had a meaningless fuck last night"

"Lee-" she snaps, the furious rise in her tone indicates that I was pushing the right buttons. So I don't stop.

"Why deny it when that's all it was?" My sharp stare lingered by her exposed collar, then lower- to finally back up at her face. shin squirms faintly in a chair- not with discomfort. But with something else "Love failed- I guess lust didn't"

Apart from my terrible mood swings, It was the imbalanced sugar levels that emerged with the onset of such prolific stress that made it impossible for me to consider driving us back to vegas in rental after we took the ferry. Edmund suspected the visible friction looming around as he was stuck with us. Aldo stayed on the island to wrap things up with his sister's abusive boyfriend. Edmund was kind enough to ensure him of support if he needed any.

Once we reached the port he wheeled off to Los Angeles. Without a question asked and a very friendly goodbye where he hugged shin as she smiled for the first time in the day.

So I individually decided to transport our luggage through the joint courier and got into the first bus that will take us to Nevada. We received looks and stereotypical side glances from the passengers which were predictable because of our sophisticated dressing and east nationality. I wouldn't have given heed towards such subtle behaviors if it wasn't for Elzina who dissected it out for me during our high school years. Since she had lived both the lives – the rags to riches phenomenon, she knew what she was theorizing.

And true enough- her observation skills were seldom invalid. Her prediction was a reality waiting to happen. she was like the genius psychic among us- and I wonder what will she see in shin that could enlight me more about her.

That stubborn girl was busy gawking at the interior of a private bus, cooking things in her own world while I was beside ranting inwardly. She had that awful-looking goldfish in a jar by her lap- she got curious stares for that which she wasn't aware of because her eyes were fixed on what rolled outside. Nature, road, sushi stalls, demolished paintball centers- everything that excludes and cancels me.

Then I fell asleep with my arms crossed, woke up to catch her staring at me. It would've made me feel good if she hadn't gone on to add an alibi-

"You are talking in your sleep"

And that's how we ended up choosing verbal violence to grind the tension in the air.

"I don't recall asking for a reason" it wasn't a snap- the more stable I looked further I saw the resent in her eyes. I wasn't going cold inside- I was merely maintaining a façade to put her off. Maybe not doing much would help her lose her guard one day. But I gave up on my cool that night when she started to gather her pillows so that she could sleep somewhere else- because from today on, I refused to leave the bed I paid for.

"Take one step towards that couch, I'll set it on fire before you reach them" with the advice I look over the comforter to see her scrambling back to bed. Once she tucked herself in she became a scientist.

"Technically it's not possible- I would've reached the couch earlier than you could've used a lighter or oil to set it on" I could understand where this was coming from. We were tired from the journey that took us a total of eleven hours, so it was sensible that we communicate about acceleration and inertia instead of- instead of something as useless as what the fuck happened to us? if everything would have gone smoother- I don't think I would have let her be tonight. What happened to the shy good girl from yesterday? "You really are terrible with maths" she had to go on and add.

"Maths yes. But what about the thing I was good at?" she can't see me with the raised brow. Not even the bitter smirk I had. But I could sense her abrupt silence- she doesn't have to answer that.

Neither she did.

The next day I got a call from Clarissa- since she was my friend and my lawyer, she professionally informed me that-

"You won the case- you can now die in peace"

A part of me didn't die- but came alive with the realization that this was the incentive for which Moreno acted in recklessness, he sublimed low enough to check through Shins records to see if he could blackmail me with anything to make the prosecution a failure. As fiercely as I wished to celebrate the win that could get me back my racing license- I couldn't bring myself to. Cause my head spins with a single assorted query-

What is it that Moreno knows that I don't?

And why do I love and respect her so much to leave her be when I could search for it myself?

No- with a cinch I throw away such ruthless ideas. Abusing my power when it comes to her will lead us into a state of distrust when all that seems to tread us was her odd trust in me despite her blunt admission of calling what we had so far to be a mistake.

Mistake?

Oh, how I loathe the word. It should get banned from thesaurus and dictionaries. In the whole of existence. Just should be wiped it off.

When the day of departure rolled in sooner than the anticipation for it- we were late on schedule. It was our last day here in the city with us running around summing up the chores. I had the head start because I wrestled into the shower first-

"You take ages to come out" she screamed at me once I closed the door on her face.

"Come in and let's shower together. It'll be quicker" I barked fumbling with the temperature screen. She was quiet after that, but by the constant bickering that rose at unexpected rootings- the flare in her eyes as she consents to her defeat usually never died down entirely. I bet she killed me multiple times in her head as a form of coping mechanism. Because that what Inara does.

In fresh clothes I sat on the couch with my sock on, preparing to wear my shoes when the door parted slightly- then came her frustrated and desperate demand-

"I forgot my clothes on the bed. Can you-

"Come out and get it your self"

There was a noticeable silence.

"Then you go out"

Seriously?

"Fine. I am going"

I don't. I sit there with my shoe in hand as she came out wrapped in a small white towel. She yelped clutching onto the towel by her chest as if her dear life depended on her. Her wet hair cascaded down her shoulder, the ever porcelain skin glistened with the steam from the bath. Her eyes- were furious and pointed. She stood her ground instead of going back in. I regretting staying when she had politely recommended me to get out.

But my mouth proceeded to blurt facts before I had control over it-

"I paid for every single brick that this room is made of. I wasn't going anywhere" she shakes her head frowning in disbelief. But I smile with an intention of irking her- I succeed "And also It's not something that I haven't seen"

Her eyes narrows as she walks and picks her clothes, I watch her step, my eyes fixed on her moves, hair, lips, and every inch that was her. Then I shift into a jerk the second she turned to snarl at me-

She was going red.

Good.

"There is this thing called modesty. I sometimes like to believe that you could be capable of it"

Her sarcasm stirs something in me- tilting my head I bite in a smile.

"Where was yours the time you confided to me about your cuff kink when you were on anesthesia"

Her jaw falls, I might end up in a customized hell for the lie I was spewing at such a helpless girl who only wanted to collect her clothes.

"I don't" she whispers,

"You apparently do" I stood my ground as she gritted her teeth.

I hated what I was on to, but I also loved how she was impersonating a tomato for me.

"Why are we arguing?" she whines, shattering the barriers she had for so long. But I don't give up. I won't until she- herself will shatter the wall she had built between us.

"I don't know. But at least you talk to me when we do" a coarse of sadness whiffs through her. But just like any other time with her cascading form, she walked away. I was used to it by now- so I put on my shoes and brace myself for the long flight ahead.

In haste we left the house, it was chaotic, a chauffeur who with his fatherly gestures helped us up with all the stuff that we had to assort. Since it was an Asian reception- I don't know what to expect. The flight wasn't an easy one with us seated beside for good twenty-two hours with connecting flights in between.

It was a private business cabin, so there was little to no one to fill the silence so- when then aircraft coordinator came it. He smiled at us- his posh uniform and mechanical face were enough to tell me how much he despised his job. Nobody would ever want to cater to snobs like us. It must be a curse.

So for the next half of the hours, we discussed what he was here for, when I signed the document he lets out a breather. Losing his tie and posture. He can expect a hefty commission out of this deal. Once he was gone after assuring Shin and I about how he will make sure that there will be the best treatment given to the passengers- the first thought from poor shin who had been watching us, two men, by recliner in the corner discussing things unknown to her was-

"Why is he informing me of what he going to do with the passengers?"

Her peak sassy remark earns a chuckle from me. I haven't laughed in days and by how raspy it came- it shows I hadn't been living much this weekend.

"He wasn't mentioning the present passengers. But the one from my private list" twisting my wrist I check for the time. Four more hours for us to land- great. I stop short when I turned to see her already looking at me with curiosity.

"What private list?" she asks as I tuck her hair behind her ears, I hadn't touched her in so long that even doing that felt like an intimacy.

"I booked a charter to fly my friends for the reception"

As I say it, the confrontative shake of the head wasn't a surprise.

"Why would you do that?" she hurried- I was calm. "You didn't invite them to the wedding because it was staged, why would you-

"You speak- I listen"

Resting tighter against the seater I run through the magazine I was previously reading through-

"But it won't change a thing. I won't let it change" flipping to a new page, distracted but confident I declare looking deeper into her, pinning her with my stare "All I can do Is give you time to come back to me, by then you'll realize that you married a man who doesn't take it easy when he is played at"

CHAPTER 28

S HIN

    I want to scream, rip off a couple of pillows and shred them until they resembled nothing that they used to be. The wild sentiment seems enticing. To destroy things I had control over.

Sweating profusely I ran on the mill, boosting its speed to a level that I won't be able to keep up with. I exert my leg and body to go on, to focus on momentum and rhythm instead of the phone call that shrills through the gym room. The screen blinks with a missed called memo- then soon another call wakes up. Same number, The same person.

Four days ago when we landed in Seoul – I met my family, Hwan ran over to me with open arms. I was fatigued because of the long flight I had- but nevertheless, I opened my arms to be welcomed when he jogged past me to embrace Lee in a manly bro hug. My jaw fell open when I witnessed the exchange and spotted the arrogant amusement dancing in his eyes as he ruffled my brother's hair.

"Thanks for gifting me the gaming studio. You are the best" the little devil wheezed at Lee as my parents shrugged when I threw a questioning glance at them. But then Dad came over to us and after some good parental hugs and forehead kisses they filled me in.

"We received some thoughtful gifts from our son-in-law a week ago" Mom said from right, while Dad shared his observation from left, Slipping his plain silver glasses, his lips curves "By the look on your face- you don't have a clue about this do you?"

A lamenting sigh leaves me. My parents changed their perky demeanor in an instant- like an attire as soon as Lee greeted them with a bow. They now imitated polished upper state personalities that Mom always belonged from- but seldom were accustomed to. My mother married a normal man whose parents ran a bakery in a small underdeveloped village. And instead of changing my father to fit the elite criteria- she realized there was no fun in living the life she had always lived. So she crazed up, became the girl who evokes as Head of the committee for the day and a lovably reckless mother and woman after her shift ends.

That explains why Hwan and I turned out the way we are.

But it still doesn't explain why I want to hurl myself out of somewhere after what I had done.

Mistake-

I called it a mistake- my poisoned words and the dying spirit in his eyes clawed onto me with each breath I took. I made it look like it meant nothing- but it wasn't enough to make him hate me.

Why was he doing this? Why can't he just hate me?

Maybe it needed a further push to get him there. More bitter remarks and genre of ignorance. So I went home to rest while he went off to meet his family. He pecked me on the forehead, reminding me to get ample rest and eat on time. And also to not think much.

It was a show for my family. By how hauntingly his gaze pierced through me- it was the opposite. He doesn't want me to rest at all.

As soon as I reached my room, removing my jacket and shoes I walk through my wardrobe. Rummaging through the drawers to revive my phone back. The usual one that I had left here because I wasn't willing to take even a snippet of element that binds me to this place.

I put in on charging and once full I switched it on.

Then I dropped it in the bed when a knock was heard. Wiping the sweat off my forehead I sat up alert to see Hwan's head emerge from the crack. Then he steps in as I inspect him with shock-

"You knocked?" I asked him as he poked his tongue out childishly, he even looked slightly taller than the last wise I saw him. He was growing so fast- even a month updated him.

It only applied to his body. The brain? It was an impossibility.

"Don't get your hopes up. I knocked because I was trying to wake you up if you were asleep"

I fight with a smile. He was a nuisance- but he was likable when he wanted to.

"That explains"

"No, it doesn't"

"What?"

"I don't know why- but I really want to respect you from today. It can't be excused that you are my elder sister and I treat you like-

I gesture him to shut up he grins, he crawls into the bed and sat with legs crossed and pillow to lap. I touch his forehead to check his temperature and pinch his arm as he hissed in pain. But that's it- he didn't pinch me back- or called me a small foot witch.

"If you change your ways- I'll disown you from being my brother" I scowl as he flashed his tooth. Batting his eyes he wiped his hand on his yellow hoodie and extended it to me.

"So then let's make a deal," he says as I pout with suspicion.

"What deal?"

He lets out an evil laugh that was similar to an inducting engine collapsing.

"I'll treat you the same. But you'll never stop your charitable husband from sending me more presents"

Dumbfounded I gape at him as he resumed-

"He had been such a gentleman. Calling Mom and Dad up every week to know about their well-being. Adding me in his gaming chatroom and introducing me to his cool American friends. If you haven't noticed yet- Mom and Dad are smitten by that dude. He is the embodiment of a typical Asian son-in-law in the modern world. He almost makes me want to get married and become one"

Is this what he had been doing? Building a flawless image to win my family over? For how long had he known that he wanted our marriage to be real? For how long had he been playing with the idea? It was a strategy- he is using my family to get to me. Bathing me in guilt while he stood there righteous and humble.

A wave of sudden anger soared in me- my head falls on the pillow as I slept on my stomach whining.

"Get out Hwan" I squeal for dramatics.

"But what about the deal?"

Why was he related to me?

"I curse you stab your little toe by that monitor he gave you" burying my face entirely I announced, my voice muffled. I heard hwans terrified utterance a she distanced from me, backing of-

"You have officially gone crazy. Poor Mr. Kim got himself a batshit-

I scream louder as he ran off into the vast closing the door behind him with a loud bang. I looked at my phone to see the missed calls. Every other day- even a day before- I had been gone for a month, and he still was personally concerned about me when our relationship had been purely professional.

I throw the phone aside and drowned in misery.

The week that followed was rough- Dad hosted a dinner for us. I didn't made effort to dress up, in my shirt and jeans I came out with a messy bun. It scarcely changed a speck in how bright Lee was smiling at me. My appearance was proof that I hadn't been thinking any less.

That night he stayed home, he had connected with my family, I vouched it firsthand as they held the conversation with ease without me joining them. I felt his eyes on me every single time when I refilled the wine – I wrapped up my dinner earlier than others and went to my room to clean up. When he walked in I still was busy stacking my dresses from the unpacked luggage.

I sat on the ground, when he - as if a monument of obedience sat opposite to me by the vacant space- I finally looked up at him.

"Can I help?" he asks innocently. For a moment I forget what he was capable of as the alcohol in my system was hazing me up. It was worrisome to think what had happened two nights ago. It was like weeks in between the hours that ticked. But with him, it was punishment without a crime.

It freaking hurts. Love hurts.

"No" I snatch my heels that he had taken out from the bag to arrange them in a slot.

"Your room. It's cool"

Don't talk to me. Don't behave as if nothing happened.

"Since it's mine- I'll sleep on the couch. We don't let our guest struggle here"

I plunge my hand to grab my winter glove, he goes for it too. Both of us hold the other ends, he tugs at it. I don't let go. Neither does he. We share the uniform bratty attitude- uptight and poised.

"You know where your said guest's struggles ends" I yank it from his hold as he lets me. He lets his guard down as his pretended demeanor crumbles. I gather my things in the basket and got up. leaving him to be as I worked on my wardrobe with tears clouding my gaze.

The week was a blur- with fittings, family dinners, spa appointments, and his constant absence. He left the next morning stating he had some urgent job- and since then I hadn't seen him. I must be celebrating this act- it just added up. He should've got tired of me earlier- it took him long to realize the piece of trash I was.

But it was impossible for him to desert me today.

Tonight was it, the gown was delivered by my hotel room this morning, the accessories, necessities and ailments, all resided in the suit. It suffocated me to think how true I want this to be. So I had to hit the gym to get a reality check- to know why I shouldn't dream beyond a limit. The phone rang again- I almost cursed at it. But as soon as the tone went dead- so did the cycle of the machine I was running in came to an abrupt stop. Gasping I almost fell, my balance staggering as a strong arm clasped me.

Breathing harder from exhaustion I looked up to. For a second I don't believe my eyes, then I made amends. Of course, there is nothing that goes according to how I yearn for them to be. So when the man who had been ringing me up nonstop showed up behind me, I scarcely let the surprise show. I jerk away from his clutch in an instant.

He hasn't changed much since the last time I saw him. how long was it? Two months- Three months?

Cropped hair, rimmed glasses, and a dimple that comes with the sympathetic smile of his. He was in his formals, crisp blue shirt, trousers, and black blazer sharp over his shoulder. I don't think I have seen him in normal clothes other than his uniform. Like ever.

"Why weren't you picking up my calls?" he asks, with tinge of softness in his voice as he glances at the abandoned mobile by the counter. Stepping from the system I use the towel hanging by to wipe the sweat from my face.

"Why are you here?" my voice was as vice as it could be, it was odd to be asking something I have a fair notion of. Dowon was diplomatic, learned and experience, he should know when to not intervene. But since he did, I speculate the reasons aren't something I should be looking forward to.

"I was invited by Dr.Han. I was a tad bit hurt, I expected you to do it before her" it made sense. But I don't want it to.

"she is hospitable. Inviting young colleagues as if they are a part of some close circle"

The choking sensation by my throat overwhelmed me as I kept swallowing the painful tears. I can't let them get to my eyes. Sim Do-won had done his part, I don't want his help anymore. But then,

I don't know where else to go- and he knows that. He is the only one who knows.

He was young, just reaching his thirty. But wise and civil to anyone who needs his support.

"She can't help but be on my good books, I am the best she has" he smiles with pride as I roll my eyes. Then he does something unexpected in the midst of smile, he walks over and hugs me. Pampering my head gently as I lay my side on him. dDrained of energy from keeping it to myself. "I am obedient so I am here three hours before the ceremony"

He was here because he searched for me, it was mere an excuse. I break the hug to look at him, sniffing as I smile at the stubborn and strange acquaintance I have. He was a faithful nerd. I was a crazy dork. We as friends would've instantly harbored, only if I had given us a chance. But I chose to run away. while he waited for me to be back. Faithfully.

"How have you been doing?" he scours my face curiously, for signs and changes he couldn't see. Scanning me as I shrug with a chuckle. tears "Were you able to complete those wishes?" he squints his eyes playfully as my voice breaks with a laugh. I nod.

"Most of them. yes" I whisper because I can't strain my words, I was afraid I might break "worms taste like almonds"

He laughs heartily with his sides crinkling as his gaze thinned. He had anticipated knowing their flavors since the day I had mentioned it to him. He knows them, my wishes- every single of them.

"So how was the US?" the gym was an empty place in the noon. I still had an hour before the make-up artist and hairstylist arrives so we sat on a bench, shoulder to shoulder facing our reflection in the far away mirror wall. Playing with the pockets zipper in my hoodie I sat with my head cloaked with the hood. At his interest, my mind sweeps over the memories of last month-

An unconscious smile plays by my lips, impressed his lips twists into an approval.

"I get it. You had fun"

Rubbing my palms I nod as I chewed on my lips hesitantly, the smile he had was short-lived with my confession.

"I fell in love with him" my lips quivered as I detested my next words even after watching his face fall "he doesn't know about it"

"Shin-" he breaths, but nothing follows with my name. It's where it ends.

"He doesn't know. Just like my family. Like everyone else"

The silence ropes us. with the discomfort, he opens his mouth to weave the kind of witty advice he always has up his sleeve. But for once even the nations rising neurologist Dr. Sim Do-Won had no window to escape the truth. No words to pacify a soul. While all that Lee helped me was with the things I wanted to do, Dowon had been there since the beginning from letting that one ill-fated day from happening.

He had been finding ways to keep me alive.

Because that's my last wish- I don't want to die.

But a wish is what it is, Dowon wasn't God- Love wasn't enough. It doesn't change the truth. I was dying.

CHAPTER 29

SHIN

When waves crash on either side with you in the middle-You learn to stroke, strive and survive. I had a past that stopped me from living life to its vast, It wasn't an intended one. A warning from the future had me digging up the last resort where I can fix the time I lost. A remedy. A concession.

While hanging in the presence I had two choices. It was either pathetically waiting for the end or getting back on my own feet to embrace the moments I had lost so far to my apprehension.

It's surprising how promptly the old fear fades when prominent ones are established.

Internal trauma from years ago had caused the nerves on my brain to quit their systematic cycle occasionally. Constant black-outs, weak stamina, and numbing joints almost to the point of paralyzing were some symptoms that shadowed if I wasn't on my medication. Not that it will work from the day my brain decides to die entirely leaving behind a useless body.

For six months it had been a crucial research, Dr. Sim Dowon, the 31 year old neurologist had been the supportive liar to me. Distributing hopes that had no surface. Tests after tests, therapies after therapies, we atleast came to a conclusion. It was an outward injury from the past meddling with the future.

The revelation was so severe that I couldn't recall the times I had a head injury. Except once. The only wise I had collapsed and fainted as a child was when I fell off the chair when the kidnapper had punched me. It was the he first time the woman with him had realized that the psychopath she was teaming with might actually pan out killing me.

Guess she wasn't wrong.

It was three months ago when I had screamed at Dowon, bargaining my anger to ampute a fact I was ready to face.

I was informed that my mortality rate falls by eighty-nine to a hundred. And the life rate and what struggle might befall with a successive surgery sounded worse than death to me. I have been treated differently my whole life, so when I know this will change everything that I had worked so hard and grown over, I kept it to myself.

I don't cry myself to sleep.

I don't think of what I will do or be like in the next two hours. I had ceased to worry now. and it felt phenomenal to not get lost in a maze when you don't attempt to free yourself. For now, I was relieved that my parents are proud of me, Hwan still had his vengeance on me and Dowon still hasn't ratted me out.

As for Lee, I admired him more with every passing minute. He gave me the space I yearned, stepping back only tonight, clad in his elegant tuxedo and gelled hair after a four-day hiatus. It's what

I had absolutely craved from him. Then what authority do I have for being mad by his absence? He affirmed me with a nod as he picked me up from the hotel- then drive from there to the venue had been a sensitive one.

We didn't talk.

Not a word exchanged.

The atmosphere was so fragile that I even held most of my breaths to keep it ventilated. He did his part well, opening the door for me, lending his hand, smiling for the camera, and adjusting the trail of my maroon embellished gown when it needed to. Interlacing our fingers tighter when we walked through the crowd reassuringly. The details of him were the same, but not him.

Deep beneath those brightly shining smiles as he greets and talks was pulsating exhaustion. His smile dropped with a heavy exhale as soon as a guest retires from a conversation. Only for another to come as he dons his mask.

There was no room for him to rest.

For an hour it rolls such, the repeated congratulatory speeches while the soft music from orchestral soprano stirs by the grandiose party hall. I looked at the floor, the opaque reflection on the glossy marble stared back at me. My hair looked lengthier as it was straightened to the tip. It's been so long since I had a portion of my hair braided into a crown, it was soft and angelic on my features with messy strands framing my sides.

I looked so young.

I was young.

Too young for this shit.

So when I suspected that Lee was on a quest to grill an assemblyman with his private doubts, I escaped to the food desk to do the one thing I had itched to do. Eat.

The mountains of delicately conserved savories and the view of it was enough to gain my respect. My stomach was empty, a glass of milk had been my sole meal for the day as I wasn't able to actively scoff the food owning to my rising anxiety.

When I realized that Lee hadn't ditched me tonight despite having valid reasons to do so, I sensed the weight back on my feet. So now I couldn't think of anything else but food. The fountain hiding me from the main hall was a holy grail, so I picked up the croissant and opened my mouth wide to shove them up, I successfully get it halfway in when I heard a request.

A profound, cold, and vague form of request that sounded more like a order.

"May I know how this golden dessert tastes like?"

I whirl to look at the person. A person was not he. Sculpted to Italian standards and with blue eyes that most philosophers dream of, he regarded me with them as if I committed a crime. I solemnly was chewing on my bite fast to help him.

"Yes you may"

I say when I was done. He squints his icy gaze with plight. I felt as if he might freeze me if I kept my blabbering up.

"I mean. You can try one and see" I croak blinking, the sensation of crust that gets stuck increases as he lifts a glass of drink and offers me. I grab and chug it down in a go with my free hand.

He still wasn't done. Though he spoke casually, he still wasn't any less daunting. So I listened to the man and his story that I didn't ask for.

"I would have done it if I already hadn't tasted the other three. It's for my wife" he eyes the line of caramel delicacies as if he demanded them to bow down to him and reveal their flavors. All his movements were sharp and deliberate, so to see him smile slightly- very lightly at the mention of his wife has me wondering what breed of sculptor was she is to mare this block of glaze. It was moving, so I smile at him "What do think tastes the best?" He asks.

For the next five minutes I help him with the Korean cuisines, he nods and listens to my personal opinion on them. I fondly look at my most favorite one and suggest him.

"You should go with this. She'll love it. It's like honey pastry but made with wheat extracts and milk" at that he picks the transparent glass bowl carefully with a tissue down to it, suddenly the low chatters dissolve into silence as a divine voice fills the room. the man next to me smile, full-blown smiles as he walks to the side - he was following the sweet voice of the gorgeous woman on stage by the piano singing into the microphone. Every single soul on floor stared at her amazed. The symphony from her voice played with the listeners, she was playing us with her beauty and charisma.

The candles lit around her seem to have lost their charm to how bright her aura was, the song and chorus that came out of her was just as breathtaking as her. I lost count of how long I was lost in it until she tipped her head to her audience as she finished with swift notes. Applause and amazement erupts as she walks down smiling at everyone under her vicinity.

Like a queen to her kingdom.

"The person who hosted this party made her do it for free," remarked the man next to me as I frown. He still had his gaze hooked on the brunette beauty as she shook hands with someone I don't know. Not that I know most- or any. So when he stonily regarded Lee who stood with Edmund laughing but occasionally searching around - I duck a little behind this strange dude in hiding in order to steal some more time alone.

"That's ridiculous of him" I comment as the man sighs shaking his head with a chuckle- it was astonishing to see that such a face was capable of it.

"That dude is creepy" by the reflexive attitude I decided that this man was it. I can share the sentiments I have for Lee with him- he seems to be a box of secrets visually, so what could go wrong.

"Tell me about it" I grunt. Glassily he tilted his head in listening. I snort "I mean, look at that innocent face. I bet he goes around fooling people"

His shoulder squared as I nervously coughed. He turned to me a questioning stare-

"You think?"

Why did it sound defensive?

"Ok- no. I mean. Maybe he really is a nice person- I-i

"You couldn't be more right" he declares as I exhale with my might. "You have an admirable sense of judgment"

"You mean observation?"

He looked at me as if he was disappointed at my correction. The negotiation died in my throat.

"Judge them. Unless you share what you think. It's fine"

With how complicated he seems he shouldn't be worried about Lee. Because I thoroughly feel sorry for his-

"Quit judging me"

"I wasn't"

"I am inevitably buying your words" he smirks sarcastically, but they soon dissolve into a genuine one as he stared ahead. The woman from stage walked over to us, to him. He leaned down to kiss her and she grinned when he compliments her-

"Outstanding," he says passing her the dessert he had been holding.

"When am I not" she mumbles spooning the edible into her mouth. The demeanor of the man changes from fondness to challenging as it transcends from her to me. I bet this man makes enemies even when he sleeps.

The humor dances in his eyes as the lady slowly looks at me with a greet on way. It halts as her gorgeous grey eyes go wide.

"Shin-young?" she exclaims as I crack an awkward laugh. Do I know this lady from the west, have I ever met them som-

From west?

My gaze snaps to them both, then at Edmund who still had Lee by the intersection I stared at them as the woman discards the bowl by his confused hands and wraps me in a hug.

"I finally got to meet you" she exclaims as I gawk halfway with a polite nod. She grabs my hand as the man's gaze went skeptical and then alert. "I am Elzina. Lee's chingu if he still goes around mentioning me like that. And that's my husband Alexander. I wonder if Lee told you about us"

I ball my hands into fists to keep them from trembling as I put on a brave front.

"He did" I steal a glance at the mighty Alexander White that I had heard so much of. By the wisdom, I would've preferred to keep

my path steer clear of him. But who would have thought that he would make such a cool bitching partner. Even for a while "But he didn't tell me that you could sing like that" I state helplessly as up close I was basking in her environment. She was the show while we were the bystanders. Her humble smile was cherry on the top. But by the top of her head, I saw him- Alexander. I swallowed my questions as he should know just how harshly I was judging him. It was kind of adorable how restless he looked, was he worried that I would spill the education he gave to the little ol me?

"You are more beautiful in real. Lee didn't let us meet till now. I guess he wanted to keep you for himself" her statement gets a sad laugh from me, but when a hand snakes by my waist from behind and when his signature fragrance engulfs me as she hugs me to his side, I quit laughing at my misery.

Elzina wasn't wrong though- he won't let me go. Even when he isn't around.

"That's was phenomenal. I would've canceled the musicians- you could've done the job for free won't you Chingu?" Lee was a different person with them, his horizon seem to dissolve as he heartily winked at Alexander who looked at me and then at Lee with the shake of his head.

More people joined this circle- I memorized their faces and names with just the tinge of personality to go with. There was Mike- tall, lean and always on the phone with his wife whispering where he had stacked his infant daughter's diapers and food at. Then we had the stunning Clarrissa who saved her number on my mobile to call me in case Lee ever committed a crime. Apparently, she was a lawyer and her personal fusion to roast Lee at any given time was entertaining. Hailey Howard couldn't come because of her filming, which had Edmund sighing in relief.

But I suspect it was a surreptitious dismay beneath his act.

Edmund went on to add our professional relationship to them, and also something that wretched my composition for a second.

"This girl is Elixir" he wiggles his brows as elzina was the only one to get it as she watched me with surprise "I am turning her book into a motion picture. Its also something Alex is investing in as a producer"

Smiling reasonably at them at first till a siren went off in my head as I snapped my neck to catch a glimpse of Alexander's white to see him sip on his wine with a sour look of regret. I could only imagine the zenith of assessment and examination he might slide around the script.

Lee had intimidating friends whose existence makes me feel small. By assets and by literal BMI. They were diverse in persona, raging from firey to cold, lively to enigmatic. And when Elzina White stared at me with a curious smile, my legs almost gave out at how subtly distinguished her study was. She was sucking the stories out of me with a comforting shock latched on her face. None of her moves wasted.

Alexander and her were match made in heaven and hell combined. They were too powerful in presence to even breathe by.

"I am a huge fan" she breaths in awe, her utterance flowy "That makes us some kind of business partners, doesn't it. You should visit us when you come to Orland"

Then she zips me in one swift motion by placing her hand atop of mine. The light from the chandelier dims slightly , the music around us morphs into contemporary acoustic. Lee was occupied with Clarissa, while Edmund, Lee, and Mike dived into a monetary conversation.

It leaves us two, I couldn't fend on to trust my mouth so I stay quiet as she proves me right-

"Don't let Alex bother you. How radically we behave shows how different we are than what we project" she gathers her skirt shifting to watch Alexander- the love in her eyes for him had me in a province of trance, but when he looked at her perplexed, sensing her stare on him was even more captivating. His were intense- probably even more promising than hers. He was like a puppet drawn to her- with her he was leveled, dare I say humane. He was for the moment the most vulnerable man I had ever seen- not the untouchable piece of marble he was a while ago "See, not everything is as stereotypical as it seems"

Sadly, I sigh a laugh looking at left to see him smile. Lee- he was happy to have them here, any I see why. But the hurt and indecisive pain behind him- they weren't buried that far. Just tucked for later, as if he decided to throw the tension from his work for once tonight in a week. It's better like this, a temporary ache to cancel the permanent scar he could bore. I would rather die without his love, I can't let him see me perish while he had been the only person to treat me right.

Different we are than what we project-

As she symbolized.

I wasn't different much. Pathetic either way. I could only erase as many regrets of mine, I know how hard its to live with hope. I just don't want him to go through that one that links him with mine.

To be in his arms was like coming home. We gently swayed to the slow music by the dance floor, it could be the final act we were putting up for them, but I was so grateful as this activity only involved us. My heart pounded with the recap of how many people I had communicated with, and how I wasn't relapsing into a repeated pattern.

I was moving ahead, moving on.

I kept my gaze tied on what was happening behind Lee- just couples dancing like us. Nothing special. I don't retain- I can't look at him. I can't- but there wasn't a restraint on him. He had his hands locked by my waist, while mine was neat on his shoulder.

For valid reasons our last night from the island resurfaced in my memory, provoking a series of needs in me that wasn't decent. But I am a potato, too timid to acknowledge them so I jointly decide on behalf of my hormones that I was losing my sanity.

Lee loves me. and he had a cruelly kind manner of showing it despite my rude ignorance so far-

"You look beautiful tonight," he says as I conclusively meet his eyes, the gel in his hair seems to have oxidized as they appeared much softer under the luminous. Our moves remind me of the party we had after the wedding. The realization of how far we've come was a commencing nostalgia.

"You too" I mumble lowly, his lips twitch into a smile. that smile, god I had missed him so much that expressing it with words might just be futile.

"I am beautiful?" my fib was obvious, he knew he affects me. So I didn't bother to try correcting. Simply settling to focus on my steps. He seems to have noticed my advancement too-

"Is it me or does it feel like you are getting good at this?" he spins me once, pulling me back to him in one simultaneous motion. But curving my body to his into complete closeness this wise "Have you been practicing?"

My voice got stuck on its course up. Dowon suggested and demonstrated a couple of tips today when he came to meet me at the gym, I accidentally ended up mentioning how I was certainly going to mess up the dance tonight. He was sincere with his hacks, but also with a fiery warning. He expects me by his clinic in two days. Regardless of how tired I was with the running tests and observations- I was human. I was going to fight for survival as long as I was alive.

"No"

It wasn't a planned lie. I don't want Lee to even spot the speck of shadow that leads him to my relation with my fellow Doctor. He was quiet for the minute when he spun me around and hugged me from behind, I felt him lean and enquire by my shoulder-

"Do you know that man?" he angles me as I saw Dowon by the bar counter speaking with the bartender, for a brief second our eyes met- but he was quick to look away. Not that he could see us with how dark the lighting was by where we stood "I caught him staring at you multiple times tonight"

I bite on lips hard, so much for overshadowing a truth.

"I don't," I say "I don't know him"

Waiting for Lee to buy and believe me I turned to find him ardently furious. He grabs my wrist, pulling me along as he strides past the other guest who was too deep into the night to care. It feels forever till we reached an abandoned corridor next to a fire exit. He pushed me against the wall, cornering me with his hands buried on either side of me.

"What the hell are you doing?" I scream at him, terrified and astonished at his actions.

"Don't raise your voice at me," he says, his utterance clipped and drenched with command. A shiver treks through me as he grabbed my arm roughly, shaking me up "Why did you lie to me?" he demands as I stood there useless with dread.

"You know that man. You were with him today" I push him away with shock latching on to me as he staggers off- he doesn't make a move, standing there in disbelief "Isn't he the one who gave you the dance lesso-

"You stalked me?"

"I came to meet you" he spits the terms bitterly with a crazed smile, a raging madness rings through as he continued "Do you even realize how much I had missed you this week? I was waiting for your calls and texts like the stupid person I am. Anything that could sign me that I wasn't forgotten by you"

It shreds me into layers until I couldn't stop the tears from welling up. Was he doubting me of infidelity? Is this what this is? But isn't it also the most suitable counterfeit to get him to hate me. But my legs had a mind of their own as I near him- he clenched his jaws, but he tensed further as I hugged him.

"I am sorry"

My ear picks up the rapid beats of his frantic heart.

"For what?"

He doesn't remove me from him, neither does he hugs me back. Don't I have his open permission? To hug, talk and hold when I needed him? I embrace to shatter him.

"For hurting you" I suck in a deep breath "You are better without me, and so am I. Don't wait for me" parting with conviction, I stood my ground. But finishing on a losing note wasn't what he seem to be used to, so when he claims my lips out of nowhere, impassive I held my breath until he teased me into kissing him back. It lasts till our breath gave up. Moving me to the wall, he places his arm above my head while his other rests calmly against my hip.

"Who do you think you are to decide it for me?" He rests he forehead against my mine. Regaining his breath with me "It will even suffice if I get destroyed by you. I will still love you the same"

CHAPTER 30

L EE

    There was this vast feeling of satisfaction to see the piece of ornament I gave her two nights ago by her wrist. The silver chained bracelet hung loosely on her, faintly crinkling when she moved her arms. Reassuring that sound was as I chiseled my hearing to overhear my family discuss and opinionate the episodes from the ceremony. The gossips that sizzle among them, it must be diplomatic- because from where I saw her seated next to Sera, her highlighted curiosity seem to pique with each word that my sister said.

For a brief moment she looked at me, then she turned to exclaim. I couldn't hear them, but with the dissected analogy of how they behaved- sera was onto something. My best guess was, she was narrating the top listed events that involve me and my embarrassments.

Chewing on a nonexistent gum and pride I surf through my phone to look through the countless emails that I wasn't able to attend to. Each more important than other- but none than the issues I have with her.

The hammering complication which led me into confronting her of her loyalty was vicious when she has been convinced on defying her actions. She gets me, she knows how lenient I am when it comes to her. But I have had enough- why wear the bracelet that I gifted her today when she could've thrown it away?

Why confuse me?

Why the faux?

I don't care who that man was. But the lie? Do I deserve them, after she knows what she means to me?

But forgiving her became a norm, so as we sat with mementos huddled around us for the said family culture to be wrapped. Shin and I have been sharing the room and bed by my family home on the third floor after the night of the reception. Not that I have seen her awake and active since I was seldom home, when I was back she was asleep with an open book on top of her chest. What could I give to hold her and tell her about my day? To see her smile at me and flirt with her philosophical humor. The final court hearing and prosecution of a decade-old nemesis had been keeping me up and off. Now that he was sentenced to life imprisonment I could see the relief in my father's behaviour.

He even shared a warm hug with me this morning, it caught me off guard so we ended up butting his forehead against mine at first. He wasn't impressed by it. No one ever seems to appreciate the efforts I make- so with a grumpy attitude, I crossed my legs by the mattress on the ground. We waited for everyone to join us- Shin who scooted to me with small unnoticeable steps whispered hurriedly.

"What is going on? Why are we on the floor?"

I stared ahead at the mural in the wall as I answered her.

"It's a tradition. We unwrap the presents we receive with them"

I hear her gasp in shock- I could relate to her. Out of all the aspects that confused me about her- this was something I could understand. Invasion of privacy- the Kims don't heed at it.

"Why are we all on the floor though?"

This wise I look up at the chandelier. The large ball of crystal hung there proudly.

"Because it's humble. A symbolism that we are grateful for the love we are amassing through these tokens" maddened, I laugh. Looking at her quizzical gestures I agree with her unsaid notion "Yes, it's irrational"

But so were the thoughts of what was packed within those mysterious boxes. Because as far as I know my friends- I don't want to admit. But they were a bunch of assholes at the end of the day- so the chances of me receiving a genuine one was a farce. Not even with Elzina- not when I pranked her with a live tarantula encased in a jar for her own wedding present.

Now that I think back, it's karma.

Aaron was inching with excitement as sera splits up the crates and cartons in numbers so each member could get an equal number of them.

"Do you have Hwans?" shin was careful not to imply her nerves as she smiled at my mother. She blows air out with a pout once she was free of my mother's radar, her small face snuggled by the fluffy turtle neck top as she softly blinked at me. But then the realization strikes as she monitored off. Refraining to hold a gaze or conversation with me.

I sigh, grazing the tip of my nails with my thumb as I watched them eagerly tamper with the coverings. Revealing sets of exported wine, valid passes to luxury villas, promotive technologies, gold bars, handcrafted invocations from known artists, and many more that were entirely for connective purposes. Half of the names on them, I don't even know of their existence. Then it was my turn to do so-

Inspecting the nearest one that I had, I fumble with the wooden beige box- the size of my palm. My heart began to race with ecstasy when I flip it open. My clutch stiffened against its covering. Shutting it with a snap I blinked, morphing my flushed nature into a composed smile.

"It's a gift card. So Clarissa like" I mumble shoving it inside the pocket of my jeans as shin projected me with a concerned gaze. she didn't have the right to do it- but it was comforting to know that she knows me well.

Then Aaron ripped open a bag of boxers with small animal prints on it. From my place, I announced it was from Mike. There wasn't anyone else who loves animals more than him that I know of- I could see the disappointment clouding my father's features. My mother smiled lovingly. Aaron was probably planning on stealing it. And shin thought that they will look adorable on me.

Good thing she whispered her mind to me.

Bad thing- she whispered her mind to me.

Worse for her- because she realized what she said after it was too late.

But too late also was it when my grandfather, who had been quiet for a prolonged duration picked up a case. The room fell silent in the mark of his respect as the wrinkled corner of his mouth curved into a smile.

"Alexander White and Edmund Sargent" his raspy voice read "Aren't they your American friends. White? The one who runs Elite Cooperation?"

My throat dries up in an instant as I nod lightly. What on earth presumed them to even join in on a gift. Don't they have enough money to do it separately- Aaron crawls and picks a note that was attached by the outer layer.

"Because we know you too well- written with a heart drawn at the end" Aaron grins, his bunny teeth wide on display as I reached my hand out to grandpa. Apart from not being able to hear well, he seems to have forgotten the hint of a body language. Because instead of handing me the box, he slapped me a hi-five with a laugh and proceeded to gut through the content inside.

Before I could jump onto it- he pulls out leather-strapped hand-cuffs.

With it, a major silence befalls that outdoes that one that we gave out to grandpa earlier.

Closing my eyes and sucking in a deep breath I fall into my spot, I sit my conscience going numb.

"This coming from a reputed man like Mr. White- beautiful" a croaky, quick squeak leaves me as Grandpa weighs them on his palm with scrutiny "His taste in art is phenomenal. I wonder how much this piece is worth"

Stunned, I watched my eighty-nine-year-old savior. His inno-cence seems to buy me validation from my parents. But when Aaron doubled over with sera hauntedly popped the bubbles from the discarded rap did I realized the generation gap saved me from a disaster only for the other to the surface.

It was too much pressure until the small voice of shin soon garnered everyone's attention as she desperately wheeled the focus on her-

"Does anyone want to see the potato peeler my bother got me?"

The curly-haired guard beelines towards me the moment I walk through the gates. The drill chopper could be heard from afar as I get walked through the prison's desks, the officer reads me the information- the reason why I got called to convene a convict.

"He asked to meet you. we tried investigating his motives- but he was relentless" scanning his permit by the reader he opens the iron door for me. behind the one-way glass panel, I could see him. "He says that there is something he has that you must know"

Scantily I run my gaze across the empty room with a chair and microphone to talk through. Cha Jung-hoon, the man too malignant and psychotic to be faced without a barrier. I remember him from my childhood memories, chaotic and jumbled- but he had been there around my younger days working tirelessly as my father's associate.

Tireless yes. But faithful?

When he was caught leaking information to the opposing committee he was executed from the existing forms of official disciplinary. His crimes meddle with the nation's policies and he deserved what came his way. A hefty sentence that he escaped as a fugitive.

But when her only surviving parent- committed arson and died within the property. He targeted my father for the murder when it was nothing but a framed homicide by people he betrayed my father for. But he would never believe that because we never found the evidence, but neither the clearance that could stop him from flipping out completely.

So now when I faced the once handsome, cultured, and groomed man in shackles and prison clothes with scars mapping his features, it colds my nerves to think of what has become of him and how he had been the cause of my family living in dread for so long.

Just a soul like us, but impaired with malice and hatred.

"He also confessed to some new crimes that weren't listed" I hold my breath , taking a seat facing him- he looks up, his dead and deranged stare is tight on me- he can't even see me. He reflection is all that he will speak to "He revealed this by his last therapy session, claims to have abduction, abuse, money deflation and laundering, and pedophilic tendencies though he never engaged in the act. I will be outside if you need me"

An acidic disgust prickles my throat as I noticed at him. He was far gone- I couldn't have withstood to be in the same room as him. It was a good thing he was shielded. People like him are the reason why I have been so protective of Sera and Shin. even thinking of them with him in a visual length felt precarious.

But I can't help but get drawn to how I had left in a frenzy when Shin made an endeavor to speak with me. After she diverted the nonexisting attention span of the people in the room to her potato peeler, there wasn't much interesting commodity in there. once we were done with dinner, her monotonous question, once we were strolling by the pool side in silence, had me in a fit of unrest.

"Did you mean it?" she watched the water with a distant look as if she was fighting through and over "That none of it, no matter what happens. Your feelings- they'll remain the same"

The luminous from the water creates a lucid hue, she looked elegantly beautiful with the soft lights highlighting her features. Removing a hand from my pocket with the box that Clarissa modified to be in the likes of a present, I pass it to her.

Initially skeptical but vividly curious she unlocks it. I memorize her flaming surprise and fidelity with how brightly she smiled-

"Is this- is this what I think that I am thinking?" she rambles, the element of her I cherish ardently.

"Is that my license?" regardless of my smug stance, she grins "I look hot in the picture don't I?"

She ceased to comment as I lift the card, a whiplash of emotions fogs in as I struggled to form a sentence.

"I-I wanted to show this to you first. It was you I thought of when I was at the peak of my success and elation. Does that answer your question" the spark in her goes flat, but not the life in her eyes. They were intense- "I am sorry for how I behaved. I wasn't on my right state of mind to-

"There's something I want to tell you"

There was a sea of apprehension in her utterance- but then her form relaxed as she took a step near me. Not close, neither far from. A civil expanse between us kept me sane. But then my phone rang, I pull it out to disconnect. But ended up receiving it on an important note. It was from one of the high post officials who wouldn't have bothered to call me if it wasn't an urgency.

And then I left-

I freaking left her hanging there asking her to wait for me while I have been waiting for her since lasting days that didn't seem to faze. But here I was encased in an interrogation cabin with my fingers pressing at the microphone so that I could have a chat with a convict.

Why did he want to meet me now?

Weren't all these years enough for him to acknowledge my presence? I was sent to the US because of this bastard's threats, he kidnapped my father on my eighteenth birthday, he attempted to poison my grandfather by saturating his medical prescriptions. He got caught four years ago-

Why meet me now?

"Shaun Kim Lee" he drawls out my name as if it was sweet on his tongue. Too lunatical to consider him humane. "Grew up so well I see"

I don't let the creep play around. I wanted to leave this place as soon as I could.

"Why did you want to see me?"

He closed his eyes with a shake of his head as if my question was like a lullaby to his ears.

"What's the hurry?" leaning on his seat his orbs fixed on his own introspection. But I could sense him on me. The stare of his was conjuring the patience in me. I only listen- was there anything else that I could do? "Ah- you must be forlorned to get back to your bride. What a lovely couple you both make"

My whirling thoughts, every bit of them freeze in speck. Clench- ing on the thin neck of the mic I speak- my voice comes out sharper than I intended to. The inkling of a man like him even knowing about shin was making me sick.

"What does this have to do with it?" My toes press by the sole of my left shoe as I lift my heel. My body kept tensing with each second that passed with his silence.

"I saw her image in the newspaper. My little shin-young grew up into such a beautiful lady, you are one lucky guy"

The echo of the chair scraping promptly against the concrete is all hear as I stood up, nothing constitutes to make my fuming anger dissolve- to hear her name from his filthy mouth, what the hell was going on?

"Why the fuck did you want to meet me" it was me, the thundering growl- the severe voice. He better shut up about her before I lose control like an animal. But he in prior was it- a filth- so when he laughs with his corners wrinkling I found my inhalations deepening.

"Look how fate plays Lee. I am sentenced to life here, but you are free on the other side of me. Conceivably expecting me to break down and beg for mercy. But why do I smell that you are restless, furious, and afraid" with each word he breaks the walls that were saving me from his toxicity- he riddled in my mind until I found myself whispering weakly-

"What are you even trying to say?"

He looks at the ceiling with his cuffed wrist holding his head. For a second I think I saw a shadow of misery sweep by him- But that was just an illusion.

"She served as a bait when I first tried to kill your father when he was treated by the Han's health center" stunned to the brink of breaking apart I stood there uselessly deciphering the hoax this was. Imploring ridiculously for this to be a nightmare. "She was a smart girl even when she was just eleven, won't give in despite the trauma she endured. Now that I see it this way, she saved the life of your father. That's heroic- it makes me fall in love with her more now that she is all grown up"

"SHUT UP" I scream punching the glass, it rattled with resentment as I kept demanding him to shut his fucking mouth up - with each repeat my voice cracked harder until I had to grab the edge of the plank that hoisted the microphone.

"You won't see me much Lee. But you'll see me in the fears of shin-Young" he pressed the red circle as a guard stepped in to take him "I used to be angry at my sister who released our hostage, but now that I hear you, I am contended with how things turned out"

Frantic I hit my palms against the glass in rapid knocks as he got up-

"What did you do to her?" I wanted to kill him, rip him shreds as he looks through his shoulder-

"My confessions that are new for you, are my oldest sins"

I don't waste my time in ponderation as I turn around- I step out to see him being escorted from the compartment, he falls to the side as I punch him. He smiles, the side of him bedded by the corridor's wall. But before I could grab his collars and choke him until the life left his eyes I got yanked back by the security. They don't let me go, he walks free as they pulled me away and out.

With each forced backed step, I go weak.

I think of all the alibis to this. But found none.

Of all the people he could have ruined to get to my father. Why her?

Why the innocent girl?

Why me?

CHAPTER 31

S HIN

It was sour luck. To find a public restroom with a lock on its main door. I found one- my fingers kept tearing sheets after sheets of tissues from a roll mounted to the wall. My hands tremble when I mashed it firmly against my nose. But the cycle seems to be the most spontaneous one so far. My anxiety shot up at the view of stained tissues bunching up in the dry marble sink of the venue. The music from the after-party of the runway show I attended and participated in could be heard without a miss.

I scoff and laugh at the same time, the word participated and the runway coming off in one sentence boosts my sarcastic mirth. I cough when the metallic taste of blood slickly stimulates my tongue. And before I know, a thin trail of blood trails by the corner of my lip.

It began to feel like a punishment. For one good thing that happened today to remind me of why I shouldn't be living in an illusion. When sera offered Edmund and I with the incredible idea of a spring collaboration with a style inspired by the book and using it as a stage to cast the official announcement for the movie- there wasn't any objection to it. But when she offered me to be the stopper of the show with her- I couldn't move a muscle in my body.

I thought she was joking.

She wasn't.

The one mystery that always came with the Kim siblings is their mode of comic. You don't know when they switch- a second they joke, the other they don't.

"I know a good walk when I see one. The command you have over your heels- I envy them"

But envious was her faith in me that got me into the ramp. The eyes on me would have been spears on skin if it wasn't for sera who sneakily mumbled when were getting our makeup done.

A stroke of peach blush on my cheek-

"Lee is among the audience"

I pale under the layer of foundation.

"He won't miss this for anything. That's so sweet"

It's not sweet, anything else but. Not when we haven't had a proper conversation in weeks, he either doesn't look my way or doesn't stay in the city so our paths aren't crossed. Scratch that- he doesn't even let our paths to intersect, let alone walk together in the same lane. So when I faced the crowd, I selfishly wished for his absence. If he was planning on letting me fend for myself- I might as well not depend on him. But to rejoice the last of my wishes without him was curdling my insides.

It was unnatural to be on the other side of his monotonous stare when I was ready to risk it all for him. I don't want to hide anymore. For once I wanted to throw myself into his arm and cry my heart out. Let my tears speak the pain I can't fathom myself. I want to tell him everything.

But wasn't to be heard a chore too- I can't bind a person that kept slipping away farther with days. All I could do was wait till I can't-

I thought of my family. Mom and her smile, Dad her his charms, Hwan and the boy he is today. Stupid, but with the right amount to go with. He is splendid when it comes to studies, his academic growth was a genetic gift from Mom. He might follow in her footsteps someday. Become a doctor- carry the legacy. But now I cannot take him seriously, but again- he is the first person that came to my mind. He was there by the shadows backstage- with a fruit bar and water. Asking me to not embarrass him by fainting or tripping. He was gruelingly concerned, fixing his emotions with occasional jabs.

I had pulled him into a hug, he was getting taller and taller by the day. But with the heels I had on, he only stood inch more-

"Thank you"

I whisper resting my cheek on his lean and boney shoulder. When he doesn't respond Is when I was sure of his guilt. He wasn't bleached with it, Hwan still thinks it was his fault. If I wasn't so keen on saving him- I could have ran off to safety that day. Sometimes it's evident how he treats me the toughest means possible so I could feel less vulnerable.

My brother was an living act with a kind heart that is traumatized by his own annoying brain.

So it's him I thought of calling first if the nosebleed won't stop. He was out there – he can help me. Fiddling with the clutch I surf the small canister of medicine that I always keep at hand for the headaches, when I find them I exhale with relief. Once I swallowed the pills without water I craned my neck up until the flow tamed after ten whole minutes holding up. When I heard a knock, my moves ascended frantically. Dumping the sheets into the bin I scrubbed my fingers and face till the only trace of redness on my face was my rash skin as a result of brittle wash.

I took a minute more to touch my make up recalling how this happened on the wedding day too. I was cooped up in the wash-room striving not to get the stains on the white dress- it was a déjà vu but with a black one. I can't seem to spot the change on my dress as the dark shade camouflaged them. and when I opened the door to see him-

The clearer did the day became.

It was all the same- except us. We weren't.

"What are you doing here?" the arena was open to the sky, from where I could see- the visitors were having a fun night with how goofy the music was. The lightings were brisk for a moment and lunged the next with a beat. since they were the only illuminative source so with it, Lee and I got plunged into darkness too-

But as I walked to him, the apparent lines of distress morphed into the calculated analysis. His suit was crisp as always, his hair styled ideal on him. But he was dissolving into someone that was an alien to me. I don't see my Lee here- he would've grilled me with questions the instant I stepped out.

Like he did before. On the random most doubts he had.

But the fact he knocked on the lady's washroom in search of me must mean something.

"Let's go home. I had a long drive and I can't wait to crash" he rubs his eyes as if making a point. If I could, I would like to split his skull in half to see what's going on with him. But by how I have behaved in prior with him- I learned my lesson.

But was he willing to even listen to me?

"Is that all you have got to tell me?" a wave of unexplainable emotion passed through him, then he sighed. My heart falls at his nonchalance.

"How about we get your tattoo done and then go home. Now that I think of it- there's something that I want to say"

I grit my teeth seething in a breath-

"Why do you want to? Don't you have important commodities to carry out?"

The radiance from LEDs paints him in a breeze, then it flails off. But not a speck of him changed. He was too steady to be factual. He asked me to wait for him that night- I waited for him, so long that I fell asleep on the couch. He wasn't there when I woke up, I was informed that he had to leave the town for some development procedure.

No calls.

No texts.

When he came back after a week- he was a hollow shell. So legitimately closed that attempting to even touch him was fruitless.

"I want to keep my promise" a full-blown wind rattles our hair and clothes, but I was too transfixed on him to care "I intend to be there since I was with you from the beginning"

I chuckle humorlessly, my passion drying with his.

"That promise of yours sounds like a hassle than an inclined one. You aren't as genuine about them as you were before" when he doesn't deny it, I look away when my vision blurs "Let's get this done with them, the faster. The better"

He doesn't oblige, so once we reach the fancy parlor he turns to me with a forgotten façade-

"Do you know what you want?"

The lack of reply from me seems to electrify his gaze into understanding. He doesn't coerce me into a talk- contrary to it, he lets the artist and I explore the symbols and designs.

"I know I want my name in a curve behind my left ear" browsing through the catalog I smile at the bearded man in a leather suit and whole tattoos peaking through his neck, the feel of Lee behind me intensifies as we talked "As for other, I want the symbol of promise by the inner corner of my pinkie"

He nods smiling, professionally detailing the fonts and measurements that he believes would fare me. While he prepares the equipment, he makes small chats once he realized how spinless Lee was with this whole situation. It was as if he was battling in his world to even open his mouth for suggestion.

"What's your name?" he finally asks me, tying his pepper gray hair into a bun "I haven't seen you both here. Ever" though he motions a glance at Lee, he doesn't divert the conversation to him. Lee was mutually mute for us.

"It's Shin-Young. If you haven't noticed yet- I am not familiar with this scene. It's my first time"

I shift when he asks me to- in the angle I witness a pinch of frown on Lee, it was gone the sooner he was a victim of my stare. He probably was wonderous of my tipping confidence. Even I was- the growth I've had since my diagnosis was profoundly impressive. When your future gets fogged, you cease crying over the present.

I still stagger.

But they don't have me in a vice.

"I can tell that" he hums as I add quickly.

"I also have an English name. it's the name I want to get inked "It rolls off my tongue gently "Elixir. It is"

He pauses his input with the needles and swivels over in the chair to look at me.

"Elixir- like the portion for eternal life?"

I jerk my head in agreement.

"You must be full of life to wish for an infinity"

Inhaling a quivering breath I let my head fall to the side, lifting my hair to reveal the canvas he has work with. I jump mildly when his hand enclosed atop of mine, his utterance came next.

"I will do it" I retreat my arm, letting him hold it for me. But Lee wasn't done yet "Will it hurt?"

It was indescribable since the inquiry came from a person who takes three shots of insulin a day. So when he gets told that it might slightly sting, the tripping tension on his face has me fuming. Wasn't grief and isolation the worse forms of pain than a physical one?

Wasn't he hurting me more?

When it got done, the artist plastered the raw patch with disin-fecting tape. Provided me with an ointment that I was instructed to use on before I go to bed tonight. So when I changed for the night in comfy shorts and top I stood in front of the dress struggling to get the gel across without my hair getting on its way.

I yelp when the tube gets yanked from by clutch with an undi-luted scold from someone who doesn't have a right on it-

"Can't you just ask?" unlike me, he was still in his formals excluding his tie and suit jacket. His brown dress shirts sleeve were rolled to his fore arms. The top buttons were undone. He reeked of frustration. Now that he wasn't wearing his coldness.

I try to snatch it back when he grabs my wrist and swats it away. Exhausted from the day and the loss of blood my lids droop into closure as he applied the icy balm on me. It's not him that was magical, it was the chemical composition of whatever was in it that soothed the burning reactions I was having. So I sigh, pleased at the relief.

"Does it hurt that bad?"

The audacity of him-

"Which one do you ask?"

The mighty Lee decides to meet my eye at that. His gaze fluttered as he swallowed in. He steps back pocketing his hands, neutralizing the unbalanced hope that flared in me.

"There has been a problem" he licks his lip, formulating more concerns in me "A federal prisoner managed to escape during transportation. He has been a threat to our family for a long time now"

It was scary to witness the zenith of hatred that seems to house in him. His jaw clenched in accord with his rigid stare. If it happened with my family- I might be in worse shape than him.

"Why did no one told-

"It's not safe for us to be here. We shall leave for US in shortly coming days-

"I am not going back to Vegas"

He moves collecting the sweatpants and shirt he had out for the night as if he had predicted my answer.

"Good thing. I wasn't even planning on it. We leave for Olando. It's more like my second home- I grew up there" in two steps I near

him and spun him into withstanding me. He turned with motive because there was no way I would be able to handle him with my strength.

"What I meant was, I don't want to go anywhere"

His gaze hardened, but voice remained passive as he changed course, simultaneously speaking his intentions.

His frigid and throbbing discretion that he seem to have decided for both of us.

"It's the best for us. It's temporary, only till he gets caught. By then let's pretend what we are doing so far" Was there the remorse that ailed me on his voice? No. Because all I heard was a Lee displaying facts- not a tint of sentiment he let pass. Was I too late? Do I even have the right to hurt when this is what I have been jeering him through all this time?

So I accept it.

Like a fool I stood obediently listening to his indications.

He was straight at it. No subtle corners. Too frontal for me to take in. But I do- Because one can only stop a mouth from speaking, But not ears from listening.

Or a heart from breaking.

"Let's end the marriage when we return. It's what I want too"

CHAPTER 32

S HIN

I had strolled aimlessly around and over by Elzina and Alexander Whites marble mansion. It was a layout that seems to come straight out of a fairy tale, with white and golden detailing, modern parlors, vintage study centers, and a diagonal guest sector. The ceilings were magnificently high at certain proportions making the hallway look spacious than it was. The pastel coloring gleefully enhanced what they had attempted to do and convey. The essence of heaven.

We were in Orlando- Florida. And by how precise my architectural admiration shone out, it's quite obvious to where Lee and I are staying in. For how long? Technically for that to be known I might have to convince my bouldering pride, so that I could talk to Lee.

I could do that.

Easy as a breeze by ocean.

But to get him to disclose why he was doing this?

I might probably have to threaten him with a mallet to his head. Or a gun from Alexander Whites collection to his liver. Or probably seduction to the bed.

If none of it works, I would simply pull my hair out and scream in frustration. Not that I don't see the imagery that far from morphing into reality.

After all this time he was hell-bent on waiting for me- he now decided to leave me be?

Leave me and now he goes around acting with his friends as if everything was splendidly blissful between us. Why does Edmund struggle with casting his actors when his friend delivers an Oscar-worthy performance on call? Lee became chirpier. The moment he rang the doorbell with balloons in clutch to wish Elzina on her birthday- his guard was intact.

Bitterly I felt the echo of his request from the morning as we drove from the airport.

"I don't want them to know," he said lowly, in rally I snort.

"Know what? That you have been having mood swings?"

It doesn't faze him. If only I could punch him- slightly to let the steam go. To let my hurt soothe. Is this how he felt when I had been through on avoiding him?

"It's better we stay with them. You'll have someone to kill your time with. Elzina also has a son- smart kid, you'll like hi-

"Are you afraid to be left alone with me?" with a disbelieving smile I turn to the window, watching this new city pass by. This is where Lee grew up- and is this where we grow apart? "Don't worry. I will behave"

This seems heat his kettle as he grunted.

"I didn't mean it like that. Isn't this what you wanted Shin?"

Shin- glad to know he still uses my name.

"Not until someone tried to convince me otherwise. Only for him to change his mind later"

Elzina did have a son. A little boy of five. Isaac white. Lee wasn't bluffing when he said I will like him. But what he forgot to mention was how critical It could get while you are conjuring tasks to get liked by him. So when Lee grumpily requested after his ageless goofy boy born with charming smile act for all to see with occasional loving gazes at me- I couldn't say no.

He wanted me to style Isaac for his Mother's birthday party tonight thrown by some business coordinator for her by the up-town. Since it involved the complex boy who looked so disinterestedly interested during the lunch we had with Mike, Riley, Elzina, and Alex- it took to the mentioned fact of me being a renowned author for him to express his thoughts.

"So you work with words?"

He looked at me with a piqued curiosity that was controlled, his big blue eyes blinked at me through his mane of a blonde hair. He looked like a tiger's cub. Fathers eyes and Mother's wit. I recall Lee addressing him as such.

He was going to break many hearts when he grows up.

And as for now, I can't break his faith in me. Something tells me every choice and move of mine were being judged by the boy who sat by the edge of his bed with his legs dangling mere the quarter from the corner. He had had a navy blue t-shirt on and some black striped shorts with socks. So as I searched his party wardrobe for a tuxedo he sat there chilled with eyes trained on the content I was piling by my arms.

Then I realized he was just a kid. I had no job or self-respect being so nervous around him. So I made small talks-

"You excited to go to the party?"

I lay the beige blazer and white shirt next to him on his bed.

"Do I look excited?" he muttered grumpily, stifling a smile I raise my brow as his eyes slightly go wide. I wasn't prepared for what came next "My apologies. That was impolite"

"It's fine. You can talk your mind with me" I wave off as he bobs his small head in a short nod. His eyes filling up with a mild childlike sentiment for the first time since I met him.

"No one is excited to go there. It's a business event- I am only attending so Mom won't get bored on her birthday"

I almost drop the pair of socks in the clasp.

"How old are you?"

"I turn six in four months" his brow furrowed.

"You are adorable" I exclaim as his face neutralizes in under-standing.

"I know" he looks down and stretches his hands by the lap "I can't wait to grow up. You are not going to pinch my cheeks or ruffle my hair are you Aunt Shin?"

Grinding my teeth from letting an awe slip through I remark-

"Aunt Shin?"

He shrugs again.

"I address uncle Lee as- well Uncle Lee. So logically that makes you my Aunt"

Organizing my inner new born Aunthood I place the suit in front of him to analyze the things I had put through.

"No, I won't certainly pinch you or de style your hair. I won't like that on myself"

I hear a soft sigh of relief from him.

"Finally someone who knows the value of privacy" then he adds as he collects his clothes and walks to his adjoining dressing room. "But poor you, uncle Lee just can't let someone adorable be. He has to hug them and keep playing with their hair. I sympathize if he treats you like a kitten too"

And when he was gone- it took me a minute to realize how true that was. Then I wait for him to step out -he took his time. And when he did come, it was a miniature of his father.

"I think you captured my style" he comments smugly, his tiny nose rising proudly as he smiles. It falters when he sees me tearing up unconditionally. It wasn't because of him- it was the chain of emotions wrapping me up. I needed someone to talk to-and this little boy was at the wrong place and wrong time. With Wrong me.

"I am sorry" I whisper shifting to wipe my tears.

"It's okay, Mom says one shouldn't be ashamed to cry. I cry too-"

"Why do you cry?" I was quick to display my worry as he rolled his eyes.

"I am just five. Remember?" then looked down at his untied shoelaces as if suddenly shy "Not many find me fun. I don't have many friends except my parents"

I got on my knees, at last facing him literally as I tied his shoes for him.

"It's enough. You'll find true friends as you grow up and you are more fun than anyone else I've ever met so far in life" I was surprised at how genuine I meant it. I've known Isaac for less than seven hours and I can trust him with my secrets. So I tell him-

"Your uncle Lee is being mean to me" his thoughtful frown earns a laugh from me.

"Uncle Lee? Mean?"

I nod gulping.

"Like how you smiled for me but not for all at lunch. He smiles for all and not with me. What should I do to gain his trust like I gained yours?"

For a minute he doesn't reply to me, while I do his tie I gave up -he probably didn't even understand what i-

"Don't attend the party. Get him to talk- Dad refuses to shower until Mom's anger cools down. Though what he does is unhygienic- you can use some other ways to get him to talk- Mom tickles me to get me laughing. I do laugh for her, but tickles don't work on me"

I blink at the man trapped in his body, He blushed deeper as I watched him. To ignore me, he adjusted his cuffs and checked his hair on the mirror-

"Please don't tell about my Dad to anyone. He honors hygiene more than anything- but he loves Mom just too much" he pockets a little vial of hand sanitizer inside his blazer and turns to me. I was still on the floor with my legs crossed and ears attentive "And if my advice works out, please help me with my crossword puzzle later as a payment"

I close the door with a loud bang once I am in the room. Lee looks up from his phone, his body tight in a tux, gaze startled but stony when he saw it was just me. I was in a gown- a dark purple laced gown with a thigh-high slit. My hair done and make up smooth on the skin. I was ready even before I left to help Isaac with his attire.

So the only job to be done now was to leave.

"We are not going to the party"

I announce as Lee stood up, unclipping the watch and slipping it to his wrist.

"From what I see you already are dressed and-

"I'll take it off. Shall I? right where I stand?"

I smirk in victory as his back goes stern with reaction to my words. When he turns, I sigh inwardly in ecstasy to finally see that confused, passionate but dark shadow in him. something than nothing-

"And what do we do here?" he gazed out into the empty spaces in the room as if the view of me was overwhelming him.

"We talk"

"And what if I don't want to?" he leaned by the bed table, seizing his car key and not waiting for my answer he walks to where I stood "You can stay here if you are tired from the journey, I'll go"

I watch him, with what I hope was coldness and unpredictable madness. Because the second he stepped to move aside I fisted his collar. He grits a what the hell are you doing with a seeth- but doesn't force himself out of my hold in fear of hurting me. It was a relief- so when I drag him to the washroom, with him gently holding on to my wrist in an attempt to slip it off- I use my shoulder to push through the glass door of the shower both. With freehand, I press on the digital screen letting the complete room rain on us.

He tried to push me away before the water could engulf him, but I was quicker with plans. I kiss him, hugging him closer with all I had. My strength and passion, fuelled by the steaming water on a cold night as he gives in.

But when he returned the kiss, my corporated thoughts became clumsier. Before I knew I was pressed against the booth wall and his coat was off- his soaked shirt a transparent mess as he broke the kiss with heavy pants. The water weighs my lashes as I whisper breathlessly with a smile.

"Your tux is ruined. Still want to go?"

He curls his finger down my chin, lifting my face until our lips were a hairs breath away.

"I have few others, but something tells me you'll find a way to make them useless before I could get my hands on it"

Then he was kissing me again, I gasp at the unnerving ferocity of it when he lined lower to the crook of my neck I whimpered my question out.

"What is it Lee?" he stops, he moves to look at me- the lust vanishing as something else sets in its place. Sadness? Anger? I don't know- I wouldn't until he tells me. "What changed?"

He reaches for the padlock, and with a touch, the fervor of water comes to a halt. He cups my face and pressed his drenched forehead against mine.

"Why did you marry into a family that had given you nothing but pain?"

It stuck on my throat, the last of my sensible breath. This is not how he was supposed to-

"How do you know?" he closed his eyes as I mirrored him, better to not see into each other than fall ill to a vulnerability that we can't afford now.

"That wasn't my answer"

"I married you. Never had I held grudge against the people who didn't know of my existence"

"Why not tell me?" he bounds me into a hug, burying my head into his chest I let the current of his scent ail me. hHe was here- he just needs to know, he won't leave me. But what was I to do?

Wish and pray to not leave him? Fight and live? Will my fate have such pity for me? "I can't even apologize to you when I can't even forgive myself"

"It wasn't your fault"

"It was my family that bastard was after" his chest trembled with hostility, his tone sharper to it's edge. "Why didn't you tell me?" He asks again. Much softer and tired in utterance, running his hand through my wet hair he coils me in firmer. Warmer.

For how long has he been blaming himself?

"I am sorry," I say, but froze when a striking headache spheres through me when I tried to make sense. How much does he know?- Because if he knew it all he wouldn't have –

A cough fights through me as the taste of metal fills my mouth. I cup my mouth with a gasp-

"Shin- Are yo-

I saw it, the perplexed worry in his eyes. A rising panic when I looked down at my hand that came out slick with blood. All I could think of was- He didn't know it all. Lee didn't know.

And once more- he wasn't supposed to find it this way. But late it was as I hear him scream my name. My vision becomes a series of blur, his desperate calls a faraway echo. It was his arms holding me- and I scarily was contended with dying in the embrace of a person I love.

Maybe not today.

But if ever the time comes- if ever Lee stays. I will die happy.

CHAPTER 33

LEE

Dr. Sim Do won, he is the one who came up when I had whisked through her belongings to find her medical files. Anything that I could get my hands on as the medics from the center had asked for. Buried beneath her piling books and editorial documents I had managed to pull out a thick binder etched with the logo of her family's medical facility.

And also a bag packed with cans of pills and pain shots.

The feathery feel of her fainting into my arms still remained fresh, the choking dread when I saw the blood by her chin and neck had only increased until I saw the lack of surprise or wonder in Shin's eyes. They were sad and tired. And I hated it.

I hated the fucking idea that folders into me.

Has this happened before?

Is this something that was also hid from me?

What was even happening?

That was when my gut kicks in, deranged and crazed I had carried her, sensing the rising temperature in her skin as my friends erupted in action to get my destination straight. I drove the car while Elzina sat by the passenger seat doing her best with the anatomical knowledge she pursues to stop Shin from bleeding out.

A look through the rear, I saw the plight and worry in her eyes. The pale stack of napkins she had used to press on, all drenched.

The silent glances that Alex kept nurturing from the side while ordering up a team of qualifiedly ranked doctors to join in were the only reason I was able to keep up with driving. My heart lurched for reassurance, for Elzina to whip up her intellect and tell me that it was nothing but some dehydrated imbalance.

But the bottle of pills and the package of test reports from recent dates lying by the conference table as the two doctors trade what it reads with a stoic silence has me in an iron hold. Shin was stable, the bleeding had stopped. She was rushed into intensive care as soon as we arrived. They wouldn't tell us what's wrong because they couldn't till they ran tests on her. Elzina and Alex never left my side, though Alex kept coercing Elzina to get some rest- all she did was use her membership card and used the nearest guest room to get the blood from her top.

It was Elzina's birthday. Shin and I were to be at a party- with how gorgeous she looked tonight with her bold eyes glowing and actions charring through me- we were supposed to ditch the gala and spent the night in each other's arms. We should have talked each other out of the pain and hurt we were diligently putting through. Not- not this.

This night was not this.

"We have to contact Dr. Sim Do won, the neurologist from south Korea who apparently had been looking after Ms Shin Young's case.

We are preparing for the video meet and we need someone who is-

I hadn't even listened to the end of the nurse's reasoning, I was on my feet and to the conference room. A woman with sunset red hair and a tall man with a sharp nose and wise eyes stared up at me when I had entered.

"I am Shaun Lee, I am her husband. How is she?"

I don't have time to read their badges or memorize the name to see who in the world is tending to her. All I want to know was that she was fine. As fine as everyone is in this room. But they smile politely at me as they asked me to take a seat.

I sit with my gaze still questioning them,

"We would like to know for how long have you been accompanying and following up with Ms shin Young with her medical –

"I haven't"

Their lips clip as I swallow the bitter truth in and puzzle them in a sentence.

"I am not aware of what happened today. I don't even know if this had happened before"

But what I starvingly wish to know now is that whatever it is- it is okay.

The doctors were quick to mask their opinions of me. But I wasn't backing off- I had been a terrible man to her. But hasn't she been the same? Hiding it all from me? Before they could swap out a new query a young-looking male who I presume was his assisting intern declared that Dr. Sim Do-won was live from Korea.

The blue screen on right to us lights up and neutralizes with a man in his wrinkled white coat and disheveled hair. His rimless glasses peaks halfway through his pocket. It was bright on the

other side- early in the morning. But his eyes were sharp and too familiar for me to brush off.

He was the man I saw shin with, the one she denied to know initially till I had confronted her morbidly. She had called him her friend.

For a second our eyes meet- a flash of recognition passes through him. But he recovers quickly only to blurt out-

"How is Shin?" then he waves it off and dives into the heart of it. Nothing that I seem to understand at first- But soon I do. Bit by bit, Pieces by pieces. Scraping as they discuss the internal trauma that had resulted in what she has been suffering throughout the year.

A year.

I almost laugh at the immense physical anguish I felt at that. They spoke of surgery- and the success rate, and it's when I burst out.

"What do you mean by success rate?"

I didn't realize how hard I had been clutching onto the armrest of the chair till the doctor's voice resonates through the screen- I only wanted to burn my finger through its leather.

"As difficult, it is to state, we can't keep you in the dark Mr. Lee. We have to be prepared for the worse. Even if we succeed to stop the internal bleeding- the rate of shin falling into a stage of coma is-

I don't think I heard him after that.

I didn't want to hear him after the nonsense he was spewing. So when the Doctors left me so I could make my decision up I stared at the man on screen, I watched his professional demeanor slip off as he rubbed his eyes, a flush of fatigue seem to fall on him as he spoke-

"I didn't want to meet the man shin spoke so much about in such circumstances. But I can't help but see why she said she can't have found a better person even if she used her whole life. She would laugh later making jokes about how short her life could be if everything goes wrong" he chuckled with a sigh, "I hated how she had such a dark sense of humor" his smile was grim as I finally saw it for the first time. She wasn't lying. He was her friend.

"I can't let anything happen to her"

"She won't like that false hope. I also disliked how much of a realist she was"

"And I don't care what she thinks"

His smile in amusement.

"She also was right about your stubbornness"

It soared my anger as my teeth grind in a clinch.

"If so, can I expect to ask a stranger the reason why a girl who claimed to love me would hide this from me?"

His answer caught me off guard.

"No one she loves knows. Not even her parents" he exhales with might, as if telling me that was a relief to him. I think I had stopped breathing. "It was her choice to keep it a secret. She didn't want her last healthy days to be monitored by her loved ones with pity. She wanted to live and be loved for who she really is. Its what her wishes were all about"

He pauses and adds, the room seems to trap me inside as I seem to be trapped within my own body. To many layers to feel the light on me. I wanted to throw the monitor away, Watch it shatter into a useless entity. Wanted the person gone from my view who seem to have made amends with something that shouldn't even be real.

Last healthy days?

What does the fuck even mean?

"I am glad she had someone to share her wishes with"

Of course, he knows of them. He probably knows more of how she felt about me than me myself. When she wakes up I have to see to it that it won't be this way in the future.

In the future where everything is perfect.

But I had one last question that I have been burning my throat. If not now- I would never be able to face it. Despite how desperate I was for this to be a nightmare, I know I have to know how this began.

"You said Shin sustained the internal trauma when she was young. Do you know how?" the sentence ends with a whisper as I saw his shoulder square with hateful malice. It was the first minute I had seen him lose the purposeful coolness in his mannerism.

"She got It from her kidnapper when she was abducted at eleven of age"

It finished there. Our conversation. I couldn't move from my spot, I couldn't feel the realness of the situation I was in. After the day I came to know of her abduction- I hadn't been able to eat, sleep or think. Estranging myself away from her.

How naive I was to think that freeing her from me would solve all our problems when every element of us seem to bind us with a past where none of us could have helped each other.

Every inch of me screamed at me to react with the blinding agony they were hoping I feel. I was alone, I was alone here with the fear of losing her. A fear that was paralyzing me like nothing that ever had.

I inhale a mouthful of air at first, then soon my racing heart joins in. My hand tears against my hair as my elbow rests by the desk. My lips quiver as the tears gather by my vision. A scream leaves me, soon morphing into a desperate sob.

I don't stay still. My body shakes with each breath. I can hear the door being opened and someone rushing to me.

I don't understand why.

Alex embraces me into him.

I don't know why.

The cries don't stop.

I don't feel the pain.

Not when the grief was so intense that It kept drowning the reasons I was breaking down for.

Chapter 34

S HIN
   I had time.

It's what I was told. Hoped. Wished and prayed on.

I thought I had it. A year maybe. More even.

It's when I had stamped on, finalizing my deal with a man I barely knew. An angelic face with a skeptical frown, cautious but comical when need be. Stanger then, but a silhouette that embraces my happiness now. He was no one back then, but today he was everything that I wanted to live for.

I thought I had the f-king time.

Dreams that came and went, in them, I was aware of it, receptive of it being an illusion. A series of a blurry mess, they were half-conscious and mostly sedated. I know they were dreams. I saw my family, my dog, my fish- the warm cup of genuine chocolate drink that I love so much from Gangnam clutched between my hands, the pleasant smile of my brother as a kid while we made sandcastles by the shore- it was the only time we got along with respect.

Even in fantasies, my breath slows down when I see him. This wasn't a dream- it was a memory from a night. It was the day before we had our first fight on the island. He had his head rested on top of my belly as he read his favorite parts from the book. My book.

Though his face was hidden by copy, the soft enthusiasm in his tone was almost as if he was reading it for the first time.

"I can never get over this," he says as I play with his hair, they were so smooth in touch. almost like silk. I would be envious if mine weren't better than him.

"Really? If I told you what inspired me to write that- you won't be able to see It the same way again" chuckling I watch him peek through the top of the binder, his eyes getting big and curious. Then he shakes his head. The very copy that he had forced me to sign for him in three different colors in his clutch. It wasn't a new edition, in fact, it was the special one- it even was worn out at the edges. It was his copy.

And he was a fan .

You could see it from the way he seem to realize in intervals that I was the person behind the characters he treats as his own. He blinks at me before accusing me of homicide. Then he expresses his wonder at how I gave birth to so many different characters while still being so young. He was convinced that I had a hidden serial killer in me. And also a passionate lover – a maniac scholar or a short-tempered blacksmith.

He loved Shin. But with Elixir. He was an avid negotiator. Didn't hold back from criticizing or praising what fascinates him. Which was a lot.

"I don't think I want to ruin the emotions it carries by asking you" there was a pause, and then "can I ask you something else?"

"Go ahead. It's not like you'll pass if I deny"

"You know me too well by now" he laughs. I lift one of my shoulders in a proud shrug.

"Why Elixir?"

It caught me off guard. Especially when he dropped the book beside me and rolled to the side, Spanning his entire attention on me. All the lies I know I was capable of constructing died inside when I saw the earnest manner with which he regarded me. I went with the truth.

"The idea of long life use to fascinate me"

His brows pinched in disbelief.

"Used to? What about at present?"

I couldn't help the smile on me. Mimicking his position I cup my face with my elbows digging on the mattress.

"I think it lost its focus to a man who seems to give meaning to my whole life in just few moments"

Gasping as I tear my eyes open wasn't the hardest part, waking up from a beautiful dream was. Because I was living a nightmare. I was a nightmare for him. For my family. For everyone who seems to care for me. Love me.

It was calm. Too quiet and cold in the room. I was alone here lying on the bed with the faint beeps of monitor breezing through. I breathe with my lips parted. Slow and steady, I feel no reminiscence of pain that I had felt every single wise I had woken up from my slumber. Each wise only to slide into the darkness.

Was it morphine? Fentanyl?

Or the usual Dr. Do-won strategy to keep me sedated until I had temporarily healed. I know he was here- I saw him put me back to sleep every damn time I woke up. I know my mother cried from somewhere when I lost consciousness. She felt so far away. The voices of the medics talking, dictating, or simply reading things out drowns out. Then gone. Completely.

This time it does happen that way, even the room was different.

I tried moving my fingers and my toes and it did do as I command, I sigh, my craned head falling back to my pillow with a smile.

I was still alive and functioning.

"Only you could smile like that after waking up from a three-day nap"

I turned to look at the source of the voice, he was there – seated by the window on the far corner that I seem to have skipped during my survey. I wasn't alone here- I think I never was since the moment I fainted in his arms.

"Lee" I breathe, my lashes weigh my vision. He was by my side in two good strides. Perks of long legs I reckon.

"Don't talk" he urges, pouring me a glass of water and helping me up, and the rim to my lips. The taste of water on my tongue makes me realize how thirsty I was- I don't listen to him when he advises me to take it down slowly. I chug it in.

This wise a huge sigh heaves me up as he uses the tissues to dab it down my soaked cotton gown and chin. I close my eyes letting the thirst quench. Like a child, I lean on him when he assuringly runs his hand over my hair. He sat on the bed, close enough to embrace me so carefully that in a sudden blast of anger I grab his shirt hook my IV stabbed hand by his. Pulling him into a hug with a strength that required my sum.

"I am not that weak" I grumble, my breath hot as I sense his nod by my ear.

"Who said you are" shoving him away slightly, I look at him in the eye.

"Then why do you look like you haven't slept in days?"

He searches my face as he answers,

"You did sleep for both of us"

Despising the quickness of how my eyes teared up to see him fighting everything he probably was going through because of my lies I provided him with my useless-

"I am sorry"

-apology.

"I am so sorry" I repeated angrily. Also falling apart in front of him.

My face was soon grabbed by his hands and his thumb wipes away the caged frustration I had for so long. To let this go was freedom. he doesn't stop me- all he says was,

"You don't have to apologize" unwilling, i try to deny when he firms his hold "You heard me? There is nothing to apologize for"

The golds from the lights reflect his brimming tears, but now that I see them in clear they weren't pained or mad. But under-standing and brave.

"It did hurt a lot at first" he saves me the stress, he smiles as he spoke "But I think I saw the reason later, or at least I try to. Good thing you were asleep for three days until I got back on track. But I also hated how peacefully knocked out you were while I didn't know what to do or how to feel. I shouldn't be saying this- but I don't know what else to do. Can you even get me?"

I nod frantically with a tight smile. he was still the same Lee – despite our lack of conversation for days, he still seem to bring me the light or be the light I fell in love with. Confused and confident, vulnerable but brave. A wall of hope that he is- and he seems to stand his ground strong enough to let me lean and rest. To let go. So I do it.

"I am scared" I whispered " I am so scared Lee"

When I say it. I seem to see it. see everything in a clearance. A liberation from the misery I carried for so long. Alone.

"I know" he whispers back, leaning his forehead against mine. "But I won't let anything happened to you"

No.

I don't want that.

"Please don't make such promises" all I could do was beg, but still selfishly hope for him to save me. I was young, I am at the peak of my life to demand that my wishes be granted. But young was he too. I can't burden him with something he-

"Stop thinking Shin. I am not making promises here. Promises are for things we are forced to keep or have faith in. I believe in us"

A moment passes as we let it. But when I take his appearance in finally my eyes go sharp.

"How can you expect me to be healthy if you look like a disaster?" I scold sniffing, scanning his wrinkled shirt and pale face.

He looks down at him with a chuckle. Our stares are still moist. We are both aware of the sensitivity of the situation. But still attempting to defy it with what we have at hand. Each other.

We have each other. Without lies or secrets.

And that was enough.

"A handsome disaster?"

"I may be even regretting marrying you now as you speak"

"I can go, fix myself. But I don't want to leave your side. I have been waiting for so long for you to wake" his tone dips as our fingers find each others in a grasp. He brings it to his lips, his long lashes were damp and eyes red by the corners.

What if I don't wake up one day?

What happens then?

I don't want him to wait like this.

I also want him to never let me go.

Holding my head up I narrow my eyes accusatively at him.

"If I get better and live for good long years and you die early, I'll make sure to kill you myself"

My remark buys me a surprised frown until I add-

"When's the last time you took your shot?"

His mouth parts in understanding, he lifts his hands in mock surrender with a face that was preparing for excuses. But it was too late before his reflexes worked. My knuckles had already connected with his forehead.

In that seconds I had made my mind up. I wanted to fight with what I have, if he believes in us. The most I could do is believe in myself.

I was never the one to accept defeat before the battle commenced.

And he was the one who I know would never stop striving even if there was no light to begin with. Together, we were bound to find a way out of this.

Because there is no way I am dying early only for him to join me soon up there.

Two more chapters and an epilogue. Oh God.

CHAPTER 35

S HIN

My brother wasn't as interactive as I had foreseen him to be. He stormed off the room when I had disclosed the childish reason behind why I hid my status from them. I explained why I yearned to live on my own terms and not had them worried during the earlier stages because that wasn't going to lead me anywhere. They had been on edge their whole life because of me- I couldn't bear it any longer.

They didn't get it. I didn't expect them to. I envisioned myself in their shoes- I might have been pissed beyond scripture if I was them. Understandable. But when they took some days to pacify and reach a belief is when it got tense. The shift meant how real this all was.

The week at the hospital I was treated with utmost devotion and care- the lighthearted conversations we shared while Lee attempted to soak in all the Korean humor that he was clueless about. We all laughed while he frowned on his mobile screen deciphering the meaning of what we meant. Dad had the most fortunistic quotes at his disposal as he occasionally hugged me goodbyes during the night. Years of importing fortune cookies had taken a toll on him- he was a living motivational Pinterest page and it helped me so much with sleep along with the countless drugs that they pump through me.

I wake up to see the bags under the eyes of Lee, his fatigue and stress glossy as he greets me every morning. His comforter crumpled beside the visitor's couch. The only time he breathes in solace is when I kiss him and assure him of my Well Being. It's then the guilt weighs me down- he was always quick to notice it as he tries to cheer me up with an unpredictable strategy.

Smuggling homemade food or letting me dye his hair to ash blonde, we even solved a jigsaw puzzle of a panda having spaghetti along with Edmund. It was something he brought along with him when he visited me- Fischer was there too.

They both were the loudest of all the visitors I had so far.

There was no sympathy, just support, and faith. They were convinced as they spoke of my cameo in the movie, the actress the production plans on casting, my input as a scriptwriter or everything on the project that was a promise of future, and it's then I saw the radiant grin occupy the gorgeous features of Lee and so on me.

I did get discharged with still no response from Hwan.

"Why has he stopped being the annoying prick that he is?" curiously I asked Lee when I spot him by the door. He was just about to enter aiming to find some peace in our room. The one which still came under the guest sector of Elzina and Alexander Whites domicile.

Lee cautiously walks and sits next to me on the bed, plucking the wrappers of crisps and chocolates that lay decorated on the bed after I had them.

"Probably because he is still- I don't know, angry with you?"

He doesn't look at me but directs his interest on sweeping off the crumbs with his palms.

When I ceased to reply for a while, he diverts his gaze at me. The love and anguish that swirled in them has me in a vice. His smile never colors his face- I pale within realizing if this is how he had felt. Still feels. Betrayed and hurt. With so much that happened, with the rest of the dominant meds I seldom had the stability to think of the aftermath. Of what must have happened when I was asleep. What he must've gone through.

I saw him assembling hope.

But I never saw him break. Or what piece of him change during the course.

He must've seen the regret, tempting me to peel away from him, his brow arcs as his arms wrap around me pulling me gently flush against him.

"You overthink" he warns.

"What if you hadn't thought it over" I had to argue no matter how much this guts me "What if this is just sympathy and you might not even like me-

"Love shin. And quit trying to believe anything else because all you are doing right now is hurting me" his honesty seals me up as my lips pressed into a thin line. His sharp stare checks for some crack, he nods satisfied "With that set, give him some time. He will come back around" I yelp when he scoots me into his lap, hooking his arms beneath my knees. Sighing in ecstasy when he nuzzled his nose against my neck, I weave my fingers in his soft strands.

"I missed your warmth so much. I missed everything about you when they didn't let me in to see you" in response I bit back a moan because apart from what he was saying, all I could feel was his lips trailing fire down my collarbones then by my jaw. When our lips meet- I know I could commit arson for this man and won't think twice about it.

A month- in thirty good days I was scheduled for the surgery. Dr. Do Won was scheduled fly here as well since he was the one who graphed my proceedings so far. Lee and his connections led us to some of the most reputed practitioners in this field with impressive records. They made sure to still fill us in with the downside.

They were humans. Not God.

But it did little to blow out the happiness I felt with these people. Elzina was an amazing woman- and Isaac was a little ball of einstinely genius which had adults fuming and scowling at their own intelligence when the scrabble tiles constructed by the Elzinas child was too sophisticated and classy than their own.

Fischer, Lee, and Edmund- it took three men to come up with the word swan while Isaac single-handedly spelled out pelican by the point booster hence giving us a win. Elzina and I merely sat there deluding to help and watch the three grown men call out Isaac for luck.

"You are such an Elzina" commented, Lee, at the young boy's smug face. "But that smile looks so much like your father" his glare only fed the cheeky grin of Isaac. We all reclined on the ground with our legs tucked, the luxurious rug that spread by the floor of the study delicate beneath us. We were also gathered here because Elzina was too bored and desired to watch her friends sweat their language off to her angelic child.

Also, her husband appeared nakedly pissed and sick to see the numerous people lounging at his home. He- how should I put it? He wasn't much of a people's person if I may say so. But when found alone in pass- he does gives you a nod with a short smile. Asking how the day was and if I need something if he was feeling refreshed that morning. Or it could be the sympathy for sick in my case. You may never know with that man. So when he asked me if their was some requirement during my early morning walks-

I did had one. We did ran out of toothpaste, he was kind enough to bring me a hand sanitizer from his supply cabin and a mouth wash too.

It made me wonder if he thought of me as an unhygienic hazard. Lee was quick to remind me of Alexander and his sanity obsession. Alexander white looked the happiest ever when I complimented the fragrance of the disinfectant that he gave me the next morning. I finally saw his teeth.

It was an achievement.

I received a handful of packages through Elzina sent by him the next day.

"This is embarrassing" Edmund mumbles.

"I am used to that" shrugged Fischer.

"Actually no. The most embarrassed I have ever been was when Lee forced us to get our cards read during a vacation when we were sixteen" Edmund sprawled his limbs rolling to his stomach and stared up at Lee with a grin. Lee wasn't entertained.

"ooo- I know of that" Elzina snorted tugging the collar of her dress and throwing a glance at me. "It's something that still haunts Alex" she whispers as Lee rolls his eyes casting a sly glance at me.

"Isn't that a bit dramatic for him?" Lee states. Fischer and Isaac were on a duel player phase already- this conversation was just a rim for them. Elzina runs a loving hand through her son's hair- the kid groans and combs it up with his finger as she giggles.

She certainly was adorable, the mystery of how she ended up with Alexander was a dark fairy tale that Lee narrated, it only increased my respect to think of what they had been through. She was kind but powerful. It was intimidating and beautiful. So was Lee. So were they all.

"He is a drama queen. But so is Lee. I wonder what Shin thinks of this incident" as anxious it was, when she spoke I couldn't help the amusement at the stories that map the young Lee and his shenanigans. He had a vicious and theatrical childhood. He still was same if you dig deeper.

"He dragged Alex and me to this shady fortune tellers parlor because he was desperate to know who of us three was bound to get married first"

Lee ignorantly played with the alphabets, casing and uncasing them as if it wasn't him that braids this revelation.

"I never pegged him as someone who believes in astrology" I exclaim as Edmund bursts out laughing.

"I don't" sterns Lee whose voice fell so small that I could barely hear him.

"Then why was it the only thing you read before exams and not the syllabus?" this wise it was Elzina and at last Fischer seem to flip out after losing another game as he sat up to judge Lee with his full potential.

"Don't worry. I don't judge" Fischer remarks.

"Oh well Fischer- but its written all over your face" I grin- this man can always ease my nerves and he knows it so he grins back at me feeling the roast that bubbled in me "You are happy that you aren't the only one in the room radiating weird vibe"

We even hi-fived at that, it earned us calculated frowns from every pair of eyes in the room. None here was clinically aware of the relationship Fischer and I share- he was like Hwan to me. We text and discuss oninon rings and we do it with pride.

"Oh come on Shin" began Lee smiling with cunning dignity and rolling the sleeve of his shirt to his elbows knowing exactly how this affects me "I stopped believing in constellations when Alex got married. I believed in self- when I did"

Though the tension was crisp on-air while Edmund seem to enjoy it through the view of the director, Elzina came to rescue her block of ice.

"Why? What's wrong with Alex?"

Lee looks at her with a charming smile, it was his most danger-ous trait.

This was answered by Edmund through sideline-

"Well- for instance, the psychic was positive that the energy she receive from Alex was a bit alien. So I was supposed to get married first and then Lee- Alex had no scope. We paid her double the price because of how furious Alex looked then" this laugh was shared by them all with an exclusion to Elzina who squinted her eyes passively.

"Are you alright?" I ask controlling my grin, she doesn't answer- when the room sobered up she had the attention of us until It seem to hit me. "wait- what did Alexander tell you?"

She slowly turns to me, her eyes sparks with mysterious strategy. They seem to smile and plan at the same time.

"He said he was told that any woman that marries him was the most blessed bride of the three. Lee was the alien. And Edmund liked men"

There was a crackle of a laugh from me in the silence , soon Fischer followed, then Edmund- who seemed a bit tipsy for a man who lost the game. When my eyes met Lee's, he has the faintest smile igniting his way to those brown orbs. The gaze seem to drink in my happiness and I didn't fall short of how much these people kept me on my toes during the smelting days.

It seem to be a rocky journey and the ship I was in waddled with how low my mind dunked when I was alone.

But for that to happen often, I must be alone. And they had figured out how to seize every opportunity they got to come and help me and Lee with it. Edmund and Fischer made me laugh until I couldn't hold my tears in. The hug from Isaac I received when I returned from my stay at the hospital was the start of my healing. Elzina was the woman who seem to put the sense back on my feet by not trying hard to reach me- but reminding me that -when ever in need, she is always there for me if I craved to talk.

When I first broke down to her a few nights ago when I had to reach her for the things I can't tell Lee, she impaled me with a comforting hug and maintained the mess I was with an under- standing and acceptance that none could have done. She was an angel.

And if I ever wished for an elder sister in my life, it would be someone like her. I have enough undermined sibling to ask for more immaturity crawling by.

But the talk I had with her, it was the instant note that rattled my heart. The moments of bliss seem to make me forget the fate I must face. And in few seconds nausea hits me- every fiber that made my body slows down painfully with fear and awe at how my thoughts affect my body. The clock was my enemy.

Be it during the dinners with my parents or when I see Lee awake at night by his laptop, his fingers tearing through his hair, and the vulnerability he seems to mask through the day coming undone only because he thought I was asleep.

Every night I feel him coming back to bed, closing in, and wrapping me secure in his arms. Sometimes he would rest his head on my shoulder. In others, he would kiss my forehead. I don't know when he falls asleep, while pretending I - somewhere between guilt and love seem to prefer the state of unconsciousness better. At least that way I don't have to see the Lee I fell in love with fade.

But that didn't stop us from going on those fun unplanned dates, he took me to his schools. Boasted in and over the tales of his image as a popular kid. We went to a musical and decided that we either sucked at appreciating a classic genre or that the musical was indeed really bad. It was the latter, so we screamed our hearts out at a karaoke booth. I learned that Lee was good with joystick and I somehow wasn't allowed to buy alcohol because I looked younger than twenty-one. They won't accept my ID.

We wanted to buy the drinks not because we decided to get drunk, it happened so that Lee was sure that I would be denied that pass. He too thought that same when he saw me first.

But with weeks due to surgery, my stamina plunged and our trips elasticated to that one that involved short strolls by the garden and daily chores by the house. And with just five days that remain, I could think of nothing else but having Lee by my side. so when Elzina and Alexander White announced that they plan on having dinner tonight at some business advocate's birthday party, my first instinct was to devour shrimp and ramen for the dinner.

It was Sunday and since we had the house to ourselves I desired to relive the moment spent in vegas again.

"You can order me around, I will do it the exact way that you-

Lifting my index to his lips I squint my lids seductively. I noticed it's one of the many and quick effective methods to get him to do things my way. Like always, it does the job.

"You just have to manage the mess before your friend comes back. God forbid what his reaction will be he noticed oil sprinkles in this aprons" I whisper, the sultry smile in his face cemented my victory.

"Anything else for my queen?" he asks with a bow. I adjust the headband like the queen that I am.

Curving into the cabinets I surf for the spices. The kitchen in this mansion was a maze in itself, the areas wide, the equipments sophisticated, the interior grandiose. The kitchen was a high-end forensic lab until I open the drawers to see the jars of ingredients and vessels lined inside.

"You can watch me as I sexily cook for my husband" flipping my hair over my shoulder I wink at him, bad choice since I got lifted into the island, I fiddle with words to say but strangely I don't when he cuts me off with his.

"Why watch her when I can have her?"

I loop my arm confidently by his neck pulling him closer, If I had to I can write poetry on how addictive his fragrance was. or how enchanting his skin felt against mine, or how in such moments of intimacy he gives me life and love that could last me an eternity.

"Then what's holding you back?"

My heart could explode if it was possible, instead, It was a ring of reminder that I was alive. But when he kissed me the gentle consummation made me smile into it. He breaks the kiss to rake me questioningly-

"Am I funny?" the hoarseness in his query tingles my insides, to know how my simple gestures consume him was not funny. It was sexy, he was a symbol of it when he wants to be.

"No- but to think you used to trust the astrology reading is"

His chuckle was music to my ears so I nod my head like a child waiting for him to defend.

"I used to until my destiny started being a bitch to me," he says, it kills the diverse thoughts that were spiraling through me. when he noticed his mistake he shook his head in warning. His warm hand holds my face vicely "It's also because I realized that I am the only one who can change things over. I want to look at you in the eyes while I talk and not think of what my mind or stars align for. I want to love you with my heart, and heart is the only part of me I am willing to trust on. It led me to you- and it's his responsibility to get us through this"

Smiling through the relief and passion we end up kissing again, making out by the counter even after a mug crashes down the floor as a sacrificial trait of our feral movements. It was the loud footstep and a mechanical o sorry that brought us back from the high land.

We both turned to look at an amused Alexander white in his sleek business suit standing in a cross dilemma by the entrance as if contemplating to leave or not. I push Lee away and slip to the floor combing my hair into place as I heard Elzina call her confused husband from somewhere far-

"The car keys are in the bowl Alex" is what she says- "And what was that noise" this wise it was nearer, but Alexander had a tactic and gentlemanly decency so when Lee rolled his eyes annoyed at his friend – his response was to stop his wife from coming in-

"Stay wherever you are Elzina, there are two wild cats on lose here" it was a piece of new information- so Immediately I scanned around till Lee nudged me on the side and whispered that he meant us. I had to remind myself that I wasn't stupid- I was simply startled to the point that I was acting like one. I swear I am smart.

"What? I instructed Marie countless wise to keep the windows shut but she-" babbled Elzina from somewhere- Alexander picked his key up and after a sweep of faintly humoring and icy glance at Lee- it stops by the mug we broke-

"Honey" he calls-

"What is it now?" calls a desperate Elzina. I could feel my nerves in my neck, Lee was calm. But suspicious.

"The restless cats seems to have targeted isaacs favored milk mug- we might have to hunt for a new one"

I speculate that it was a play of light, I saw a glimmer of a smile on his lips before he pockets the keys and finally leaves. And when we were alone once more, we had our respective questions diverted at no one in particular-

"What now?"

Was mine and it made sense.

"Why cats?"

Were his- which made more sense.

I might relish to theorize that he was secretly a cat enthusiast. But mostly I knew that they left for the night so we could have some alone time before the time to our big day cease by. The whites were one great family. They just weren't anticipating the improper use of their kitchen and their son's favorite mug ending up in the floor in pieces while they played their role of a hospitable host perfectly.

CHAPTER 36

L^{EE}

Her beauty enough was capable of distracting me despite the dire tension that lurked by the corners of my heart. I found out that my survival depends on hers. That laugh of hers, they mold my sanity. If anything was to ever happened to her, I would live for the sake of its responsibility. When I spotted her after my conversation with the surgeons I stayed cemented by the doorway. The dull cotton gown was sized large on her thinning frame, her skin shone with her smile the second her brother hugged her. Whatever the differences he had carried came to an end last night when I got these two to interact in a safe zone where Hwan wasn't screaming at her and she wasn't dissing him out for being the impolite younger brother.

She gets intensely feisty when she speaks her home tongue. And for the sake of Hwan and his pride-

I had to make them reconcile. Especially when she described her relationship with him.

"He was the only person who treated me without a care. I was normal for him- I can't bear him look at me the other way"

Two hours prior to the surgery, the room sluggishly started to host the visitors. Her parents were the worst of all-they seem to have doubled in age while Shin kept her stance strong through it. I had chanced to distract myself with everything I possibly could- I didn't seem to occur in the moment. Because when she had hugged me and I had ensured her with the practiced promise to endure for her- I couldn't memorize her voice.

I know that she spoke of how much she can't wait to come back, the crack of it and the trembling whisper of her love for me. Too numb to mean it then I had kissed her- the words I could comprehend died in my mind. My tongue parched and my throat constricted- my heart that went into frenzy and my body that seem to have stoned itself seems to work as two different commodities.

Childishly I fist my hands to savor her touch that she left on them right before they wheeled her through the theatre. She had closed her eyes then, I wonder what she thought of. I despise what I can't seem to fathom now.

My denial was stark. Stubborn and aggressive.

Hwan sat beside me in silence, unlike me- his jittering legs kept restlessly tapping against the floor. His focus seems to hauntingly reach for the panels through which they took his sister. When he finally addressed her- I wish he hadn't.

"She gave me the keys to her car" he spat, licking his lips. "She said that they will take her license away because after this surgery she'll be deemed unfit for the activity"

He scratched his thumb against the leather cover of the ignition key, he looked sick at what else she could have implied.

"She also said that she will kill me if I got very much of a chip on it" he lets out a humorless chuckle, his eyes brims with hot tears when he looks up. I couldn't look away despite it being my first urge- I cannot because he mirrored every emotion that ate me. Everything that I craved to let go.

"Sounds like her" I force out with a nod, passing the bottle of water that Edmund had brought me before he left for the cafeteria to grab some food with Shin's parents. Hwan seems to have inherited her subtle features- not prominent, but a critical look and I saw the bridge of her nose and small ears that they seem to share along with the color of their eyes.

He chugs the water down and exhales, the tension in his neck dilutes as he smiles at me.

"She also told me to take care of you if she takes a long time to recover"

"That also sounds like her"

With little to no time spent with this boy in person except when we log in as a multiplayer, apart from that the silhouette of his existence is only mapped in my head by the times when shin had brought him up. complaints, debates, and good laughs are what we had shared around his name. Shin and I had this in common, we had people who had our back- but seldom a permanence with them, the only forever with a person I seem to have thought of was after I fell in love with her.

"Thanks for taking care of her. she is the happiest when she Is with you" He honesty only puts me in a new low. But with the desperation he seem to latch this conversation- I know he was trying to forget what might be happening inside as we conversed. Even if it's for a little while.

"And she is the craziest when with you"

I wished we could talk more, but when time escalates we drown further into an unsaid apprehension.

I can't even seem to recall the last few days with her. Unable to remember even the events of last night or the day before or even the week to it as I sat there sunken and bitter. It soared, when the doctors walked out they presented me with their professional results. From somewhere far I heard a low sob erupt from Mrs. Han. A hand- who I suspect was Edmunds placed by my shoulder. Hwan clutched those darn keys tighter with an angry scowl.

When I sensed Edmund following my movements- I gently pushed him away with my arm.

"I want to be alone for a while" I don't sound like me. I wasn't me.

He respects me and nods, the sadness that lines his face till he walks away etches within me- and soon everything comes back in sight. The night when I first saw her, the said naïve and platonic wedding, our first kiss, the silly nose scrunch she does when she is offended, her wild hair when she wakes up, those savage takes on Fischer, her timid shyness when she realizes her slip, her mornings, her nights- the friendship and promises. They all come back.

Even the memory of her last night that I had buried, the one which seem to have taken everything along with it.

She had asked me to move on if something goes wrong.

"Promise me that you will find love and happiness"

I slip into my car and close the door shut- I think I had refused to answer her. But then the tears in those big brown eyes had held me captive as I had lied my last promise to her, a lie before she decided to rest. A long slumber that no one knows an end of-

I lied to her- I agreed I will move on if things go wrong.

I won't. I cannot.

I will wait. Days, weeks, months, or years. No matter how long she takes- I'll wait- It wasn't a time I bargained to stay alone and weep my loss. The fact that she was alive and asleep was what keeping me cruelly sane. She will wake up, she has to.

I smile while I cry.

I hate my fate for doing this to me- but Ironically I thank it for not taking her away from me. It was maniacal- but it was enough. This was enough- for now.

Who am I kidding- I have been breaking into pieces every single day with dread this month, tonight I seem to have shattered beyond repair.

But still- it was enough.

But still I hope.

CHAPTER 37

Her tattoos, he dreamt of them vastly. In them she would bracket the silky brunette strands behind her ear, revealing the nape – the inked letters elegantly stark by her pale skin, Lee would always be torn between perceiving her details or her charms. Panic would engulf him when she would look at him- some times they would sit by the meadows watching the sunset, in others, it was by the coastal island listening to the songs composed by the waves. All they did was sit, with her fierce gaze on the nature ahead while he had his on her.

He hates it when she looks at him, even in the dreams he was aware of its end. He wakes up with a jolt because it is where it stops, when he gets seen by her. As if it was forbidden or sinful for him to be there with her while she was supposed to be alone.

He slept in strips, calling it a nightmare he would start his day by dragging himself out of bed- leaving it unkept. Periodically he would step on the messy entities that lay around- staining or denting the epoxy flooring of his penthouse in Las Vegas. He would cuss at himself but seldom bothered to clean his lavish pigsty up.

Sometimes he would walk straight to the closet and shove his washed clothes in, while in another scene he would pick one less greasy shirt from the ground and buttons it up by his half-naked body. But not on Tuesdays. He can't risk the wrath of a certain young boy who never misses the date to get him to-

Lee groans when Han Hwan walks in, his collage backpack slung lazily and his disappointment appropriately valid.

"I shouldn't have told you my passcode" Lee muses glumly walking to the washroom. The boy follows him with his patience visibly compressing. He might explode if wasn't given what was needed. And he needed an explanation for so many things that he had lost count. But the start was-

"Where are your fresh clothes that I got it done for you last week?" Hwan throws a murderous look at Lee- he had been doing what he can while he balanced college and this degenerating man from the past two years only for him to confess-

"I think I used it to clean the kitchen yesterday" the onset of guilt that panged by Lee's stomach was overpowered by his pride. So he squeezed a good amount of paste by and began brushing his teeth. Hwan stood by the entrance not a bit surprised. Lee was aging backwards mentally while his face did the opposite. His once styled and trimmed hair was now overgrown mane that curled by his ears. His roguing beard could help him pass off as a member of a drug cartel, or even worse, a homeless man if it wasn't for the logos from the brands he wore.

Of course it's Hwan who forces him into ordering them.

Though stained and dirty, he still had the delightful laugh and quirky smile when he turned to acknowledge a pissed off Hwan.

"I am just kidding, I kept it safe so that I can wear them to the hell hole you drag me to every Tuesday" he adds a wink and proceeds to spit out the salty taste of foam. Hwan sighs in relief, if not a step ahead at least he had the decency to save them.

"You know how expensive these therapies are? If you manage to open up a little- your tic tac sized brain might realize that It's not a forensic interrogation and it's perhaps something that could help you"

Splashing the cold water on his face Lee felt his drowsy infers waking to a memory.

"Expensive? Of course, you can own a black card and still want to save money, it's what she did as well"

Hwan had no response to that. He has seen this man hurting like no one else, when Hwan had his family to help each other, Lee had his self-loathing that took him to the bottom of what none could have foreseen.

"I can live here if you let me. I always wanted to move in. Pent houses are my scene" Hwan sniffs, crossing his arms and leaning by the frame. Lee frowns in horror.

"And do what? be my Mom? No- thank you"

Hwan could only roll his eyes and sigh at his tantrums. He was skeptical he might be the only sane person left in their household. His Dad had thrown himself to a series of work overload while his mother seem to divert her cure to alcohol. While Lee had many friends that were there for him, he did the one significant thing he seem to be good at. Running away.

In fact it's Hwan they consult and call when they desire to know of Lee's whereabouts. Lee made Hwan lie, if not- he would threaten him with the idea of never letting him in his life more than he already has.

Lee moved back to vegas, had cut off the ties with his family. Ran a sketchy garage and dismantled his penthouse worth millions of dollars to somehow making it look like a haunted seaside cabin. He was the ghost that plagues in it.

Hwan was the angel or paranormal expert who seem to keep the spirit in check within regular wonder if it was fine to pull out a tooth or two of this man to get him to make work again.

When Lee got presentable enough Hwan tossed Lee the key to shin's car, Lee wasn't impressed by how it hit his face. He wasn't prepared for a catch or to drive her car.

"You driving today, I cut my thumb chopping broccoli"

Lee enters switching off the voices that sprang up in his head using the subtle breathing tactics that the therapist had advised him of. He hates how It assists, he despises how he was unconsciously striving to find a cure when he deserves to suffer.

"That's illegal. To eat that thing" Lee offers his useless output to a boy who didn't care enough. His thumb was fine- he wanted to get this coward to drive. Hwan noticed the longingness in the eyes of Lee when he takes the wheels. It was her car- it didn't even smell like her anymore. And as it was hard to admit- Hwan couldn't seem to forgive himself for how he seemed to not do the same.

Was he forgetting his sister?

He can't remember someone all the time, but the number of times when she houses his thoughts, seems to have declined by the past year. By now, he solely thought of her when he had to assemble Lee into a semblance of normalcy. It was a responsibility she gave him till she recovers, And it's been long enough for him to give up on it.

He can't seem to. Lee could be annoying and broken too frigid to use your time on. But he wasn't a stranger- living in the same city he would swing by his apartment when Hwan would fail to call him or simply call him with a flu-infused voice. It was mostly a load amount of scolding and barked orders to eat healthily and stay warm that Lee did. Sometimes shoving a thermometer into his mouth and buying him a meal included.

Hwan secretly knew what his gestures were for it was his favorite part where Lee seem to acknowledge him. When the line between being his brother in law and brother blurred was when Lee agreed to share his password to his house and allowed himself to be dragged by Hwan to get some psychological aid.

"How- how are you?" Lee croaks, failing to hide the genuineness in his tone. "You didn't come last week"

"I had exams"

"It's not the season"

"I had a date"

Hwan Lied, the last Tuesday he was at the hospital to meet shin. He had gone to see her after two months- though Lee had transferred her to vegas and despite Hwan and Lee were the only ones who get to see her often, Hwan hadn't visited her for a good sixty days. Lee knew- he wouldn't remark on it.

But when Hwan received a call from the doctor stating a mild motion movement from shin- he almost dropped the egg he was to crack by the pan for dinner. Shame and distress crowned him at his neglecting behavior. Was he so weak to have given up on her so soon?

But was it even humane to hide this progress from Lee?

Hwan had advised the assigned medic to not inform Lee of this- though there was a motion detected, it still wasn't anywhere near a recovery. It could even have been the trick of a night- Hwan was intimidated of what would happen if nothing heals in the future.

Lee was learning to breathe again, he can't afford to plug him back into a supporter where nothing was promised because of a speculation.

After the therapy session, Lee and Hwan went for a dinner that none of them seem to be dedicated to. Hwan could taste the change in environment and he suspected that it had to do everything with Lee. In a Korean BBQ restaurant, Lee emerged to occur more American than the Americans themselves. His jersey overcoat and rugged man bun earned him few flirty glances from young aspiring girls. Hwan looked like a child in comparison to this tall and broadened man stuffing his share of food.

"Have been working out I see" comments Hwan- they have been doing this every week for a year. every time Lee would make fun of what the psychologist had suggested to him, but on rare days he would silently contemplate the logical reasoning it withheld.

Lee makes no effort to talk, usually, it was another way around when Hwan would ignore his snarky remarks- tonight the station- ing pose of Lee seem to bore a level of strange aura that Hwan hadn't come across.

When they finished, Lee drove them to Hwan's neighborhood. By the time they reached the sky seem to have unbolted into a pour of merciless rain. The street was empty with a couple of residents running inside their house. Lee got out after shoving the key by Hwan's lap rather heatedly.

Whatever it was that he had been bottling up uncorked in the dark.

Dumbfounded at such attitude, Hwan pursued the trait and got out. The rain soaks his clothes wet In a matter of seconds.

"What are you doing?" he shouts through the sound of tapering water as an equally drenched Lee ran a hand through his hair with a bitter chuckle.

"I am walking home" he states. Hwan wasn't naïve to Lee and his uncalled actions. But this was something else- this was alarmingly serious as he took a step forward simultaneously questioning Lee and his antics.

"What is it? What happened?"

It cost him so much to build the relationship he had with Lee. he can't let it dissolve like this when-

"I am not your responsibility young man," Lee says, his eyes narrowing down to slits. "I know you are not here for her"

Hwan had to pretend to be offended despite how true it was.

"You have no right to accuse me of healing from grief-

"I don't. I am not accusing you of anything you fool" Lee spat his terms with anger, his voice rang like thunder that the storm lacked. "I am accusing you of staying here for a man and tending him when he and his forsaken family is the reason behind what happened to your sister"

This fused Hwan into exclaiming out once more.

"For how long are you going to blame yourself for this?"

Lee had the quick answer conjured.

"Until you will stop wasting your life on a deranged me by staying here"

"I am here because I opted to study-

"No person in the right state of mind would choose vegas for education when they have better entries at the disposal"

With that a silence falls upon them, the rain had entirely absorbed into for them to feel its nuisance. Right then, they were in enough trouble for each other.

"What about the promise I made to her then? She knew what would become of you without her around" Hwan had treaded carefully by the mention of her for so long that it took his whole to do it with pride. He was proud of what she was and is. And he wants her to feel the same about him. even if it means playing a carpenter with a job of constantly knocking some sense into Lee.

"I can take care of myself. I don't need anyone. " defends Lee, Hwans calm smile fuels his irk.

"Maintaining your insulin and building a body is keeping you alive. You are not living, you are surviving"

Lee for a moment, even a gist of it realizes how credible that was. Then he also reciprocates how he doesn't care. So he turns around to leave with the last punchline, silently wishing that it will keep Hwan off his hair.

"Then let me survive. I am good at that"

Lee strides off the street with no intention of getting a cab or getting shelter. The rain panned out to a suitable pour as he looked up at the starry and clearing sky- it was a tight rope, the dreams he gets of her sweet laughter, her voice that soothes his pain as in those dreams that felt more like home than when he wakes up.

He prays on each day.

The minute he wakes. But nothing ever happen. The world moved while his slept. Slept on a cold hospital room foreign to his ordeals. He didn't ask much.

He just asks her. The fate can take his soul the moment she wakes. He will be happy with the idea of her living for them both.

If only it was that easy to trade.

If only it was the prayers that were blessed.

To see her quiet and cold, pale and thin by the crisp mattress, so unaware of him and the days that flew and fell like the dried autumn leaves only angered him more. The first couple of months went by with him pulling the strings and connections to get the culprit back behind the bars. He received his punishment, but it wasn't the end to the trauma that Lee was hit by.

And when Lee stumbled with a curse that brought him back to present, when he felt a hit by his shoulder, he turned around to a panting Hwan. The hwan who had ran to him so that he could stop Lee from going any further with his grouching stamina had his phone clutched in a death grip while his useless lips only spewed out heavy exhales Lee waited for him to compose.

But hwan didn't seem to mere physically lost his breath, if anything he was spellbound and stunned.

Lee had so many questions that came with such behavior of Hwans- but before he could open his mouth Hwan wheezes out.

"She's awake"

If that didn't stopped the heart of Lee. What came next sure did.

"They- They called. They said She woke up And you are the one she is asking for"

Epilogue

People speak of dreams and hallucinations. The region of deep slumber in which the illusions are so rational that they almost ascertain of it being true.

Shin-young felt the same. She had seen the handsome man in her trances. Always generous and kind, always happy.

Leaving him behind in her barren sleep was what gave her anxiety when she woke up. To her- this seems to be a new world. Bright lights, beeping monitors, and a touch from the people who observed her were so warm and real that it felt unnatural.

She was confused, she was scared. She couldn't remember how long it had been since she had been awake watching the pace and exchange words that she cannot understand.

But as the minutes passed, it came back to her. The senses in her fingers, the colors in her vision, and then the sounds in her ears. But they were too tight, sharp, and loud as her eyes tear up.

She was like a child out of a womb. Unknown to her surround-ings and helpless to what was going on. She was frightened and cold, breathing heavily when they aided her to sit.

Her limbs ached, her heart rang by her ears. And her fears wept silently for a man who she had left behind in her dreams. But when minutes expired and her perception came to life she looked around frantic at the woman who had been piping calm musing to soothe her anxiety. When the female nurse rushed to Shin's service- she opened her mouth to feel and utter the one name that she seem to recall.

Nothing reverberated.

She tried again, but her throat burns with such trauma that a shocked gasp left her body. The nurse, grasping the need of the situation presented shin with a note and pen.

At first, it took shin her pathetic strength to curl her fingers by the slender body of the pen, and in a sluggishly crooked scripture, she wrote the one name she had remembered first.

A name she seem to had remembered even before her own.

The name was Lee.

He ran,

He trotted as he rammed into people. He ran in his soaked clothes leaving watermarks on the clean hospital floor to the dismay of janitors. But when they saw who it was, they exchanged surprised glances with their colleagues.

A community doctor who passed by them grinned, hollering the two words that the old cleaning ladies prayed for since they had met Lee two years ago and heard his story. The Lee to whom this sector was a second home. The Lee who reminded them of their sons. The Lee who became an embodiment of true love among the staffs here.

"She's awake"

These words were loudly thrown around by one to another. The remeding patients who were new were confused. While the old helped them with the narration.

The old ones were already celebrating with hugs and cheers as they made path for a breathless, gleaming Lee to pass through. When Hwan followed tenderly- his eyes scanning the hallway. An inquisitive smile lights his ever gloomy face up as he realized-

'The son of a gun was never alone, he just had his harbor racked somewhere else'

But no assistance prepared Lee for such a reunion. When Lee tore open the door to her room he wasn't ready for it. Despite years of wishing, praying, and screaming for her to open her eyes- he wasn't in any manner orchestrated to see her.

Like a small ball of fur, she sat there cocooned and wrapped in a cozy blanket. Her head inclined to her lap as she thought grimly of something.

Rather Of some one.

Of him.

Of if he even existed!

When the doors uncrocked, she had expected to see the face of the same doctor who had been for the last ten minutes notifying her of her surrounding. Checking for pulse by her wrists or a torch to her retina. But it wasn't the young intern who she was competent to furrow her brows at.

It was him.

He was here. But yet not the same. This version of her intuitions seems to have aged like a fine wine. The charm in that lidded gaze was tainted, but so intense. His steps slowed down as if he was scared that this would end in a dream if his movements were harsh. But, the closer he got to her the further he lost his mind.

And he didn't want to keep track of it. He was willing to let go of his tears or laugh or words. But nothing happens. He just watched her- even afraid to touch her.

She looks up at him, her excitement overpowering her anxiety. She was shin, and he was Lee. But who were they?

Who was he?

Then a series of washed memories surfaces. All a jumbled mess. She still was confused. She still wasn't awake entirely.

But when his hand reached out and cupped her cheeks, its warmth colored her cheek as she unconsciously leaned into them closing her eyes.

Unlike in dreams, his touch ignites her with spirit and life. But just like in a dream...his voice remained the same.

"Thank you"

That is what he said. She didn't know what she was being thanked for - but she accepted it in silence. Because unknown to the cause it's what she wanted to say to him the moment he stepped in.

Thank him.

For everything that she couldn't remember or say.

Remember for now.

But couldn't Say...quite literally.

Lee didn't leave her side even for a second. The doctors had advised him and Hwan to cease clean of any forced interaction that could lead to her recalling an involuntary memory. They were asked to behave in accordance of a stranger with her while she sat silently watching them like a curious kitten as they took care of her.

Though her parents were there they weren't allowed to meet her until she expresses her development.

She did try to express once, verbally. Using her mouth. Her lips moved and a tired sigh escaped.

As for her legs, it took her an embraced support from Lee or muscle therapist to even get up from the bed.

It had been two days since Lee had been metaphorically dying to get her attention but all she does was distantly stare at the buttons in her wheelchair.

She can't speak, she can't walk.

Was else was useless about her- what's the use of such recovery when she couldn't remember -

Well- her suffering was short-lived because on day third she recollected her clasped memories. They came in investments. The portions at times big and in others - a dent of mere flashes.

But she was great at jigsaw. The puzzles soon began to form a bigger pictures. And soon she wasn't as clueless as she was a couple of days ago.

"Shin" Lee inquired her for the first time, even her tilt of acknowledgment filled him with gratitude as he lost his breath and forgot the reason for why he called her. She viewed him quizically but it was enough. "You look worried, is there something you want to speak- I mean write about?"

If Lee learned anything in those past years of maintaining his patience was that every hurdle could be tackled if given time. Her voice- she might have lost them, her steps may stagger today. But to him, she had never been so whole and perfect as of now.

She was getting healthier by the week, she ate well and slept well. Though he still got his panic bolted every time she took a nap. He had seen her sleep enough for him to last a lifetime.

Though it did hurt like hell to know that she might have forgotten of his existence he was unaware of how much she had been organizing her recollected memories and the stifled smile that she hid when Lee and Hwan bickered.

She was happy that her husband and brother had gotten along so well.

So it was on day five she sat on the bed when the two idiots woke up. She had the nurse help her to a shower and a new set of clothes that Lee brought. After grinning in the likes of a lunatic by the mirror she Got her hair and nails done by using the generous nurse's makeup kit. The shirt dress she wore on was slightly loose on her, but the feel of soft silk fabric on her skin instead of the cotton gown cured her of dreadful nostalgias.

The two girls in the bathroom shared a mischievous glance. Never had the nurse anticipated that she would get to play pranks and share laughs with the gorgeous ex-comatose girl that she had been assigned to eight months ago.

Lee woke up to an angel smiling down at them as shin sat there by her bed. While Hwan thought he saw a naughty glimmer when shin blinked at her brother.

Hwan felt his heart clench with giddiness as he grinned at shin. Lee on the other hand was still an idiot. So shin had to roll her eyes when she saw the confused frown that reflected the face of Lee.

'Just what low of bare minimum was he satisfied with?'

She thought.

She waved her hand asking both of them to walk over. They both somehow managed to not fall face-first to the ground tangled up in sheets by the couch they shared last night.

The note she gave Hwan was for him to get her parents here. Hwan was stunned to his core and he traded his glance back and forth to the paper and his sister. He looked more alarmed than last night when Lee read out his stock market report... While he was asleep.

Shin noticed that Lee still talked in his respite. It had been two years. Yet he was the same. Well except for-

She passed her second note to Lee with her two fingers clipped by them. Lee looked at it expecting it to be her common needs. But boy was this personal.

"Shave off that damn beard and kiss your half-paralyzed wife already you fool"

One year later

SHIN

How can someone look as gorgeous as me and not be boastful of it?

I question myself direly as I squinted my gaze by the floor-length mirror attached to the trial room.

My winged eyeliner rests coolly at the impatient knock by the door. Lee stood there in his tailored black suit and equally black shirt- his designer shoes polished to sparkle. It now didn't bore the coffee stain that Lee accidentally dropped on my dress and his footwear right before we were to enter the chapel.

Lee took an en route and found us the nearest dress store to the church so I can get a change of clothes and he could get to-

"I can't believe I got a supermodel for a wife. You can wear a plastic bag and still make it work baby" his glassy face gleamed while I glared.

The doubt resurfaces again. How can I look so gorgeous and not be boastful about it?

I just cannot.

He does it for me.

And as humble as I was for that, it didn't pass my vibe. This wasn't an honest compliment. He rather was trying to stall my attention from the fact that I was a bridesmaid and he was the best man. And we both were horribly late because my husband was a caffeine addict.

Since when?

I have no idea when it began. He always blamed it on Hwan. And Hwan seem to have matured in a way to not defend on his behalf and just accept his fault with a shrug.

What happened to my brother?

I wouldn't know.

Probably hard puberty and trauma from baby sitting my husband for so long .

I bring my fingers to the level of my face and angrily sign him my heart's desire.

"You are screwed. You are never touching coffee again"

He understands it better than I intended to.

"Oh, darling. Please stop screaming at me. People are looking at us"

He signs me back.

Even when I can perfectly hear him. He likes to put his newly learned skill to use. The terrible of them all is when he uses to seduce me with his naughty thoughts in public where no one gets what he suggests.

I do a fresh twirl for him. I stop to wiggle my brows asking his opinion on the maroon laced dress I had changed into.

"Sexy" he breaths hoarsely. He chuckles smirking when he notices my blush. But instead of ruffling my hair like he usually does- he engulfs me into a hug and kisses the top of my pinned-up head.

I melt in right there. But manage to somehow realize that he was still stalling.

So I step on him as he hopped back grunting. It turns out that when you have lost your time to a comatose stage, you as an individual start to screen all sorts of emotions. I haven't been holding back since the day I woke up.

I have been demanding, so had he. I have been wild and so is he. We had been a prisoner for so long that now we merely walk around in as civilized citizens only to remove our facade once alone.

The journey of healing had been challenging to say the least. They mostly were thorns than solace. I was a child learning to walk, my hand was my mouth retaining to talk. The communication Lee and I had lost would always put us in a strange place.

But every single time we bounced back into the crazed people who were willing to defy the odds.

We made our disability a weapon. And soon we could joke, talk and live without the impression of remorse over what we can't do.

Though he occasionally admits to missing my voice. It turns out it wasn't an aspect that we want back. We have more than we solicited for.

"Lean" I indicate.

When I suspected his innuendo in making. I tugged at his tie in turn causing him to slouch.

Bad choice.

The proximity had my breath taut. So I work on his weak tie and push him away before he could smile and enjoy my flushed nature.

"I think it's now you whose stalling," he says.

"I am not" my hands were determined to deny.

"You know I can hear your voice and emotions in them?" He takes a step near grabbing my wrist. Unfurling my fisted fingers he kisses my palms and settles in a loving smile "I can read you like a book and write you like a story Shin. I know it's the first wedding you are attending after our own"

If that is not it he interlaces his hand with mine and gets us moving. From the aile and from the store where he already seems to have purchased this attire for me.

Once in the car, he helps me with the tag on it as an eerie silence seems to house between us. Then I ask-

"Have you been to one?"

His lips thin into a dismal smile. Then he looks ahead at the sunny Californian street.

"I would skip them even in screens. Let alone be in an actual one"

I don't pry him further. Not when we drove, not when we met everyone. Not even when Isaac White seem to understand just what I was saying.

"It's been so long since we met aunt shin" he fills in as soon as Lee turns to greet Alexander White with a hug. Unlike Lee who's face remained young as soon as he got rid of his awful beard. The shadow of it seem to work for Mr. White who had just entered his thirties. And as for his son-

"I don't know if you know. But I have a certificate in ASL. So does my Mom. We can interpret what you say. That is-" the boy who's once cheeky chubs has now given a window to stark details blushes shyly "That is if you ever want to talk to someone"

Isaac was nine while Elzinas daughter turned three. And I couldn't believe it when Isaac understood when I spelled kangaroo for him.

Then it was a series of periods where I told him how much I missed him. He said he had been busy with his high school syllabus. I looked at Lee for correction. Turns out there wasn't a need for it- Isaac was a prodigy.

And it wasn't a surprise for many who knew Elzina Winston.

"Alex seems to be more relatable to his daughter now" Lee mumbles coming to stand next to me as soon as he checked on Edmund. While I on another hand was too scared to even move a feather - what was I to do when asked to be the bridesmaid of my celebrity crush Hailey Howard?

Say no.

In ASL?

I screamed in Caps lock asking Lee to agree with the arrangement. But to know that Edmund and Hailey's story began when the producer casted Hailey as the main lead for the book adaptation that I wrote was a revelation that took me days to get used to.

They had made a trilogy on it. And it had been an enormous hit among the audience. But wider the hit was when in between the shootings and commercials, something else sparked apart the artificial glamour of Hollywood.

The story of two rival Exes coming back together resurfaced.

It thought of it as a farce.

But here we are. In a secluded wedding where Fischer stood by the podium grinning widely in anticipation to start the ceremony.

"What's his daughter's name again?" I ask squinting at Alexander who had his little girl tucked by the arm while his wife applied her coat of lipstick. He seem to guide her verbally and she lacked a mirror on her.

"Iris"

"Such a pretty name" I state.

"He wants her to fail few exams in school" I snort at that, Lee chuckled as well "Alex wants someone in the family who he could relate to"

When Lee turns to me I nervously ask him something that I have meaning to do for months now.

But subtlety wasn't my forte and Lee seem to grasp my hesitation even before I could put it out for him.

"Not now baby" I exhale with my shoulders sagging. "I want this to. But I want to wait until-

" I am healthy. I got myself checked- I swear I am alright"

He nods sideways with a soft smile. Taking my hands in his, we both ignore the roll bells signalling the arrival of the groom.

"Just a year more. I promise" he says pressing his thumb against me. Simultaneously we turn to watch Edmund confidently make his way to the higher floor and we also watch it disperse the second he saw Hailey walking down the aisle.

His smile falters and his eyes fixes to her veil and it trains on her tenderly until she was there up with him.

When the ceremony commences Lee whispers to me with his hold never flaying from others.

"Do you want to get married again? Like a real one! May be- wait a year more as I resume my career in tracks and then we make lots of babies?"

Though our gaze watched a wedding. Our mind certainly dived in the past. To our day. To the one platonic agreement that led us here. I smile politely at the procession in front of us. And as for the answer -

I strengthen our hold and closed my eyes to savor the beauty of the bond the marriage held in my life.

The beauty that harvested adventures, passion, growth, love and life.

The beauty of us.